To Kaethan—for, you know, loving me and stuff.

◇

And to nine-year-old me—we did it.

CAST IN FIRELIGHT

DANA SWIFT

EMBER

Text copyright © 2021 by Dana Swift
Cover art copyright © 2021 by Charlie Bowater
Map art copyright © 2021 by Virginia Norey

All rights reserved. Published in the United States by Ember, an imprint of Random House Children's Books, a division of Penguin Random House LLC, New York. Originally published in hardcover in the United States by Delacorte Press, an imprint of Random House Children's Books, a division of Penguin Random House LLC, New York, in 2021.

Ember and the E colophon are registered trademarks of Penguin Random House LLC.

Visit us on the Web! GetUnderlined.com

Educators and librarians, for a variety of teaching tools,
visit us at RHTeachersLibrarians.com

The Library of Congress has cataloged the hardcover edition of this work as follows:
Names: Swift, Dana, author.
Title: Cast in firelight / Dana Swift.
Description: First edition. | New York : Delacorte Press, [2021] | Summary: "Adraa and Jatin are royal heirs of their respective kingdoms, masterful with magic, and their arranged marriage will unite two of Wickery's most powerful territories—except, they don't get along. Now, with the criminal underbelly suddenly making a move for control, the pair must learn to put their trust in the other if either is to uncover the real threat"— Provided by publisher.
Identifiers: LCCN 2020043214 | ISBN 978-0-593-12421-5 (hardcover) | ISBN 978-0-593-12422-2 (library binding) | ISBN 978-0-593-12423-9 (ebook)
Subjects: CYAC: Fantasy.
Classification: LCC PZ7.1.S947 Cas 2021 | DDC [Fic]—dc23

ISBN 978-0-593-12424-6 (paperback)

Printed in the United States of America
10 9 8 7 6 5 4 3 2 1
First Ember Edition 2022

Wickery

- ⊛ Cities
- ◉ Villages

adpra

lps of Alconea

Alkin

Mila

Agsa

Agsa Palace

Yadisa

The Academy

Deities and Their Powers

◇ ◇ ◇

The Nine Touches

Erif, Goddess of Fire: Rules over volcanoes
◇ **Red Fortes:** Ability to create and manipulate fire

Renni, Goddess of Inner Capability: Oversees personal growth
◇ **Orange Fortes:** Ability to manipulate and heighten senses and the body's physical capabilities

Ria, God of Air: Governs tornados and wind
◇ **Yellow Fortes:** Ability to create and manipulate air, especially for flying

Htrae, Goddess of Earth: Reigns over fields and crops
◇ **Green Fortes:** Ability to create and manipulate wood and plant life

Retaw, God of Water: Controls flooding and tsunamis
◇ **Blue Fortes:** Ability to create and manipulate water

Raw, God of War: Stands on the battlefields of soldiers
◇ **Purple Fortes:** Ability to manifest weapons, shields, and boundaries

Laeh, Goddess of Healing: Watches over the sick and injured
◇ **Pink Fortes:** Ability to heal and enchant potions to fight illness

Dloc, God of the Cold: Dwells in blizzards and avalanches
◇ **White Fortes:** Ability to create and manipulate ice, snow, and other winter precipitation

Wodahs, God of Shadow: Lives in darkness
◇ **Black Fortes:** Ability to camouflage and cast illusions

◇

I Meet the Love of My Life and Slap Him in the Face

Adraa

The door was made of ice—glowing blue, crystalized ice. And behind that door was my . . . I guess I should say destiny, even though it sounded absurd. Meeting a boy who *might* be my husband one day should not qualify as destiny.

Yet here I stood with my parents in a gaping black mouth of an entryway, with columns that jutted out like fangs to a blue-stoned palace so massive I had to turn my head side to side to take it all in. The last beams of dusk caught the glassy surface and danced. I glanced at my parents, both of them unconcerned. I guess we weren't going to talk about how strange it was to make a door using only white magic. Had that been in their lectures? And, Adraa, don't mention the creepy door situation.

My father lifted a fist to knock and I lurched forward, tugging his arm down. But it was my mother's words that stilled us both. "Maybe . . . maybe we should wait."

1

Snow flurries whirled. The winter wind howled. Then Father gave us both *the look*. "We've been talking about this for years, Ira."

I hadn't been involved in these annual discussions, obviously. I was eight. My parents had been considering my arranged marriage since forever.

"And after all those steps," Father huffed.

I didn't even want to glance behind me at the slope of stairs we had climbed. My legs ached, quivering in confusion as to why we hadn't flown here on skygliders like sensible witches and wizards. By stair twenty I had begun imagining the Maharaja of Naupure made us walk up here, not to fulfill tradition as everyone had told me, but to weaken me. By stair sixty-two, a nagging thought crept in like the cold—I approached a prison, not a palace.

I could see from the crinkle of my mother's crooked nose that she was about to laugh. And my one opportunity in this nightmare of steps and cold and weird doors was about to slip away.

"I'm with Mom. This is a *bad* idea!" I said.

Both pairs of eyes shot to me. Father immediately bent down and clasped my shoulders. "Just think of this as meeting a new friend, Adraa."

"But, but he's—a boy." A boy I would one day be expected to . . . kiss. I knew marriage also meant living with someone in the same dwelling, but it was the idea of kissing that rattled me. I would be expected to do that regularly and supposedly like it? I tugged Father's arm again. With Mother's help this could be over, forgotten. We could turn back from this mountain, board our skygliders, and return to our own palace and the coast, where winter didn't try to freeze you to death.

But I had said the wrong thing. My father laughed and even my mother shook her head and covered her mouth with a gloved hand to conceal a smile. Sometimes I think they only had me for my unexpected one-liners.

"Yes." Father chuckled, the warmth of his breath marking the frigid air. "Yes, he is a boy. And so am I, and you like me well enough, right?"

I didn't like this logic. I had missed something stark and obvious, or my father had. My potential betrothed in all his *boyishness* meant something completely different from my father's broad frame and comforting arms. The question was a trap, so I answered the only way possible: "Yeah."

Father laughed, tilted his head to Mother and repeated "yeah" to try to make her smile again. Then his green eyes thawed. "I know this must be scary."

"I'm not scared," I rushed out, but I couldn't tell if I was lying. Naupure's winter stung and I shook with it. Rising behind the palace, Mount Gandhak pierced the sky and the last beams of daylight bled onto the rocks in a yellow-orange paint. In the far distance, from my bedroom window, the volcano appeared as dormant as ever. Up close? The light mimicked lava.

Father peered at Mother and held her gaze. "It's just a first meeting. Nothing will be written in blood. Tonight, it's just a meeting," he repeated. And before I could say anything more, even protest one last time, Father finally knocked.

Nothing happened. I was saved.

"No one's home! Let's go!" I shouted.

"Adraa," Mother snapped. She opened her mouth to say more, but the ice groaned. Cracks splintered out in branchlike streaks. I stumbled back, listening as each glacial shard shattered and fell. And when the door was done pulling itself apart, only darkness greeted us. No flesh had touched that marbled ice. Wisps of blue smoke fluttered in the periphery of my vision. I spun to catch its potency. Magic!

The dim entryway awoke with light as candles *pop, pop, popp*ed to life, illuminating a wide staircase and an elaborately dressed man descending toward us.

"Greetings!" the man bellowed. This had to be Maharaja Naupure. But he was . . . skinny and short, which was unexpected. You don't go imagining the most powerful wizard of our neighboring country as skinny or short. Both? This couldn't be the man. But on his chest, he wore the Naupure emblem, a mountain embedded in blue wind.

He strolled toward us, and he and Father pressed their forearms together before hugging. Father laughed and said, "It's been too long."

Mother placed her fingers to her throat and bowed in dignified honor. Words garbled together and I retreated, the wind biting into my back.

Forget skinny and short. Forget first impressions. I had been utterly wrong. My parents knew this wizard well. Which meant this was *more* than introductions and pleasantries. This was a decision, already decided. What about "It's just a meeting, Adraa"? What about "It's only a visit before Jatin goes

4

away to school" as I sat and memorized what to say, word for word?

Father turned. "Adraa."

I froze. Move me and I would break apart like the door.

Father didn't notice. He reached for my hand and pulled me forward, into the hall. Arches upon arches, adorned in paisley and gold, glimmered down at me. Candles burned. The smell of crisp winter air mixed with bouquets of white frost-light blossoms. Yeah, it was pretty, but fear whispered that it was all a facade.

"Come on in. Get out of the cold." Naupure motioned as though to swat away the wind. With a quick spell, blue smoke gushed off his arms, ran straight for me, and then spilled into the night.

I gaped as the ice shards picked themselves up and refroze in place. Frost crystals trailed over the wall's marble veins, weaving across the door's hinges and stopping only when they touched the bright-gold silks draped across the ceiling.

I was so busy watching the show I didn't notice the orange wisps of my father's magic thawing me. Lingering snow on our cloaks sizzled into steam. When I turned around again, everyone's attention focused on me.

"This must be Adraa." Maharaja Naupure crouched, and now even I was taller than him. It didn't help. "Pleasure, little miss."

Here, I was supposed to say "Pleasure" and maybe add a "thank you for inviting us." Silence. I would give them silence.

Mother frowned.

Maharaja Naupure continued to stare. "You are a pretty little thing, but I'm sure you know that, huh?"

This man obviously only had a son. "Pretty"? Really? He knew how many stairs I had just climbed, right? Where was my compliment for surmounting his torture? I glanced at my mother. She bit her lip, probably scared of what might tumble from my mouth. My mind buzzed with all sorts of retorts. My parents had *lied*. So I accompanied a shrug with something special: "I know."

Mother took a quick, sucking breath as if preparing a spell, but Maharaja Naupure barked out a laugh. "That's right. A pretty girl should know."

What? What kind of response is that?

Maharaja Naupure swung toward the stairs and yelled, "Jatin! Don't keep our guests waiting."

A muffled thump echoed from upstairs. My throat dried, but my hands began to sweat. That thump was him, the boy, like a real monster in the depths trying to scare me.

Naupure guided us to the open room on the right. A prayer table cloaked in red stood before us. Tapestries in various colors covered the nine-sided room, every paneled wall praising a different god or goddess. Mother grew up on Pire Island, where they have long given up the idea that the gods bestowed our magic. But even though her eyes lingered on the tapestries uncertainly, Father had taught me enough about each peering face. I knew it would be under those eyes that we would spill our blood. I quickstepped to my father and tugged his hand. *Please let him understand my concern. Please.*

6

He nodded. "Adraa's a little nervous about meeting Jatin."

Betrayal. White-hot betrayal. I dropped his hand like it had scalded me.

"Of course," Naupure said, just as I cried out, "No I'm not!"

Mother's eyes seared into me. Our alliance, however short-lived, had fallen.

"I'm sorry. She's normally not like *this*." Mother pointed to the spot next to her. "Adraa, come here."

I obeyed in a fumble of pink-and-orange skirts that I tried to straighten as I sat down next to her. I didn't know what to do anymore to get out of this. To rebel even further would mean punishment. Or maybe I was past that. Maybe whatever I did—

"Have you come into your magic yet, Adraa?" Maharaja Naupure asked.

And just like that, the anger died. "No, sir."

"She will, of course. She is a year younger than Jatin, if you remember," Mother said quickly.

"Oh yes, I remember." He peered at me, inspecting.

"She has her Touch. Adraa, show him."

I automatically turned my left hand over, palm up, and placed it on the red cloth. The fabric was itchy, with little barblike tufts instead of nice velvet softness. Why would anyone buy an itchy tablecloth? The Naupures were monsters.

I displayed my Touch, a small marking that had flourished upon my left wrist. It was a reddish branchy swirl the size of a silver coin, darker than my brown skin. It held the only true indication that one day I would become a witch, and therefore

7

was one of the only things that gave me hope as I crept closer to age nine. One day, if I was powerful enough, the design would spring up each arm, wrapping itself up to my shoulder like those of my parents, Maharaja Naupure, and half the country. Like a plant, I must nurture my Touch. I must study.

"And your other arm?" Maharaja Naupure asked.

Cautiously, I set my right arm on the table. My parents froze, because there was nothing there, only bare dark skin. The real concern, and the reason I feared I would be powerless, lay in this fact: my right arm was unnaturally naked. Everyone I had ever met reported their Touch appeared on both wrists simultaneously. There are the Touched and the Untouched. I've never heard of anything in between.

"Interesting," Maharaja Naupure said.

"Have you seen this before?" Father asked. "I thought it was all myth and legend."

I knew it. I knew my parents were concerned, and I knew I had a reason to be too.

"Well, according to legend, the gods are fighting over who should bless her."

I snatched my arms off the table and glanced around the room at the tapestries of the nine Gods: the blue God, Retaw, commanded a flood; green Goddess Htrae reigned over a field; yellow God Ria flew in a tornado; red Goddess Erif ruled a volcano; white God Dloc swirled within a blizzard; pink Goddess Laeh cured sickness; black God Wodahs concealed himself in a dark cloak; purple God Raw stood on a battlefield; and orange Goddess Renni was enveloped in muscles and strength. They looked ready to eat me before considering giving me power. Could they really be arguing over me?

"That's more reassuring than . . . the alternative." Mother sighed.

I pressed my mark, hard. Without magic, without *all* nine types of magic, I was useless. No title. No ability to lead any country, let alone mine. When I glanced up to see Maharaja Naupure still inspecting me, the weekly lectures on politeness were completely forgotten.

"Do you need to check my molars too?" I opened my mouth.

"Adraa," my mother spat. I closed my mouth quickly, but continued staring at him. *See the* real *me, Maharaja Naupure. See how unsuitable I would be as maharani of Naupure! And not because my right arm is bare.*

Maharaja Naupure again barked out a laugh, which seemed to be his only sound of amusement. "Oh my. You remind me of my Savi."

Before my parents could agree or Mother could shuffle out of the awkwardness of having to admit I was in fact her daughter, a boy, *the boy,* walked into the parlor. He had jet-black hair like my own, brown skin much lighter than mine, and shiny, glazed-over eyes. Jatin, my betro—I couldn't even think it. Here I was, goose bumps radiating up my arms and down my legs, and he was *calm.* No, he looked . . . bored.

Not looking bored was rule one, right before being excessively polite. Which, when you think about it, is the same rule, because this calmness was all sorts of annoying. How could he be calm?

"Jatin, there you are. Come meet everyone. This is the Maharaja and Maharani of Belwar."

Jatin nodded. "Pleasure to make your acquaintance." So I wasn't the only one with regurgitated lines.

Jatin bowed to my parents and then turned back to his father with a "what else must I do" expression.

"And, Jatin, this is Adraa."

Should I stand or something? Before I could make up my mind, Jatin turned to me and gave the most awkward smile ever crafted. Both of his canines were missing.

"Hello," we said simultaneously.

"Jatin, why don't you show Adraa your room," Maharaja Naupure suggested.

Jatin looked up at his father with calm obedience. No help for the cause there.

Mother nudged me with an elbow. "Go on, Adraa. We need to talk with Maharaja Naupure in private."

I twisted around, ready to pout my way out of this, but then I saw my father's eyes. They weren't crinkled in humor. They were *always* crinkled in humor. But not today. I had to let this boy show me his room. Jatin nodded for me to follow. Nodded! You would think this kid owned the whole country. Well, I guess he would one day.

I trailed Jatin up more stone steps and through the labyrinth of the palace, staring at his back. Any time he even twitched to turn around and look at me, I pretended to be fascinated with the yellow and blue entanglement of colors on the archways.

When we finally stopped, Jatin gestured to a wood door with his name etched in swirly lines. "Here it is."

I crossed my arms. I could play this game all day. "It's a very nice door."

Jatin stared at me, waiting, and then turned the handle and waited again. Nope. No way. I was not going in first. That was how I would get locked in a room and never be heard from again. My parents might trust this calm, polite boy, but I didn't. It was an act, for sure.

"Ah, you can go in," he said.

"You first."

"But . . . you're supposed to—"

"Supposed to what?" *Fall for your tricks? Think again, boy.*

"Never mind." And with that, Jatin ambled into his room with me right behind.

I expected massive, like everything here, and while the furniture appeared oversized, it was because the room in fact was not enormous. It could hold a single elephant instead of an entire herd. The clutter might have also had something to do with it. A library had exploded upon the desk. Parchment dripped to the floor. Orbs and bottles glowed with tiny balls of magic on every flat surface. I stared, captivated by the glowing swirls of color. In one row sat all nine types of magic, neatly arranged and gleaming like a rainbow. A small red fire, an orange mist, a yellow glimmer of air, a bundle of green mossy material, a blue wave, a purple spike, a pink ball, a black fuming shadow, and, finally, white frost crystals. Was all this *his*?

It had to be. When first learning and trying to cast spells, young witches and wizards create each individual and godly color. Only at age sixteen is one's forte determined. Then every spell filters through your particular blessed color. Which meant

11

with the array of hues surrounding us, Jatin could already cast *all* nine!

Jatin grabbed a white orb, whipping my attention back to him. "Do you know magic yet?" he asked as he spun the translucent container. Snowflakes and frost crystals shimmered inside. His Touch swirled in an intricate design up the back of his right wrist.

"I've been studying."

"No, I mean can you do it yet?"

"Well . . ." I searched for something to distract him and found only orb after orb of colorful smoke. Is that all this boy did—study and spell?

"You can't!" His eyes bugged out in surprise and then shrank down into pride. They sure weren't glazed over now. He looked at my hands. Cheeks flushing, I shifted my right arm behind my back slowly. *This is why boys are the worst.*

"What? Are these really yours?" I sputtered, but I already knew the answer.

"Yeah. Wanna see?" He jerked the container up. "This was my first freeze spell."

He would open it *in here*? I knew this boy was dangerous. When one is first learning, magic either needed to be confined in an orb or cast in an open space. His room suddenly felt even smaller.

"Don't! You can't."

He straightened. "Yeah I can! I'm a wizard."

More like spoiled brat.

"I'm a witch too. I just haven't gotten my powers yet," I said.

He crossed his arms. At least the orb wasn't about to be opened. I had saved myself by that much. "I bet you are not even a witch."

"Am too." I reached for my left sleeve to show him my Touch, but his laughter stopped me. Heat flushed my cheeks, hot coals pounded in my chest. "Take that back or else!"

"But if you can't—"

I didn't let him finish. I hurled myself toward him.

I meant to just make him lose his balance and maybe his grip on his precious orb, but in my frustration my hand slapped his cheek—with force. Jatin stumbled backward, falling to the floor with a thud. He yelped and the crystal-filled orb tumbled across the room.

Feet thumped up the stairs. I crouched, my anger wilting and blooming into fear as the footsteps approached.

"I'm sorry! I didn't mean it." My throat constricted in regret. I really didn't mean it.

Jatin held a hand to his cheek as he stared at me wide-eyed. At least he wasn't crying.

"Let me see?" I edged closer when he continued to peer at me like a lifeless statue. I peeled his hand from his face and sighed. Nothing. No mark. No nothing. Well, it had only been my open palm.

"You *hit* me."

"I'm sorry." He was nowhere near crying, but I felt the hot press of emotion about to erupt in my own eyes. I had hit the future maharaja of Naupure. Even though it was an accident, *I was as good as dead.* And I guess a part of me deserved it.

Jatin's door was open, so our parents had no trouble hustling over the threshold.

"What happened?" Father asked.

"Is everyone okay?" Mother asked not a second after him.

I scanned between Maharaja Naupure lumbering over us and Jatin sitting there, still shocked.

"Adraa?"

"I . . . I got mad and I didn't mean to, but I—"

"She didn't do anything," Jatin said.

For one breathless moment, we all stared at him as he snapped out of his daze and got up off the floor.

Like they were going to believe that. "No, I . . . I hit him."

My parents glared, my father's eyes in particular shooting green icicles.

"You all right, Jatin?" Maharaja Naupure reached out one long arm to his son. Jatin didn't meet anyone's eyes as he nodded at the ground.

"Sir, I cannot begin to apologize," Mother said, turning to the maharaja.

"Adraa," Father snapped.

"I'm sorry," I whispered.

"Why did you hit him, Adraa?" Father's voice was firm, and filled with warning.

"He . . ." I glanced at Jatin. He finally unglued his eyes from the floor. And they were anything but calm.

I dropped to my knees in front of Maharaja Naupure like my prayer position to the gods. "I'm sorry, Maharaja Naupure. It doesn't matter what happened. I should not have hit Jatin."

After a terrifying still minute, I peeked through my hair, which had curtained around my face. Maharaja Naupure was shaking, and I trembled. We were going to die. I had hit Jatin and now, as payback, my parents and I were going to be killed.

An abrupt snort broke the tension. The maharaja was . . . laughing.

Maharaja Naupure bent down and raised my chin so I met his gaze. He peered at me in a way that skewered me to the core. Then he smiled. "Strength is more than standing." With my chin still in his hand, he looked up at my parents. "She is made to be a Naupure."

◇

CHAPTER ONE

An Unromantic Love Letter

Adraa

It is morning when I hear the news I have been dreading for nine years. I'm eating upma, my mouth and heart functioning properly, when my father trips them both with a single question.

"Did you know Jatin is coming back home today?" He glances up from the mounds of reports that fan out in circular stacks like a topographical map of the northern rice fields. Refusing to choke, my mouth revolts, and I eject the porridge instead of breathing it in.

My sister, Prisha, drops her spoon into her bowl and it clangs. "Ew."

Mother's face tilts in disgust. "Adraa."

I place a hand over my mouth to create a barrier so nothing else can escape as I cough. It feels like various organs have arisen in a coup. My heart, the leader, lurches, trying to make a break for it or at least to rip off the surrounding ropes of my arteries.

My father's eyes seize mine as they hum with insinuation. "I'm guessing that's a no."

Nine words, one for each year I had not seen him; that's all it takes to wash away my peace. After all this time, Jatin is coming home.

The sun has decided it's going to play peekaboo with the clouds, so in cyclical intervals the dining room glistens with warmth and then dampens into gray hues. Of course it would be during a piercing blaze that the consistency of my life breaks apart. My mind tries to pick up each individual word my father uttered, but drops them like a clumsy toddler.

Jatin.

Coming.

Back.

Today.

"Today? As in like a few hours from now?" I cough.

"Yes, that is what *today* means." Father sets aside a large report without looking at me.

"Maharaja Naupure didn't tell you last time you visited?" Mother asks, clearly satisfied I won't ruin the finely embroidered tablecloth.

"No," I say. "I mean, he might have . . ." Since that first night years ago, Maharaja Naupure and I have developed a friendly relationship, beyond the role of future father- and daughter-in-law. It is upheld by my monthly deliveries of firelight, which we both use as an excuse to discuss everything—politics, economics, a special project I'm working on—anything besides his son. Sometimes he slips up and I then pretend my brain has slipped up. But I couldn't have truly skimmed over this news, right? I'd be impressed with myself if anxiety wasn't drowning out all other emotions. Ignoring the idea of Jatin and being his wife is a second job.

"Oh, Adraa," Mother sighs.

"What? I haven't been summoned or anything and I'm not scheduled to send my firelight today, so . . . so I'm *not* going." I wrap my voice in confidence so maybe they won't push me. An unpleasant shiver runs down my spine. Going to the palace, being part of a welcome home parade I'm sure all of Naupure will attend, seeing the boy who would one day be my husband. My heart gags, one more tremor to note it isn't done freaking out. After nine years of me being here, in Belwar, and Jatin a hundred miles away training at a fancy prep school in Agsa, the engagement was finally . . . real. Now only Mount Gandhak would separate us.

"That's fine," Father says.

Mother frowns. "Don't you think she should at least make an appearance? After all, he's coming *through* Belwar to show his support. Half the city will be there."

Father looks up from his reports at last and shrugs. "If Maharaja Naupure did not summon her, I'll leave this one up to Adraa."

Mother grabs a piece of naan and rips it in half, her crooked nose flaring. When Father makes sense and advocates for freedom of choice, Mother really can't argue. Victory soars through me.

"I think Adraa should go!" Prisha exclaims, head buried in

her spell book. But I can spot the smirk nestled in her tone. *The little . . .*

"We'll leave this one up to Adraa," Father reiterates, and a thick silence slides around us, indicating the matter has been concluded. I look at my breakfast, able to breathe again. I won't have to face him today. And tonight I'll craft better excuses. Though I've been running through all the good ones lately.

Father shuffles some more paperwork. "Did you also know he stopped an avalanche on his way home?"

This fact, unfortunately, I do know. "Yeah, a *small* avalanche. Whoop-de-do." I spin my spoon into the upma, pushing the vegetables around, appetite officially lost. Prisha grins at her spell book. There is nothing amusing about the logistics of witchcraft, especially in fifteenth year. She just loves this, loves when I can be proved wrong, when I can be outdone in magic. And Jatin is always there to prove that.

"Stopping an avalanche of any size is impressive, Adraa. It saved half a village," Mother interjects.

"I'm glad people are safe." I relent. It's just . . . did it have to be Mr. Arrogant, Jatin Naupure, who did it?

"That boy is very proficient at snow spells—exceptionally so, in fact. I heard during his royal ceremony Dloc threw a blizzard at him and he took it down in seconds."

White magic is his forte, Dad. Is he supposed to be bad at them? That's like being impressed that, as a red forte, I can start fires. I almost remind my parents of the stable inferno I stopped last year, or even, dear Gods, what I do when I sneak out at night, but I hold my tongue. Because that needs to remain se-

20

cret. And who am I to talk, really? I have never saved so many people. And I have yet to battle through my own royal ceremony and prove myself capable in all nine types of magic.

The next moment, Willona bursts into the dining room holding a bowl of mangoes and sets it on the table. Our oldest and dearest servant runs her hands over her apron and I just know she is contemplating something. Why does she look so . . .

Oh no! Wide-eyed, I pivot fully in her direction and wave my hands, but it's too late, the words are already spewing out of her. "What did his letter say, Lady Belwar? I know everyone in the kitchen has been dying to hear."

I cover my face. That is—I mean *was*—supposed to be our secret. Do I need to start bribing the palace staff? But even that might not work. I cannot trust anyone when it comes to Jatin. Our engagement is common knowledge, too public in the palace to try to rein in the rumors.

Mother sits up straighter. She is such a sucker for romance. Except, she has no clue what lies between Jatin and me is not romance. It's fierce competition. And it can only end in disaster.

"He sent you something again?"

"Um, no," I lie.

"Adraa?"

Prisha smiles from across the table, daring me to lie again. How can someone who looks so young and innocent in all other features have such a mischievous mouth?

The note burns hot in my pocket. I had just gotten it this morning and had not felt like opening it. I know about the avalanche. He is going to rub it in my face.

21

I sigh. "What? Should I read it aloud?"

"That would be lovely."

Willona brims with excitement and then claps. "I'll get the kitchen staff."

"No, Willona, don't!" The door swishes into place behind her retreating form as I'm completely ignored. I tear the letter out from its useless hiding spot. The sun sinks behind a cloud once again, casting the room into dusky light. How fitting. I peel apart the seal and scan the contents to make sure nothing is too disturbing to say in front of everyone. The letter is short, but still gag-worthy, as always. "Really? You guys are going to let this happen . . . *again*?"

"Let them have their fun," Father says while signing something important.

"Yeah, Adraa, let us have our fun." Prisha looks me square in the eye.

"Fun?" This was my love life, or lack thereof. It should not be . . . fun, especially for our entire household, staff included.

It takes only four minutes for a quarter of the witches who work in the palace to tumble into the dining hall. They all appear giddy to the point of combustion. I might feel the same if I believed one word of Jatin's nonsense.

"Okay, everyone ready? I'm only reading this once. Zara? I'm looking at you." My maid rolls her eyes and then nods for me to proceed.

"*Dearest*," I begin. The women sigh in one heaving breath. Oh please! I give them a stern stare over the parchment and start over.

Dearest,

    If you haven't already heard, I am in Alps of Alconea, where a terrible avalanche nearly destroyed the village of Alkin. I was able to stop the destruction and hopefully further solidify my honor in your eyes. For one note of appreciation from you is all I'll ever seek in this world. One day I hope we can walk side by side on these beautiful mountains. How I long to be near you again! My heart punches in anticipation.

                   Wishing you my love,

                   Jatin

It is a complete farce. I have not seen the boy since that night I "punched" him in the face. Thinking back, what I did should be categorized under a shove or a slap, not a punch. I barely grazed him. But details get exaggerated with time. Or better put, Jatin likes to exaggerate. In reality, we don't like each other. And we certainly *don't* love each other.

Glancing up, I watch the kitchen staff hanging off each other and melting into the rugs. "Really, *every* time, guys?"

"He is so passionate and romantic," our cook, Meeta, says.

Zara croons, "Read the part again about appreciation in your eyes is all he seeks."

I push off the table and turn to go. Most of my audience heeds the signal and slips back to work in their designated parts of the house. Only Willona and Zara stay behind, probably to talk to Mother or Father about some chore or other.

"Where are you off to? Aren't you going to help me in the

clinic today?" Mother asks, annoyed at my rudeness. "And you need to deliver firelight to the East Village, right?"

I swivel back. "Um, I need another hour to get the firelight ready for the East Village."

Her fingers full of upma stop midair. "You didn't finish last night?"

"Ah yes, that is what I'm saying. Didn't finish."

"Oh, Adraa." She releases her frown, the signature one. "That's the fourth time in the past two months you have been behind."

"Training first, then one hour of work, and I'll be right on schedule." I put on my best "it's no problem" face.

She sees right through me. "Training first? Adraa, *no.* Basu expects a thousand firelights by midday."

I shove at the swinging door, desiring escape. If Mother pushes about why I didn't get the firelight done, she might start to piece together what I really do at night. I can't let that happen.

Willona saves me, with a joke at my own expense. "Oh, Miss Belwar gets so enthusiastic for training after getting one of Jatin's love letters." She grins and places one hand near her heart.

"Probably to burn off that blush." Zara fans herself and giggles.

I gesture to my face. "I'm not blushing." Although it might be hard to tell even if I were. After Mother I'm the darkest in the room, sometimes in the entire palace.

"Oh, guess you aren't," Zara says, sounding way too disappointed. A blush lies over her own cheeks, however, which makes me smile. She will surely sneak out for the festivities and I could ask her later how Jatin's parade went. Then I could ask about more than just the parade; I could ask about him. Did he look kind? Did he look nice? Did he look as powerful as he must be?

Ah, why do I even care about the jerk? Walk side by side on the Alps of Alconea? He knows I've never truly traveled, didn't join him at the academy a year after he started. I'm the oddity with a one-armed Touch and thus have been bound to this part of the world to preserve the Belwar reputation. Can't have the heir to the throne running off to the academy, a place to show-case the next great leaders of our generation, and embarrassing herself. I push at the door again, thinking about training. Maybe I am an embarrassment. Unlike Jatin, who at nine could cast all nine types of magic, my white magic casting is bloody awful. If Alkin had had to rely on me, that village wouldn't have survived.

"Fine, one hour to train, one hour to make the firelight, and then you are getting down to the East Village," Mother says.

"Thank you. You're the best, Mom!" I call.

Father looks up from his reports and raises both his arms. "I'm still here, you know."

"You are the best too, Dad." And he was, for getting me out of seeing Jatin today.

"Can I go to the parade, then?" Prisha asks. "If Adraa doesn't want to see Jatin, I do."

I hold my breath. In no way was *that* a good idea.

"Prisha, you have an exam," Mother argues.

Thank Gods. I could take Zara's giddy reconnaissance, but Prisha would deliver me lies or half-truths and I would be left to decipher them. Or even worse, she would walk right up to Jatin and introduce herself. Then I would have to explain my absence was due to fear and annoyance, not obligation to other duties.

I push through the door, glad to leave my sister's protests behind. Once alone in the hallway and on my way to the training yard, I whisper and touch my fingertips to Jatin's letter. *"Gharmaerif!"* A warm red glow spreads across the page and one icy clear word in Jatin's messy script, for my eyes only, unfreezes and steams into life. *"Winning."*

Blood. It's true.

CHAPTER TWO

◇

Homeward Bound and Hating It

Jatin

Up. High up, where clouds start to flirt with the sun, Kalyan and I fly. It is a freedom like no other. My skyglider, whiter than bone, glides under my control toward home. I am heading home. Huh, I thought I would get used to thinking that after the eighth hour of travel or so. But it's not like I have ever escaped the cage of my name and title. School had been only an extended prison, reaching out hundreds of miles from the palace to confine my heart and bind me to ambition. *Learn and train, you must, because one day you will rule. Messing up or giving up means not only personal failure but also your country's demise.*

I sigh, and think of the avalanche for the hundredth time. All that training had barreled into meaning something other than future obligation. I had saved people's lives. It felt good. It *feels* good. And thinking of the avalanche rears my brain into Adraa territory and I cannot help but smile. She should be getting the letter today. She should know what I accomplished in Alkin. This feat tops everything we have ever bragged about before. I'm definitely winning.

My personal guard drifts his skyglider closer to mine. "Okay, I know you don't like flying this much and returning to Naupure isn't exactly going to be the best day ever, so what is it? Why do you have that ridiculous smile on your face?"

I glance Kalyan's way. The wind whips his black hair and carries his white magic from his skyglider sweeping behind him in gusts. White trails my skyglider as well, but mine blends with the puffy clouds; Kalyan's saturates the sky with a straight grayish stream.

"What are you talking about?"

"The smile, the one you have been wearing since Alkin."

"I'm just happy I was there. Able to save all those—"

"You sent Adraa one of those senseless notes again, didn't you?" Kalyan shakes his head at me. "I know I'm right."

Adjusting my kurta, I meet my head guard's piercing look. "How do you figure?"

"I told you. Because of that ridiculous grin of yours. You are so proud of yourself. You think you are beating her."

I unglue the smile so my face discloses only seriousness. "I have a lot to be proud of. Look at this beautiful land." I gesture in a vague downward motion and then take a gander myself so I can keep my smirking in check.

A couple of miles to my left, the ocean sits, washes, and flows in an unbelievable mass. I can only comprehend it because I'm high enough to understand just how far into the forever it stretches. For some reason, miles of ocean seem more daunting than the endless snowcaps and greenery of mountains that rise to my right. Maybe I'm too used to the mountains: I was born within them, so their rise to meet my flight is like the peaks are trying to tickle my feet or clasp my shoulders, a warm familiar greeting. In the last six hours of flight the ocean has stayed constant, but the mountains grew and I know I am almost home.

"Proud of? We aren't in Naupure yet. Or are you insinuating this will be yours because we are nearing Belwar?" Kalyan asks.

"No, I do not plan to conquer."

"Of course, it will be practically yours anyway once you marry."

I don't feel like responding. If it weren't Kalyan, if I didn't know he was joking, those would be dueling words. Kalyan leans back on his skyglider, the wind catching the kited tail at a different angle. "Do you think she will be at the palace?" His tone is curious, interested. If I had voiced the question, the words would have drowned in anxiety.

I shrug.

It is so easy to think of Adraa as someone to tease, to challenge, but that is where our affection for each other ends. Truthfully, I don't know her that well. There are only a few variables I can nail down. One: she's competitive, almost to the point of vicious. Two: she's easily annoyed with a temper I have experienced firsthand. Everything else dwells in the land of supposedly. Like supposedly she's beautiful, supposedly she's brilliant, supposedly she's kind. All my father's words. But I guess he has a right to those opinions. She has practically grown up with the man, while I on the other hand had been sent away. I'm the foreigner in this situation. But now, I will finally figure her out myself instead of reading about her in palace reports. I turned eighteen months ago. If we are going to get married, it will be soon. My mouth goes dry. Do I want her to be at the palace? The "no" staggers before me. I don't want her there yet, don't want to face my future the moment I step through the ice door.

Kalyan glides close, too close really, but we are skilled enough to do it. He slaps my shoulder, obviously aware of my sudden unease. "Hey, we've been over this. She can't be too bad."

I sigh and pull a hand through my hair. "Yeah, Father just loves her." Which in truth makes it worse, so much worse. How can I escape this arrangement when the man whose respect I crave more than anyone's in the world admires a temperamental hothead who is all wrong for me?

Kalyan doesn't respond. He likes to find his words, make sure they convey something of importance or at least set up a joke. Mere talk for talking's sake is senseless garble to him. School was a real quiet time having him as my closest friend, but in the air, facing home, I cherish that silence. Wordlessly, he extends his forearm. I quickly knock mine against his before he whooshes out a few meters for safety. It's enough.

Ahead of us, three of my older guards fly, a small procession considering when I left for school at age nine I had twelve guardsmen. Not that we expect any danger, but it's a long journey. Someone could burnout. Accidents do happen. Only four flying stations, yellow-magic-fueled platforms for rest and recuperation, hover along our current route.

Mostly, though, it all comes back to me being the only heir,

30

not just my father's only son but his only child. I was supposed to have a sister. I was also supposed to have a mother. By now I've almost stopped noticing the cage of precaution. Almost.

From here I can only see the whip of cloaks and the guards' magic. Orange, yellow, and blue jet streams spout from the end of their skygliders and disperse before reaching Kalyan and me, thus prohibiting the potential cross of magic that could send us all barreling toward the mountain's feet.

Suddenly, yellow drops and my body tightens. *"Vardrenni."* I rush into a spell to make sure Samik hasn't been hit or fallen asleep, to make sure I can still save him. White smoke blurs my eyes for a second and my vision zooms in, magnifying Samik, who is descending and falling back on purpose. I sigh. Just a report then, but I stay alert regardless. I should be paying more attention, not thinking of Adraa or my father.

It takes Samik only a minute of hard flying to swoop under and then rise to fall in line beside me, the skill of a yellow forte. "Raja Jatin." He lays his index and middle finger to his throat in salute. I mirror the action.

"Yes?"

"We are approaching the East Village of Belwar, where we will meet the carriage."

Great. Just great. Not just paraded around for my father but for the Belwars too. One in particular, I'm sure.

"Thank you, Samik." I press my fingers against my pulse point again and he copies me, adding a deeper bow. Then he waits a moment to catch the wind and drop. So much honor and tradition; so much respect. But who is Samik beyond that salute?

31

Something seems to whisper I'll never get to know. Partly, it's the Naupure way. We are formal by nature. But it's more than that. We don't discriminate based on one's forte, unlike my uncle's country, Moolek, but propriety is still ruled by how many types of magic one can cast. In a land in which the majority can handle four types at the most, I'm a novelty. A nine. I'm also the heir to the throne. To a few people, I'm the embodiment of a god. That last bit has always been overwhelming. But it doesn't stop everyone from bestowing his or her ultimate respect and that means I get guards, I get loyalty, I get reverence. Never friendship.

Kalyan veers closer instead of shouting. "Think we should switch when we land? After all, we are doing the whole carriage thing to parade through the village."

I touch my simple blue kurta and look at Kalyan's fine embroidered jacket with my family's emblem, a mountain constricted by wind stitched into the fabric. We look so similar, like brothers: black hair, dark eyes, a light-brown complexion, even matching square chins. He is my guard for that reason, impersonating me whenever we travel or for laughs back at school. The real difference lies in the fact I'm a head shorter than my friend, but that disguises me even more. Everyone expects a maharaja to be tall, looming. Only my Touch gives me away, the power of my studies and blood racing up both my arms to meet my shoulders. Concealed in cloaks and a long-sleeved kurta, only the five of us surfing above mountains can identify me as a raja.

"You don't want to pretend to be me for one last time, for humor's sake?" I'm grasping, and we both know it.

Kalyan sighs, letting me grasp anyway. "Fine, but as soon as we pass Mount Gandhak we are switching. I am *not* riding up to Azure Palace and knocking on the ice door wearing this."

"Deal." I know I will never masquerade as a simple guard again. I already ache for the easiness, the simplicity in pretending I will not one day rule the country.

CHAPTER THREE

◇

A Little Thief

Adraa

"*Himadloc,*" I chant. Red streams of magic slip off my fingers and streak toward a bowl of water. The liquid stirs and slowly, way too slowly, hardens, cracks, and finally freezes over. Sighing at that pathetic attempt, I walk back to the covered porch, where the fattest book in history sits upon a podium. I flip through it, searching for other simple white magic spells.

A door to the training yard slams shut, which can mean only one thing.

"Hey! Your ceremony training isn't for another three hours. Why did you start without me?" When I don't look up, my best friend slaps her hand down on the page I'm reading. "Adraa. What's going on? Did something happen?"

"No." I shrug and push Riya's hand away.

She peers down at the paragraph. "Snow spells, really? Might as well show me the letter now."

I finally glance at Riya, who's shaking her head because she knows I only turn *this* desperate with white magic when I'm reminded of my royal ceremony. And Jatin in any form is the ultimate reminder. Oh Gods, he's really coming home today.

"What? You are easier to read than this ancient thing." She lifts one corner of the book and lets it drop for emphasis.

"I resent that. I'm complicated, mysterious, and . . ."

"And fretting over a boy?" Riya arches one of her thick eyebrows.

I jerk the letter from my pocket and hand it over. "I'm not fretting about him. I'm fretting about . . . about . . ."

Riya holds up a hand, my stammering explanations puttering out as she scans the letter. She finally meets my eyes again. "I guess he is kind of winning."

I tear the letter from her. "Aren't you supposed to be supportive?"

"I protect your life, but the job description doesn't say anything about being nice to you." Her hand rests on her knife in implication, but she also smiles.

It's a bad joke. Seven months ago there was no job description. Seven months ago Riya only had to worry about being my best friend. Then three Vencrin criminals cornered my personal bodyguard, Mr. Burman, her father. They blasted him with torture spells until he was comatose. Riya took up her father's mantle to protect me without hesitation. But it wanes on us, stiffening our once comfortable relationship.

And sometimes it feels like all I can do is change the subject. "I have to make more firelight and deliver it to the East Village. You in?"

"Of course. Could I even get out of it?"

A joke again, but this one bites because I think part of her means it. "Don't fret over petty things like a couple of words." I pat her arm playfully as I fetch the orbs for the firelight, hoping she knows just how much *I* mean that.

She takes my distraction, though, and helps haul the bowl with hundreds of small spheres over to the huge courtyard. Frostlight petals crunch beneath our feet, perfuming the air with the smell of crisp snow even though it's summer. These blossoms like to saunter into my training grounds like they own the place, which they kind of do. Hundreds grace the floor, taking over and leaving nothing but a sheen of white-speckled blue. One time they caught fire and almost burned the arched wooden pillars that surround us. I learned an extinguishing spell pretty quick after Riya and I saved the palace with a wave of water from the bubbling fountain. I chuckle at the memory as I wipe some of the blossoms away to reveal the dirt underneath.

"You want to try again?" I ask, gesturing to the pile of orbs and the bare spot I created.

Riya sighs. "You know I'm not good enough with red magic."

I mimic her sigh. "Yeah, just wishful thinking."

"Fine, fine."

I brighten and place two orbs on the ground. "Repeat after me and remember to raise your voice as you go."

"This isn't my first time, Adraa."

I don't apologize—Riya wouldn't want me to—and I begin the spell. Whispering at first and finishing in a shout, Riya and I coax our magic out. *Erif Jvalati Dirgharatrika . . ."*

Purple smoke billows off Riya's fingertips, red bleeds from mine. Both color streams hit the orbs and fire bursts inside each sphere casing. My heart erupts as I watch Riya bend to pick up her orb with its tiny flame glowing inside.

"You . . ."

She blows hard on the little life and a smoky ghost floats upward in passing. "Didn't do it."

I grasp my own orb, blow as hard as I can. The life doesn't flicker. The bloodred flame actually seems to rejoice at the challenge, flooding my hand in light. With a click I shut the orb. "One done, three hundred to go."

"I'll keep you company."

I roll my stiff pink sleeve up to let my magic breathe.

◇ ◇ ◇

I had lied to my mother; it took well past an hour to make three hundred orbs of blazing and unwavering light. But since Riya stopped my sad endeavor to try to get better at white magic, I'm ahead of schedule. I sit down to rest by the central fountain dedicated to Retaw. Riya hands me a cup of water, and I chug.

"You know, I can see why you can't do much of anything with snow and the cold. Watching you make these"—Riya picks up a sphere of firelight—"it makes sense."

"Uh-huh." The ice door of Azure Palace flits into my memory. I'll never be able to do anything like that, and a fire door just sounds dangerous. My magic forte *is* dangerous. A rani is meant to snuff out problems, put out fires, not start them. And that's what I want, to create, not destroy. That little ball of red light she holds is the first good thing I've been able to make.

"I'm serious. What's so great about the cold anyway? Who likes to be cold?" she asks.

I give a tight smile. "Thanks." I can't voice my lack of progress with white magic again. When I turn eighteen in a month and a half, forty-five days to be exact, I must showcase my talent to all nine gods and request their blessing. And while it's all well and good that I'm more powerful in fire than anyone I have ever met, the fact of the matter is that Dloc, the white god, may not accept me. And no one wants to be blasted off the podium by a blizzard. It could kill me. Or better put, the gods could kill me. If I were a normal Belwarian it wouldn't matter. I wouldn't attempt the ceremony, because being talented enough as an eight is amazing. But I'm almost a royal, a future maharani of Wickery, and I can't rule unless I can control all nine types of magic and prove it to the gods and to my people.

At first, I neglected white magic because it came hard to me. Then I schemed that being an eight my whole life meant I could get out of my engagement and arranged to marry someone else, but a few years ago I realized how important helping my country, or rather its people, was to me. I may not want to marry Jatin Naupure, but I do want to become a maharani and lead Belwar in some capacity. Passing the ceremony is more about gaining the title than gaining a husband.

However, long ago I recognized how much everyone wants this arranged marriage to work, how good it would be for Wickery. My parents and Maharaja Naupure decided to wait until

Jatin and I were older before uniting us with a blood contract's holy and binding seal, which is normal protocol little eight-year-old me didn't comprehend. However, that didn't stop a verbal agreement, which is almost as binding when it comes from wizards of such power. What doesn't help is the fact Jatin Naupure writes me "love" letters. From their perspective my parents have no reason to discourage the arrangement. One more reason to blame Jatin for this mess. Plus Maharaja Naupure actually loves me, wants me as his daughter-in-law no matter my weaknesses. But he doesn't grasp how deep my weakness in snow delves. I stare down at my arms. One is soaked in swirls and designs, the other plain and as dark-skinned as the rest of me. *Can you do it yet?* Jatin's voice jabs.

It's times like these I wish I were Naupurian. Jatin's ceremony was at the academy without a big to-do and where passing is all anyone cares about. He's been presented as the heir of Naupure since birth, both arms shouting talent, doubt unheard of. In Belwar it's different. On my eighteenth birthday, my ceremony will be my first grand entrance to the people. I will walk the streets of Belwar wrapped in the nine colors and I will do my trial at the heart of the Belwar temple, during which I fear my one arm will convey only doubt.

I get off the ground and pace. *"Himadloc,"* I send out to the bowl of water. The red strains of smoke streak through the water, and then nothing. I'm tired, I try to tell myself. I just finished three hundred firelights, I reason. The lies don't work.

"You sure you aren't practicing so much because you *want* to be with Jatin?" Riya asks.

I spin to give her a dirty look. "Why does everyone think that? Like it's odd I want to be a rani and not a wife."

She laughs and points at my hands. Sometime during my pacing I pulled out Jatin's letter again.

I flinch and let the parchment drop. Then I flail as I snatch for the paper as it floats over the bubbling fountain. "Blood." I rub my temples and slide down the closest pillar.

Riya chuckles at my dramatic wilting and kicks my foot with her boot. "Are you still having those red room nightmares?"

"Only one last night. But it's not that. It's . . . he's . . . he comes home today," I groan through my hands.

"What?" she yells. I've surprised Riya, which is an unusual development. I peer up to take in her confusion, happy someone else feels like this is serious enough to warrant stress.

"Gods," she gasps, before reeling in her shock. "But we still have time." Riya is the only one who truly understands the extent of my problem. Of course, my parents know to some degree, but they believe I'll pull through with more practice. It's why I'm still allowed training time in the middle of the day. I would explain to Maharaja Naupure, but a little thing called pride gets in the way, and I refuse to tell Jatin, ever. He cannot have another thing to sneer at. That's how I imagine him writing at his desk—sneering. The boy needs an ego boost as much as I need another reminder that I'm losing. That I may lose everything.

"Let's get going. I want to fly, to forget about all this for a while," I say.

Riya nods as she examines her timepiece. "Yeah, we're running late anyway."

The little stumps of our skygliders hang in the training yard attached to a wooden post. With a quick green spell, the post unravels and releases Hubris in condensed form. Riya keeps glancing at me, worry drawing her full eyebrows closer to her dark eyes. I proceed as usual, trying to convey through my actions I'm well and unafraid of my impending ceremony or my marriage.

With a hard flick and a simple spell, the eight-inch-long wooden tube enlongates. The handle, bound in interlacing wicker, extends, and at the tail two kitelike pieces of red fabric unfold and stiffen with a snap like when the wind catches a sail. I smile at Hubris's full form as I chant the flight spell that will cast us both air bound. Red the color of blood pools into the woven wicker, finding and soaking its way into the wood's slivers. I add a little extra magic to take the additional weight of two saddlebags filled to the brim with firelight.

Before settling atop Hubris, I adjust my belt and redo the knot of my orange skirt over my pink pants as Riya pulls on a purple pair. Around the palace I normally wear pants under my wraparound skirt because, well . . . let's just say I've been so active and forgetful in the past that Zara never creates an ensemble without them. Riya, however, is more proper and elegant. Any outsider, though, might think I'm the more modest and traditional one, with my dedication to long sleeves. They would be wrong, of course.

When you're under eighteen, it's best to wear your parents' colors while in public. So while I'm doomed to pale-orange and bright-pink attire, Riya, who's three years older, gets to wear whatever she wants. Like most days she sports her parents'

41

purple and a soft blue that looks fantastic with her light-brown skin. One day the nine-pointed sun will also be stitched to my clothing, but the royal emblem of Belwar is only donned after the ceremony. I can't seem to get away from the fact that I'm not ready for the throne.

I crisscross the straps of two large saddlebags around my shoulders. Riya does the same, heaving them over her head before mounting her floating skyglider.

"Ready?" she asks. I fix the curled strap of one of the feisty bags before nodding and punching my feet hard in the ground.

"*Makria!*" Riya and I shout. Frostlight petals explode into the air as we jet upward. The sticky grip of humidity loosens as the wind ruffles my blouse. The aroma of frost lingers until Mother's factory of smells takes over. Years ago, Mother seized the east wing of Belwar Palace and converted it into a pharmacy and patient station. It can smell of anything, from rotting seagull feet to spring flora. As I glide by the roof of my home and Mother's potion galley, the smell of lemons and fish circles through the air. Not too bad, since everything near the coast smells of fish anyway.

Already fifteen meters in the air, I can see the line of people amassed outside the palace gates and curved around the corner. A baby wails. The elderly hobble forward. Younger kids anxiously bounce around, sent to fetch my mother's potions. A bittersweet smile pulls on Riya's lips as she catches my eye. I know how the lines of people looking for medicine can unwind her. They unwind me too.

We are flying right over her father. Mr. Burman's room is

near the east wing, close enough to all the potions and pink magic to remind us that he needs my mother's expertise to keep breathing. She knows how much it destroyed me too. He was my tutor before he became my bodyguard. He taught me how to fly. He taught me how to fight. And nine years ago, after I came back from my visit to Naupure, he's the one who caught me crying about my Touch. He's the one who took me aside and said, "A true rani doesn't have to have magic or a god's blessing. A true rani just helps the people."

He is one of the reasons I am the way I am, that I'm doing what I'm doing when I sneak out at night. He always knew what to say. Sometimes I do too, but today, like most, I'm lost for words for my best friend. We stream upward and eastward in silence.

Anchored between lush mountains lies the cavernous valley of Belwar, my city and home. As we rise, I can see just how far my country extends to include the smaller villages nestled in the northern mountains and among the rice fields. But the majority of the population that my father and mother protect is here, bustling and moving beneath me and Riya.

It's the most diverse place in all of Wickery. Belwar has always been a shipping port calling to travelers and hagglers and foreigners. Then, five years ago, the Southern Bay Monsoon tore through southern Agsa and refugees fled here. Pire Island, right off our coast, was left without the usual shipments of agricultural goods, which sent another wave of asylum-seekers. With Mother being Pire we welcomed them with open arms.

It would be easy for my country to segregate itself like Moolek does, based on religious tradition and forte color. Or by any other facet along which hatred likes to divide. By skin color like Agsa does, by gender like Pire Island, or by power level like Naupure. We don't. While we might have a problem with the long perpetuated stigma against Untouched, with half the populace powerless, I'm proud. And I'll do anything to be a "true rani."

Belwar may be small, a pond compared with the lake Maharaja Naupure controls or the ocean of land Maharaja Moolek governs, but it is home. The four villages, denoted in simple geographic terms—north, south, east, west—all splinter outward from Belwar Palace. I live in the center of a compass. Maybe that's why I so fiercely want to retain my title. Being a Belwar gives me direction and purpose. Without it, what am I, really?

I gaze westward toward Mount Gandhak, the towering volcano separating my land from Jatin's. It is a foreboding but dormant landmark of distinction that casts a wide shadow. Was he there already?

It takes only seven minutes of focused flying to get to Basu's. Not enough time to clear my head of Jatin or the looming royal ceremony. As we descend into the East Village, I spot Basu's shop immediately, a stacked, bushy fortress. Basu tumbles out and waves me down, which is quite annoying. *Yes, I see you!* I want to shout. Riya and I land with only a slight whirlwind of air swooping and swirling around us.

"I was worried you would be late again," Basu says, his tone spiked to critical capacity and tinged with impatience. What a wonderful combination.

I smile. "I wouldn't miss your charm and warmth, Basu."

Riya shakes her head, but to the untrained eye it appears as if she is only shrugging off one of the heavy saddlebags. I haul my own bag over my head, but it tugs in protest. The strap smacks my shoulder and I spin to find a little boy, about seven years old, holding one of the firelights. He reached into the bag and took it.

"Hey! That doesn't belong to you!" Basu roars.

The boy's eyes widen, clicking between fight or flight. He chooses flight. Thieves always choose flight.

"Stop him, someone stop him." Basu bounces into the road, waving his hairy arms to indicate the boy.

Firelight is three coppers, literally one of the cheapest things in our country—I made sure of that. So why steal? Was the boy that poor? I drop both saddlebags into Basu's arms. "I'll get him."

"Adraa!" Riya yells.

"Five minutes, I'll be back." I wave in reassurance.

I have to know.

"*Tvarenni,*" I whisper, and send orange magic to my legs to catch up. But the boy is fast like he's memorized the twists of each alleyway. This might be more challenging than I thought. He ducks into a dark side street where a strand of villagers are washing and dyeing clothing. They yell in protest as the boy blows by sheets billowing out to dry. The path turns into hundreds of steps, pebble encrusted and moss coated. I can still see him, bouncing up, up, up.

"Hey! Boy! I just want to talk!" I yell. He turns around, jolts, and flies even faster up the stairs. "*Zaktirenni!*" I shout, shooting energy into my muscles.

I thump up the stairs and my orange magic brings me within four steps of the thief. I reach out to hook a hand around his arm when, *whack*, a dusty rug slaps me in the face. A woman leans out the doorway from which she threw the dust-covered thing into the stairwell. "What the—"

I'm knocked sideways and my lungs knocked into turmoil. Hasn't my throat already had enough of this today? Coughing and gasping, I watch as the horrified woman pieces together the person-sized object her precious rug has run into. "I'm sorry, Miss. . . ." She begins a trembling bow, but I wave my hands.

"Don't worry about it."

"But—"

I spot the boy at the top of the staircase, peering down at me. Then he dodges to the left. "Ah no!" I spring forward, taking two steps at a time until I reach the top. And then I'm careening onto my tiptoes as several goats strut past. A bustling town square lies before me, market day in full swing. People in colorful clothing jostle one another. Vendors shout from open stalls. Large, wide bowls of fruit and different-colored spices lie on the ground before kneeling merchants. "Watch it!" The goatherd yells roughly at me for almost colliding with his livestock. This just got harder.

"*Vindati Agni Dipika*," I whisper. Tendrils of red mist unleash from my hands, searching for my own creation, for my firelight. More than intuition forces my head to the left. I catch the boy sneaking around a vegetable stand, hugging the ball of light to his chest. I run forward, tumbling past people who are just standing there. Why is the market this crowded? Why aren't people ambling around, shopping? They all stand there, frowning, as I swivel among them.

The boy sees me coming, but I'm already close, within two body lengths. He darts into the open square. Too late I realize why no one is moving, just standing around and staring at the center path. A coach, bright blue, gold trimmed, and pulled by one large elephant, rumbles along the path. The boy glances back at me, not what he is about to run into. Everything slows.

"Stop!"

The elephant startles, trumpeting to the clouds. No green magic spells to combat or halt an animal come to mind. "Tva-renni!" I scream. People around me can foresee the tragedy, the bloody mess the boy is about to be turned into. Their gasps and cries drown out my own voice. Some make way for me, dodging to the side to create a clear path for interception. I push past others. Again I scream the speed spell and my body is enfolded in red. "Tvarenni!"

The elephant jerks skyward. The boy's hands rise. My fire-light gleams, the first thing the elephant will smash. And I pour every ounce of magic I have into my muscles. I must have moved faster than ever before, because somehow I slam into the boy and twist at the same time. The elephant stomps down, an arm's length from my head. I wince and roll myself and the boy farther to the right.

"Matagga Zantahihtrae," a male voice chants.

I roll again, the boy and me, tumbling in the dirt. The elephant no longer moves a muscle, but trumpets softly in frustration. Yeah, me too, buddy.

I sit up, dazed by the amount of magic and fear lingering in my bloodstream. The boy whimpers when I move. I process the noise of his heavy crying at the same time a male voice shouts, "Is everyone okay?"

I can't exactly turn around with the boy fastened to me like a leech, so I raise one weak hand. "Yes, we are alive." Faces in the crowd gape, hands stretch out. Thank Gods I'm not eighteen yet, that these people have no clue this dirty mop of a girl may be their future ruler.

Someone bends over me, blocking the blinding sun and the blur of faces. It has to be whoever was in the carriage. Before I see his face, an emblem stitched onto his jacket greets me, a snowcapped mountain with blue wind encircling it, the emblem of my intended. Raja . . . Raja Jatin.

I scramble like I've never scrambled before, both brain and body afray. "Ahhh."

Again, he speaks, with a rich voice that can only be described as masculine. "Are you all right?"

The boy cries into my side. The crowd murmurs. But the noise should be louder, should be as pounding as the questioning voice. *Am* I all right? Something in me seems to be malfunctioning. Another man appears behind Raja Jatin. "The elephant and everyone else are fine," he says. "Are she and the boy okay?"

"I think she hit her head," Raja Jatin says.

"I, um, I'm good." Good? Really? That's all I can come up with? Embarrassment, because it knows it has the right to invade this situation, creeps into my cheeks and spreads over my entire body. I must be dipped in a different, fuming red.

Raja Jatin steps back and turns to the crowd, letting his guard, or whoever he is, take charge of the situation I have so amazingly created. The guard ruffles the crying boy's hair. "Hey, it's over. It's okay. Your sister saved you."

The boy finally looks up and peers into my eyes. "You did save me." He sniffles. "Why?"

"Ah." I'm unable to be articulate right now, let alone answer why I value life. The simple answer—*because*—seems underwhelming and foolish. What actually spills out of my mouth is much worse. "Just answer my questions, okay? Don't run off."

The boy nods. In one motion he unwraps his arms from my middle and pulls my firelight into view. "Here, it's yours."

I reach to take it, but my left arm falls to my side, limp like jelly. It aches as if the nerve endings have been snapped. Blood, not again. Not now! I grasp the orb with my right hand and let it fall in my lap. How am I going to escape this mess? To burnout at this moment . . .

I glance at Raja Jatin, who looks stiff, like a statue at a podium addressing the crowd. His guard, however, is enthralled by my exchange with the boy. Confusion lines his features.

He stands and the boy follows. Everyone is waiting on me. Even the crowd strains to catch a glance at the foolish girl who ran toward a royal carriage and now can't seem to get up.

When I don't stand, the guard raises his eyebrows and offers his hand. I peek at Raja Jatin again, who is talking to the carriage driver. At least he's not paying attention to me and has no clue who I am.

"Can you take this?" I gesture to the orb.

"What is it?" the guard asks.

"Firelight," the boy says before I can answer.

49

The guard's eyes widen as he pockets the red magic before reaching down again and grabbing my good hand. With a majority of his help, I'm able to haul myself up. The crowd cheers. I can hear it, but the faces are smudged. My vision swims like I've dived into a murky pool. I sway and the guard grabs both my forearms to stabilize me. "Are you sure you are *good*? I think you burned out."

I laugh at his puzzlement. Burned out—the term is particularly accurate for me even though it applies to all witches and wizards. I clench and unclench my left hand. The designs on my wrist don't glow, and deeper, under the skin, my blood chugs along fast and scared, but not spiced with energy. I haven't burned out since . . . ah, wait, there was that time last week.

"I've had a busy morning," I murmur, striving to sound confident. It's a mediocre attempt at best.

This is why I'm supposed to create firelight at night, so sleep and time can renew my magic. I love my invention, but it's powerful and energy depleting. And currently I'm having time management regrets. I sway again, my body practically slamming into the guard's. He catches me, this time by my shoulders.

"Yes, definitely burned out. You're going to pass out soon. I promise you'll be safe when you awaken."

"No I won't."

"I can assure you, by the honor of Raja—"

I interrupt so I don't have to hear the full name. I can't bear the reality of it in full. "No, I mean I won't pass out. I just need a few minutes." The dizziness should fade in about five minutes. It always does. Blackness clouds my vision, but it won't take over.

The guard's hands still hold my shoulders. Another bout of light-headedness hits me. I grab his forearm as an anchor. His skin is cool. I'm not only burning out but burning up.

"Do, um . . . do you mind if I . . ." He finishes with something, but I can't make out the words. Blood, my brain's swimming. I need to sit. Thinking I could stand in this condition was foolish. As I release the tension in my legs to crumple, the opposite happens. This man . . . this *boy* has the nerve to pick me *up*. I am in his arms, pressed against him. His left biceps digs into my back; the other arm hooks around my legs. Huh, he smells of frost. My nose notes it as if that's an important element to life right now.

Oh blood. What's going to happen to this guard when Raja Jatin finds out this man is carrying his betrothed? It's too late. I've messed up. I can't say anything anymore. I'm swimming. Guess I won't need to ask Zara later how the parade went. I have become a part of it after all.

CHAPTER FOUR

The Burnout Girl

Jatin

Of all the wild things one would expect at a homecoming parade, like an assassination attempt, for instance, a peasant girl throwing herself in front of an elephant is low on the list. Deep, actually, as in, I hadn't planned for it. Hadn't been watching the crowd for speed spells that would propel a girl into our path. I mean, what a way to go, death by royal carriage. Gods. A moment after she rolls to the ground and I calm the elephant, I understand. Not a suicide gone awry; a rescue gone well.

And now, somehow, I'm holding this burned-out witch in my arms and carrying firelight in my pocket. When her arm spilled to the ground like it was paralyzed I knew. Burnout. It's drastic, but I guess for a peasant one act of bravery can use up a limited supply of magic. Still, I haven't seen someone suddenly deplete themselves of all their magic since seventeenth year, when one of my classmates was trying to create a fifteen-meter wave. He fell to the sand like a coconut and had to be hauled off to medical.

She will surely pass out too, but I refuse to leave her in the street. The plan to take her to Azure Palace formed before I could reflect on all the potential downfalls. Like if Adraa is there already, what will she say when I bring in this dust-covered, unconscious girl? What will Father say? At this moment, I don't care.

"*Zaktirenni,*" I whisper, to give myself a little strength. I don't exactly have a good hold on her, having had to do the whole catch-and-lift motion all at once. I adjust and feel my orange magic take hold. The silk of her skirt shifts under my hand. Thank the gods she is wearing pants too.

I don't carry her far, but those six meters ooze intimacy. She heats my chest like the sun has melted between us. That's probably the burnout. Probably. I've never carried a girl before, never done much of anything besides talk to a witch. That's the problem with a long-term engagement. You always feel obligated, guilty to do anything or form anything but friendship with the opposite sex. Besides, I had studying, and that was always more important.

The girl's eyes are closed, but by the way she clenches and unclenches her hand against her forehead I know she's still awake. The sun blankets her face, a dirty face. But under the dirt . . . I can't help but stare. She's beautiful; thick black hair windblown and scrambled, long dark eyelashes over even darker lively eyes. With my magic, the girl is light, but even if she were heavy, I would like this. She smells of mud and grass rippled by wind, fresh and real, like when rain wafts spring through the air. And the warmth, it's . . . nice.

"Watch your head," I say.

She leans against me, her soft breath tingling my neck. A shiver dances down my spine. I don't know why I have such a strong reaction, but I hold her closer as I crouch and shift to enter the carriage. I place her on the plush blue cushion and suddenly, just like that, I'm not touching her anymore. The humid summer air strikes me—it's freezing.

"I'll be right back."

She nods, then seems to register something and grabs my arm as I move away. "The boy, please. Make sure he doesn't run. Bring him here."

I bend forward. "He's obviously not your brother. So, who is he to you?"

She shrugs. "A thief."

What? I know my surprise shines through the mask of calm I'm trying to wear. But who can blame me? This is more than I anticipated. The academy didn't provide training on beautiful girls who run toward enormous elephants to save criminals.

"All right," I answer, schooling my features. It's one thing I can honestly say I did have daily practice in at the academy.

"Thank you," she says, before leaning forward to hold her head in her hands.

Once I'm sure she's not going to say anything else I ease out of the carriage. Kalyan frowns as he talks to the boy. Kalyan frowning? Never a good sign. When my friend spots me, he walks over, leaving the kid with Samik.

"Jatin, I think the boy is a thief and the girl was running after him to get back what he stole."

"Yeah, I know. And this is what he took." I dig the orb from my pocket and hold it up.

"Simple red magic?"

"No, it's firelight."

"As in Lady Adraa's invention?" Kalyan inspects it. "Doesn't look like much to me. Maybe a little redder than normal fire."

"The boy said it's firelight. Now I want answers. Those two have piqued my interest."

"That could be their plan, to get close to the maharaja or to you."

Or this could be orchestrated by my father: a test to prove myself before I reenter the ice door. Doubtful, but the thought hovers, overbearing and cloudy. "I don't think so," I finally answer.

Kalyan shakes his head. "She seems too pretty and too powerful just to be some girl on the street. I don't know if you saw it, but she was *glowing* with magic; had to be, to run that fast."

"I'll take my chances."

"You mean take *my* chances. I'm not letting them know who the real raja is now."

I pat Kalyan on the shoulder. "Thank you."

I walk over and squat next to the boy so he and I are eye level. Equals. "Hey, so if you don't mind coming with us, we want to ask you—"

"No." The boy's tone is firm, but his eyes dart sideways first, then everywhere. He's looking for escape, no doubt.

"It's not for me. She saved your life. You owe her."

"She has the firelight back. Let me go." Blood, whatever I say next will sound like a kidnapping. I guess that is what I'm doing, in a roundabout way. Maybe this is a test. You're going to take a kid in for interrogation because one of the most beautiful girls you have ever seen wants you to?

My voice hardens and gets gruff, to unnerve the boy. "Get in the carriage." Well . . . I'm going to fail this test.

"Let's get going, Samik," I say.

The boy slips inside the carriage and I follow, Kalyan right behind me. The coach totters into motion. While the cushions aren't hard, the boy acts as if I've forced him onto live coals. One day I will be conducting and rectifying grievances. It seems fitting that as soon as I begin my journey home I have to deal with things of this nature.

I turn my attention back to the girl, who's still bent over. She clenches her left hand. The little part of her Touch I can see on her left wrist glows a faint red. Magic must be returning to her. I watch intently, but it's Kalyan who blurts out the question that loiters on the tip on my tongue.

"How is that possible? You were burned out three minutes ago." He may be suspicious, but I'm fascinated.

"I'm used to it," she murmurs, without looking Kalyan in the eye. She is obviously uncomfortable in Kalyan's presence, but of course that's because she thinks he is a raja. This moment perfectly encapsulates my hatred for my title. The slight dread that stiffens her spine irritates me and makes me restless.

"So, you always go around throwing yourself in front of carriages?" I ask.

She directs her gaze at me. As a guard I'm safe. "Not on a

daily basis." Her expression is deadly straight; no wrinkle to let me in on the joke, just dirt and dust. I can read the beauty of her features, that part's easy. Reading her? This might be a long ride.

The girl twists toward the child. "Tell me why you stole the firelight."

He squirms, looking like he wants to drift into the woodwork. "Because Mom keeps talking about them, how we could heat the stove quicker or light the porch. But they're hard to find and too expensive. I didn't think you would miss one when you had so many." He pauses, wringing his hands. "Please, don't tell on me."

"Expensive! They're three coppers. Could your mom not afford that?"

Three coppers is extremely cheap. A loaf of bread averages about fifty or so in this part of the world.

The boy looks at her strangely. "Three coppers? Firelight is five silvers."

"What the blood?" The girl punches the seat cushion. I've never heard a witch curse so bluntly. I have to cough to conceal a laugh.

"Who sets the price?" Kalyan interrupts.

The girl stares at Kalyan, willing him to look at her. "Your fiancé," she answers slowly.

The mere mention of Adraa charges the air. And then, suddenly, I'm watching a staring contest unfold before me. Kalyan is a master of solemn looks and quiet contemplation. If either of them would turn to look at me, though, they'd notice the sweat and the anxiety of homecoming getting the best of me. I feel for the firelight in my pocket. Adraa's magic. Would this be news to her?

As I predicted, the girl breaks first and refocuses on the boy. "It's five silvers in all of Belwar?" she asks.

He shrugs. "I'm not allowed to go beyond the central square," he says like it's obvious information and we should be ashamed of our interrogation tactics.

"Where do you live? What neighborhood?" Her tone turns desperate.

"East Village, down by the docks."

"Blood, Vencrin area," she whispers so softly I almost don't catch it.

"Vencrin?" I ask.

"A local gang, bunch of criminals who sell drugs like Bloodlurst to anyone with a piece of silver to their name."

I've heard of Bloodlurst before, a red powder that can enhance one's power. One medical report at the academy detailed how addictive and destructive the substance is. It's killed people. I try to remember its exact effects while the girl continues.

"I don't know why they would be interested in firelight unless . . ."

"What?"

"Unless they're trying to undermine the Belwars."

"Or simply turn a profit," Kalyan suggests.

"Yes." She nods. "That's more likely. But this feels personal."

"Personal?" I ask.

She doesn't answer my question, just gives Kalyan a determined look. "I need to go."

"Are you sure you—"

"Please, I can't go to Azure Palace, or wherever you are headed. I need to get back."

Kalyan turns to give me a look, then thumps on the carriage three times in Samik's direction. The coach slows and then lurches to a stop. The boy scoots close to the door, ready to burst from his confinement.

The girl glances at the boy and then shuffles closer to me. For a moment, I believe she wants help out of the carriage and I reach for her extended hand.

"Can I have the firelight?" she asks. I pull off an awkward maneuver to mask wanting to hold her hand. Read that one wrong.

"Oh, ah, yeah." I give the firelight to her and feel cold again.

"Here, kid." She tosses the orb and he catches it with fumbling hands. "Tell your mom if she has any red magic to add a little every day and it can light a whole fireplace for *more* than two months."

"Thanks." The boy smiles and then plunges into the street.

The girl hops down. "Well, thank you." She pauses and I can see she's clearly deliberating. "I'm sorry this was such an . . . awkward meeting."

"Are you sure you're feeling okay?" I want her to say no. I want her to keep talking. There is obviously so much I don't know, about firelight, the Belwars, and her.

"Yeah, I'm fine. You could say I'm the kind of person who when knocked down can get right back up again." She stares pointedly at Kalyan. Then something amazing happens: her eyes shift to me, and she smiles, a laughing smile, like we have shared some kind of joke. In the next sweep of a second she's gone. It's like magic vanishing into thin air as you're still trying to determine the spell. The carriage pitches forward again as if nothing has happened at all. *Did any of that just happen?*

"Blood!" I curse.

Kalyan starts. "What?"

"I never asked her name."

CHAPTER FIVE

◇

An Interrogation

Adraa

I can't believe he didn't recognize me or at least suspect who I was. While I'm shocked, pride also slithers in. I'm winning this one. I have the upper hand after all. But how could he not have figured it out? I gave him such clues, practically waited for him to ask.

At the end, a part of me wanted to tell him, let him off the hook so our next meeting wouldn't be even more awkward. But I couldn't do it. I'll let the awkwardness fade, the memory settle so that it can wear away a bit at the edges. I only now seem to process that I met Jatin, sat across from him. It's almost laughable, but my anger at the Vencrin balances the scales or absolves the embarrassment. Five silvers! *Five.*

It takes me ten minutes of hard walking to get back to Basu's. I had hoped the hike would calm me and get my head straight so I can properly threaten Basu and get to the bottom of this. Nope, the issue dwells for half a mile.

Children run up to me, materializing from the alleyways and into the bright streaking sun. I'm dirty, with a tear in my skirt, but the gleam of my silks must still smell of opportunity.

"Ten coppers, ten coppers," they say, all smiles and big eyes. Hands reach upward, some with a Touch wrapped around their wrists, others naked. I search for my small sack of coins. But it's gone. That boy, whose arms wound around me, tears rolling down his checks. That sneaky little—

"I have nothing," I say, happy I don't have to lie. I try to not give away any silver and gold like this, for it will find its way to funding Bloodlurst. Some of the older children, near my age, already wear the splotchy red sign of overuse in the crooks of their elbows.

Vencrin drugs have infected the East Village. Yes, they feel good. Yes, Bloodlurst in particular can make you more powerful for a limited time. And that can mean a day's work down at the docks, making skyglider deliveries, or even illegal cage casting. But the drugs are slowly draining my people of their magic, of their lives. And now the East Village isn't getting firelight either. Which means Basu, a bizarre old man who has been a family friend for years, has betrayed us. A man who let one-fourth of my city suffer due to vastly unfair prices and slide further under the control of criminals and druggers. Firelight is the first step in bringing light to the darkness, protecting people from the Vencrin who roam the streets and dispense quick boosts of power to teenagers. Without it . . .

My chest hurts. I feel like I'm going to explode.

I round the corner to Basu's street and the kids slink and

shuffle away. When Riya sees me, her shoulders unravel, but when a closer look confirms my safety, she breathes in anger.

"'It'll take five minutes,' she says. 'I'll be right back,' she says. What the blood, Adraa? You are covered in dust and . . . and . . ." Her speech slows. Gods, she knows. "You *burned out*?" Her voice trills up in a question, but she only needs a jerk of my head in verification. The shame of losing my magic creeps back in like heat. I'm sticky with the disgrace of it.

"I'll apologize in full later. Right now, we have a problem." I step closer to her. At the word *problem,* Riya shuts down her irritation, open for what is coming instead of yelling about what has happened.

"Tell me."

"The Vencrin are stealing my firelight and up-charging it. Three coppers is five silvers for those near the docks."

"What? Those—"

"Also, I ran into Raja Jatin." I brush a hand through my hair, suddenly aware of its tangled state. And I had considered telling him who I was!

Her jaw unhinges. "Wait, what?"

Under normal conditions I'd probably laugh at her gawking. I drop my hand and even the leftover embarrassment evaporates. *Five silvers.* "We can talk later. Right now, I need to speak with Basu."

I step into Basu's shop, and though I'm not trying to be quiet, it's unusually soundless. Nice new purple door. Hardwood floors. He doesn't have bells hanging over the threshold or even fabric cloaking the doorway. Both are normal precautions against

63

thieves shrouded by black camouflaging spells. I watch him as he frantically grabs orbs out of my bags. He inspects, places, inspects, places each ball of light into boxes. Greed gleams in his eyes. How had I never seen it before?

"What's going on, Basu?"

"Oh, Lady Adraa! So glad you have returned. Did you catch that thief?" He extends one hand, waiting.

"Sorry, too fast," I say, my tone biting.

"Huh, well, you do look worn, my dear."

"Don't call me 'dear.'"

"Oh, my apologies, Lady." He continues his task. Inspect. Place. Inspect. Place.

This isn't working; in fact, this process is boiling the anger, cooking it. If he didn't hear the edge in my voice the first time, I need to make it sharper. "What's going on, Basu?"

"What, my d—" He restarts after a long look at my face. "Have I done something to offend you?"

"If not you, then someone you work with." I might not be able to cast ice spells, but my voice drips frost.

Basu stops his inspection. "I don't quite follow."

"I know, Basu. Five silvers for the firelight. *My* firelight."

"I sell them for three coppers, like you ask." He lifts his hands in one of those open shrugs. "Nothing funny."

"Basu."

"I have been a friend of the Belwars for two generations. I wouldn't dare tarnish—"

I grab his kurta and push him against the wall. Empty orb canisters clatter. My left arm flames red and his collar singes. So does my sleeve, but it won't hurt me like it will him.

"Adraa! Calm down," Riya warns. But she doesn't know how often I do this, how I've perfected it.

"He's responsible, Riya. Let me deal with this." Sometimes I wish I could control my anger better. I'm suffocating, the lump in my throat making it difficult to say the next words, but I can't stop. The girl I pretend to be at night emerges. Five bloody silvers, Vencrin, betrayal—each detail pumps through me. "I know it's you." There is literally no one else in the East Village I distribute to, which kind of narrows down the suspects. "So talk," I command.

"It's supply and demand, Adraa. Even if you worked all night and all day you couldn't supply the entire country or, blood, the entire continent. It's a cute experiment for Belwar. But this is commerce and profit."

I shake him against the wall when he doesn't continue. "You disrupted an entire market; you cannot control something like that. The rest of the world wants to see in the dark too."

I give him a cold, hard stare, and the flames on my arm jolt.

"Okay, okay, there is this one distributor. Said he would pay triple for half of my firelight supply. I have a family same as everyone."

"Name the distributor."

"I don't know the man in charge, just the guy, practically a boy, who picks them up."

"Name. Now."

"Goes by Nightcaster, obviously a cage-casting name, but I didn't ask. The money . . . it was more than I had ever been offered for anything. Please."

"Nightcaster?" I drop Basu and he tumbles against the counter. He really is working with the Vencrin, then.

Riya gives me a look of wide-eyed confusion. "Who is Night-caster?" she asks.

I deflate into stumbling surprise. I know the name all too well. Once a sport, cage casting has turned into an illegal fighting ring where wizards and witches battle and the audience gambles and soaks up the violence. The biggest ring in the country, the one run by the Vencrin, is only a few blocks from here. It's called the Underground, not the most creative name given its where-abouts, but Nightcaster is one of its prime contenders.

I know because I am too.

"You bloody bitch." Basu pats down the sparks on his kurta. The skin around his neckline is no more than sunburned. I'll show him how bitchy I can—

Riya grabs my arm. "Rani, don't." She's using the Rani talk on me? I glance between her and Basu. In both their eyes I must look enraged, a fire needing to be extinguished. I relax, and be-hind me, Riya sighs.

"You won't sell to them ever again," I command.

"I can't do that. They expect—"

"You seem to think I care about what the Vencrin expect."

"V-V-Vencrin?" Basu stammers.

"You don't even realize who you are selling to?" Pathetic, just pathetic.

"Please, Rani." Basu steps around the last saddlebag of fire-light, protective and fatherly. Fatherly protection only looks nice when it's a living being; any inanimate object and one just looks absurd. That's Basu, greedy and ridiculous to try to plead for something that is not his. *I'm* firelight's mother.

He continues, oblivious. "Give me this batch and then I can work something out with them. I need time. I *need* this shipment."

"I'm stopping this now."

"Expensive firelight is better than no firelight. You would be destroying the East Village if you take it. They count on *my* supplies, *my* deliveries."

"They count on *me*. *You* are the one who has failed them."

My left arm extends and before I can think about the spell, I cast. *"Yatana Agni Tviserif,"* I chant over and over until the first word spills into the last. I don't know exactly what I expect to happen, but when the orbs start to quiver, I chant a little louder, a little angrier. Maybe I could make them defective or something. But in my head I imagine it: the firelight leaving their containers and Basu's control and coming back to me.

"What are you doing? Stop!" Basu shouts.

Then it isn't just the orbs vibrating but also the magic inside them. An orb-filled box crashes to the ground. The clattering drowns out Basu's cries. Even Riya tries to yell into the rattle of noise. The orbs, my magic, they are obeying me, trying desperately to reconnect. It's only a few at first, but with another chant, hundreds burst from the orbs or ghost through the sphere's seams and fly toward my left hand. The fire turns into red smoke as it amasses and slithers up my arm. So much power! I've never tasted such strength. This came from . . . me?

I breathe for a moment as Basu and Riya stare in silence. Then I reach toward the last saddlebag and Basu panics. I see the spell on his lips a moment before it's cast.

"Noooo!" Basu and Riya both roar. Riya thrusts herself in front of me as I begin the counterspell. She pushes me to the ground and hurls a purple shield spell. It's too late. Basu had three seconds on her, easy. His yellow light breaks through Riya's half-crafted shield and swerves around her, blazing toward me. It would be easier to concentrate if I weren't falling through the air, but whatever. Riya had good intentions and I can see everything, feel every drop of my magic hovering on my Touch and ready to explode. I hit the ground as Basu's yellow spell hits my counterspell in midair. I can taste his magic like it was uttered from my own mouth. A knockout spell. Oh, Basu. You really thought you were going to get away with this.

It takes only a second for my rebound spell to swallow Basu's magic and redirect itself. In this moment my Touch seems to have a personality of its own, and it can feel easy victory. No contest. The red smoke smacks Basu's chest and blows him against the counter. A moment passes in which he staggers to gain his footing. I sent a minimal counterspell. It shouldn't even knock him . . . Basu's eyes go wide. He slumps, and slides down the counter, and with a thump his butt hits the ground. Never mind, I guess it was enough to render him unconscious. Riya was right. Maybe I don't realize how powerful a red forte I truly am. Maybe I could have really hurt him.

"Adraa!" Riya shouts.

"I'm fine, I'm fine." I wave her off. "Though this is the second time today I have rolled in the dirt."

"I was only trying—"

"I know."

She helps me stand and I brush dirt from my sore hip. I'm going to need a little pink magic today to ease the bruises.

"What in Wickery did you do? Before he cast."

"I took it back." I clench my left hand. It's the opposite of a burnout; it's a renewal. Instead of feeling like jelly, my arm is solid steel.

"That was dumb. You don't know what reabsorbing all that power could have done to you."

"Yeah, I know," I admit. I hadn't exactly meant for it to happen.

"How did you do it? I don't remember ever learning that kind of spell. I don't even know anyone who has done that."

"I . . . made it up."

"Made it up? Gods, you and your experiments."

"I created firelight, it responds to me. I just kind of did it." Though I don't think I should ever try it again.

"Well, you freaked him out." Riya stares down at Basu. "That worm! Doesn't he know he could be arrested for casting against a Belwar?" The anger seems to have migrated. Somehow, the fight calmed me, but Riya's failure to protect me ignites her, must bite into her self-worth.

"You did great, Riya."

"I failed. If that was anyone with a higher Touch or if you hadn't seen it coming . . ."

"You won't let it happen again."

We share a long look.

"So what now? Should I arrest him?" She kicks at Basu's boot.

"Guess so. Bring him to my father's attention, ask him for help in the matter. He was my parents' friend, after all."

"This is such a mess."

I squat next to Basu, feel for the rhythmic beat of his pulse. "It'll be my job one day, right? To clean up messes?"

Riya smiles and rubs my cheek with her sleeve. She shows me the dirt. "You look the part for sure."

I rub at my face too and the sleeve comes back dusty. "Gods, and I met my fiancé like this."

CHAPTER SIX

◇

I Have Some Explaining to Do

Adraa

It is not always pleasant to work with the Dome Guard. Formality drips from the interaction, or maybe *saturates* is a better word. Riya and I explain the entire situation, and the leader, an older, gray-haired guard, shrugs, having to trust me when an unconscious wizard sits at our feet.

I would like to request that Basu be delivered to the holding orbs below the palace, but they were abandoned after Mother's arrival on the mainland years ago. She couldn't stand sleeping above criminals. I can't blame her. On Pire Island, prison cells dangle off the cliffs, just in case, you know, someone should break free. In Belwar, the only prison, the Dome, lies in the northwest, far from the coast and the ships, and close to Mount Gandhak. It's a stone sphere of a building standing in the shadow of a volcano, hence its name. It's daunting enough to be frightening. When Basu awakens he's sure going to have a bad surprise.

Two guards restrain Basu with Dome cuffs, which prohibit

him from casting any type of magic. The cuffs glow bright yellow as he's loaded into a windowless carriage. One guard, with a sharp, strong beak of a nose, stares at me throughout, even as he casts orange coils to help him with the weight of Basu's limp body. It's a little unsettling, his staring, like we are playing an uncalled-for game. If he asks me to smile I'm going to lose it.

"Your father might have to hold trial if the truth cannot be cast out clearly," says the leader, who's taking down my story.

I turn my attention back to him and hope Nose Guard finishes his job quickly. "I understand the casting accords with truth spells. I do not care about his spell against me. I care about the corruption."

"Will you inform your father?"

"Yes."

"Thank you." The guard ruffles his graying hair, which makes him look young, almost childish. "Saves me a lot of paperwork."

"Well, thank the gods. The paperwork." He doesn't grasp in the slightest what Basu has done, does he? Doesn't realize what five silvers would mean for a poor family. How much harder life is without fire; how vulnerable my people are to those that lurk in the shadows.

The guard clears his throat and places two fingers near his Adam's apple. "Lady."

I'm this close to not paying my respects, not placing my fingers against my throat, but in the end I do. They *are* moving a body for me, after all. That sounds grim. A part of me kind of likes it.

◇ ◇ ◇

Riya and I are not nine meters into the air and away from Basu's hut before she salts me with so many questions I could be preserved for a century. They string between my father, Nightcaster, and Basu, which only serves to remind me of how the latter has changed sides.

"Riya, give me a minute to think. A whole lot has happened in the span of three hours. We are going to tell my father immediately; I have no clue who this Nightcaster is; and yes, maybe I'll question Basu further. You good?" Guilt about lying snakes up my belly. I don't think I need to question Basu. He gave me what I needed when he dropped Nightcaster's name. But to explain would blow my cover. I cannot let Riya know that I sneak out at night, let alone what I accomplish.

"All right," she agrees.

Exactly sixty seconds pass before Riya slowly slides into "So, what was he like?" Her voice is curiosity mixed with disbelief, a tone children use when they see my dad fire off his magic at the Festival of Color.

"Who?"

"Who else? Raja Jatin."

"Oh." I resettle on Hubris and look toward Mount Gandhak. He must surely be there by now or very close. "What you would expect: cold, arrogant, and quite tall . . ."

"*Annnd?*" Riya drawls.

"And what?"

"*And what?* Are you kidding me? And, did you like him? Did he seem to be a good person, a good match, a good anything? Give me something of substance here."

"I shouldn't fret over boys, an older, wiser friend recently—"

73

"Oh, come on."

I sigh and let the wind talk for me for a minute. Finally, I twist to face her. "The truth is I don't know, Riya. Both he and his guard had no idea it was me they were talking to, but considering they thought I was some East Villager, they didn't treat me badly. The guard was easier to read and seemed friendlier. He . . . well, he carried me after I burned out."

"He picked you up? Like carried you in his arms?"

"Yeah."

"Blood, you must have hated that."

"It was horrible and not so bad at the same time."

Riya shoots me a weird look, one that signals she wants to crack open that answer and get to the bottom of my emotions. But I can't reason out how being held was both embarrassing and nice in its own regard. I yank myself from the memory. I shouldn't be thinking of Jatin's guard or the warmth of his arms wrapped around me. So I focus on Jatin. He had seemed so . . . I search for the word. Controlled? Calm? Then the right word slaps me in the face and I offer it to Riya in sacrifice.

"Raja Jatin seemed unfeeling."

"Unfeeling?" She pauses, mulling over the word like I did. "Huh, maybe that is a good thing."

I laugh bitterly. "I should be happy to marry a cold and unfeeling man?"

"He didn't know who you were, right? It's good he wasn't too friendly. You are Gods-blessed beautiful and he didn't do anything, didn't *care*." She stresses the last word, and I finally latch on to her logic.

"You interpret this as loyalty to the engagement or his faithfulness to . . . the real me?"

"Well . . . yeah."

I guide Hubris closer, lean in, and raise an eyebrow. "That's a whole lot of assumption for someone who doesn't even like men."

Riya rolls her eyes. "Don't be jealous, Adraa. We can't choose who we are attracted to." Isn't that the truth. As a royal, there isn't much of a choice of who I could marry, much less who I'm attracted to.

I snap my fingers. "Perhaps his unfeeling demeanor means he wasn't attracted to me? Maybe he thought I was ugly." I laugh and cannot seem to stop. That would truly be something incredibly ironic. After all these years of stress and rivalry, it comes down to Jatin simply shaking his head and walking away.

"Please, get ahold of yourself."

Hubris sways with my laughter. "Imagine Jatin objecting to the blood contract because he thought I was hideous."

Riya makes a show of looking me up and down. "Yeah, don't hold your breath." She huffs and grips her skyglider tighter. "Besides, it's a positive assumption, and I need positivity. I want to keep my job, and that means one day living in Azure Palace. I would like to think I will serve a good raja, just as I serve a good rani now."

The raw compliment settles my laughter and I hiccup into silence. Riya was always supposed to be my guard and accompany me to Azure Palace. Mr. Burman had been priming her for it. If this were seven months ago, I would make a joke about her assumption that she can keep her job after failures like today, but I hold back. I like to poke Riya, but I love her too much to slap.

"Thank you."

The concept of attraction sticks to me as we land, latch our skygliders, and walk to the grand hall. I'm throwing open the doors and all I can think is, what if Raja Jatin could look beyond our past and really get to know me?

Father's voice knocks me out of my thoughts. "Behind schedule again? That's my girl."

He's at the head of a long table, surrounded by what he dubs his second family. I've grown up seeing our advisors. But today it is a small counsel, and the five chairs for the Belwar rajas remain empty. Riya's mom, head of security, sits to the right of my father with her usual elongated frown. That frown embodies her entire demeanor. A couple of the guardsmen are here, including Hiren, Prisha's guard. Willona and the cook, Meeta, have both awkwardly taken seats too, which means it is a palace security meeting.

I go tongue-tied. Riya was right to question me about my father before, because what am I going to tell him? Sorry, Dad, but did you realize your friend Basu is a lowlife who sold my product to the Vencrin? Even worse, how do I indicate how bad this is without telling him how I know about a cage caster named Nightcaster?

I take a deep breath. "I need a private audience."

Father tilts his head. "Serious as dawn or dusk?"

I smile at his code. "Duskish," I twist my hand side to side. "We aren't in the dead of night yet, but . . ." I hold his green eyes, trying to convey what has happened with only a look.

"Well, then." He turns to his companions at the table. "Everyone please leave. I need . . ."

He looks at me expectantly.

"Five minutes," I supply.

Willona and Meeta tumble from their seats thankfully. They tell me they hate these meetings so much because they don't want to imagine a harmful spell sealed in any of the letters sent to the palace, or a poisonous potion that could lace our porridge. They don't want to think about treason and murder. Well, I'm going to have to tell Father about Basu's betrayal. Maybe he'll be readier than I was, since he has been contemplating people trying to kill him all morning.

Riya's mom lingers outside the door and stares Riya down. The real interrogation will be later tonight, for my friend. I wish I could squeeze her hand or apologize. I understand Mrs. Burman's paranoia and worry for her daughter, but that critical gaze is why I can't confide in my best friend. It's my only real reason to dislike her mother, but it's enough. I can't trust her because she can't trust me. And around the circle we go. Mrs. Burman finally steps out. Gods, every move she makes is so dramatic.

Hiren, on the other hand, slides smoothly from his chair and walks toward us. He winks at Riya, a reminder that he got to sit in this meeting and she didn't, even with her promotion.

"Lady Adraa," he says as he walks past, his black cloak, a tad too long for him, dusting the ground.

I nod in indication that he should hurry it up, but he stops instead with a grin. "You've got some dirt on your forehead, you know." He reaches out a hand.

I push his shoulder and he chuckles. Hiren may be older than I am, but he still acts like a child. I don't know why Prisha respects him so much.

"Move it, Hiren," Riya says.

He gives a little salute, and I think I catch another wink before he disappears.

I sit a few chairs away from Father. Don't really know why; feels more official this way, I guess. He eyes Riya as she sits beside me.

"She stays," I tell him.

"All right, what is the dusk-level emergency?" he asks.

"Basu is in the Dome."

Father's eyebrows knit together. "Go on, you've learned how to hook my attention."

◇ ◇ ◇

On the way in, this felt like such a long story because of its heaviness, but after a few sentences, with some details omitted, I'm done.

"As a future maharani, what would you do next?" Father asks. Gods, everything, even life falling to pieces, is a lesson. He continues after seeing my irritation. "Or better put, what are you requesting of me?"

"Nothing. I wish to consult with Maharaja Naupure to see if he can give me more information about this Nightcaster." I don't mean my tone's sharpness. But I can't help it. When I talk to my father of politics and agendas, it feels that's what I become too. He wants me to learn the game. Right now, I'm playing it. I already know how I will investigate.

"Why Naupure?"

Another question to which I can't tell the whole truth. I need my answer to sound good and convincing. "As our greatest trading partner and the man who helped me set up the firelight distribution, Naupure might know more about any connection between Basu and the Vencrin. He could provide a clue I'm missing as I begin my investigation." It's a lie. What I need to do is talk to a man by the name of Sims, who runs the underground cage-casting ring. But I can't tell my father how I will put myself in danger. How I will lie and manipulate and bleed so everyone can access my light once again.

"Granted. Talk to Naupure."

"Fine. Thank you." I hate counsel with this version of my father, when the political raja emerges. I'm just another witch requesting another thing. I place two fingers on my neck and search for the laugher in his eyes. It's unsettling that I don't find it now, but I reassure myself it will return at dinner. The idea that one day it will be gone forever frightens me. I walk to the door. After all, I have a letter to write.

"Adraa?" Father calls.

I turn back.

"I'm sorry. I know how much your firelight initiative meant to you. Bad people are always trying to corrupt good things. This setback shows us how good firelight is for Belwar, though. Don't let this deter you. Don't let it—"

"Basu was *your* friend. How can you be so . . . so nonchalant?"

"Basu was another trading partner. The term *friend* is used loosely to craft allies. Truthfully, I always thought he was a mucky little fellow."

The crinkle around his eyes appears and relief tugs at the corners of my mouth. There he is. There's my father.

CHAPTER SEVEN

◇

Delivered to Destination

Jatin

The incident with the girl has become a distraction, a center-piece on which to focus so my mind doesn't wander to the peripherals where the anxiety of homecoming gobbles up space like air, invisible and all consuming.

We have tumbled through Belwar's East Village, North Village, and a bit of the West, and then, finally, entered the mountains. We trudge along Freedom Pass, which skirts the foot of Mount Gand-hak and then stretches across my country. It's named for the trail that people seeking religious and social freedom used to flee from northern Moolek. Those trailblazers believed all nine gods should be respected equally and each forte had a place in society. The people of Moolek think some gods, particularly Htrae, Retaw, Ria, and Erif, deserve privilege over the others since they are the original four fortes. It's been four hundred years since this path was used for freedom and I'm still glad I'm not my uncle, who rules over Moolek's lands, however vast they may be.

As a white forte, I might have been banned from ruling Moolek. There, being an orange, purple, black, white, or pink forte is a mark of inferiority from the start. Naupure might have its own problems with judging and devaluing people based on how many of the nine they cast, but right now white ribbons and brocade banners frame doorways. One fountain glistens, frozen with sunlight charging through. All in my honor; all for my name.

The academy resides in the flowing fields and lush marshes of Agsa, which means that for nine years I lived in the open. I forgot the cluttered squish of people when they mob the capital's streets, blurring in a faceless mass. One hard bump knocks me into Kalyan, and I straighten my kurta, the heavier one with the Naupure emblem. Itchy and constraining, that's all I can think about it.

The carriage jolts again as if the wheels have caught a stone in their shoe. We limp along painfully. It was a miracle when we broke through the mountain terrain, but the cobblestones might be even worse. I can understand a little of what my ancestors must have thought after traveling so far to find their place in the world, but I had forgotten what it would be like coming back to my own city.

I have only skimmed along Mount Gandhak, an hour by sky-glider at the most, and yet, Naupure is different, the air not as thick with the smell of fish, spices, and dyes. The houses are squatter and angled to climb the slopes of mountains. The streets are narrower, stair-entrenched and brighter, both in colorful paint and lack of litter. My people are louder in their hails, not only because I'm their heir but also because Belwar has a different sort of reverence for those chosen by the gods, one that makes their voices and cheers softer and themselves less hungry to see my face and know me. If the girl were to have saved the boy here, the crowds would have knocked us over to find out what was happening. And that difference in mentality stems from Belwar having the largest population of Untouched in all of Wickery. When half of a city can't do magic it naturally separates itself between the haves and the have-nots. Naupure teems with talent. Our ancestors were the outcasts whom Moolek tried to segregate and still does today. We slowly discovered this mountainous land and spread out, finding its pockets of habitation. Belwar grew from coastal opportunity, melding Pire Island explorers, Agsa businesspeople, and Naupure adventurers.

"Can't see why they're this happy. My return doesn't mean they're saved or any better off," I whisper to Kalyan.

"No, but it does mean their children could be," he says casually. Why the blood does he have to make such heavy statements? The sheer bulk of it presses on my shoulders. No wonder my family is short. Maybe the weight of the kingdom has pounded down my bloodline.

"We are going to have to climb that mountain of yours, aren't we?"

I look to where Kalyan points. It's a mountain, Mount Gandhak's miniature that hugs closely to its mother's side. Hills and slopes flourish into the rest of the city, but nothing stands taller than Azure Palace. It's so proud up there. I can make out the glint of the sun reflecting off the rooftop. Samik turns the elephant left and the carriage slowly follows. More faces, more waving hands.

"That would be the tradition for a homecoming or one's first arrival," I say.

"Tradition is important, I guess."

◇ ◇ ◇

"Next time I say tradition is important, remind me of this!" Kalyan shouts over the wind. The path up the mountain is a few miles of sloped zigzags, but after reaching the outer gate, it's a straight incline of stairs. For all of Kalyan's height and strength, his endurance when it comes to rough climbing could use some work. I'm sweating and cursing my legs too, but his huffing raises laughter in my chest.

"It's summer, Kalyan."

"So?" he pants.

"Imagine doing this in winter, might take your mind off it," I yell.

"Whatever the season, I'm sure most people who climb this thing have two legs."

"Then shouldn't I hear half the complaining?" I tease.

Mountain goats jump from the staircase. "They make it look so easy," Kalyan mutters.

"We are almost there."

"Can't see this blue palace of yours yet."

I scan upward, searching the stretch of stone. "It's there," I whisper, mostly to myself.

Behind us, Samik and two gate guards follow. My other men, who have flown above the carriage the whole way to provide air support, are still flying. In the future I'll be flying, but right now the people need to see my face, need to believe I am home for good. Disembarking from the carriage and showing myself to the swarm around the market hadn't been a disaster. I waved, people cheered. I cast some snowflakes in the air, people cheered again. They never stop cheering.

Still no Adraa, but she could be next to my father, beside the palace. Maybe that's why my muscles ache and my heart beats fast. Not out of shape, but bent sideways by anxiety of the unknown.

Climbing the last step and taking in the palace leaves no time for rest. My father and thirty advisors, nobles, and servants stand before the entrance. Behind them, guards in full armor stand at attention in a giant V. The tip points to me like an arrow aimed at my heart.

Kalyan whistles under his breath. "I get to live here."

I clap him on the back, take a breath, and step forward. I haven't gone nine years without seeing my father; he visited five or six times when I was at the academy, and came months ago for my royal ceremony. Still, even though I recognize him, and his smile, I'm onstage in front of all these people. No one has exactly given me my lines here. Am I expected to make a speech? Do I hug him?

"Welcome home, Son," Father says as he presses his forearm to mine. The guards fall to one knee, each with two fingers to the side of his throat. The staff bows, each one also saluting me.

"Thank you," I say as I glance around for any girl who could be Adraa. I refuse to be caught off guard.

Father watches me. "Lady Adraa isn't here. I thought she might come, but I didn't summon her, so I presume she carried on working like any normal day."

I smile, the first true one. She wasn't here. Thank you, Gods. I straighten my expression to a neutral one. "That's fine with me."

"Here, you remember Chara."

I turn toward an elderly woman and the second true smile erupts. "Chara."

The woman who practically raised me as a child lifts her shoulders as if to say, *Lookee here, I'm still alive.* She comes in for a hug, and I return it. She squeezes a bit, and that jump-starts my nostalgia. After my mother died, how many times did Chara hug me like this? I could probably cry on demand in this embrace, a habit easy to retrigger. But I'm glad to say that upon my release, my eyes remain dry. Kalyan walks to my side and I step aside to introduce him.

"Oh my." Chara blinks. "You boys look so alike."

"That's why I have a job," Kalyan jokes, bowing.

I introduce Kalyan as the palace staff greets me. Some new guards, some new servants, but all in all, most faces have changed only in age. A young servant, probably my age or close to it, lingers after his bow. "Raja Jatin, I have to say, um . . . thank you for Alkin. My sister, you see she moved out there—"

This is what that girl must have felt like when the boy thanked her for his life. What exactly do you say to something like this? "Of course," I whisper, and offer him my forearm. His face brightens as he presses his arm against mine.

After I've greeted everyone, Logen, the lead guard and my

father's bodyguard, takes Kalyan in like a lost chick and steers him toward the garrison and training fields in back. The servants disperse to other duties. Within minutes it's only Father and me walking through the ice door.

"Long journey?"

"Yes, you could say so."

"Sorry you had to do the carriage for so much of it, but people want to know you are back, want to see you."

"I understand." What's a son for if not to be paraded about?

I cannot seem to face Father head-on, cannot hold eye contact for more than a few seconds. I thought I had forgiven him long ago for sending me off, but now, home, seeing the servants and the guards, I hate that I had to leave.

"Jatin, about Alkin and the avalanche." I face him. "I'm proud of you."

"Thank you." And like that, the emotions bubbling in my chest simmer down. Proud. It isn't the same as love, but it's close. Maybe he is as nervous and awkward about reconnecting with me as I with him.

Now I glance around to truly take in my home and not just to avoid eye contact. Everything is the same and yet . . . new. Like losing an old toy only to rediscover it years later. Something is different, though. Fire glints in the corner of my eye. The candles are gone, I realize. I walk toward the grand stairs and pick up an orb with a small fire blistering in light.

"You have firelight too?" Something in the way I say *firelight* must sound puzzling because he smiles and replies, "We thought the name was fitting."

"We?"

"Let's sit down and talk." He walks toward his office, not even wondering whether I will follow him. Of course, I do, still holding the orb.

We take the staircase on the right and wander through a long hall until we reach the end. For some reason, I remember Father always saying he liked the view here, even though the room doesn't have a balcony or windows. Must have been a joke my young brain didn't grasp at the time. More firelight orbs light up Father's large central desk and the half-dozen chairs strewn about.

"What you hold there is Adraa's invention. I helped her start the distribution process and gave her a good discount on large quantities of orbs. She crafted the spell on her own. The light will burn for two months straight."

"Two months?"

"I know; it is quite impressive. Belwar doesn't need to trade with Moolek for ghee for lantern oil, meaning a newfound independence and stability. Various industries and craftspeople now work after dusk; thieves are more easily caught; and the number of household fires has dramatically decreased. Adraa has changed the entire economy. It's a new era, an age of light."

"Who produces them?"

"Adraa, of course."

"Just her?"

"That is why she only supplies her kingdom and our capital, but we will have to change that soon. Only, she is having a hard time finding a witch or wizard powerful enough in red magic to copy her spell."

"You cannot copy the spell?"

"Unfortunately, no. But then, Goddess Erif has never particularly liked me." He laughs like there is some inside joke I'm not allowed to be a part of.

"Adraa never mentioned firelight to this extent in her letters." Even Father cannot produce firelight? By Gods, this was winning. She had been winning the whole time. When I was nine I had wanted to impress her with a freeze spell. Naive me had wanted her to praise me, wanted her good opinion. But I'm a fraud compared with her. I only learn spells and recast them to perfection. She invented an entirely new one. I had never even thought of trying that.

Father smiles. "So you still write to her, then? I know I made you when you first went off, but you continued. I'm glad."

"Yeah, I wrote." I can't tell him what our letters consist of, teasing and competition, nothing of real value. I was so pleased with myself earlier knowing she would have received my letter today, but now? I desperately want to take it back, rip up what has already been sent.

Then again, the letters weren't completely terrible. In the beginning, I wrote just two lines—how are you, or such nonsense—because Father made me. I don't think I could have endured anything more, what with me still harboring embarrassment from that slap in the face. Adraa replied with questions about school. I think she was jealous I went off to the academy to learn magic, while she had to stay in Belwar and be tutored. I read those letters all the time. They smelled of sea salt and reminded me I was the lucky one. How could someone be lonely and homesick knowing they were winning in the game of life?

And answers to her questions came so easily, what with being a year ahead of her in training.

Adraa: *I learned how to fly. Have you flown yet?*

Jatin: *Yes, of course. In Agsa we get to fly over miles of flowers and fields.*

Adraa: *I learned how to fix a broken femur. Can you do that?*

Jatin: *Yeah, that's simple pink magic.*

Then it became about earning top marks in our studies. Who was best in every subject? She got potions hands down; I was better at subtle, tricky magic like growing fruit.

Adraa: *My tutor says I am number one in his class.*

Jatin: *Yeah, because you are the only one in it.*

Adraa: *That's not true. He teaches others. You're unbelievable. You think you are so great.*

Jatin: *Probably because I'm number one in my class.*

A few years later, we moved on to acts of bravery or feats of prowess. I protected a kid from being bullied; she joined her mother at the clinic and started healing villagers. She saved a dozen horses from a stable fire; I helped people, including Kalyan, in the aftermath of the worst storm Agsa had ever seen.

Then, after a dare from Kalyan, I turned the letters into love letters with taunts hidden in ice. I also did it to get Fiza, one of the ladies of Agsa, off my back. When rumors spread about me writing love notes to my fiancée, it stalled her flirtation.

But I had agonized over the stupidity of that decision until Adraa had sent back a blank letter I had to freeze to read. She was all sorts of irritated I had claimed victory. She didn't even say anything about the confession of love. I had been so relieved she hadn't taken it seriously, I kept it going to tease her further. I don't quite know why she is so fun to mess with. Probably because she tries so bloody hard when it comes to magic. Or maybe I liked the fact that I was winning our little competition and wanted to keep that going.

In truth, I have no idea what kind of student or wizard I would be without Adraa. I was one of the best because I couldn't let a girl a year younger than I was and hundreds of miles away win. And maybe I pushed her too. Maybe we would be great together—pushing each other to be better in magic and life. Or . . . we might argue all the time about everything. I can't tell, and that's what petrifies me.

Father interrupts my thoughts. "I was thinking about a proper meeting, but not quite sure what would be best. Your mother was always better at things of this nature." He rubs the gold wedding bangle wrapped around his wrist. Fourteen years and he still wears it. He stares over my shoulder at the huge map of Wickery covering one wall. What is he thinking when he looks at that map? Naupure's vast land, our oath to our people? Or about our future alliance with Belwar?

I open my mouth to respond, but stop when someone knocks on the door. We both turn.

"Yes?" my father asks.

"A letter for you, Maharaja," a man's voice calls through the door.

"Come in."

The young man who thanked me for his sister's life holds out a note. I take it and my father thanks him. I look down and stare at Adraa's name, and the envelope addressed to the maharaja.

"Like she knew we were talking about her." I give Father the envelope. I imagine it's some apology about her not being here today, but Adraa surprises me again when Father reveals the contents.

"She says she has recently found out about a corruption in firelight distribution and wants to set a time to meet with me." The girl from the street had already gotten to Adraa, then. She worked fast.

"I'm going to respond. Maybe this will be an opportune moment for you two to meet again?" Father raises his eyebrows in question.

"Fine by me," I lie.

◇

CHAPTER EIGHT

I'm Caught in Azure Palace

Adraa

Two full excruciating days pass before I have the time to visit Maharaja Naupure. Re-creating and distributing firelight, and questioning people in the East Village, takes up most of the hours, but I have other responsibilities as well. And during it all I have to act normal and sit on the one lead I have that connects Vencrin and my missing firelight.

I distract myself with training with Riya in the courtyard, each session getting me closer to the final test and no nearer to mastering white magic. I also observe one of Father's meetings, which went particularly poorly considering Hiren's father, the raja of the northern mountainous region, asked why I was so out of it. So with my leftover hours I help Mother in her smell factory. I cook up most of the potent potions, boiling them just right to be mixed with some other herb or by-product. Riya always tells me she doesn't want to hear about the bitter herbs or goat eyes unless it is a potion she should learn for her father, so I don't. Much of pink magic is used to heal ailments like a broken bone or an open wound. This is the type that, as a guard, Riya is trained for. But disease and sickness need potions infused with a healing spell. That is the type my mother excels at.

Pink magic might be the rarest on the mainland. In our coastal homestead, most study blue water magic to catch fish or green vegetation magic to produce bountiful crops. Everyone wants to learn yellow to be able to fly and orange and purple to protect themselves. For an average citizen, the ability to do up to three or four types of magic is a blessing. Healing spells are hard to master, and the materials difficult to acquire. But injury and sickness are rampant in the harsh wilds of Pire Island, so pink magic is a necessity there. Thus, the best healers come from Pire, and Mother might be the best Wickery has ever seen.

And yet, when one's fingers fish for the liver of a goat, one doesn't feel high and mighty or grateful for the opportunity to work under the best. Zara, my maid and Mother's top apprentice, is sure grateful, though. I've seen the girl up to her knees in sheep dung and the happier for it.

"Your mother wants to know how that liver is going," Zara says, rounding the corner from the patient room to the workroom, where jars of everything imaginable line the walls and kettles filled with thick liquid bubble.

Half a goat lies on a smooth metal table before me. Its head is missing, but I don't want to know what's happened to it, especially the eyeballs. "I've got one lobe." I point to a platter.

Zara nods, all smiles, and turns, ready to report.

"Hey," I call. Zara bends back around the door. "Tell her after this I'm leaving. My appointment with Maharaja Naupure is in an hour."

Zara's eyes go wide. I'm sure she can't imagine jetting off to another country to meet with a maharaja. She can't fly either, so the prospect must seem doubly inconceivable. I think she sometimes forgets she doesn't work only for a powerful pink magic user but also the Maharani of Belwar. Though sometimes even I forget how hard it is for most. The trip might be only an hour away, but some wizards can't make the journey without resting at one of the three flying stations floating over the city.

"Yes, of course, my lady," Zara replies, before doubling back. "Oh wait. Does this mean you'll be meeting . . ." She claps with excitement. "Want me to do your hair?"

"What's wrong with my hair?" I start to reach for the braid and remember the goat's blood.

"Ah . . ."

I point a finger. "*You* did my hair this morning."

"Ah," she repeats, and then ducks away with a smile. Never mind. I can't begin to comprehend Zara. She's an amalgamation, code switching based on her duties so fast I can hardly keep track.

Someone knocks on the door on the other side of the room, where the palace hallway connects to Mother's area. I withdraw from the goat's intestines and shoot a purple magic lever that flips the locked hatch. Riya barrels in, blowing my fading red mist into chaos before it disappears.

94

"Hey, Adraa, we better get—" She stops upon seeing me covered in blood. "Gods, couldn't you have warned me?"

"Not exactly."

"You should clean up. We need to go." She pulls out a time-piece. "Hope the wind is with us."

"Or we can make some," I say as I dive back into the goat. I've cast a purple spell to materialize a thin knife, but my red tools are hard to see amid all the goat blood. I slice away at the fat and at last I dislodge the rest of the liver. "Got it." I place the meaty piece on the tray.

"That's really great, Adraa. Really great."

I take off my apron and wash my arms in a water basin, bathing away the blood.

"Adraa?" Mother rushes through the workroom door. "You're still here?"

I point to the goat. "'Adraa, don't you leave until you get this last piece of liver for me.' That's what you said."

"But I didn't realize the time." Mother wrings her hands and then reaches forward to tuck a piece of hair behind my ear.

I jerk away. "Zara can help me. But Maharaja Naupure already knows I'm a mess." I smile at that. "So you don't need to—"

"Just Maharaja Naupure?" she scoffs. "Raja Jatin is home from the academy. You will surely see him. It's very important you look . . ." She frowns. "Oh, you are going to have to change at once." She points at my silk orange blouse and the slash of blood dripping down it. It looks as if I walked into the middle of a gruesome murder. I had been careful too.

"Blood," I swear.

"Don't curse," Mother reprimands.

Riya laughs behind me. "I think she meant it literally."

◇ ◇ ◇

"You look fine, stop fussing," Riya commands.

"It's not the style or fit; it's the . . ." I unleash my hands from the folds of my lehenga and the wind whips the ornate orange fabric into my face. "This." I gesture to my half-covered face, then thrust the skirt back down and pin it as I hold Hubris tight. I can't even see my skyglider in the mess of skirts. Of course, it's not only the outfit. With all the firelight business, I had almost forgotten about Jatin, but I don't want Riya to know that. "Have you ever flown with a long skirt?"

"Yes, I have."

"Well, I dislike it, immensely."

"I can see that."

I shoot her a look. Then the pink fabric wrapped around my hips and thrown over my right shoulder hits me in the face from the other direction. All the pins holding the silk in place are about to fly off, if they haven't already.

"I think it's great you are wearing traditional dress. You desperately need the practice wearing one on a skyglider."

I detect something in Riya's voice and spin toward her, which throws more fabric in my face. "You! You hid all my flying pants, didn't you? No wonder Zara got confused and nervous."

"You can't prove anything."

"Which is basically an admission of guilt. I hope you are happy. Maharaja Naupure is going to have a big laugh."

"I bet Raja Jatin will like it."

"I won't be seeing Jatin." Maybe if I say it enough I can conjure it into truth.

"Yeah, right. That's what you think. Your mother knew better. And I know a setup when I see one."

"Riya, I have important business to discuss with Maharaja Naupure."

"Yes, I know that, and you know that. But Naupure and Jatin probably think this is a ploy to get to the palace and meet."

"Oh Gods," I breathe. Riya is right. And once again fabric slaps me in the face.

◇ ◇ ◇

I'm worried Riya is right, so when we part ways on the front stairs, I don't wait for Naupure to come get me. Hughes, Naupure's main associate, asks me to wait in the main hall, but I can't linger there like a sitting duck.

"I'm going to go up. Save him the trip down."

"Lady Adraa, I insist!" Hughes calls after me. I lean over the thick stone banister. I do feel bad after seeing his panicked face. Hughes and I have had several great silent conversations as I've waited for Naupure in the past. We're practically best friends.

"He's expecting me. I promise you won't get in trouble." And I continue to climb, one set of stairs, turn, and then the other. I have to pass Jatin's room to get to the office, or at least what used to be his room. The carved Jatin upon the door appears worn and reminds me too much of the nine-year-old I once knew. He sure doesn't look like that anymore.

I'm so stupidly nervous that I consider muffling my footsteps with black magic so Jatin won't hear me passing his room. He's probably not even in there, I tell myself, but I still hurry by the door and make it to the end of the hallway. I knock and pray Naupure answers quickly. I'm still vulnerable out here after all.

"Yes?"

"It's Adraa."

Papers stir, a chair screeches against stone. "Come in."

Naupure gives a little start of surprise as I enter. "Hughes didn't tell me you were here."

"I'm sorry, I ditched him."

"Wondered when you would start to do that." Naupure's eyes widen a little as he processes the parade of fabric I'm wearing. "You're all dressed up."

"Yes, well, I got blood on my other clothes."

Naupure bursts out laughing. "Not yours, I hope," he says as we both sit.

"No, I was cutting out a goat's liver before setting out."

He smiles brightly. "Some days I just can't wait until you are living here."

I squirm in my seat, fixing how the lehenga falls around me. Naupure and I hardly ever talk about the impending marriage. That's why we get along so well. I should have expected this, though. Jatin home. Me in fancy attire. Suddenly, it all seems real. I *would* one day live in this palace instead of my own.

I gesture to my outfit. "Don't go expecting this on a daily occasion." I don't mind more traditional wear like lehengas or saris, really, only flying had been too difficult for words, and I know I can't train in it either, meaning in one single day I would have to change three times to get anything done. That sounds like the most absurd waste of time.

Naupure's chest shakes as he chuckles. "I'll be sure to set my expectations."

I sense a pause and go for it. I need to change this conversation before I can't think properly about what really matters. "There has been a new development in Project Smoke."

"I assumed when I got your letter."

"Oh, good. I was thinking . . ." *How should I word this?*

"What?"

"Nothing," I say. I can't tell him how all the women in my life assumed he didn't want to listen to me, but only reintroduce me to Jatin. A warm fluttery feeling soars through my chest. For Maharaja Naupure, Project Smoke is more important than me as a marital piece to maneuver around a board. But by now I should know better. It was Maharaja Naupure who comforted me when I broke down in this very office after Riya's father was injured. It was Maharaja Naupure who hugged me tight and said, "Do you want me to help you find the culprits?"

I start by telling him the story of the thief, bypassing the carriage interaction altogether, but sharing my interrogation of Basu. "I got him to admit he was selling my firelight to a boy named Nightcaster."

"As in—"

"Yes, I can't imagine who else it could be. Which means Basu was selling directly to the Vencrin. I need to go back into the

Underground to fight as Jaya Smoke and I'm going to find out why the Vencrin are hoarding firelight."

"Hoarding? In your letter you said they were taking it and selling it for five silvers."

"I thought so too, but I was in the East Village all yesterday giving shop owners orbs of firelight. I mark the orbs to let people know how long the firelight will last. Basu was either wrong or he lied to me. The East Village hasn't received a shipment of one thousand firelights in two months. Firelight was up-charged because it has become so scarce. The North and South villages were affected too."

"So, you question Sims, maybe even Nightcaster. If they say nothing or don't know, what then?"

"Then I'm going to follow Nightcaster, see who he reports to. And I'm going to shut this corruption down."

"Adraa, this mission was dangerous enough the first dozen times. And now you want to go outside of the cage-casting ring? If you push hard enough, you will be discovered."

That's a risk I'm willing to take. I want to prove myself, demonstrate I'm more than a one-armed Touch. But Maharaja Naupure works on logic. "Sims gives me more information the more I win. I'm doing well, well enough he might give up meeting times, shipments." I pause, awaiting Naupure's acceptance to my plan. Knowing he is behind me in this gives me a safety net. One I don't think I could live without.

"So this mission isn't about Mr. Burman or the drugs anymore."

"It will always be about that. I'm not going to stop until the streets are clean. But I know what they're doing with the drugs. What could they want firelight for?"

Naupure rests his chin in his hands. "I have a guess."

I lean forward, eager. This is why I was so desperate to come here. "What do you think?"

"It's only a guess and a troubling one at that."

I stare at him until he continues.

"Maharaja Moolek." He pauses as I absorb the name. Naupure goes on to explain before I can grasp the entire implication. "Why else would the Vencrin overpay for something so cheap? It's not their style. Vencrin would steal it. Mounds of money? That's my brother-in-law wanting his hands on firelight."

I have to get up and move. It helps me think. I pace in front of Naupure's desk. "Moolek was angry a year ago when Father told him that firelight had replaced lanterns, that we no longer needed to import his ghee. And I wrote the letter saying I couldn't supply his country, *his enormous country.*" I gesture to a map on the wall; the one of Wickery, where Moolek's lands stretch above Naupure and the even smaller Belwar. Moolek sits upon us both like a shoe crushing an ant. "I can't do it until I find more witches or wizards who can perform the spell."

"And Moolek isn't about to send you his best red magic users to help find candidates."

"Of course not." I'm past the point of pacing, my hands accentuating each word. "I guess he is just going to hire criminals to take it for himself!"

"This is only a guess, Adraa."

I turn to Naupure and lean forward earnestly. "A good guess. One that is logical and sound." *Why hadn't I realized it before?* "I just need proof. Let me get it."

101

He pauses, probably to judge my anger. I stand upright and lean back on my heels.

"I don't control you. I don't think anyone could," he says.

"But you don't approve?" I ask with as calm a voice as I can muster.

"Let's go over the plan step by step."

I sit again and Naupure pulls out my report. Fifty sheets representing six months of trying to understand and ultimately destroy the Vencrin.

"Let's start."

$$\diamond \ \diamond \ \diamond$$

An hour later, I inspect everything again and smile. "I can do it."

"There is so much that could go wrong."

"Then I fall back. I go home. I can bail out at any moment." I point to several places on the map.

"But will you? If you see something going awry, will you leave?"

I know Naupure needs a definite answer. So I pause, look him straight in the eye, and chill my voice. "Yes." I can't exactly tell if it is a lie.

Naupure sighs. "I think you should take your guard."

"We've talked about this." Riya being there would cause suspicion, and she can't keep the secret from her mother. But I don't blame Riya. Blood, if I were Riya I couldn't keep the secret from Mrs. Burman.

"What about someone else, one of *my* trusted guards?" Naupure asks.

I shake my head. "It would cause suspicion in the Underground. The fact that I don't have friends there makes Sims think he has the advantage."

"And how very wrong he is." Naupure stands and extends his forearm.

I maneuver and press my left arm to his. "Thank you."

He has always trusted me, believed in me more than my own parents do. I may not want him to become my father-in-law, but he is practically my second father already. A bang on the door breaks the moment.

"Yes?"

"Maharaja, the Raja of Warwick is waiting for you," Hughes says through the door.

Naupure glares at his timepiece. "My brother is early, which means I'm late."

"I can see myself out." I've never felt luckier. Happy relief flies from my worry-bound shoulders. Naupure frowns and I know what's coming. A nervous chill slides down my spine and suddenly I'm cold and sweaty at the same time.

"I was hoping you and Jatin could meet again today."

"Um, I should be going." I fiddle with my belt, checking that Hubris is attached securely. Riya prepared me for this and yet I'm an ice sculpture pooling onto the floor.

"You don't come here that often, so I was thinking it would be convenient for both of you. If the wind is against you it's more than an hour of hard flying."

Jatin hasn't told his father about our first meeting, of course. Why would he when he had no idea who I was at the time? I meant to use that to my advantage, but what was I really going

103

to do with it? I know this, though: I don't want it taken away, with me left awkward and foolish for not announcing who I was at once.

"Maybe your parents would prefer a more formal introduction." Naupure gazes at the map of Wickery. I know for a fact that his wife's portrait used to hang there. Every time he stares at it, I have the feeling he looks past the squiggly lines of Wickery's borders and at her face. He once said I reminded him of her, of Savi.

Maybe this whole thing is uncomfortable for him as well. When I was a child it must have been more entertaining and interesting to meet and assess me. Now the process is a whole lot of work for all of us. But I guess marriage always is.

"Perhaps," I say at last. My parents only want me to make a good impression. Want there to be some chance, before I ruin it. But what do I want? I want there to be a way for Jatin to meet the real me first before seeing me dolled up like the Festival of Color. Maybe underneath everything, that is why I didn't reveal myself in the East Village.

Maharaja Naupure checks his timepiece again.

I motion to the door. "You should get to Raja Warwick."

"Another time, then."

"Of course. I'm here every month. And in two weeks I'm bringing firelight." I gulp. Two weeks, then, that's how long I have to think about everything. I bow and salute.

Hughes stands at attention as I open the door. I give him a guilty smile and he makes no visible motion, but I see disapproval written on his face. A fair trade I'd say.

"Goodbye, Adraa. Be safe." Maharaja Naupure clutches my shoulder and then turns for the throne room.

I don't breathe easy until I pass Jatin's door. I can't help but feel it's going to burst open like he and his father have laid a trap for me. But nothing happens; it remains sealed and ghostly quiet just like it has been for nine years. I take the stairs breezily, even with a little hop in my step. I have more time. I was going to figure out what was happening to my firelight and then I was going to take down the Vencrin. There is hope, a plan, and a path that will lead Belwar to success. And if Moolek is behind the firelight shortage, then my first political move lies before me.

I round the second staircase. A man is making his way up. My eyes meet his and we both stop on the same footfall. No!

Once, when I was little, a fly landed on one of my burning training candlesticks and got stuck in the hot wax. I blew out the candle to see if that would help him, but it was too late. He buzzed in panic and yet his death was so quiet. It would have been unnoticeable if I hadn't witnessed the whole thing. I never quite understood the sheer terror he must have gone through. But now I understand, because the eternal gooey silence that the two of us have stepped in creates a deathlike panic within me, one no one will ever notice and I can't escape.

◇

CHAPTER NINE

Casual Chatting Turns Chaotic

Jatin

—•—

After an hour of training on the practice fields, I can't take look-ing casual and acting surprised if my future wife might suddenly emerge with my father. I motion to Kalyan, who is working on his purple magic. A grayish wall surrounds him as he stands qui-etly casting a spell on repeat so the surrounding bubble builds on itself. *I'm going in*, I mouth through his shield.

A few layers of the bubble burst and he glances up, sur-prised. "Want me to come?"

"No, this is good work. Keep at it to see if you can run and sustain it."

He nods and I track across the dirt. I thought Father and Adraa would come out thirty minutes ago and it wouldn't be that awkward. Now? I'm sweating. A lot. I don't think it can be explained away by training anymore. Actually, it probably looks like I have a condition. I wipe my brow.

What's the worst that can happen? I ask myself for the thou-sandth time. *She hates you, you hate her, and you marry someone else*. The peasant girl flits into my mind. Yes, someone exactly like that, who saves people's lives without hesitation. I choke the thought down as I step through a side door and into the palace. What's wrong with me?

I thump up the main staircase. About five stairs from the landing a flutter of pink twists around the corner and I freeze. It's her, the peasant girl from the market. How in Wickery . . .

She's in a lehenga, one with an orange skirt that brushes the floor and a pink sash that wraps around her waist and over one shoulder. No dirt in sight. In fact, I'm the bedraggled one. My mouth goes dumb.

She finally breathes and removes her hand from her chest. Then she laughs with what looks like relief. "Blood, I thought you were someone else."

How . . . What? I stumble into question, but then realize I haven't yet vocalized the words. Probably because so many questions are running through my head. Who is she? Why is she here, alone? How did she get word to Adraa so fast? She can't be a peasant. There is no way in Wickery she is an average commoner, not wearing that outfit.

"I was just leaving." She indicates the stairs I'm blocking. The ones I will keep blocking forever if that's what it takes to be able to properly talk to her. *Say something before she disappears,* I urge myself.

"I'll walk you out," I'm finally able to articulate. It's a small but important accomplishment.

The girl has another excuse at the ready. "I've got it. I have someone waiting for—"

"I'll be happy to. Please," I add when she doesn't look too

thrilled at the prospect. I breathe, trying to remove the awkwardness of our last encounter. I can still feel her in my arms, the heat of her body. Blood, I may be blushing.

"All right," she says.

We begin down the stairs, a descent into another world. I'm unsure how to break the silence. Should I say something about the street incident or maybe inquire after her health? I go with something simple and significant. "So, I never did learn your name."

She hesitates and not in the timid, five-second kind of way. I undergo a solid brick of silent calculation. I am talking ten cold hard steps that clack against the stone.

She finally relents. "It's Jaya."

Victory wells up from my stomach for a split second before her counterattack lands. "Yours?" she asks.

I hadn't even thought . . . "Kalyan," I supply, and twist to offer her my forearm. I should have told her who I really am, but I can't. I can't give up the facade just yet. She hesitates for half a second, then presses her right arm against mine, Touch to Touch. And there, within the ultimate sign of respect and equality, the lie seals itself.

Too late I realize how sweaty and dirty I am, how I might have ruined her brocaded sleeve. She looks down at her arm and I want to die.

"Sorry, I've been training. . . ."

"What? Oh no, you're fine." She doesn't wipe her arm on her skirt and I'm so thankful. Two more stairs of awkwardness.

"So, what are you doing here, Jaya?" I hope that sounds casual, not desperate. She squints at me as if I'm a servant who spoke out of place. Guess I kind of am in her eyes, but what about her? What does she do to warrant a private audience with my father?

"Some business for Lady Adraa."

So Adraa wasn't coming. She had sent the girl who had discovered the problem instead. But does that mean Adraa is avoiding me? I need answers.

"So you work for her?"

"Well, yes." Jaya pauses. "I'm practically family."

Three more steps. I'm running out of steps.

"You don't need to look so concerned," she says. "I mean, I have already been cleared entrance; I've already had ample time to kill Maharaja Naupure if that were my intention and now I'm leaving." She gestures toward the ice door, which lies ahead.

What the blood? "Implying murder and treason isn't exactly reassuring."

"Sorry, that came out wrong."

"You implied—"

"I'm a friend to Maharaja Naupure, a good friend."

Good friend? Private audience? My brain clangs. Oh Gods, could this girl, this girl who must be my age or younger, be sleeping with my father? Sudden rage snaps behind my eyes. No. It's been ages since Mother died and normally I would be disgusted at the notion of Father eliciting young commoners into his bed, but not her. Not her!

"Good Gods, now you think I'm sleeping with your maharaja." She rubs her temples.

Is she *admitting* it?

She waves one hand at me. "I'm not," she practically yells.

We have both stopped right outside the staircase's mouth. For the first time since the street incident I look into those fiery brown eyes. Without dirt on her face I can better see the fierceness in her features. We are almost the exact same height. That spurs a fluttery lightness in my chest. We are eye to eye, which somehow grants us equal footing and intimacy.

She breaks the gaze and walks forward. "I'm not," she says more evenly, staring straight ahead. Relief wants to restart my heart, and I let it; I believe her. Why am I jumping to such wild conclusions about this girl? I jog to catch up with her.

"I'm sorry if I insulted you in any way."

She meets my eyes. "Let's restart. I'm just a girl who is not a murderer or a mistress."

"Same." I smile at her and she laughs. And with that, I feel powerful. We walk the last few steps to the ice door. I don't want to let her go, but I also don't want our conversation to erupt into awkwardness or horrible implication again. She touches the door, something I've never seen anyone do before. But that was nine years ago, a lifetime. Maybe this has become a thing.

"I love this door. It's marvelous, isn't it?" she says. I used to love it too, probably the reason I spent most of my time on white magic. Now, all I can think is that I had to walk out of it a decade ago.

I reach forward to pull her back. "Yes, but you don't want to touch it for too long, it can give you frostbite."

Her hand steams. "I've always been careful." She keeps staring at the door and I wonder if she is trying to see her reflection in the ice. The warped image doesn't do its owner justice.

I wait a beat, then jump into action. It occurs to me she might not be able to open it. "Here, let me." I cast the intricate spell, and the door breaks apart, allowing buttery light to flood in. My magic floats like lost fog.

"A white forte," she says as if noting the weather. Maybe I gave myself away, but Kalyan is a white magic forte wizard too, so this shouldn't blow my lie.

"Yes."

A girl sitting on the stairs bounces to her feet as Jaya and I step over shards of ice. She is pretty in her own right, but she doesn't have Jaya's eyes, her rich dark skin, her cheekbones, hair that— Oh no, I'm staring again.

"This is my friend, Riya."

I quickly bow and smile. She sizes me up and seems pleased to be doing so. She's laughing at us, I realize. Well, at least me.

"Riya, this is Kalyan."

"Oh." She gives a little start. "I just thought . . . Never mind."

She thought I was Jatin. Oh Gods. I should admit it. I'm being so ridiculous. I'm going to look like a fool, but I open my mouth anyway.

Jaya starts talking before I can say a word. "I—I did want to thank you for the other day. I realize most people black out when they burnout and it was nice to know if that had been me you wouldn't have left me in the street." She breathes as if blowing through a rehearsed speech.

"You're . . . you're welcome."

111

She nods, turns, and unhitches her skyglider from her belt. "Come on, Riya, let's go," she says as she trudges down the stony path. I would have to yell for her to hear me now. I can't force myself to do it.

Jaya has almost reached the stairs that stick out of the mountain when a voice interrupts my reverie. "Raja Jatin, is there anything I can do for you?" a well-shaven guard in vest armor asks from behind me.

I cross my arms and lean against the pillar that spouts from the entryway. The air up here is thin, but fresh and cool. The sky shimmers with wisps of pink, dusting the blue palace walls with a purple glow. "No, just enjoying the view."

"Yes, me too, sir." The guard smirks. I follow his gaze to Jaya walking down the path.

"*Zitadloc,*" I whisper, and point my white magic in his direction. It wisps up his leg and into his spine. The guard shudders. "Good Gods, man, decency."

◇ ◇ ◇

I don't know what to do after an interaction like that, so I stumble to my father's office, only to find it vacant. So I go back out to the practice fields to watch and help Kalyan as he sprints with the multilayered shield around him. But my mind has been warped. If the girl was a distraction before, she's become all I can think about now. What had Jaya and my father talked about for so long? What plan was being implemented without me? *Good friends,* she said. It hits a sore spot I thought had healed long ago.

I wander back to Father's office over the next few hours in between more training and a cold bath. He's properly swamped, as any maharaja should be. And yet I have way too much time on my hands with nothing to do. It's Hughes who comes for me in the end.

"Maharaja Naupure wants to see you."

My head jerks from the spell book I was no longer reading. "I'll be right there."

Three minutes later, I'm standing in front of the man I've been trying to talk to for hours. While my head has been swarming all day, my father looks as if his has been swarming all month.

"There's been a skirmish near the Naupure and Moolek border, in Warwick territory," he says bluntly.

I stand straighter, completely focused for the first time in hours. That area has been in turmoil for years, but the look on my father's face tells me I should be concerned. "How bad?"

His face doesn't crumble; there's just a tightening around his eyes. "Six dead so far. A couple of fields of crops plundered." He throws his hand in the air. "All in the name of the four gods, I imagine."

I nod and try to process what he's told me. Six dead, not close to the worst I've heard, but it could get worse. There might be fighting at this very moment.

"Jatin, with you home, I'm not as worried about leaving the capital."

I understand immediately. "I can do it."

"There is a lot you already know, of course, and you now have the title of raja for authority."

I repeat what will probably be my mantra for the coming weeks as I take care of my capital and country. "I can do it."

"Yes, I believe you can." Father starts arranging folders and paperwork in the cabinets on the right wall. He tells me what is what. It's a long hour with no time to interrupt about firelight, Adraa, or Jaya. I try to concentrate. After everything has been pointed to or addressed, Father leans back to gaze at his wall of work. Or now, *my* wall of work.

He clears his throat. "I'm sorry I couldn't introduce you to Adraa properly. It will have to wait until I get back." He pauses as he contemplates the calendar on his desk. "She's delivering firelight in two weeks. I'll have to write to cancel."

"I can handle that without you."

He raises an eyebrow at me. "If you are sure."

I don't want Adraa to feel like I'm avoiding her like she's probably avoiding me. "We need the firelight, right?"

"Yes, but the meeting is more so I can talk to her."

My stomach clenches and my throat tightens. She's more of a daughter to him than I am a son. Maybe we should let *her* run the palace for the next few weeks.

"Don't worry. As long as no one gets slapped in the face it will be an improvement. Besides, I know you'll like her."

How does he know this? How does he know what I find attractive? He doesn't know me, not truly. Jaya pops into my head and this time I don't smash the image away.

"May I ask you something?" I ask.

He is so overwhelmed with the situations at our borders I can pretty much ask anything. I could probably even ask about Mother. "Always," he says, verifying my theory.

114

"I want to know more about the Vencrin." It's been running through my head since getting back, how much I don't know about Belwar's troubles. Seeing the girl again reminded me of my ignorance. Adraa sent Jaya here to talk to my father about the Vencrin firelight problem, but I wasn't included in the meeting. And I need to know, especially if Adraa is coming and might expect an update.

"The Vencrin? Adraa wrote to you about it?"

My father severely overestimates the substance of our letters. "No, I heard about it in the village."

He rubs his chin. "How much do you know?"

"Only that they're criminals in Belwar who sell drugs to the Belwarians."

"And Naupurians too. We are affected as well. Just in the capital at the moment, but it's enough to make anyone concerned."

"Why wasn't I made aware of this, then?"

Father frowns. "I thought it would interfere with your studies. Knowing something bad is happening and not being able to do anything, that's practically torture. Besides, the Belwars have helped. Especially Adraa, she wants to get to the bottom of it. It's more in their territory, their domain."

I pause. *Especially Adraa?* She never bragged about this in any of the letters. She didn't even mention her role in firelight. What else was everyone keeping from me? "I want to help too, or at least know everything there is to know," I say.

Father assesses me. Only for a second, but it's a second Adraa Belwar probably never had to endure. "Recently, Adraa discovered the Vencrin are no longer dealing in drugs only.

They're also buying up firelight. I think they may be doing so under Maharaja Moolek's instructions."

"Uncle Moolek?" I say, too loudly. First the skirmishes and now I learn my uncle is tampering with my fiancée's invention. "What would Moolek—"

"I just think that it *looks* like Moolek is involved. I suspect he wants firelight to replicate or destroy. Firelight has made Belwar less economically dependent on Moolek. It is also an insult to the Moolek ideology. Firelight lets any commoner with no skill in red magic wield fire and light. Meaning wizards and witches who are not blessed by the four main gods, or even the Untouched, are able to grasp that power and be equal to others. What if Adraa invented a green spell that could let anyone prosper in the fields, or a yellow spell that allowed anyone to fly a skyglider? Your uncle's control would collapse."

"You're right." I sit down with a thump. My father doesn't need to explain further. Moolek's social hierarchy is built on taking advantage of those with less magical ability and crafting barriers and stereotypes around certain colors so that they remain inferior to the original elemental types. All of that makes sense to me—how could I not have seen it immediately? In the carriage Jaya said the theft of firelight felt personal against the Belwars. She sensed it, then.

"It's still only speculation. When I visit the border, I hope to meet with Maharaja Moolek. Currently we are in the middle of everything, both geographically and as the country with plans to unite with the girl who created a spell that threatens Moolek's way of life."

Holy blood! "Maybe I shouldn't marry her." It's a bad joke that hits too close to my true thoughts.

Father goes quiet, painfully so. His next words are whispered harshly. "Jatin, if I'm correct about your uncle's motives, he will try to control Adraa somehow. And that would be an alliance that would break our land in two. He would have her power, her brilliance, and her firelight."

I don't know what to say. Never have I imagined how political my marriage might be. Yes, fulfilling family expectation, and yes, an alliance with Belwar, those were given. But now? I run my hands through my hair. Does the whole world revolve around the fact Adraa invented a fire spell? Feels like it.

"And if I hate her? Or she hates me?" Maybe I should tell Father about our letters. Because I think she does hate me a bit. She's not avoiding me because she's shy.

"Get to know her before you start a political crisis." Father laughs, but it's a dark one.

He pulls a stack of papers from his desk drawer instead of the cabinet. This one must be special. "You are right, though. You should know everything." He hands the stack to me.

I flip it open to find page upon page of handwritten notes. "What is this?"

"I have someone on the inside, someone undercover, in hopes of learning about and bringing down the Vencrin. And now that also means figuring out whether Moolek has a role in the firelight shortage." Father points to the notes for emphasis. "This is their report."

I examine it. The first page marks day one, with the agent's name, Smoke, written across the top. It looks like Adraa's handwriting, but then I realize it's too neat. Adraa's writing swoops and swirls like a ten-year-old on a skyglider; this person swoops with smaller flourishes like a seventeen-year-old flier. But my guess is the writer is female.

I want to learn, but this is more than textbook material. This is insider information, the secrets of an undercover operation. "What do you want me to do exactly?"

"You asked. You care. Adraa cares too." Father points at the report again. "Learn what there is to know. If you want to be a part of it I won't stop you."

"A part of it?"

He motions toward the papers. "You'll see. She could use backup."

◇ ◇ ◇

At first the notes scramble to explain everything. The entire process of the investigation, the theory, the goal, the beginning, all are laid out in a jumble of details. But within five pages, the important pieces start to float above the garble. I turn a page. Vencrin and their marked attacks on ships on the Belwar coast. I turn another page. Vencrin and their marked hits on the streets of Belwar.

The next few pages explain Bloodlurst. *Extremely addictive and pleasurable to the senses on initial use,* it says in large print at the top. I had remembered correctly; with recurring use the drug enhances one's Touch. Another page, more reports of incidents in which an addict burned out or killed someone. I stop at one sentence. In the majority of cases, taking too much Bloodlurst burns out the user . . . I reread the next word to make sure I'm seeing it correctly. *Permanently,* it says.

I leaf through more pages. Agent Smoke discovered a connection between the Vencrin and a place called the Underground, a hidden arena for cage casting, with weekly matches. There's a calendar. The next date circled on it is in two days. The only other item emphasized with the same pugnacity is the name Sims, underlined with three bold strokes. Then there are name after name of cage casters. Next to some are *V*s. The members proven to be Vencrin, I realize a second later as I scan down the page.

Nightcaster: Rakesh: Black: V
Tsunami: Beckman: Blue
Thunder: Tenson: Yellow: V
Lightning: Kuma: Orange: V
Streak: Amit: Orange
Ax: Anik: Purple: V
Quake: Navin: Green
Mist: Sonna: Blue

I shuffle through a few more pages and a smaller page falls out. I grab it off the floor. It's another city map, with six points marked by red dots. Next to each dot is writing. I peer closely at a dot. *2 V, 30 packs destroyed.*

I look up and realize hours have passed. I've read twenty-five victim cases and thirty fighter profiles. I rub my eyes, but can't wipe away the headache behind them. So much was kept from me. I knew my country wasn't perfect, but I thought it pure and clean compared with Moolek. Nothing like shattered illusions to make you feel both sick and exhausted.

Adraa was doing something, Jaya was doing something, and Agent Smoke was doing something. I hit my desk, and the first red magic orb I ever created falls and rolls under my bed. Over the years it's lost all resemblance to a flame; now it's only a wisp of red smoke. If I opened the thing it would puff into nothing. I bend to get it, and when I set it back in line with the other eight orbs, resolve hits me in the chest. I'm no longer a pathetic ghostly spell sheltered in an orb. I am a raja in the nine gods' eyes.

Now I know what Father meant.

I will be a part of it.

CHAPTER TEN

◇

Into the Underground

Adraa

Being undercover, being Jaya Smoke, means I must constantly live in confidence; must wear it like my Touch and let it grow and coat me like a second skin. The persona keeps me safe. But I can't help but like and admire the woman I become when I'm Jaya. So much so that it seeps into other parts of my life. I curse more in the Underground and thus can't hold back saying "blood" on a daily occurrence. I'm pretty sure I swore five times in front of Raja Jatin in the carriage and hadn't even given it a second thought.

I like Jaya so much that I have become my persona, which over these past months has confused me. Have I changed myself forcefully, to the point that I have lost myself? Who was I really before I took on this mission and became a cage caster and then a night stalker? Blood if I can remember, but that person feels weak and alien to me now. These are the thoughts that lurk in my mind when I use black magic, when I paint myself in it so I can't be seen. As an invisible entity of the night, I sneak into the East Village and hunt for the landmarks that guide me toward the Underground.

I round a corner, still expecting Basu to ambush me. But I shouldn't worry. He's gone. Two days ago my father finally read the update. After the interrogation, the truth spells revealed Basu didn't know he had been selling my firelight to criminals. He's been banned from selling firelight again, but that's a whole lot better than time in the Dome.

Basu begged for a guard to protect him until he could leave the city, my dad said. That's the part that draws shivers down my spine and makes me keep glancing over my shoulder. The Vencrin started cropping up slowly about a year and half ago. From what I've learned, most if not all Vencrin members are nothing more than thugs dragged into the drug-dealing game by the lure of power upgrades, money, and protection. But I can't ignore all the evidence that points to them destroying Mr. Burman, one of the most powerful men I knew. So maybe I am wrong. If Basu is that scared of the Vencrin, should I be as well?

That's why tonight is so important. It's taken me months to track down one drug den and stop a handful of drug transactions. And I'm nowhere near finding Mr. Burman's assailants. If Moolek really has a hand in this mess it could take me months. Months I don't have. Jaya Smoke's days are numbered. Thirty-nine days and it'll be my eighteenth birthday and the royal ceremony. And after my face is plastered all over the country as a rani, entering the streets in the red mask and breaking up drug deals won't be easy. Without the information I gather as Jaya, I will basically be wandering around alone in search of illegal activity. I have to find new leads on what is happening to my firelight, and soon, before the royal ceremony, before I'm forced to be *only* Adraa Belwar for the rest of my life.

The entryway into the club looks like nothing special. Several times I've had to double back to make sure it's the same dull and litter-filled dead-end street. At the end of the grime, well, there's more grime, and beyond that is your average broken window. Only after delivering a few harsh taps and dusting some of my magic over the opening does something interesting happen. The broken glass and the frame grow, elongating like a jaw dropping open. A huge wizard pushes aside the curtain behind the glass and throws open the window door. I no longer need the password because I get the nod, smirk, and sneer, in that order, indicating that I'm allowed entrance.

I lower myself into the cesspool of smoke and haze. The stickiness of sweat and heat due to lack of ventilation hits me like an awkward hug. I've heard a few wizards exclaim, "Ah, back at home!" as they walk in. So yeah, the clientele who likes to watch cage casting isn't the most profound or hygienic.

In the dark recesses of corners, wizards and witches press the fine powder of Bloodlurst into their Touches. Their eyes flash a brilliant red for a brief second and then dull. The healer in me has to hold myself back, still myself from lurching toward them and explaining the pain that comes with burning out forever. *It will happen in three stages!* I would yell at them: Beads of sweat. Endless spasms. Limp weakness. Then, magic finally gone, permanently, and all for the happiness and power it brings them now. I turn away from the laughter and sighs.

Along the wall, the names of fighters and their stats flash

in sequence. I catch mine emphasized in red. Next to my fake name are the more important betting opportunities and stakes, which flicker, constantly fluctuating. Ten to one, it says, I will win against a fighter named Ax, whose name flares in purple. A lot of money will be lost tonight.

I take two steps toward the back room where I change and prep for fights, when Sonna, the bartender and a fellow fighter, calls to me. "Smoke!"

I push past the clog of consumers and amble up to her. "What?"

"Sims was looking for you."

"Yeah?" I try to read whether this is good news or bad.

Sonna looks as disinterested as ever. "Said something about you fighting first."

"First?"

"Yeah, that's what he said," she says as she presents a row of fresh drinks and sweeps up leftover condensation circles with a wave of blue smoke.

Sims likes to sandwich his event. Give the audience big shows at the beginning and the end to hook interest and keep the people here betting and drinking. So first means a good level of respect. Guess I didn't lie to Naupure after all. I *had* joined the big leagues, which means I have more to leverage with for tonight's needed information. Perfect.

◇

CHAPTER ELEVEN

Getting into Trouble

Jatin

Agent Smoke has given straightforward guidelines to finding the Underground. A list of objects and clues notify fighters and audience members of the hidden location. An upside-down hammer, which I find on a rotated sign outside a metal crafter's shop. An arrow on a dyed sheet hanging in a yard directs me down an alleyway.

Soon the rest of the signs become unnecessary because I'm able to follow a group of wizards who are obviously heading toward only one thing. They smell of pent-up violence, or maybe it's body odor mixed with alcohol. One wobbles into a wall and the others laugh as they pull him forward. I sustain the black magic just in case, but I don't think these men would know they were being tailed even if I went up and introduced myself.

They lead me down several alleyways before they slosh to a stop at a dead end, where only a broken window peers out into the night. One of the wizards rattles his fist on the glass, right near the shards of razorlike teeth.

"Hello!" he calls, then laughs with his friends. They're drunk. I'm going to have to backtrack and navigate from scratch. Stupid mistake. I'm a few steps away when I hear it, the groan of a wooden frame bending and the snap of glass breaking. I turn to see the window has expanded to a door, and a man is opening the wicker crossbeams and cracked glass like a screen.

I retreat into the shadows, then whisper in order to be visible again. When I round the corner I spot the last man tumbling through the door. The gatekeeper is about to close the elongated window frame as I rush forward.

"Hey, entrance for one more?" I slur.

His face twists as if I've made an uncomfortable joke. "You aren't a regular and you aren't on the list," he says.

"Yeah, but a friend invited me and I've got the money."

"Friend, huh? What's the password, then?"

"A bloody place like this doesn't need a bloody password," I quote from Smoke's files. Gods, I hope that was the actual password and not Smoke ranting in curse form in her research.

Unbelievably, the guy nods and holds the window door open for me. *Two for two! Thanks, Smoke.*

"Four gold." He holds out his hand and I surrender the outrageous amount of money. But I have much more pressing matters as I enter the Underground. For one, the smell—a mixture of mold and body odor—presses on me like a damp cloth thrown over my head. If at any time I get used to this frontal assault my olfactory glands must have been obliterated.

126

After a few stairs, I duck under a low-hanging exposed beam and am confronted by the sight of mobs of people in the dusty gloom. The number of beings mushed into this giant open warehouse calls for a moment of proper gaping. No one gapes back, though, and I realize with a start that I'm anonymous for the first time in my life. Even if I were to make a scene, this is Belwar and I've been gone for nine years. It feels good.

To my direct right, a bar stretches and then hooks around a corner. In the middle of the room, barrels of bright light shine upon a giant sphere five meters high. It sits on a raised platform, with an attached runway leading to a black-curtained doorframe. All attention is fixated on and reaching toward the sphere. I shove my way closer, squeezing between pressed bodies.

Inside this rounded cage, two dark figures zoom around. So that's how they control the spells from hitting the audience. They have amplified an orb, made it as thick and strong as a Wickery prison cell. Transformed it into a playground of destruction. As I think this, a blast of spikes fire and stick to the walls of the dome before bursting into purple smoke. One fighter—a woman— whooshes to the left to physically hit the other fighter in the face. Why do people want to see a girl, or anyone for that matter, get beat up? This is disgusting. Isn't there enough suffering and death already? The purple magic wizard leans backward and backhands the witch. She crashes into the side of the dome closest to me and I finally see her face, her beautiful and bloody face.

Jaya.

◇ ◇ ◇

Jaya stands and wipes her bleeding lip. "You want to play? Let's play!" she yells. The crowd shouts in response. Some who were cheering for the wizard have turned. A man screams in my ear, "Destroy him, Jaya!"

I have made a lot of ignorant judgments in my life, but never have I been so oblivious. This girl. This girl, who burned out in my arms, cage casts.

Jaya casts a spell I can't hear, but everyone sees the blaze of red shoot from her left hand. Her opponent, who based on the cheers is called Ax, ducks, rolls, and manifests a shield to block any residual magic. And there is magic to spare, because Jaya's power smashes against the sphere where Ax once stood and spatters outward and against his crouched defense. Before he can rise, Jaya is standing over him. With orange magic no doubt, she beats down on the shield like a red-hot hammer and it breaks, allowing Jaya's fist to plow into Ax's arm. *Crack!* Something shatters and the audience bursts into another horrid roar. All around me, wizards surge forward. My body's sweat and smell meshes with those of the crowd. I've become one of them. Even if I wanted to, I can't turn away and retreat.

Jaya glides backward, giving Ax, who's nursing his freshly broken arm, space. She's drawing this out. In a real fight it would have been best to cast another spell to defeat him. This is all for show, a painful, bloody game. How can this be the same girl who threw herself at death's feet to save a thief? Does my father know she does this?

Ax stands, cradling his broken arm. It's already swollen to twice its normal size. He's casting, shooting pink healing magic and orange morphine down to the bone to override the pain as he and Jaya circle each other. So that's why she retreated. She wanted him to mend the damage she's done.

Ax sends off small spells that Jaya either ducks or blocks. They become a tangled battle of purple-red movement. Now it's just a question of who will get hit first. It's Ax. A stream of red strikes him in the foot and twists his leg. He sways a bit, but nothing else happens. The two continue their fight. Ax looks restless, though, glancing frequently between Jaya and his foot. He's probably wondering what the spell was as much as I am.

Suddenly, Ax seems to have had enough. A purple blast ignites the air. Flames burst from Ax's good arm and swallow half the dome. All anyone can see is Ax pelting streams of fire in Jaya's direction. Jaya throws both hands up, and then disappears from view. I jolt forward, but can't go anywhere. *She gave you a chance, you bastard!*

Ax falls to one knee, but keeps chanting the fire spell. It's about to engulf the entire dome, Ax included. The idiot. Wizards and witches on the other side of the arena holler. A red halo blooms over the sphere. Jaya, she's containing it, making an orb of yellow and purple magic to suck away at Ax's spell. The red streams streak the ring, so bright many cover their eyes. I raise a hand, but I don't dare look away. She's there in the brightness, walking forward, chanting, arms outstretched and swirling in a circular motion.

In one blink, both color and light disappear. The purple flames vanish and the red container evaporates. Jaya stands, while Ax hunches, panting.

"Smoke, Smoke, Smoke," the crowd chants. Their voices toll in thumping unison.

"What?" I shout to the wizard next to me. "What are you saying?"

"Smoke!" he yells, and points to the girl in further answer. "Jaya Smoke."

Oh my Gods, why hadn't I pulled it all together sooner? Jaya was Agent Smoke. This girl was an undercover agent in the underground cage-casting ring. What had my father done? Or worse, what had Adraa *made* her do?

Jaya sends one last puff of red magic at Ax, and it nuzzles his cheek before making him slump sideways. What the blood was that? The dome clicks free at the top and pulls apart into two halves, like an egg cracked open. When it has completely collapsed, a bearded man comes forward and raises Jaya's left arm above her head. The audience cheers, claps, makes any noise it can to signal its appreciation.

"Smoke, Smoke, Smoke," people continue to chant.

Jaya Smoke beats the air with her fist, victory splashed across her features. Then she walks out of the dome and toward the black hole where fighters enter and exit. And that's when a new emotion runs across her face. She doesn't like this, does she? I look at the wizard Ax, slumped in the dome. If she had wanted to kill him he would be dead.

Who are you really, Jaya? I push against the crowds. I am going to find out.

◇ ◇ ◇

I can't very well follow Jaya into the black hole she has disappeared into. That would involve jumping onstage. Too public and noticeable unless I use powerful black magic. I spot the only other entrance that might lead to the back. A large wizard stands in front of it. I can't squeeze by him, even cloaked in a conceal spell. Black magic confuses the eyes, not the sense of touch or physical mass. Black hole onstage, it is.

I wait for the next two fighters to enter the ring. While the announcer calls out their stats, I cast the most powerful camouflaging spell I have. In this dim, smoky environment, I fade from existence. A roar reverberates behind me as the two wizards begin dueling. I climb the platform and slink toward the curtained threshold. The curtain is probably only here to notify people of a black magic user. Most homes typically fasten hidden bells at the top of the doorframe so they ring at any movement. There are no bells here, and yet I still lift the curtain fast, not wanting anyone to notice fabric moving on its own. Behind the material a few meters of hallway stretch to meet a door. I uncast the spell and power walk. If I get caught now I can talk my way out of it. Get caught in black magic concealment spells and you are guilty automatically, no matter the circumstance.

The door is locked. Typical. With a quick blast of air under the frame, the metal plate on the other side swooshes back with a clang. I open the door to find more hallway, with noise brewing from a door at the end. The best camouflage is acting like I belong here, no doubt.

I'm walking toward the noise when a bulky hand grasps my shoulder. "You're not supposed to be here. Fighters only." I turn to find a wizard even taller than Kalyan. He's got a lot of meat on his bones, muscles with a padding of fat. I don't want to have to fight him.

I shrug off the hand and face him chest to chest. "I'm looking for Jaya."

"Yeah, you and every other stalker I've found back here." The words pull at me. Gods, how much unwanted attention has she received from cage casting while on her mission?

"I'm a friend." I hope she vouches for me; that is, if I ever get past this beast of a man. She had thanked me the other day for helping when she burned out, so there's that. We might be friends in her mind. I hope she deems us friendly at least.

He laughs. "Yeah, we all have that fantasy. Now get the blood out." He pushes my shoulder and I let myself stumble. Distance is better for purple dueling spells.

I pivot to another tactic. "I want to talk to Sims."

He starts a little, then regenerates the stern frown. "You friends with him too?"

"Never met, but he'll be interested in what I have to say."

"Oh yeah, what would he be interested in from you?"

Blood! I wish Agent Smoke had furnished a description in that report. But at least I know whom I'm dealing with now. I open my mouth.

"Hey," a voice rings out.

Sims and I both turn. It's . . . her, standing there. No bloody face. No confused air. In fact, this girl is way too pretty and way too put together for someone who almost got burned alive. But here she is. Jaya and Agent Smoke, wrapped into one, and again barging in for the save. Guess it did look like I needed rescuing. She takes a few quick steps forward so she is the third point in our hostile triangle. "He's with me, Sims."

132

"With you?" Sims asks. I think he means it sexually, but she blows off the insinuation.

"Was going to introduce you, but he wandered off." She turns to me and holds my eyes for half a second. The message is clear enough: *Shut up and don't contradict me.* She shrugs and stares Sims down. "He's got a good arm and he's a white forte. You've been looking for one."

Sims gives me the standard up and down. How classic, I'm being summed up in a glance. "He doesn't seem like the fighting type."

"That's what you first said about me, too." Jaya gives him one of those long stares, primal and unnerving. Unspoken sentences flow between them as they maintain eye contact. I want to understand what they're saying, to see the memories burst forth in their heads about a past in which this girl, this Belwarian peasant girl, came here and requested to fight. And she's still a fighter, still here tonight knocking out a wizard who has dubbed himself Ax.

Sims breaks eye contact and says gruffly, "Fine. If his arm is so good I'll put him against Beckman. He's been itching to taste new meat."

"Beckman? You drugged, Sims? I wanted you to meet the guy, not kill him."

What in Wickery have I gotten myself into? I calm my face. Can't let any uncertainty through, or else I'm going into the ring with death.

"Best I can do on short notice," Sims snorts.

"Fine, I get it. But I just wanted you to take a look at him. We can come back next week." Jaya seems relieved for a second, not

133

in her voice, but something about her shoulders unwinds from tension. She is working a trap or a plan, something that Sims is obviously falling for.

"You know that's not how it works. He came here to be seen? Then he's going to fight," Sims says.

"Fine." Jaya smiles. "Let him have my second fight—Tenson. And next month I'll take Beckman."

Sims's whole demeanor transforms. A black happiness bubbles inside him. I can see it sweat out of him like sludge. "You and Beckman?"

"Me and Beckman."

Sims's mouth does this weird half smile, half frown, like he's weighing these options on his lips. He rubs his hands together. "I need time to publicize that."

"That's why I'm saying a month."

"All right, deal," Sims says as he thrusts out an eager forearm.

"I still get my payment for tonight." Jaya jams a thumb at me. "I get his contribution too."

Sims glares at me as if he forgot I was still standing there while they negotiated. "Once I see he can still stand afterward."

Jaya turns to me. Now she's the one summing me up in a glance.

"No problem," I say before she can cast any doubt or give Sims more leverage.

"I won't be cheated, Sims, either way." Jaya presses her arm against his. "That's the only thing you can count on."

Sims pokes a finger at both of us. "You've got thirty minutes. I like to be impressed."

CHAPTER TWELVE

◇

Getting Him Out of Trouble

Adraa

Interacting with Sims is like watching someone try to peel off your skin. You want to scream, to yank away, but either action means more torture. He is not Vencrin, but he works for them, allowing the Underground to be a meeting place and a way to funnel drug money into the system. Because of my hatred, our relationship is . . . strained. So getting myself involved in anything beyond our agreement is risky. But then I saw him, the guard who carried me when I burned out, being confronted by Sims.

I don't know why I wanted to save Jatin's man. Well, I guess actually I do. Jatin and I were bonded, or would be. His man was my man. The resemblance between them is uncanny too; it makes me feel as though letting one be destroyed would kill the other. If I don't fight for my people now, what good am I as a future rani? Besides, I know what would have happened if I left Kalyan to Sims. He would have been beaten in the alleyway,

135

three or four against one. Those were the odds that had been stacked against Riya's father. And this had all started because of what happened to him. I won't chance that happening again, to anyone, especially Jatin's friendlier counterpart. So I cloak myself in a thick skin and trade myself, my fight, so his blood won't be spilled on a dirty street.

The actual trading isn't so bad. I thought I would probably have to offer up something big like that to find out about my firelight and Nightcaster's involvement. But now my plan hinges upon this guard's ability. Already the lack of control pokes at a level of anxiety I haven't felt since my first night here.

Sims walks away in the direction of his office. Or he might be heading to scout out Streak and Thunder, who are near the end of round one. A bell dings in the background and the audience's roars quiet down.

I turn to Kalyan, who is staring at me.

"Thank you. I—" he begins.

"Not here. Follow me." I walk in the opposite direction of Sims, toward the locker rooms. The noise of several fighters flits down the hall. This is going to suck. The others are never happy about fresh meat without some sort of announcement by Sims.

"Don't say anything," I whisper to Kalyan, before pushing through the curtain.

Five heads twist at my entry. Beckman, easily the largest man in the room, returns to his meditation. But the others are all eyes and a torrent of emotions at Kalyan's presence.

Rakesh stands and steps into my trajectory. "Who the blood is this?"

I try to hide my hatred. Nightcaster. As he speaks his arms flex. He's had ink sketched into his upper arms, trying to present himself as an eight or a nine. Everyone knows, can see the color difference. He's also the only one who fights shirtless. The muscles and abs in full view are as intimidating and disgusting as ever.

"A friend, new fighter. He's taking my place against Tenson."

Tenson, with his scruff of brown hair, pops up. "What the blood? Sims didn't clear this with me."

"Go talk to him yourself." I gesture to the door.

Tenson slides around Rakesh and then pushes past Kalyan and me. "Knew you would be scared when you got to the big leagues," he scoffs.

I turn to Rakesh. "Get out of the way. I need to prepare him for the fight."

"Friend, huh? All the times you could have had me, Jaya, and you chose this?" Rakesh gestures to Kalyan as if I have brought in trash off the sidewalk.

Could have *had* Rakesh? I don't want to even touch him. He's been like this since I arrived here: harassing me, insinuating his sexual prowess. It's sickening. One would think after I beat him in a match a few months ago it would have settled the sexual fantasy he has cast upon me. Instead it's gotten worse. He doesn't want only sex anymore. He wants domination. More than any Vencrin in here, Rakesh rattles my blood. Can make me shrink back into the younger and less confident Adraa. I hate him for that.

I've never been fearful of my looks or power before, but when people like Rakesh exist it's hard not to wonder whether looking any different could lessen my burden. It's his fault, not mine. I know whatever I looked like he would harass me. But I can't help but wonder, could his foul tongue and fouler mind be contained if I changed anything?

Kalyan tightens behind me. Oh Gods, I forgot. He's a better, kinder person than I am. He might try to defend my honor or some crap, even not knowing who I really am.

"Get out of the way," I repeat to Rakesh.

Rakesh shifts into a fighting stance, but it's Kalyan's eyes he meets over my shoulder. Oh blood no! I don't get to be dismissed for a fight just because now I have a man at my back. No matter how much Rakesh scares me.

"We don't have time for this." I step to the right.

Rakesh shoots out an arm as a barrier. Everyone pauses except Beckman, who stands from one of the wobbly wooden benches Sims provides.

Then Rakesh speaks. "Hope she's softer and wetter on the inside."

The scene erupts, mostly because I'm pissed. *"Kavacraw,"* I cast, and a red flurry of magic smokes into a blockade between Kalyan and Rakesh. Then I grab Rakesh's wrist, the one right in front of me, and twist and bend it upward with force. My shield catches Kalyan's fist, barely. He hadn't cast any spell behind it, which I was counting on. His punch sinks into my shield like sand, and flecks of red magic splinter off.

I have only a second to examine my handiwork because with a yelp of pain Rakesh swings for me with his free arm. I release his wrist, duck, and push further into the locker room. Far enough away and he'll have to cast something instead of taking a swing.

"Leave the fight for the ring!" Beckman shouts in his deep voice.

Kalyan bats away my shield, which is already dissolving. I throw my hands up in the air in surrender to Rakesh, but mentally prepare another shield. Red magic floats down my left arm in warning. Rakesh is steaming with fury. He would have rather taken Kalyan's punch than my wristlock, I'm sure. At least then he could have said a man made him shout in pain.

"Listen to Beckman," I encourage.

I glance at Kalyan, who is assessing the situation in silence. He doesn't look like he will throw a punch again, but his body angles like Riya's sometimes does. Protective, guardlike, and, most important, ready to insert himself in the middle of a magical brawl.

"Rakesh!" Beckman shouts again.

With that, Rakesh shoves himself toward the curtain. "Bloody bitch." This time the whispered phrase doesn't bother me as much as Basu's, because I've won this round.

Kalyan slides out of Rakesh's way and toward me.

I find Beckman's eyes and nod.

"Gods. She always that fast at casting?" Navin, one of the young fighters who has remained quiet, asks.

Beckman replies, but I don't have time to listen, or care. I'm already marching toward the door on the far left.

I slam the door securely shut as soon as Kalyan is through it. With a flick of my hand I soundproof the doorframe. The room is a third the size of the main waiting area. It used to be the storage closet, and various like-minded tools are stacked on the far side. The rest of the space is for me and two other female fighters, who come around every once in a while. So the space is mostly mine. I have a locker, a bench, and all the firelight I need to make out the dirty corners and dusty nooks.

Kalyan has the good sense to wait until the magic clusters around the door's perimeter. As soon as the square red halo completes its ring, he's off. "What was that? Does that happen to you every week?"

I think back. Not *every* week. "Normally, I don't have to protect people who have no right being here."

Kalyan recoils. For a second I'm glad if it hurt him. He has jeopardized my entire undercover operation. I wait a beat. "That was an opening for you to tell me exactly what the blood you *are* doing here."

"I understand if you are mad."

I throw my arms up. Understanding won't fix anything. "Congratulations, you are intelligent enough to understand anger." I look at him and immediately regret my words.

"I came here same as you. To get information about what has happened with the firelight," he says.

"Because Jatin thinks he owns it? It's Belwar business."

"No, Maharaja Naupure gave me the reports. He wanted me to help you."

"*My* reports, you mean! My mission, my life on the line." The words echo in the small enclosure. Even though I'm risking my life, it's the mission that feels vulnerable right now, exposed. I was going to stop it after all, the Vencrin and the drugs. That was going to be my legacy. And if I fail . . .

Then two words sink in. Maharaja Naupure. Maharaja Naupure gave this guard the reports, wanted him here. He never thought I could do this alone then. He had pestered me about a guard and now here one was, standing in front of me.

"Yes, you're right—your life. But if I had known it was you I—"

"Known it was me?" Oh Gods, does he know who I am? Would Maharaja Naupure have told him? I must be such a joke in his eyes. The silly, rich girl who thought she could be tough and help her country. We both draw into a long pause.

"I would have come no matter what, Jaya," Kalyan whispers.

I take in a breath. He doesn't know. Regardless, it's a nice sentiment. Even if I were only Jaya, an average commoner, he would help me. But did I bloody ask for his help? No. That's the point.

It's as expected, then. He's here under orders and obligation, an ill-informed soldier reporting for duty, but doing a wonderful job screwing things up. He stares at me intently. I have to break eye contact. His eyes suck me in with their kindness and genuine good intentions. He threw a punch for my honor after all. But maybe that was for Jatin's honor too? Ah, this is such a mess.

I look at the clock. We have twenty minutes. "We don't have time. You're here now. I just hope you can fight, because that's the only way we are going to salvage this."

◇

CHAPTER THIRTEEN

Lessons Learned

Jatin

Is it possible to start to fall for someone when they're fuming at you? As soon as Jaya asked, "Known it was me?" my brain did this weird dance; it clambered for words, and picked up affection instead. If I had known Jaya was Agent Smoke I wouldn't have just come, I would have run. I don't care who she is in society. I've seen her save a boy's life. I've read her month's work to stop a horde of drug criminals. I've witnessed her hear a man utter disgusting slurs at her and she rescues *him* from *my* anger? Who does that? Not to mention the extreme skill it takes to cast and move that fast. That young fighter who was incredulous and a little terrified at her swiftness has a right to be. I'm not sure if even I could have foreseen and cast a boundary shield that quickly.

I like her. I want to fix my interference. Want to help her rebuild her mission.

"What do I need to do?" I ask.

"You have fought before, right? I mean, you're a guard. You were taught?"

"I was taught, but this is different. Cage casting is . . . minutes ago your opponent tried to burn you alive."

She gets defensive. "And what, real fighting is all nice and honorable?"

"Sorry, but at least we try. We are expected to be honorable."

She shakes her head. *What is she thinking?*

"Yeah, you're right. I forgot what I was dealing with. Okay." She paces a few times. "Okay, um . . . try to hit me."

"What?"

"Try to take me on and I can see what you're missing."

"I don't—"

"Look." She points to the door. "In about twenty minutes you are going into the ring. Honorable walked out the door when you stepped in. I won't get hit, unless you are some master wizard."

I make a swing. She's right. If I'm going into the ring I should start fighting, not talking. I make contact and immediately retract. *Blood!* I thought she would be fast enough, like with Rakesh, or she would at least duck. Maybe she wasn't prepared. Red smoke disperses, revealing her hand covering my fist. I didn't hit her; she caught my punch.

Jaya releases my fist a second later. "Good. At least you keep your wrist straight and can aim."

I rotate my shoulder. Is this what Ax felt like out there? Where did that magic come from? "Did you . . . did you cast a spell?"

"Of course. What, you think I can catch a punch like that naturally?"

"But I didn't hear you. Can, can you . . ."

"Oh, Gods no. Wait, have *you* ever met someone who can mind cast?"

"No." To be honest, I have been working on it for ages, but nothing has come to fruition. In theory, mind casting, casting without saying the spells out loud, could work, but no one has proved it yet.

"I haven't either, but cage casting is the closest it gets," Jaya says. "You must chant under your breath so your opponent doesn't know what to expect. Here, watch my lips and listen."

While the directive gives me an excuse to look at her, I don't want my gaze to tell her anything, like, for instance, how bloody beautiful I think her lips are. She steps closer for me to hear. That's the only reason she stepped closer, I know, but I can't stop something inside me from roaring awake and pushing for me to do something. Something . . . charming.

"Did you hear the spell?" she asks.

Blood. Focus, Jatin. "No. What was it?"

She sighs. "A shield spell. Please tell me you know those, both physical and magic."

"Of course I do."

"Okay, good. Your opponent, Tenson, is a yellow forte wizard. He likes wind bursts, so either throw up a bubble shield or combat wind with wind. Like me, he also favors orange magic, particularly speed enhancement."

I nod. "Got it."

"Cage casting is also about letting the magic flow continuously." She touches my hand and traces up my arm. Even over my cloak it feels amazing. "Pick a finger and focus. Let your Touch flow up and down your arm and not all at once. Okay, chant with me this time, and actually cast the spells. Each one should appear at once and disappear as you start a new spell."

She steps back. "Ready?"

For fifteen minutes we build shields crafted for strong gusts of yellow magic. I've trained to cast continuously, but never quite like this. A white shield spell isn't even fully destroyed before Jaya tells me to start the next. She taps my arm to indicate when I should change. It's an advanced teaching method and I wonder where she learned it.

A knock on the door whips our attention back to the real world. I almost forget there was anything beyond this closetlike room.

"Hey," Sims calls.

Jaya pulls back the soundproofing.

Sims bashes the door open and charges in. "Two minutes!" He pounds on the wall in emphasis. The way he looks, I think he wishes that wall were my head.

"He'll be ready, Sims. I got it!" Jaya yells back.

"You better. What's his fighting name anyway?"

She turns to me in question, and I shrug.

"Do I have to do everything?" she whispers to herself. "The White Stranger!" she calls.

Sims spits. "Weak."

"Then anything you bloody well please, Sims."

He grunts and turns to go, waving two fingers at her. Only two minutes left. That's all? I don't even have time to be nervous.

"We'll probably regret that later," Jaya says. "Take off your cloak and pull up your sleeves."

I unfasten the cloak. "Why the sleeves?"

"Because this is as much of a show as a fight. Now roll."

I almost comment on how bossy she is, but stop when I realize it's leadership, natural bloody leadership. She must be frustrated, angry, nervous, and Gods know what else, but beneath all that she is under control. No wonder Father employed her. I should probably take notes.

She seizes my cloak from me and hangs it up. When she turns my sleeves are rolled to the crooks of my elbows.

"Good Gods." She starts and stares at my arms. Giddy pride flows through me. I want her to keep looking. She blinks to snap out of it, and the slight movement is intoxicating. "Do, ah, all men in the academy have that much"—she coughs—"power?"

"I got to be Raja Jatin's guard for a reason, right?" The lie comes easy enough.

She is thinking something; the wheels and cogs are churning in her eyes. I want to know what exactly. Did my Touch give my birthright away that quickly?

"You must be, what? A seven, an eight?"

Only rajas and ranis can harness all nine, so it would only make sense that I were lower, much lower. Kalyan is a six, but with my markings . . . "Yeah, seven." I throw out the number hoping it is both low and high enough to make sense with the intricate designs of my Touch.

She doesn't miss a beat. "What can't you do?"

What can I afford to give up in the ring and still stay undercover? "Red and pink." I'm surprised even as I sputter out the

146

half-truth, red and pink having always been the trickiest magic for me to cast. But potions won't be used in the ring and I don't want to burn someone alive like Ax tried to, so I guess the partial truth works.

Jaya nods. "All right. Now, off with your kurta."

"Excuse me?"

"We have one minute," she says as she turns from me. I huff so she knows how annoying this is, then pull the kurta over my head. She holds out one hand, still facing away from me. I pass it over. Without a second thought, she whispers a spell and the fabric tears. The long sleeves rip off easily enough, right below the biceps. She hands my kurta back without looking and waits for me to put it on again. "You good?"

"Yeah."

She faces me and nods. Her eyes linger on my arms, and despite the situation I smile.

"You shouldn't—" She pauses. "You can't wear full sleeves. And this will give you more mobility anyway."

"What about you, then?" I gesture to her outfit. Both black sleeves stop right at the wrists, so all one can make out is the slight Touch that curls up the back of her left hand.

"Yeah, well, if I were to show my arms to these men . . . For you it's an act of aggression. For me it invites challenge. Trust me."

I'm going to have to trust her to get out of this, but a part of me relishes the idea. I want to trust her, to know her. Know everything.

"Time's up! Bring this good arm of yours!" Sims shouts as he bustles into the room.

147

CHAPTER FOURTEEN

◇

I Watch Snow Fall

Adraa

While Kalyan marches onto the platform that leads to the ring, I take the back route. Pushing through the crowds, I find the wooden ladder that ascends to a platform that runs the entire circumference of the underground warehouse. Only fighters and employees are allowed to watch fights from here. We call it the upper deck. I heave myself up and scan to see who else watches from this balcony-like walkway. Looks like the entire group came to observe this one. I spot Rakesh at once and veer away from him. There has been only one time I was trapped up here alone with him and it scared me into intense wariness from then on.

Across the raised walkway, Beckman nods for me to join him. I walk toward him guiltily. Beckman is the best cage caster here and one of the only wizards who is not Vencrin. Cage casting is what he likes doing, is good at doing, and can make money doing. He's savage in the ring, but he's still one of my citizens, whom I swore never to harm. Even though he could and might break me in a cage fight.

"Hey," I say as I sit and dangle my feet over the edge. I grab the railing and slip my arms over it to hold on. "Thanks for earlier."

"That nothing blood of a wizard is getting worse these days," he snarls. "He's a psychopath in the making. Gods, if I were his father . . ."

A bubble inside my chest expands. Beckman is the father of two little girls. I've seen them once, at the market, following their giant of a dad around as if he were one of the gods. It's one of the main reasons I chose to align myself with him and he has granted me some protection here. Which only means that he doesn't give Rakesh the opportunity to be alone with me. But in one month I would fight Beckman. What had I done?

"Your guy any good?" he asks.

"He's not my guy."

"He's something to you if you vouched for him to Sims and he wants to brawl with Rakesh." Beckman's harsh bearded face lifts in a "got you there" look.

Instead of answering, I stare down at Kalyan as he and Tenson stride into the ring. The two halves of the sphere rise to reconnect like broken wings. They click into place and then clunk as they buckle together. Kalyan twists to analyze the sphere that surrounds him.

This is it. I cannot help anymore, cannot intervene. Maybe I should have left Kalyan to the alleyway. Things can get bloody in the dome too. Kalyan's gaze blazes through the crowd. Maybe he's looking for me. I wave, but then feel ludicrous. He won't know to look upward.

A voice booms, "To the right we have Thunder, a veteran of the ring at three years."

Tenson shoots a stream of yellow magic and it bundles up above him like a rumbling cloud. It's impressive and all, but when the clouds are bright yellow, they look jovial. It's like trying to be fierce with colorful cotton candy swarming above your head.

"And to the left . . ."

I sit up straighter and lean forward.

"We have the White Knight in his debut fight."

I have so much riding on this fight and yet I can't help but laugh. Sims paints all of his fighters in exaggerated personae. I'm mysterious, alluring, and unattainable as Smoke. Beckman is formidable and daunting as the Tsunami. Guess Kalyan is getting the good-guy act. How fitting.

Kalyan frowns at the name and shakes his head. He's at least confident in there. For now. He glances at the swarm of clouds still billowing above Tenson, then he casts a spell too. Good, I forgot to tell him the beginning procedure. Kalyan's spell gusts from his right hand and the frosty white stream flies toward Tenson's clouds and whips through them. It then tears itself around the sphere like some wild bird. Oh Gods.

"Whoa, already—" The rest of Beckman's sentence is lost in the uproar of the crowd cheering or booing at Kalyan's brazen prefight show of power. It's definitely not very White Knightly of him.

The announcer stalls before yelling, *"Fight!"* Tenson leaps into the air, spins, and throws wind in a razor-sharp disk. Kalyan ducks and slides to the side smoothly. He rolls and builds a shield. Good. And he needs it too, because Tenson comes flying back at him and strikes downward with one foot. But as Tenson's foot lands, the shield disperses and gathers around his leg. In a flash of white, Tenson's foot ices over and thumps to the ground from the extra weight. Kalyan isn't done yet, though. With control of Tenson's leg, he whips him across the sphere, where he smashes against the wall.

Beckman whistles. "Good, smart casting."

But it's far from over. Tenson is already rolling and cracking the ice with his own white magic. The ice breaks apart with a blast and Tenson is free, sprinting around the sphere in different directions, looking for an opening. Kalyan stands in the middle observing, which is going to give me a heart attack.

Move!

In a split second the two wizards meet. Tenson comes from the left and Kalyan ducks his fist. They both craft knives and suddenly the battle is a whirlwind of movement, with arms jetting, retracting, and blocking.

I can't tell who's winning or whether either has been cut. Beckman pats me on the back hard enough to remind me to gulp in air.

"Not your guy, huh?"

"Not my guy."

The two keep it up until Tenson twirls his arm and catches Kalyan's wrist. The shoulder bends unnaturally. Applause clamors in approval. The crowd is fickle today, can't decide which wizard they want to win. Then, still in the armlock, Tenson kicks Kalyan against the curved dome.

"Nooo." Without thinking I cast an orange and pink spell to examine the damage. My eyes blur and then focus on the muscles and bones within Kalyan's chest. I zero in on the shoulder. There is a tear in the muscle and it's already swelling. I blink to cancel the spell. When I refocus on the fight, there's been a shift. Kalyan has wrestled out of the armlock and is clutching his jaw.

"What happened?" I ask.

"Your man escaped the armlock, but Tenson punched him in the face."

I squeeze the railing hard. If Kalyan gets seriously hurt it will be my fault. He shouldn't have come here. Fighting in a bubble of five meters is drastically different from any training ground or battlefield.

Kalyan and Tenson circle each other. At least Kalyan's movements are still calm. The fighting restarts in a blink. Wind tunnels, Tenson's favorite, volley against Kalyan, but instead of shields he uses yellow magic too. White and yellow streams hammer against each other. The wizards' hair and clothing ripple as if caught in a storm. Kalyan withdraws and lowers his injured arm. I can see Tenson's smile from here. He thinks he has won.

Please. The word beats against my brain. *Please don't mess this up.*

One of the spells connects directly. This is always dangerous in the ring. In the small space of the dome too much power can build up and the magic can be uncontrollable. It could kill them both. I've never seen a white forte wizard in the dome before, but the white-and-yellow mixture appears holy, and as if a god will manifest among the rays of color. Kalyan and Tenson look about equal, but the energy continues to build. One of them is going to have to let go, and soon.

Tenson mutters continuously and each new wind spell builds with rhythmic pulses into a collision. But then I realize that Kalyan, silent and one-armed, has cast only one spell. Wait, that can't be right. *One* spell against the dozen Tenson has thrown?

I turn to Beckman. "Are you seeing what I'm seeing?"

He nods slowly. I don't think he can believe it either. "Tenson has no clue. He can't see it."

In a snap it's over. Kalyan says one word, one small enhancement to his spell, and Tenson is thrown against the wall. Built-up yellow magic bounces off the sphere and clusters into clouds. Tenson is down, the match is over, but for the first time no one cheers. No one can grasp what's happened. Snow cascades over the two wizards, one passed out and the other catching snowflakes in his outstretched palm.

Beckman whistles softly. "If he isn't your guy, are you sure you don't want him to be?"

"What?"

"I know that expression." He nods to my face.

Beckman knows nothing of my real life, so I don't care or listen when he doles out advice; like when he scanned me in the locker room my first day and blurted, "If you are here to escape abuse you came to the wrong place with that face."

Yet, for the first time he has deciphered my feelings and

emotions before I can even properly sort them. I do *feel* something, and it is more than happiness that Kalyan is safe and that I will get information from Sims. It's something close to awe.

Beckman is still shaking his head at the snow scene when Sims appears behind us. They both look as stunned as I feel. "Where did you find him?" Sims asks me.

I didn't find him so much as he was ordered to follow me here. I can't say that, though. "Doesn't matter. You got a good show out of it."

Sims grunts in agreement.

"Now, let's talk payment."

CHAPTER FIFTEEN

◇

Fixing a Friend
or Flirting with a Stranger

Jatin

Fifteen minutes I wait in Jaya's solitary closet of a room nursing my shoulder. After that, I succumb to the dread that Jaya might not return. Officially ditched after winning for her and her mission? Gods, that's rough. I contemplate going home or wandering around like a lost dog to make sure she doesn't get into any trouble, but that sounds pathetic and a little too much like the stalker fan Sims first believed I was.

Then she appears in the doorway.

"Hey." I jerk upright, sending a wrenching spasm down my back.

Jaya straddles the bench beside me. "It feel as bad as it looks?"

I swing my leg over the bench so I'm facing her. "No."

"Yeah, I'm sure." She looks at me expectantly, like I'm suddenly going to admit it does hurt, that my jaw feels as if unhinged and smashed onto the floor or my shoulder is about to

155

tear off. But her presence makes me lighter, happier. I wasn't forgotten or abandoned.

Jaya sighs. "You did well."

"Because I didn't die or because I won?"

"Because you didn't die." She laughs and rests one hand on my hurt shoulder. I look at it, then her. The world pauses and my breath hitches. She is very close.

"Jaya—" She gently squeezes my shoulder and I wince and jerk at the throbbing pain. "What the—"

"You were just going to sit here talking to me with a tear in your rotator cuff?"

"I . . ." The truth is I had already sent some pink magic in to fix it the moment I stepped out of the ring, but I can't say that. "How did you know?"

"Can do pink magic, remember?" She points at herself.

"Oh," I say dumbly. But how could she tell? What kind of spell is that, to diagnose me from meters away or through a light touch of her hand.

She tilts her head. "Does Raja Jatin know you are here?"

Oh Gods, she knows I lied. She can sense the pink magic I used to try to reduce the pain in my shoulder. "He, well, he . . ." I suck in a large breath. "Yes, he knows."

She doesn't seem to like the answer, but accepts it with a hard nod. Then she reaches into a nearby locker and brings out an orb of pink goo. "Okay, then I don't have to do a complete conceal job."

"What?"

"You can't do healing magic, right? I'm not going to leave

you like this." She gestures to me like I'm broken. "I have to clean myself up all the time." She points at her lips. Again, she makes me focus on them, and I get a little more aroused. I almost wish she would stop doing it. Almost . . .

"Ax busted up my lower lip earlier and now it's good. Proof I know what I'm doing," she clarifies.

"I didn't doubt that."

"Okay." She waits uneasily. "It's easier without your kurta."

I raise my eyebrows, and the right side of my mouth twitches upward on its own.

She rolls her eyes, but as much as she wants to hide her awkwardness, I see it. "I'm not trying to make a pass at you," she says.

Gods, I wish I didn't hear the truth in those words.

I also wish I could take off my kurta without struggling with my right arm. Jaya helps me with the last bit and I feel like a wounded animal. Yet I do get to cherish the moment when her gaze lingers on my arms before she sets her hands on my shoulder.

"This will numb the pain," she mumbles as she wipes the pink goo over the bruising and whispers a spell. While she works she's fixated on my shoulder, and I'm fixated on her. For once it's acceptable to stare and I take full advantage. Maybe others wouldn't find her as gorgeous as I do because they overlook the kindness in her piercing eyes, or the way her mouth twitches when she curses or says something sarcastic. I play with the idea of teasing her about the red in her cheeks, but she might counter with the same claim about me. My whole body is warm except for the coolness surging through my shoulder blade. Finally the pain retreats behind the tingling cold.

Her eyes lock onto mine. We are even closer than before, kissable close. "You are in a lot better shape than I thought," she says.

I sit up a little taller. I've never been the most muscular of men—I'm no Rakesh—but I'll never need to print on a fake Touch, so there's that. "I *think* I'll take that as a compliment."

Confusion spins in her eyes and then understanding hits her. She laughs. "No, I mean the tear. Your injury is only half as bad as I thought." She returns to casting pink magic as she shakes her head. Maybe it's the proximity and the view, but it's the best healing I've ever received. My shoulder relaxes and begins to thank me. Jaya works with steady hands, as though she's sewing my muscle back together. My pink magic, on the other hand, operates like an overdose, almost as painful as the initial injury.

"Okay. It will be sore for a few days, but how does that feel?" she asks as she wipes her hands on her pants. I contemplate lying so she'll lean toward me again.

"Perfect." I rotate my shoulder and it's only stiff, as if I slept wrong.

"I expect you want me to do your jaw too."

I angle forward. "If you insist."

She slides forward until our knees bump and then whispers, *"Goghatalaeh."*

I thought her hand on my shoulder was something. But this is almost unbearable. I imagine pulling her onto my lap . . . and the slap to the face that would surely follow.

As if she can read my thoughts, Jaya's gaze flits upward and connects with mine. She must feel the tension. I mean, it's palpable. In the next second we've both fallen silent. She's stopped casting and we are just staring at each other.

"You're distracting me," she whispers.

"You're the one who wanted my shirt off."

"*Goghatalaeh*," Jaya says, and a rush of red smoke dives into my jaw. I wince as the pain compacts, eases, and then releases. Yep, that's how it feels when I heal myself, and now I remember how much it sucks. I would've studied pink magic more if I knew it didn't always have to hurt like this.

Jaya bites her lip. "Sorry, I shouldn't have done that."

I rub my jaw. "Nope, I deserved it." I shouldn't be thinking about kissing her. I'm taken, by a girl she works for. And both of our countries depend upon Adraa and me marrying and standing up to my uncle's potential threat. *What's wrong with me?*

Jaya tosses me my kurta and I catch it as she stands. *No, don't leave.* I have so much to ask her. I throw my kurta back on. "How did you get mixed up in all this?"

Jaya frowns deeply as she digs through her bag. "You read my reports."

"No, I mean why you? Why did my . . . maharaja pick you as his agent?"

"First, he didn't pick me. I went to him. With Lady Adraa's blessing, of course."

"What?"

She turns to face me. "A few months ago the head security guard of Maharaja Belwar was attacked by the Vencrin, and they put him in a coma. I watched a family be torn to pieces—my friend's family." She takes a deep breath. "I also work in the royal clinic. For months I've been treating wizards and witches, hurt by or addicted to the drugs the Vencrin have been selling. Everything else is spelled out in the reports. And tonight Sims has given me what I need. And that's partly because of you." Jaya clasps my arm. "So thanks," she says while sliding around me.

She really is leaving. And Adraa has approved of all this? Just let Jaya come to the Underground alone and then . . .

"You aren't done tonight, are you? You're going somewhere else, going to trail one of the Vencrin."

She stops in her tracks. "It's not your concern."

"Let me help you."

"You've done enough, you're hurt."

"And you fixed me," I counter. Like that was going to be any excuse. "I know I've gotten in your way tonight, but I can make it up to you." I step closer. "You need backup and I'm a good fighter."

"I've been alone in this awhile. I can handle myself."

That scrap of paper flips into my mind. Jaya Smoke *was* doing more than reporting Vencrin incidents in the streets; she was stopping them. But Bloodlurst can be sold by only one wizard. If she's after firelight and it's being stolen and taken elsewhere, this is going to be bigger than one or two wizards in an alley. "Two men dealing drugs is vastly different from an operation like this and you know it."

She doesn't flinch, but I can tell she's deliberating by her expression, so I keep talking. Something I say might knock some sense into her. "Maharaja Naupure gave me your reports for a reason. And it was for this, to help you."

"How do you know what kind of operation I'm after? How do I know I can trust you?"

She's got me there. I *am* lying to her, after all. Maybe she can sense it. But if I tell her now she'll freak out and go off alone against who knows how many criminals.

She steps toward me. "Prove that it was Maharaja Naupure who gave you my report."

I scramble for an explanation. What would be unique to my father? What sign or information didn't come from her written hand? I think about the first time we met.

Got it. "You are trying to prove the firelight shortage is Maharaja Moolek's doing," I say in a low voice.

Jaya falls back on her heels. I've obviously shocked her.

"That good enough?" I ask, though I know it is.

She squints at me, a measured look in her eyes. "You're wrong about one thing. It's not tonight. In three days meet me at the East Village square, two after dusk."

Now it's my turn to go on the offensive. "How do I know *you* aren't lying?"

"I guess we'll just have to trust one another."

"I won't be late," I say, half in reassurance, half in warning.

"I don't doubt it." She pauses as she reaches for the door, turns back. "One more thing. How are you with black magic?"

I smile. That's one thing I don't need to lie about. "A natural."

CHAPTER SIXTEEN

❖

Pier Sixteen

Adraa

Kalyan is so punctual even Riya would be impressed. I'm not late—the stars have just started their twinkling—but he's beaten me here. He leans against an alley wall, eyes trained on the square. Funny enough, it's a lamp carrying firelight that illuminates his features, especially his jawline. He's watching for me, I realize with a start. Only I've come from the other direction, avoiding the openness of the square like the professional that I am. But I hang back in a curtain of darkness. He's different from what I thought Jatin's head guard would be like. I figured Jatin would pick someone, I don't know, someone mean, someone exactly like himself and not just in looks. It shouldn't fascinate me so, that Kalyan is kind. He was probably ordered to help, but the way he surveys the sky for me . . .

"Looks different without a parade and some girl hurling herself in front of a carriage, huh?" I say as I come up beside him and mirror his cross-armed stance.

162

He twitches; one could even describe it as flinching.

I can't help but chuckle. "Did I scare you?"

Kalyan collects himself nicely. "For a moment there, I thought you had stood me up."

He had a right to be worried. I almost flew past. Probably shouldn't tell him that, though. "I thought about it."

What is wrong with me?

He smiles regardless. He wears it so well too, that smile. "I guess I should thank you, then, for keeping your word."

And yet I'm lying through my teeth. For the first time, guilt climbs through me regarding that particular detail. "We're going to the docks. Pier Sixteen," I answer, bringing Hubris to life in a rush of red smoke. I can't risk the mission, no matter how kind he is.

The moon is wide tonight, but that's okay. Light creates more shadows, and that's black magic's specialty. Kalyan and I fly low under a film of concealment. For safety reasons it's illegal to even hover below rooftop level, but it's too hard flying *and* using black magic to cover the glow of a skyglider. Kalyan seems to know how a strong wind can easily break an illusion, because he doesn't contradict our unlawful maneuver. He even accepts my hand signals for turns and speed changes. Only Riya could be this coordinated with me. Must be a guard thing.

Houses spawn and collide with each other for space until the docks. Only the smells of fish and salt water signal the approaching ocean and the piers that branch into it. Kalyan and I zoom within the protective shadows of an alleyway until the wide shoreline welcomes us. We're here and we're vulnerable.

From now on it's best to be on foot. I swivel to tell Kalyan, but he's gone. I look down, where he's already landed, attaching his skyglider to his belt.

"We should walk from here," he calls up in a whisper.

I drop within the next second. How is he so good at this so fast? It took me a month to properly trail and surprise attack drug deals in the streets, and that was with suitable escape routes and shadows.

"What?" Kalyan asks, noticing my stare.

I buckle Hubris to my belt. "Nothing. Let's go."

◇ ◇ ◇

We run into a wall, the rocky end of Belwar Bay, where the cliffs raise up to form the southernmost coast of continental Wickery. We've passed fifteen perfectly fine docks, all posed and ready with hundreds of ships latched to their sides or floating just off. Now it's emptiness, a wall, and the slosh of semicalm sea.

"Sixteen, you said?" Kalyan asks.

"Blood." I knew the number sixteen sounded wrong on Sims's lips; I thought Belwar had only fifteen working piers. I'm an idiot. Months of work and blood in the ring, and Sims lied to my face. And I had thought I had put on my Bloodlurst addict act so well too. *Idiot.*

Kalyan suddenly points. "The waves are off."

I whirl around. "What?" But I'm already looking, analyzing where he gestures. And I see it. A current is bringing in the waves and they furl nicely into surf. But they aren't catching

164

the rocks. In fact, if anything is off it's that the waves are altogether too peaceful.

Kalyan and I both step back and I reexamine what's in front of us.

"A near-perfect illusion," Kalyan voices. My sentiment exactly. I'm almost in awe of this thing's complexity and strength. Nightfall helps, but still. Mere wind isn't breaking it.

"Except at the seams." I glance over at him. He really is a natural at black magic. He'll have no problem casting on his own mask, a spell I created to conceal myself.

"Except at the seams," he agrees.

We creep up the beach, guiding ourselves along the illusion, not daring to break through yet. Best to find the edging so that the two of us aren't walking in the middle of who knows what. Right past the seawall we find the fissure of a corner. Now the hard part, because the easiest thing about an illusion is breaking it. That's the opposite of what we want, however. The Vencrin are astute enough to notice two people-sized holes.

I ready myself to step forward and cast my own little illusion like a poor patch job, but Kalyan stops me. With one spell, white smoke engulfs his arms, and he reaches forward and pulls the corner apart. His nod indicates I should go ahead, like he's holding a door open for me. One might even consider this gesture chivalrous, if the other side didn't possibly lead to the criminal underbelly of Belwar. But his magic is still impressive.

The scene that appears after I duck under Kalyan's arm? Not so much. Pier Sixteen resides on the grimy side of forgotten and abandoned, just past disgusting and living alongside jagged rocks, and waves endlessly try to soften them. An average captain would perish if he set off from this location. Now the location makes sense. The Vencrin have tapered off the last section of beach, a place no one would think to reclaim due to the risk and needless danger.

Voices rise from down the pier, and Kalyan and I crouch behind the nearest jumble of wicker crates and fishing nets. A quite flavorful seaside stench confronts us, but I don't think we've been spotted. From our perch we can see a ship that doesn't appear to be in much better condition than its dock. Sludge and barnacles have climbed from the water and cling to the boat's siding. Sails with small tears in their orange fabric fan out like the scales of a fish.

Three wizards are loading a crate, one positioned on the dock, one on the ramp, and one on deck. They use a yellow levitation spell, passing the wicker crate among the three of them in a rainbow sheet of orange, black, and purple. It must be heavy and fragile to need the power and concentration of all three wizards.

There's something weird about the orange forte user. I don't recognize him from the Underground and yet his features ring inside my memory. Where have I seen him before? *Was* it the Underground?

I'm wasting time searching my nagging memory. "I need to see what's in those crates," I whisper.

Kalyan pushes at my shoulder as I begin to stand. "You're going to barge in there with no plan?"

"No, I was about to tell you the plan."

"I think we should call the Dome Guard. Get them involved. Will only take one bout of magic."

"No," I say reflexively at the thought of a jet of white magic zooming into the sky and alerting everyone to our position. But then I pause. Guard? *The guard!* Basu. The man with the nose, who loaded Basu's unconscious body and kept staring at me. I spin back to the man with a crate above his head. It's him.

"It would be better if—"

I cut Kalyan off. "Blood no. See the wizard closest to us. He works for the Guard."

"How do you know that?"

"Long story. Doesn't matter now, but I'm sure of it."

It does matter, though. Was that why Basu was released so quickly? The betrayal when I fought Basu gathers its twin and stuffs the emotion into my heart. Why! Why is everything corrupt in Belwar? Then an awful thought permeates my misery. Is this why the best swordsman and purple magic user I know is in a coma? Maybe it wasn't just a Vencrin attack that cast Riya's father into his deathlike state. Maybe it was an ambush, the Guard itself backstabbing him. I stifle the rage that wants to spout out of my mouth.

Kalyan's stunned expression reverts to one of neutral concentration. "You're right. If he's a Belwar guard we can't call them."

Good, he's with me, because I can't stop now. Forget my promise to Maharaja Naupure about retreat if necessary. I'm going to make these men bleed.

"You take the guard on the dock. I'll take the one on the ship. Whoever the black ramp wizard goes for, we take him out."

The wizards are already on their second crate. "Ready?"

Kalyan nods.

"Chagnyawodohs," I whisper, and wisps of red float off my fingers. The red mask adheres to my face in cold strokes. Then I cast a purple spell, and my magic plunges into the fibers of my black clothes, sewing thick, armorlike red swirls into the fabric. I quickly teach Kalyan the spell, and a white mask fastens to his face, turning him into a ghost come back to life. I can only imagine how freaky I must look, but it's the best disguise I've worn in all my spying and ambushing. A black magic spell I created myself.

"When you see red, you know when to attack," I say, then run and dive behind more shipping crates. Two more leaps behind cover and a jump off the one-meter-tall seawall and I'm on the beach, the sand sloshing upward with each footstep. Hubris bounces off my thigh.

"Sthairya Saritretaw," I call to the sea. A dark wave breaks unnaturally farther inland. A thick foam of unrest eddies. I run and, without a second thought, step onto the water. Stairs bubble in small breaking rifts as they jolt upward, and I climb in unbalanced havoc.

Only have a few seconds before the stairs disappear. Gods!

I jump for the anchor's rope as the water stairs shimmer and fall in one flat crash. The wet braids of fiber burn my palms as I grapple for a grip. Blood! I slide. One meter. Two meters. I tighten my hold and finally stop my descent, an arm's length from the ocean. My heart pumps in my ears. That was . . . not graceful.

The Vencrin may have heard the wave or my fumbling, so as soon as I'm level with the deck I reach over with a knockout spell ready on my lips. But there's nothing. No wizards, no levitation spells carrying crates; nothing but dead silence. *"Vrnotwodahs,"* I say, to reconnect with the shadows of the ship as I climb over the side and crouch.

Then I hear it, the clatter of a crate cracking, the yell of a spell, and the grunts of fighting. I run to the ramp and take in the scene on the dock with wild searching eyes. Kalyan has a bubble shield wrapped around him like a re-creation of the sphere in the Underground. The purple forte wizard pounds it with orange magic, shearing off sheets of dust and smoke. Inside the bubble Kalyan punches a wizard in the gut. The big-nosed wizard lies to the side, motionless.

What about my plan?

"Nizleah," I send toward Mr. Hit-It-Until-It-Breaks, then drop behind the ship's railing. My red magic flames toward his purple forte like an arrow. It misses by centimeters and splatters against Kalyan's shield. Blood. I low-crawl fast on the deck, awaiting a spell to hit the place I fired from.

Instead, the wizard bellows, "Intruders!"

In a blink, movement rips through my senses. The boat feels alive as noise vibrates within it. Vencrin, some already rumbling up the stairs to get to the main deck, are coming for us.

"Agati Drumahtrae." Planks peel away from the deck and I throw them toward the door. They slam in a random crisscross fashion, but it does little to slow the wizards. In one loud explosion the pieces burst apart. I drop and cover my head as splinters

rain down on me. The only good thing is that all the debris, plus my black magic, conceals me from the seven Vencrin who rush onto the deck. These Vencrin aren't dressed like cage casters. They're sailors, with worn brown kurtas, greasy hair, and tall boots made to walk or climb on water like I just did.

"Over there!" one Vencrin on the far side calls, and three others immediately rush onto the ramp to reach Kalyan and their bellowing friend. No! I can't let Kalyan be overrun. As the Vencrin race down the ramp I chant a green magic spell. In one heave the ramp tears and then slides from the ship's deck. Shouts of protest erupt as the three men tumble into the water. The wizard in the front hits the pier hard and falls with a splash into the water's dark depths.

"It's the Red Woman!" a wizard yells, and the sound is close, too close.

I spin, the red smoke of my magic already condensing into a shield. A black sword lands with brutal force and bites into my magic as I raise my defense. I want to absorb the purple magic, so I let it burrow deeper. The Vencrin jerks the sword back, trying to reclaim his weapon. I take advantage of the distraction and pound my open palm into his chest. *"Sphot Pavria."*

He is blown backward and over the deck, leaving the black sword stuck in my red-plated armor. Too late I realize he chanted something before my wind tunnel took him out. The black sword lurches free, condenses back into shapeless magic, and flies around my shield. I raise my arm in protection, but the magic finds its target. I yell as sharp pain pierces my arm, ripping from elbow to mid-forearm.

Another man advances in glee at my scream. His mouth moves, but I can't hear the spell. In a flick, I send out my go-to rebound spell. Red meets blue in a stream much like Kalyan and Tenson's fight earlier. But this isn't for show. I chant again, and the added force knocks the wizard into another body hurling itself at me. Too soon, yet another red-faced wizard whips something at my head. I duck, and clutch my elbow automatically when it screams open at the sharp movement.

The distraction of pain leaves me open for a second too long. A foot kicks me in the stomach and I slam sideways. Before I can take a retching breath, an orange stream slices toward my head. I jerk to the right, but the orange isn't a stream of magic; it's the inflamed wizard's fists. He lands hard and splinters the planks with his strength. If he touches my throat with that power I'm dead. With a howl I pull myself up and kick out with one foot. It meets his ribs with a crunch. But instead of toppling backward, he lunges forward and we roll into the mainmast as we grapple. Every bone in my body converts to a hard angle as I try to buck him off me. He wants my throat.

"Zaktirenni," I breathe as I lurch and grab his wrists, which are centimeters from my neck. We both grunt as his hands descend closer. Orange saturates my vision. My grip slips.

Then something white spills into my peripherals. A smoky white rope laces around the wizard's mouth and chest. His eyes bulge and his body writhes in resistance. A moment later, his weight lifts off me and he flies backward, then over the side of the ship. Peering after him as I convulse, I find Kalyan at the other end of the stream.

"Sorry I'm late. Someone destroyed the ramp."

My mouth gapes as I struggle to breathe. How can he be making jokes right now? He doesn't even look tired as he reaches to help me stand.

Purple flashes behind Kalyan. A Vencrin leers, sights set, a spell pulsing over his fingertips. *No!*

"Are you—"

I grab Kalyan's hand and yank.

He tries not to fall on me, hands shooting out to catch himself. It's clear I hadn't exactly thought it all through, especially when his chest slams into mine and we both huff out a breath. For a single moment Kalyan stares at me like I'm mad while collapsed on top of me, his entire body pressing . . .

The bolt of purple streams above us, right where Kalyan had been standing. Screams erupt as the spell hits another Vencrin, who crumples. Torture spell.

Understanding lights up Kalyan's eyes, his face very close to mine. "Thanks."

I push at his chest with my uninjured forearm, twisting out from under him. "Thank me later. We need cover."

"Sphuraw!" he yells as I call to my red magic. A shield encases us like a bubble, and a ring of fire lashes outside of that. The two of us stand to face four remaining Vencrin. Kalyan's back presses against mine, and its warmth and bulk allow me to breathe evenly for the first time in what feels like hours. I can almost ignore the pounding of purple arrows smashing against the shield, or the rage of voices shouting obscenities at us. They mostly scream permutations of *bloody, red,* and *bitch,* switching

up the words based on variation and good old-fashioned passion. Overall, it seems that I can be described as a menstrual cycle.

I clutch my throbbing arm.

"Are you about to burnout?" Kalyan whispers.

"No, it's just my arm."

Kalyan's eyes bulge as he assesses the red wetness dripping from my sleeve. "I can't take them all without you."

"You won't have to. Let me pass through the shield on three. I'll take those two." I nudge my foot toward the black forte Vencrin whose magic seared my arm, and a blue forte. "You take purple arrow and the wet one."

"On three, then."

My arm throbs. "One . . ." My back aches. "Two . . ." I'm nauseated. "Three!" I rush at the shield, drowning out the pain. On my side, the fire dies at my command and the shield evaporates. On the other, Kalyan's white magic explodes. It's enough. It has to be. I lash the rest of the fire like a whip and slash downward, between my two opponents.

I move in all directions, my left hand casting spells, my right protesting against the pain, but still holding a shield. Colors fly around me like the Festival of Color. Only instead of splattering the sky, the shooting lights spin vertically and with terrifying death words behind them.

One spell hits a crate and it explodes. Orbs of firelight tumble out, hundreds of them rolling across the makeshift battlefield. I stare after a few dancing past me, dazed for a second. It's true, then. They're taking firelight! With my newfound rage, one of my spells breaks through the wounded blue Vencrin's shield and he drops.

The black forte wizard runs toward me, an aggressive move in a spell-shooting fight. I whip my line of fire at him and he barrels over it. *Blood.*

I need time to think, to chant. But I don't have time. He's too fast. He yanks a steel dagger from his belt and jerks forward. I lean back as a flash of silver cuts toward my chest. Reflexively I reach for my own belt, but I don't have a blade on me, only Hubris. With a flip I release my skyglider from my belt and hold it up in defense. With another swipe the dagger buries itself in Hubris, and with one more quick motion the Vencrin whacks Hubris's handle off.

"Vitahtrae!" I shout, and Hubris obeys. Its remaining handle extends without the kitelike tail so I can whirl Hubris like a staff, as I used to do as a child. Smack, cut, twist, duck, the two of us dance as the wizard nicks and slashes Hubris apart, piece by piece. Splinters slice my hands as wicker frays and Hubris is whittled away.

I lunge, feint left, and then smash Hubris's broken end into his right shoulder. *"Zalaka Drumahtrae,"* I chant, and shards of my broken skyglider explode into black forte's arm. He hollers and stumbles to his knees with the pain, curling his arm into himself. I take advantage of the distraction and elbow him in the face, his teeth knocking against my elbow. Finally, he falls back.

And then it's done. My line of fire sizzles as it eats up the deck. A thump echoes as the pommel of Kalyan's sword hits the last wizard's chest. I'm relieved until Kalyan raises his pommel for a blow to the head.

"Wait!" I yell.

Kalyan stills as he holds on to the collar of the drooping Vencrin. I tumble through the firelight, bodies, and debris.

"Why . . . why do you have firelight?" I demand of the Vencrin.

He stares at me, dazed. One eye is swollen and blood gushes above his eyebrow. But the other eye appears haunted, or maybe even terrified.

"I'm not telling the Red Bitch anything."

I really need a more creative name. I mean, I get the red mask brings the color into descriptive play and the snug black cage-casting top shows I possess boobs, but still, to quote Sims, it's weak. Kalyan jostles the wizard. Clearly, he's not a fan of my street name either.

I lean in closer, steady my breath, and cast fire to my hands like I did when interrogating Basu. "Tell me what you are doing with the firelight."

He flinches from the fire like they all do, as if the temperature and height of the flames aren't under my control. "It's you who will burn in the end, witch."

"Are you delivering it to Moolek?" I yell.

His one good eye widens, then narrows. *"Kalaleah,"* he spits like a curse.

"No!" The fire vanishes and I rush to cover his mouth, but smoke swarms over his head and he goes limp, already unconscious.

"Blood." I slump down the side of the ship and start numbing the pain in my arm. Kalyan drops the dead weight and scans the destroyed ship. As I drag my hand over the sweat soaking my hairline, he sits down beside me and places his elbows on his knees.

"Next time"—he breathes heavily—"we need a better plan."

◇

CHAPTER SEVENTEEN

Truth Revealed, Mind Blown to Bits

Jatin

I watch the ship burn into the night, the smoke condensing in angry plumes. Then Jaya and I disperse the soot and extinguish the flames, because the last thing we need is an audience. Though the Vencrin's mighty illusion helps with concealing everything.

I've never been this mentally exhausted. I might have worked my magic harder at training a few times, but never before have I had to cast for my life quite like fighting a ship full of Vencrin. I mean, I was a raja in the gods' eyes and thus my people's. Unnecessary risks like this are practically forbidden. Yet, it feels good. Real, like the Alkin avalanche or saving people from the wreckage of the Southern Bay monsoon in Agsa five years ago.

Looking up at the ship from the pier, a majority of my mind still tumbles with the knowledge that Jaya and I took down ten decently skilled wizards, no, criminals, who couldn't care less if their spells were lethal. Their bodies lie strewn before us. And while I wouldn't want to leave them to be torched by the pyre, I can't spur any sympathy for their injuries or their blood-splattered faces. I heard the spells they were casting. I could have been an innocent bystander on the pier when the first three rushed in to attack me. And I didn't walk away unharmed. Bruises already bloom over my torso, the tenderness and ache verifying their color and circumference.

As soon as Jaya extinguishes the fire, it's quiet again. Only the waves brush against the shore. A loud rip tears the silence. The tatters from Jaya's right sleeve sway in the night air. Blood patters onto the pier.

"How bad is it? Let me see," I say.

"I've got it." She twists away, impeding my view. Red glows around her arm as she recites a healing spell. An intake of air hisses through her teeth and the magic disperses.

"Jaya, I have experience with this sort of thing."

"Yeah, me too." That's true. The way she commands pink magic she must have buckets more experience treating wounds than I do. And yet, I want to check for myself. Verify she's actually okay. I would never have brought another wizard or witch into the unpredictable danger of that fight. For a majority of it, I had no clue whether she was hurt, or dead. But if it weren't for her wrenching me down, I would be convulsing in a fit of pain until I gladly welcomed darkness. It was a quick moment, but I still feel the huff of her breath on my face when I landed on top of her. Just like I still remember my arms wrapped around her when I carried her days ago. It's too late for me. It's more than attraction and wanting to help someone in trouble. I care about her, enough that her winces and small gasps now stab at my concern.

She lifts her right arm and tears off the black sleeve. It's dark out, but the moon casts a wide glowing net. And in that net I extend my neck and finally glimpse Jaya's arm. I can't understand what I'm seeing at first, maybe the blood covers the designs, but no, that's wrong. There is no Touch at all. Her arm is bare.

Hesitantly, I move closer. "Jaya?"

She doesn't glance up from her arm. "Yeah?"

I step even closer, right in front of her. Strands of red magic penetrate the wound and begin stitching the skin together. She presses at the raw streak and wipes away the blood. Now I am dead sure. No Touch.

She finally looks up and staggers back a little at my closeness. "Blood, don't do that."

"Your arm . . ."

She tilts her head and smirks. "And you said you had experience with this sort of thing." When she sees how blank my face must be, she sighs and gestures back at the ship. "A Vencrin sliced around my shield. I'm going to fix it."

"N-n-no, I-I mean . . . ," I stutter, then trail off. This can't be.

Then she stills. Her eye's hook mine and slowly she pulls her arm away and behind her so it's no longer in view. The action nags at a memory, one where a young girl slid her arm behind her back as I told her she wasn't a witch.

"Oh, that, it's nothing," she says.

"Let me see your arm."

She tries to laugh. "Kalyan, I fixed *you*. I can heal a little scratch."

"Please," I say as tenderly as possible. The truth is I need to clarify what I saw more than anything in the entire bloody world, because every Touched member of society I have ever met has had at least a swirl or two on both wrists. There is only one person who has a one-armed Touch, is about my age, is a red magic forte witch, and knows my father. Adraa Belwar.

Jaya, or Adraa, or whoever she is, sweeps both her arms forward and with a quick spell her left sleeve also rips off. Her Touch is dense; swirls, sweeping lines and flourishes whirl up her forearm, and higher, I'm sure. It's an arm of power, but I've yet to see her this vulnerable. Caution lingers in her eyes as she takes me in. "I'm a one-armed Touch, and whatever you think, it's not contagious or a weakness."

She folds her arms into herself. Time teeters on what will be said next, but I'm reeling. All the pieces have fallen into place, but the puzzle in my mind is exploding. I think my brain has rebelled, because all I can hear is my voice yelling *Stupid!* over and over again. My hands fly to my head to try to shut it up, but they can't. *Oh my Gods. Oh my bloody Gods!*

First she's Jaya, a beautiful commoner, then she's Jaya Smoke, a cage-caster spy, and now! Now she's Jaya Smoke and Adraa all wrapped up in one. I was, am, going to marry this girl. This is my fiancée. Shock peels away and my heart thumps in triumph. My heart is going to race out of my chest. I *can* care about her. I can like her—blood, I'm even allowed to love her. I don't need to squash the feelings or the thoughts that have bubbled to the surface ever since she saved that little boy in the street. What have I done in my life to make me this Gods-blessed lucky?

I gaze at her in wonder. Who would have thought the little eight-year-old girl who hit me in the face would become a cage caster? Actually, that part kind of makes sense. She hasn't changed much in that way. But she has grown and, ah, developed.

Then I realize what I've done. I've freaked out, not for the reasons she thinks, but I haven't said anything. *Blood! Say something, Jatin!* What my face must look like. It's probably awful, because her face goes blank and her eyes harden. It's as if I can touch the wall she's crafting between us.

"Don't look at me like that. I don't need—" She pauses. "It's a birthmark, not a disability."

"I know." *Okay, words, words are happening. Good.* But was that the right thing to say? I move closer and reach for her right arm. She jerks a little as I lightly raise it into view. My heart may give out just being able to touch her. I stare at her wound. It's not as deep as it appeared. It will scar for sure because she didn't work on it immediately, but the pink magic has already done a great job sewing the flesh together. And finally my brain kicks back into gear and I know how to spin shock and elation into reassurance. "Okay, good. It looked bad when I first saw it."

"Oh, ah, yeah." Her expression is a mix of relief and confusion. "Told you I could fix it."

I release her. "I know about one-armed Touches. Legends say they're created when the gods fight over the blessings of a witch or wizard. The fights can get so bad that contests are held, and the victor is the only one allowed to touch that child."

Her eyes hold wonder and confusion with my religious knowledge. How many little jerks had made fun of her over the years for her to be this cautious? Oh Gods, including me when I was a heedless nine-year-old. She must hate me, the real me. I clamp my mouth closed. For now I won't tell her I'm Jatin. I can't. Not in this moment where I've royally messed up.

"Yeah, Erif must have fought for me and won." She stares up at the sky. "That is, if you believe the legends." She lowers her head and looks at me. "How do you know any of that?"

"Reading." I shrug. I know about the legends, but that's the last thing I'm worried about. My father has been telling me for years how Erif blessed Adraa with a one-armed Touch. At the time I didn't care. It was an interesting factoid that made sense later, when I learned she had invented firelight. Now, it's the key to everything. She's been lying to me from the beginning, leading me to believe she works for my future wife. Now . . . she *is* my future wife.

"And that's why you serve Adraa." I give her a pointed look. Will she continue to deny who she is?

She refocuses her attention on me. "Yes. Adraa taught me everything I know. I would be lost without the Belwars." I wait a beat for her to say more. She doesn't. So she's going to keep the charade up, then.

Having verified she is going to keep lying to me, her fiancé, who is lying to her, I don't know what to say. Being Kalyan is always easier than being Jatin. And it still might be on this occasion. But I'm at a loss. With my conscience giving me permission to like her I'm twisted and tongue-tied. I start to sweat.

"I'm breaking open the crates," she says, not knowing how life-altering this moment is for me. At least now I understand why she's so committed to discovering what's happening with the firelight. If hundreds of my spells were being shipped who knows where, I'd want to find out too.

The crates are wicker, a combination of stalks woven together. Unlike wood, the wicker flexes against acts of violence. The best way to open the crates is through a simple green magic spell that frays one spine and then splits the thing open. Adraa must not know the technique. The sound of a thousand twigs breaking reaches my ears. I step closer to find the nearest crate gutted, with orbs of firelight leaking out.

She picks one up and turns it over. "Two days ago."

I snatch an orb rolling by my feet. On its underside is a date that confirms it.

"It didn't stop at Basu," she whispers.

"What?" *Who's Basu?*

Adraa turns to me. "This operation. It's much bigger than I thought."

◇ ◇ ◇

After we open all the crates of firelight orbs, we eventually discover the drugs. In cloth patches tied with string sits a fine red powder. *Bloodlurst!* it screams at me. Couldn't be anything else.

"Careful not to touch it," Adraa says. "It's absorbed through the skin."

I warily set the bundle back down.

"Another fire?" she suggests.

"We can't exactly dump it in the bay," I counter. "You light them up, I'll disperse the smoke. We don't want any more potential signals—"

Before I can finish my sentence the crates blaze. I cast a funnel of wind to divert the smoke, stifling a chuckle as I do. She doesn't waste time.

A few minutes later, only a spot of ash marks the drugs' presence.

"Good thinking," Adraa relents.

Our gazes glide to all the firelight. She sighs. "I don't want to destroy it."

This is her magic, her invention. I don't want to destroy it either. "Then don't. Let's hide it below the pier. We'll put some black magic around it and bring it to Belwar Palace later."

"Okay." She pauses. "Don't rub it in, but you were right. I needed backup tonight." And with that, the aches in my muscles and the bruises covering my torso stop throbbing. My whole body smiles.

"I said don't rub it in," Adraa says as she heaves one crate up and chants it into levitation under a bed of yellow magic.

"I didn't say anything," I defend.

"Your face says enough."

I guess I do need to control my grinning.

The job is done before I remember beginning, feeling perfectly right working beside her, even though the night enters its menacing hour in which the sky slips into a dark sheath of oily glue.

"We should get out of here," I say after I finish casting the last black concealment spell over four crates of firelight.

"Ah, about that. I have a problem." Adraa gestures to her belt. "I kind of destroyed, no, I *did* destroy Hubris."

"Hubris?"

She shakes her head a little like she's embarrassed. "My sky-glider."

"You named your skyglider—"

"It was one of my teacher's ideas. I kind of was a reckless flier when I first—" She shakes her head again, harder. "Never mind. The point is, my skyglider is gone. I have no way of flying."

"So . . ." I don't think I would ever describe myself as giddy—until now. "You're asking for a ride?"

"Yes."

Which means she has to be close to me, and I to her. I smile and unbuckle my own skyglider from my belt. Might as well use this to my advantage. "I don't know. My skyglider normally doesn't like strangers." The words roll off my tongue. It feels so natural to tease her.

"Skygliders like me," she huffs under her breath.

I pull back our only means of transportation and hold up a finger. "One condition."

Her eyes become defiant. "I don't believe for a second you would leave me here. I was a stranger ten days ago and you hauled me into a royal carriage."

She's got me there and she knows it. I would never leave her.

She stares at my skyglider, then back at me. "Which is actually kind of risky for a guard who protects the future maharaja. I could have been a trap to hurt Raja Jatin."

You were a trap. My father couldn't have planned it better.

He always wanted us to meet again, in unofficial circumstances. But I don't think he could imagine what we have already been through in the past few days, how much I already care about her. "Are you always going to insinuate assassinating the Naupures?"

"What's your condition?" she relents, ignoring my question.

"Fine, it's not a condition. I'm starving. You hungry?"

"We beat up ten guys together, almost got killed, and your condition is food?" she asks like I'm absurd.

I feel absurd, confidence and uncertainty mixed together. "So yes, you're hungry?"

Adraa touches her stomach as if she forgot that part of her was still working. "Yeah, of course I am."

Victory. "Well, I'm stopping to eat somewhere before heading home."

She throws up her arms. "It's one past midnight."

"Ah, well . . ." I look around the pier, hoping an answer will come. This is stupid. I should have just asked her out properly, when ten unconscious bodies weren't surrounding us in the dead of night. "Do you know a place?"

She cocks her head to the side, thinking. "Yeah, maybe I do."

CHAPTER EIGHTEEN

◇

I Go on a Date (Not Like a Romantic Date, but Maybe, Sort of . . .)

Adraa

Kalyan has been acting weird since discovering my one Touched arm. Is it pity? I practically know every reaction to my ungodly and unnaturally naked limb. But his surprise, delight, and under-standing about the legends . . . Yeah, it's strange, and different from all my other experiences. I can't seem to drag it out of my head, even after we start flying.

The skyglider twitches in the air. I start and can't help but grab onto him.

"You okay?" I ask. I'm always in control of my own flying. Haven't had to rely on someone to cart me around since I was twelve. Gods, I wish Hubris hadn't died tonight. Or better put, I wish I hadn't killed her.

"I'm fine," he says.

"I can fly us if you want." My arm hasn't moved from his body, but I feel uncomfortable latched on like this.

"I'm fine," he repeats with a laugh. He seems overly happy.

Maybe he's on an adrenaline high from the fight or maybe he is still grinning about me telling him he was right about my needing help. Is that all a man needs to be happy? Validation?

The skyglider falters again and my stomach dips out from under me. My other arm wraps around him instinctively and now I'm hugging the guy. In a moment it's over and we cruise like nothing happened. "Are you doing that on purpose?" I ask.

He laughs. "Possibly."

Then the oddest thing happens. He reaches for my hand. My *right* hand! I release my hold, but instead of nudging me backward to indicate I should let go—which is what I expect—he catches my palm, lightly squeezes, and pulls my arms together so they continue to wrap around him.

"It's safer," he whispers.

I don't know what to think. No one touches my right arm on accident. My parents don't intentionally avoid it per se. But still, I've become accustomed to using my left hand for everything. Any contact with anyone and I offer my Godly arm, not the naked and alien-looking flesh. Enough awkwardness and bullying from other children taught me long ago it's a monstrosity. I still think it's one of the main reasons I wasn't sent to the academy to learn magic with Jatin and other royal children.

Yet Kalyan touches me like it's nothing. The first time he helped pick me up and the first time we had given our respects on the Naupure stairs he had taken my right hand, but that had been an accident on my part and he hadn't yet known about my Touch. But tonight, it's as if he saw my arm, my insecurity and my pain, and was making it clear that . . .

Gods, this is your fiancé's guard! He carried you and now you're letting him squeeze your right hand? But my body leaps for joy like it's escaped the palace for the first time. That one simple gesture felt safe, and right, and more intimate than I could possibly imagine. My palm still tingles with the pressure and heat of his fingers squeezing mine.

I can't let him know what it's doing to me, though. "Safer because you are that bad of a flier?"

The skyglider lurches and I hang on for dear life. I let out a yelp too. I'm not proud.

"Yeah, I'm not too good." His voice slices with sarcasm. He's messing with me.

"You know, I can take this thing over," I say.

"Not without me letting you."

He's right. It's grueling to take over a skyglider unless the original flier's magic fails or they allow it. But . . . is this flirting? Is he flirting with me? His tone is the kind filled with secret smiles. I shimmy and twist forward to try to grasp his expression.

I catch his eyes.

"Drop over there, in that square." I gesture and the skyglider dives. The world tumbles from under us and wind springs up as we plummet. "Gods, not literally." My fingers fan over his stomach and the momentum of the dive slides my whole body against his. That's when Kalyan's stomach flexes and not in some display of his core muscles. He coils in pain.

As soon as my feet hit cobblestones, I scramble to the ground.

He's laughing. "Sorry."

I don't join in his merriment. "Why didn't you tell me?"

His laughing eyes widen. "How . . . how did you find out?"

"Gods, it's obvious when you make me hang on to you like that."

Kalyan steps over his skyglider and in a quick snap it's shortened and hooked back onto his belt. "Look, I'm sorry I didn't tell you immediately. Right when I found out, which was only about an hour ago, I—"

I walk forward, cutting off his rambling. He's so used to not having pink magic he doesn't even know when he should ask for help. "It's okay. Just let me see it now." I glance down at his stomach.

He takes a giant step back. "Wait, what? What do you want to see?"

"The bruises on your stomach."

"The bruises on my . . ." He chokes on his laughter. "Those are fine. I don't need pink magic."

"Are you sure?" This must be how he felt, wanting to check out my arm earlier.

"Yeah, stop trying to undress me, Smoke."

"I wasn't . . . that's not what . . ." I clamp my mouth shut. I'm falling for his antics again. I need to get better at not letting him get to me. "The place is this way," I say as deadpan as possible, and turn.

◇ ◇ ◇

I'm pleasantly surprised the bar's inhabitants don't want to rip Kalyan's and my heads off. Respectable members of society line the wall, not black-clad Vencrin sailors or drug dealers. But I forgot to account for the fact that thanks to our ripped black clothing, that's what Kalyan and I look like. For blood's sake, Kalyan has someone else's blood splattered on his pants. How did I not notice that before?

I think it says something about me that I want to cast on my red mask and yell boo as the third suspicious set of eyes takes me in and then drops away. Or, even better than boo, *Hello, everyone, I might rule the country one day.* Imagine that.

The warmest greeting comes from the candlelit lamps dripping from the ceiling and the yards of fabric draped between them. The second-warmest greeting comes from the gleaming tabletops, oiled by thousands of hands.

"Corner," Kalyan and I say at the same time. We share a glance. Is he as paranoid as I am, or does he know his blood-splattered pants need to be hidden from this bewildered crowd? As I slip into the corner seat, it feels nice to press my back against the cushion and survey this glowing marshmallow kingdom of laughter and drunkenness.

"So, you've been here before?" Kalyan asks.

"No, I've just seen that it's open after I leave the Underground." I lean forward and he mirrors me. "I don't normally go celebrate after I beat up ten men."

"Then what *do* you do?"

A man ambles up to our table. "Drinks are at the bar. Here is what we are offering this late at night." A menu smacks onto the table as he turns away. I guess I can count that as the third-warmest greeting, but the paneled curtains, in all their brocade brightness, come pretty close.

191

"Do you think they know we knocked out ten men and burned their ship, or is it something we said?" Kalyan asks.

"Must be the way we breathed." I know it must be our faces, but I don't want to ask him how I look right now. Because it's going to end up being an awkward "You look fine," or even "You look beautiful," when I don't care because I survived a Vencrin battle, and thank the gods, Kalyan isn't someone I need to impress. Just someone I need to cover if a Vencrin walks in right now.

The waiter boomerangs back to us eventually and we order everything that sounds edible. Kalyan goes to the bar to buy Roloc, a frothy liquor Agsa invented that glows in a rainbow of colors when swirled. I ask for a continuous flow of coconut water to be dredged to our table.

"So tell me, what do you think of Jatin Naupure?" Kalyan asks as he slides back into our little corner. There he is, Jatin, the man I do need to impress one day. The man I'll have to be pretty for.

I choke on my first sip of coconut water. I'm starting to wonder if there is a mind reading spell the academy secretly teaches its students. "What? Why?" I sputter.

"I want your opinion."

"Why would I have an opinion about him?" Gods, I really don't want to talk about my fiancé.

"You seem like the kind of person who always has an opinion."

Was that an insult or a compliment?

"I mean that in a good way. I want to know what you think," Kalyan continues before I can say anything. "And I know you have *some* impression."

192

He had me there. I can't say I didn't meet him in the carriage. I don't exactly know how to answer, though. I'm speechless.

"Fine. Better put, do you think he and Adraa will get along?" He tries to catch my eye. "Be happy?" Well, that officially reconfirms it, then: Kalyan doesn't know who I really am. I'll have to thank Maharaja Naupure later for keeping my identity a secret.

I guess that means I can be truthful. I finally face him head-on. "Honest answer?"

"Of course," he urges. Eagerness lights his eyes.

"I think Jatin is arrogant and cold."

Now he's the one to cough. "Wow, so you're saying she hates him, then?"

"I don't think it would be hatred between them."

He brightens, cocks an eyebrow, and smiles. Maybe it's the adrenaline from the compact series of events that have transpired in the past few hours, but I want to release this truth, out of the thousands of secrets I hold within me. "I think it would be worse, contempt."

He pauses, looks down at his drink, and rubs the condensation off the glass with his thumb. It flashes pink to blue. Jatin is his raja! I shouldn't say this stuff to him, no matter how honest or loopy from adrenaline I am. Besides, honesty isn't my strength. I still can't seem to tell him my real name. I don't want to burst this thing, this partnership we have.

"I'm sorry if I offended you. What's he really like?" I ask.

He frowns as if he can't name one good quality. *Oh blood.* "Gods, you can't think of one nice thing?"

"No, no, just don't know where to start."

I snort, but gulp my drink to obscure the noise.

"He's good at magic."

"Ah, huh. But so are you," I counter. And Gods was he.

"It isn't a contest between the two of us." He smirks.

I smile, then look out the window for a second. Why was I trying to make it a competition? I liked Kalyan, almost everything about him. In some weird, twisted part of my mind did I want to convey he was better than Jatin, better for me?

Kalyan doesn't sense my troubles. "But really, he wants to help others. The avalanche in Alkin wasn't for show. He flew as fast as he could and after he saved all those people he was . . . happy."

I nod. Jatin's letter flickers into my memory. "Yeah, happy enough to rub it in Adraa's face."

"How do you know about that?" He smirks again as if he's caught me in something.

Blood. How would Jaya Smoke know about those letters? "Um." Might as well tell the truth on this one too. "About a year ago the Belwar staff started opening all out-of-country mail after an attempted poisoning of a Belwar raja. A staff member read this . . . well, this love note." I shrug. "Sadly, it kind of became a thing for Adraa to read them aloud. The other women think it's true love or some crap."

The color drains from Kalyan's face. I think he must know about the secret messages. "What?" he says.

"But it's all a joke. He did that, you know, probably to tease her, to make fun of her. It's all pure competition between the two of them."

He shakes his head. "Gods, I'm embarrassed . . . for him."

I suck in a breath, wondering if I should ask something. When will I have a chance like this again, though? "What does Jatin think of Adraa, then? I mean really." I wait, as I've never waited before.

"Well, she's a little annoying."

"Yeah." I gulp my drink to offset how resigned my voice must sound.

I knew it! I knew the sneering face that joked about our loving relationship only joked because I repulsed him. I remember my younger self, so jealous of where he was, and I wasn't, that I would constantly ask questions. I would try to trip him up on some form of magic I could do better than him. I think I would hate young Adraa Belwar too, with her insecurities splattered across the page and encoded in each line of text.

Adraa: *I created water today, made it rain for a few minutes. Have you ever done that? Not just manipulated water but created it?*

Jatin: *I do that all the time. Rain is easiest, but I've done all types of white magic precipitation too: snow, sleet, hail.*

Kalyan pulls me out of the letters and back to the bar. "What? You're going to agree? Just like that?"

"Oh, was that a joke? You were joking?"

"Of course." He laughs as he shakes his head at me. "Here, let's make a deal. I'll answer a question about Jatin if you answer one about Adraa."

"Why do you care so much?"

"Because they're our employers. Their happiness is practically *our* happiness." He sounds like Riya. *I want a good raja to serve,* she had said. My marriage really is important, affects thousands of people. Talking about this without telling Kalyan my identity is wrong. But I would love to know his perspective on Jatin, and Jatin's perspective on me. And I'll never have an advantage like this again.

"Okay, deal."

"So what's Adraa like really?"

"Well, she's good at magic." I mimic Kalyan's tone and attempt to duplicate his low voice, but kind of fail. I was trying to be funny, but instantly grow uneasy at the lie. I can't say I'm good at magic, because Jatin is already a raja, while I might fail at being a rani. An emotional tidal wave tumbles over my face before I can wash it away.

"What's wrong? That was good. The voice might need some work, though." He smiles and I can't help but smile back a little.

"It's fine. I'm fine." I gulp back the emotional wreckage of my life.

He places his chin in his hands. "Please tell me."

He *is* kind. Those eyes want to know; he cares about me regardless of my position. Why does that have to be so nice? I should tell him who I am.

"You trained with Jatin at the academy, right?" I blurt out.

"Yeah, pretty much."

"Will you train with me?"

"You want to train with me?" He jerks up and points at himself.

Without warning, the insecure Adraa emerges. "Never mind, forget I asked." I gulp the coconut water.

"No, I don't want to forget that. Yes."

196

"Yes?"

"Yeah, let's train together."

I know I must be beaming. I will finally get to experience how people are taught at the academy. Maybe failing at white magic at my royal ceremony isn't imminent.

Food pours onto our table at that moment. From a central bowl of rice, smaller bowls pinwheel in an array of heat and steam. Goat stew, lamb curry, wicker nuts, pepper bark, silken fish caught in the Belwar Bay, and thick triangles of naan are the first to pop to my attention.

"Okay, next question. You go," Kalyan urges as he scoops food onto his plate.

I don't care about this game anymore. First, I want to eat. Then I want to contemplate what just happened. I'm finally going to train with someone who studied at the academy. If it weren't for my arm badgering me with pain, I would practice right now.

"Oh, I don't know. Jatin's favorite color?" I offer.

"Really?"

I realize a second later I actually do want to know this. "You can tell a lot about a person by their favorite color. I knew this kid in the palace who I swear became an orange forte because he loved the color that much."

Kalyan's face twists in skepticism. "Who loves orange that much?"

"Exactly. And I've found the people who say their favorite color is their forte are either obsessed with it, like that kid, or plain conceited."

"So what's yours?" he asks.

"Pink. But what's Jatin's, huh?"

Kalyan scrunches his face as he stalls. "Why pink?" he asks. He's grasping, not wanting me to know Jatin loves white. I knew it. Mr. Arrogant must love white, be as obsessed with it as he is with himself.

"Because in a clinic, pink is the color of miracles." I don't miss a beat. "Jatin's favorite is white, isn't it?"

"Okay, maybe it's one of his favorite colors."

"That's worse than orange."

◇ ◇ ◇

Thirty minutes later and I've found out Jatin was either ignored or idealized more than picked on at school, wrote the love notes on a bet, and doesn't like wide-open places like the deep ocean. And even though the information is about Jatin, since it comes from Kalyan's mouth, I feel as if I'm discovering more about him than about my fiancé. He talks about Jatin's fears and history so freely, without any anxiety his raja will punish him for it. That tells of a level of closeness not even Riya and I could ascend to.

Then our conversation devolves and we forget our little game. Kalyan and I talk about Naupure's current poverty bill, which hopes to furnish jobs to the Untouched. We come to the agreement that thirteenth- through fourteenth-year class are tied for the worst in life. We discuss the ethics of the truth accords even though we both agree chanting someone to tell the truth is better than the past judicial system where rajas had to constantly hold trials. We eventually revert to the issue of Bloodlurst and the Vencrin. And what we did tonight comes back to me. All the stolen firelight comes into focus. I still have no proof Moolek has anything to do with it yet. Kalyan seems to be thinking the same thing.

"What are you going to tell Adraa about tonight?" he asks.

"That we have a problem." I peer into his eyes. "What are you going to tell Raja Jatin?"

He smiles. "That I met a witch."

◇

CHAPTER NINETEEN

Colorful Note Coordinates a Meeting

Jatin

Life as raja of Naupure isn't much different from being at the academy. Instead of mind-numbing history and geography lessons, I attend mind-numbing meetings about the fate of all that geography and culture. Okay, it's completely different from school. I have to make decisions constantly. I have to read reports and letters incessantly. I have to still find time to study spells, without designated training time attached to such memorization.

Life like this is what I always imagined it to be. Advisors stretching out their hands, but not daring to grab hold as I wobble along a cliff's edge. Me walking through the palace as faceless wizards and witches buzz with demands or questions, mostly both. A voice sounding like the amalgamation of my teachers and my father yelling, "Learn, train, you must because one day you will rule! Messing up or giving up means not only personal failure but also your country's demise!"

I never realized it before, but training was my release. After hours filling my brain, letting my Touch cast off spell after spell was my way to shout back at the voice, "I'm working! I'm trying! I won't fail!" So when I spot Kalyan and other guards sweating in the heat on the long patch of the training yard, I rise from my father's chair.

◇ ◇ ◇

I had gone through every single type of magic besides pink, and only because I haven't broken anybody's bones. Next to me stands a tree singed with fire, stabbed with spears, and with every leaf blown off. The ground is muddy with water and melting snow. I've lifted boulders and I've turned practically invisible. It's been a morning of release.

Kalyan plops down in the dirt next to me when I finally sit. I told him everything about Adraa hours ago. He's been quiet the whole time I wrestled with nature. But I presume he will say something now. It's like he knows when I'm ready to be talked to.

"Let me try to understand this again. You are telling me Adraa doesn't know who you really are, at all?"

"That's what I'm saying."

"And she's lying to you too?"

"Yes."

Kalyan whistles. "Blood."

That about sums it up.

"And again, *why* aren't you telling her?" he asks.

"Because . . ."

Kalyan peers at the sky. "She hates you, doesn't she? Told you all those letters were going to end badly."

I chuckle morbidly. "She doesn't hate me. She hates Jatin, or at least the idea of him. Thinks he is arrogant and cold."

"Where did she get that from?" he says, deadpan, and raises an eyebrow in case I still don't catch his meaning.

I gather some dirt and let it drizzle through my fingers.

Kalyan squints at me, then leans back on one arm. "Gods, now I get it. You want this to be like a normal relationship. You are trying to, ah, what's the word . . ." He snaps his fingers. "Court her, get her to like you. That's why you are lying."

"And you think that's so terrible?"

"I think when she finds out, it's going to cause all sorts of trouble. And what about me? Your future wife thinks I'm her fiancé. That's messed up. What if I run into her?" He pauses, then raises his eyebrows like an idiot. "What if she tries to kiss me?"

I snap to attention. "Okay, first of all, you aren't that lucky or charming. Second, don't worry, she hates you."

"Because she thinks I'm Jatin Naupure?"

"Yep."

"If I get fired over this, I swear," he grumbles.

I give him a look. "You knew nothing about it."

He lies down on his back. "You're right. I don't know a thing."

I lie back too and stare at the clouds. Summer is nice to the clouds, makes them puffy and white. And I like that. I like their freshness. What's so wrong with the color white anyway?

"Hey, Kalyan, what's your favorite color?"

My friend sits up again and gives me the "do I need to be

concerned about you?" look. I keep my attention on the clouds to maintain casualness.

"Orange," he finally answers.

"What? Really?" I have to look at him now.

"Yeah, the sky only turns orange when it's at peace."

Peace. Not something Kalyan has seen much of. My memory plunges back to the night of the Southern Bay monsoon. How I strained my thirteen-year-old body and scream-casted to calm water, wind, and upturned earth. The rescue teams pulled so many bodies from the water or from under buildings it was like we had wrenched them up from a graveyard. Kalyan was one of the last I found—an eleven-year-old squeezed between a clay wall and a wood pillar impaling his calf. When I pried the wood from the kid, it was as if I had saved a younger version of myself. He looked like my twin.

His odds of survival were low, especially during the amputation. When his parents' bodies were found, I thought he would lose hope and that would be the end of this kid who I kept skipping class to visit. I showed off my magic to him and he was only kind of impressed, but maybe that was enough, I had thought. So, I made a promise: "When you get out of the clinic you can come to the academy with me."

I remember the way he had eyed me. "That fancy one?"

"Yep. I'll even help train you, and I'm the best."

"Okay," he had said. And Gods, the way he said it—casual like, but so deeply full of hope. And he did recover. I wrote to tell my father I had found my perfect lead guard if he would fund his education. And he had.

Kalyan may think he got lucky. May think he got to be my friend and my guard only because he looks like and can impersonate me. He may even think he can be fired. But he's got it so wrong. I'm the lucky one to be friends with a guy who almost bled to death, lost his parents and his lower leg, and yet knows orange skies still exist.

And now I feel as if it is my duty to find Adraa and let her rub in the fact that one's favorite color is an acceptable and telling question. But maybe that would further present me as conceited.

"Wait, favorite color? Is that an Adraa thing?" Kalyan asks.

I face him and the fading sun. "If you are about to make a joke—"

"No, no joke. Wait, I'll be right back." Kalyan jogs over to the barracks and disappears. I turn to the palace and begin mapping out how many people I have to talk to, how many reports I need to read. Curiosity at Kalyan's outburst and instructions grounds me, but obligation pulls at me to get up and get back to work.

Kalyan barrels back across the field. "I think this is yours." He offers up something flimsy and small. It's an envelope, an envelope with Jaya's handwriting on the front.

I jump to my feet quicker than any living animal and tear it open.

Hey,
    So I have that shipment that still needs to be hauled back to its rightful owner.
    Meet me one before dusk?
        Sincerely,
        A girl whose favorite color is pink

I scrutinize the sun and its drooping form mocks me. "When did you get this?"

"Early this morning."

I grumble and wipe my neck. "Why didn't you give it to me sooner?"

"Firstly, it has *my* name on it. Secondly, I safeguard all incoming mail. But know what? I'll start handing over all the wild proposals or death threats Azure Palace receives from now on since you are so interested."

"I've got to go."

"So it's from her, then?"

"Yeah."

"Well, good luck forming a normal relationship or whatnot when the girl is already speaking in code."

"Yeah, but it's code I understand!" I yell over my shoulder as I run. I think Kalyan's call of "for now" is meant to slam into my back, but it pushes me forward instead.

◇

CHAPTER TWENTY

Listening to Torture

Adraa

The sun yawns to the east, splashing the sky in an orange glaze, which means Kalyan didn't get my note, ignored it, or couldn't get away from Azure Palace. I hope it's the too-busy one. I glance at all the firelight even though I know how much is left. I've already flown home three times with saddlebags full of it. But since I have to deliver a thousand orbs to Azure Palace in a few days I was hoping Kalyan would still appear and help me haul. But it might be too late for that.

My heart races as I reload my saddlebag. Why am I this anxious? Is it because I don't *just* want Kalyan to help haul? Maybe . . . I want to see his face again. He does have a nice smile, an amazing smile. I stare at my right hand. It's probably my imagination, but the pressure of his hand squeezing mine lingers.

For the twentieth time I wrestle with my conscience. Kalyan doesn't need to know who I really am. It's safer that way. But the truth swells to the surface and pulses where he touched me. It feels good not being a royal around Kalyan, maybe . . . too good.

"Hey," a voice calls.

I jump, a spasm that seizes my heart and flips it sideways. "Blood!" I gasp.

Kalyan stands by the wooden pier with a guilty smile. My heart hammers away. I breathe to calm it down, but it continues to pound. It's the fright, I tell myself.

He holds up his arms in surrender. "Sorry, that wasn't revenge for the other night or anything. I'm just glad you're still here."

"So you did get the letter." *Gods, Adraa, what a stupid question. He is standing right before you. Of course he got the letter.*

"A bit late. But I got it."

"Good." I nod and look down at the firelight awkwardly. I suddenly can't seem to think.

Kalyan squats next to me. "You've already taken some?"

"Couldn't wait all night," I tease.

"I won't be late again." His tone is dead serious, the chilling opposite of mine.

With those words, my hammering heart wobbles and I . . . smile. *Blood. What's wrong with me?* If he is teasing me again, I can't show it gets to me, that I enjoy it. That I really do believe he will be here next time.

Ah, what am I doing? He. Is. Jatin's. Guard. And I'm a future maharani. My heart, doing whatever the blood it's doing, doesn't change that.

I fumble for a topic change. "The palace must be hectic without

Maharaja Naupure around. And before you ask how I know he's gone, Maharaja Naupure messaged Belwar Palace asking for support if something should happen in his absence. Also to say the firelight delivery is still on . . . so that's how I know."

He shakes his head. "I never think you're a potential threat to the Naupures *until* you start rambling."

"I'm just pointing out how I know things."

He chuckles, but quickly follows it with a sigh. "The answer is yes. The palace is hectic."

I wish I had the chance to prove myself for a few weeks. Would I get a letter any day now with Jatin bragging? I've been dreading it, seething with jealousy. Or maybe our letters are over since he is only a mountain range away? I don't know. "Raja Jatin handling it well?"

"Don't think he has had to handle anything too complicated yet. I would say I do all the heavy lifting." Kalyan heaves a wicker crate off another one and rips it open with one clean swipe of green magic.

"Was that supposed to impress me?"

"What are you talking about?" he asks with a smile.

Gods, he is so easy to read. I know exactly what kind of reaction he wants. I continue to stuff the firelight in my bag, not giving it to him. "Nothing."

"I'll let you admit you find me impressive when you are ready." The comment slinks out in a sarcastic whisper, but I hear it nonetheless.

I look up, but Kalyan is packing firelight as if he didn't say anything.

"Don't do it," I say suddenly.

"What?"

"Don't let Jatin's arrogance rub off on you."

"Oh Gods, you really do hate him." Kalyan shakes his head. "There's a lot of work to be done." He gestures to the firelight, implying we should focus on our task. And yet, there is something in his tone, something I have yet to uncover.

◇ ◇ ◇

We work under the veil of black magic as the orange sky deepens to navy. An hour later, four bags are packed and teeming with orbs. Kalyan is about to lift the strap of one over his shoulder when I hear something, footsteps-atop-the-pier kind of something. The black magic drapes around us, but not on top. If the owners of those footsteps peered between the planks of wood they would see us.

Without a second thought I push Kalyan against a pillar and jab a finger upward in warning. His furrowed eyebrows arch into understanding and he places the bag of firelight in the sand softly.

After our last visit it's clear that Pier Sixteen doesn't exist to the good citizens of Belwar, so some random wizard or witch isn't going to be strolling overhead. This has to be Vencrin.

"Are you verifying it as well? The Red Bitch has a partner," a deep voice says.

Kalyan and I lock eyes. *Definitely Vencrin.*

"A white forte wizard. Tore up and burned the ship with her."

Deep Voice sighs. "Had to see it myself. Nasty piece of work she's done here. She's becoming more confident, more of a problem. We can't let that happen."

"What do you suggest?" the other man asks, his voice laced with uncertainty.

"What I have suggested from the beginning. Kill her, and this new partner of hers too."

A tremble runs through me and I know Kalyan felt it. There's no way he couldn't. I'm practically plastered to him. That is until he pulls me even closer and the "practically" incinerates.

The other man, the subordinate, shifts his weight above us, obviously mulling over the simplicity of Deep Voice's instructions. *Kill her, and this new partner of hers.* "And what about the Belwars? The eldest daughter, Adraa, knows about Basu and the shipments."

"Don't worry about the Belwars. Everything is heating up nicely. It's perfectly pressurized. You just focus on stopping this Red Woman."

Well, I guess I should be glad only one of my personae will be hunted down. Kalyan slowly runs a hand over my shoulder blade in a circular motion and I give up the act that I'm not clinging to him. His heart hammers as loudly as mine.

"How?"

"The easiest way would be to discover who the blood she is," Deep Voice growls. "Have someone at each exchange ready to follow her. Our best black forte or one of your guards."

"About that. There's something else you should know."

"Well? Out with it!" Deep Voice yells.

"Yipton, one of my Dome Guards, was loading the ship that night."

"And?"

"He is under suspicion. As well as many of my men."

A shadow falls over Kalyan and me. Even the pier boards shudder. He's *right* over us. "So we have also been compromised in the Dome?"

The guardsman steps back. "Not entirely. Just some of the men who work the city with me."

"And as the head of my guard unit you tell me this only now?"

"I—"

"Can you fix it?" The Deep Voice is hard.

A pause, drawn out. "It will take some time. And I can't guarantee—"

He doesn't make it to the next word. Deep Voice casts a spell and his "friend" tumbles on the pier in a thudding heap. Dust plumes off the boards above our heads. My heart jumps.

"We can't be compromised," Deep Voice says. Then he casts under his breath.

The pier above us vibrates as the fallen wizard spasms. The back of my throat tastes like ash. Wood-rattling, scream-piercing, illegal, and against the very nature of pink magic, a torture spell unravels above. *And never-ending!* my heart screams. Never-ending until death . . . I unpeel myself from Kalyan's strong arms and step toward the black magic veil. I can take this man out and save the writhing wizard. Kalyan grabs my arm and pulls me back. The anguished look on his face shakes some sense into me. And I realize I am shaking too.

Mask, he mouths, and gestures at me.

We both know I can't cast on my mask from right under this dangerous wizard. The red smoke would alert him of our presence, and then all this firelight, neatly packed up, would be in jeopardy.

But by the sound of the seizure's strength, the man above us doesn't have much time left; he might already be comatose. I shut my eyes and squeeze, wanting to block out the noise and frothing panic spilling out above us. Is this deep-voiced wizard the one that put Riya's dad in a coma too? I grind my teeth and hold still. I don't know how I'm able to control the anger growing in my stomach or the impulse to fight this man. I've never quite controlled my anger like this before.

Kalyan's hands are still hooked onto my arm, half hugging me, half restraining me from my own dangerous impulse to punch first and deal with the consequences later. Maybe that is what's keeping me under control.

Above, the shaking ends and the groans take over.

"I need guarantees. This . . ." Deep Voice pauses. Maybe he's gesturing to the burned ship. "Needs to be fixed now." He steps over his comrade's body and walks down the pier.

I shift away from Kalyan. He lunges for me, but I *have* to see this wizard's face. To be so close to the Vencrin leader, or at least one of the leaders, and not get any physical description would be a waste of this miracle. I scurry to the edge of our veil and crane my neck. All I see is his back in the distance. He wears a dark cloak, blending in with the growing darkness.

"*Vardrenni.*" I cast over my eyes and the image zooms in. But even with my magnification the wizard is a black blur as he sinks between two homes and disappears. So I'm left with nothing but the fact he wants to kill me—which I already knew.

The groaning has stopped. The tension breaks and silence stretches back into being. I clamber up the pier.

"Wait!" Kalyan calls after me.

I run to the fallen body and search for a heartbeat. His skin is still wet from sea salt and sweat, and under that is the faint flutter of his pulse. Not dead. I run a few spells, measuring if any of his internal organs have started to shut down. He's not even comatose. Lucky? No, the other wizard knew how long to push the torture. Finally, my eyes refocus and I look at his face, recognize the gray beard. Every feature is all too familiar. I flinch and move away, off the pier and through the white smoke of Kalyan's illusion veil.

"What's wrong? How is he?" Kalyan asks as he follows me.

"I talked to that man two weeks ago."

"You know him? Gods, I'm—"

"Not well. Don't even know his name. He arrested the East Village firelight distributor, the man named Basu I told you about."

I pace. *Did this really just happen? Kalyan and I just happened to be under the pier when the Vencrin leader threatens our lives? Did he know we were there and this is all some sort of message? Are we currently in danger? I swept the pier before, didn't I?*

Kalyan breaks into my turbulent thoughts. "But he's okay?"

"He's going to be in a lot of pain when he wakes up, but I've never seen a torture spell with that much control. I didn't realize one could command those spells like that. He should be fine."

"And that's bad?"

"No, that's power. That's practice . . . lots of practice." Maybe that's why I'm so shaken. The turmoil raging inside me stems from fear and guilt. Coincidence or not, for the first time I wasn't in control. I hid and left a wizard to be tortured.

Kalyan stills. "You shouldn't be on the streets alone anymore. You won't be able to deal with the Vencrin and watch for their spies at the same time."

"Well, I'm not giving up. After this"—I gesture to above—"I can't stop." I won't let that happen again.

"I'm not telling you to."

"Then what are you saying?" I demand.

"I'm saying, let me join you. They already think we're partners."

Relief floods me, but it's more than that. I do need someone to watch my back. And I'm also happy that it's him, that he is with me on this. I can't let him know that, though. "Okay, then."

"Really? You aren't going to fight me on this?"

"You almost sound disappointed."

"I was already formulating a whole speech to convince you."

"Yeah, well, I wouldn't say it now. You don't want to talk me out of it, right?" My sarcasm is a defense mechanism, but it's never been so evident. I'm transparent.

Kalyan chuckles and picks up the bag of firelight closest to him. "In three days we'll start planning."

"What?"

"You want to start as soon as possible, right? Well, in three days you'll be delivering the rest of the firelight."

"Yes, for Adraa . . ." I trail off. Just saying my real name shaves off a piece of our shared intimacy and refocuses it. What are we doing? What am I allowing him to do?

"Of course." He nods, confident. "For Adraa."

In three days I'll also be introducing myself to Jatin. Before we can ever train together he'll know who I am. And once Kalyan learns this, will he still want to be my partner? To risk his life?

"I'll see you then." I hope he can't hear the dejection in my voice. But I can and it bathes my mind in confusion.

◇ ◇ ◇

For the next three days I search for Basu. Partly to make sure he is okay, partly to wrest any other details from him. But he's gone. The only report left with his name on it confirms he headed for Agsa and was escorted all the way to the border. Which makes sense—that's what my father told me, too. The gray-haired guard, on the other hand? He's disappeared. When I request a report on everyone currently employed, Hiren's father, one of the five rajas of Belwar who help run the Dome Guard, tells me not one profile matches that description. Even the report with Basu's infraction and truth-spelling case contains no name of the commanding guard who took him in. Saves him a lot of paperwork, my blood.

So I'm left with nothing but threats chiming in my head, Maharaja Naupure still gone, and Jatin Naupure expecting me at the ice door in a few hours.

What's worse is I haven't been able to sleep well. The dreams like to come at dawn, not the dead of night, but when my mind drifts in semiconscious anxiety. One could blame what happened on that pier, but the red room dream has haunted me for weeks. The dreams aren't what one would call normal. I'm not running, falling, or being hunted down by the Vencrin. No, I'm sitting in a blurry red room where my surroundings bleed. It's always quiet until I'm hissed at to do one thing: "Perform the royal ceremony. Become Adraa Belwar."

When I try to argue that I am already Adraa Belwar, the voice repeats itself, until the words swirl like the walls. "There's only one way. I have only one way. Perform the ceremony."

I awaken one of two ways, shouting or with my throat hurting like I already have been.

Twenty-nine days until my royal ceremony.

◇ ◇ ◇

I enter the sick bay and turn left on instinct. I offer a wave to a few of our long-term patients. Some are here because of Blood-lurst. It's odd that only these people connect my face to my po-sition in life, at least for the next twenty-nine days. Then all of Belwar will know exactly what Adraa Belwar looks like.

Off to the left is a private room, and behind its door I'll find Riya. I ease the door open, so as not to startle her. She's wear-ing all light blue today. I wonder if she does that subconsciously when she's going through bad days.

In his cocoon lies Riya's father, Mr. Burman, my old guard, and the best teacher I've ever had. My mother's pink magic swims over his head, diving into his mouth and nose to supply oxygen and hopefully reengage activity.

"I was looking for you," I whisper to Riya.

She glances up. "Sorry, I was . . ." She gestures to her dad.

"I know. It's fine." Today's the first of the week. She always gets like this at the first of the week. Mr. Burman had a saying that good things happen even at the beginning if one embraces the start of something new. He had sayings for everything.

I pull a chair forward, roll up my sleeve, and cast. *"Pravleah."* For a moment my mother's pink magic glows a little brighter with red. Then everything falls back to normal. I've cast that spell about 196 times, not that I'm counting.

Riya squeezes her dad's hand, then gathers me up in her eyes. A look of thanks switches to alert confusion in two seconds flat. "What in Wickery is that?"

"What's what?"

"This." Riya shoves the rest of my sleeve up my arm, exposing the scar from the Vencrin ship attack. "Oh Gods, Adraa!"

The jagged scar looks less angry now, only a stoic light line on my dark skin, but for Riya it's new and surely disturbing. "I . . . my knife slipped when I was gutting a pig for the clinic."

Riya lurches backward in her chair and frowns so deeply her mouth pops open. "Why are you lying?"

"Lying?"

"Yes. Lying. You *are* lying. Unless you are saying your own purple spell cut into you for fifty centimeters before you pulled back and thought, 'Ouch, that hurts.'"

Blood, just like her mother. A small part of me is impressed and proud to have Riya as my guard and friend for her reasoning abilities. But that small part doesn't wash away my fumbling as I search for a reason for the scar and why I would lie about it.

"It only sounds like a lie because I'm embarrassed about it. I should be better than that."

"Adraa, what's going on?" She pauses. Blood, I can tell her mind is gnawing away. Her next words are quiet, measured. "Tell me you aren't bloodletting yourself to Dloc."

"No!" I pause as well, searching for a way to throw her off. "Why? You think that would work?" I joke. I haven't heard that term thrown around in ages. Bloodletting. While it might still happen in Moolek, here it's considered a barbaric practice to win a god's favor. Mother doesn't even like to give up the goats for traditional events. "A body saved from disease is better utilization of that goat than watching it bleed on the temple floor," she always says. Such a Pire Island mentality.

Riya eyes me warily. "So it was a mistake?"

"I didn't mean for it to happen," I say, knowing she will hear the truth in that at least.

"And you didn't heal yourself right away because . . . ?"

I unroll the sleeve and wipe my hands on my pink skirt. "Didn't think it was bad enough. I was wrong." I get up to leave, seeking escape. I can only lie to Riya so much before she rips the truth from me. Her mother taught her how to truth cast after the accords became law. Even I don't know the spell, for ethical reasons and balances of power. And that scares me when I guard such a horrendous secret from her. Secrets. Plural, now.

She calls out as I lay my hand on the doorknob. "Where are you going? You came looking for *me*, remember?"

"Oh, right." I turn back to her. "I have to deliver firelight to Azure Palace today. Wondered when you were free."

Riya's eyes widen as she scrambles from her chair. I guess I should have used this earlier to distract her. "You are meeting Raja Jatin today?"

I shrug, but inside I'm twisted up with worry.

"And . . . and that's what you are wearing? Flying pants?"

I smile in vengeance. "I stayed away from goats today. You can't force Zara to hide these now." I smack my thighs. "But Zara did help me with my hair and makeup." I twist my head so Riya can see the intricate braid running down my back.

"Your mother accepted this?"

"My father did." Got his approval this morning when paper-work threatened to overtake his desk. Not like I should even *need* his approval. My pink wraparound skirt and flying pants are standard Belwarian attire. Besides, Maharaja Naupure respects the Belwarian tradition of heir anonymity and, more important, the secrecy of Project Smoke. Wearing a traditional and over-the-top lehenga last time was absurd on multiple levels and probably confused the staff, who have assumed I'm just a delivery witch for ages. Though today I'm not seeing Maharaja Naupure.

"Fine. Let's go, then." Riya arches one thick eyebrow. "Mother wanted me to ask Logen a few questions about security in Maharaja Naupure's absence anyway."

"Oh, so you aren't busy?" *Please say yes. Remember anything of importance.*

She pierces me to the bone with a single word. She too can play at vengeance. "Nope."

CHAPTER TWENTY-ONE

◈

Staging a Deception

Jatin

Adraa is coming to the palace. Which means first I must convince Kalyan to impersonate me again, and second, tell every person in the palace not to call me by my name. With Adraa not out in society because she hasn't taken the royal ceremony test, only Hughes really knows her and calls her Lady. Some housemaids and a few soldiers have seen her delivering firelight, but that's about it. This isn't a guess. I spend my nonexistent free time questioning everyone in the whole palace about what Adraa might look like and then analyzing their response to know if they might recognize her. Chara gave a sheepish grin and told me she was quite beautiful. Somehow my old nursemaid giving me a nod of encouragement wasn't the highlight of my investigation. The giggles of one particular housemaid or the sly smile of that one leering gate guard weren't either. Gods, one would think as soon as we see each other we were going to get married on the doorstep and fall into bed before we hit the stairs. My mind unravels at the thought.

Hughes doesn't like Adraa, which was a change in pace from all the innuendo and reassurance of her beauty. Something about "how she doesn't obey the social code of maharaja life." Then he had sighed. "But she's pretty, so . . . ," and he let that last word drift. One would think that's the one attribute I care about. Do I really come across as that shallow?

"Yes, yes, you do. Especially when you go around asking the entire palace how she looks," Kalyan had said with such a thick layer of dry humor I didn't stick around to talk to him about the role he must play.

When I went to the barracks later to explain he must be me if it comes to that, I received more of a reaction from him. "Absolutely not."

I don't want to order him to do it. Don't know if I have ever really given him orders before, more like asked for favors. I refuse for this to be the start. "I'm going to try to make sure she doesn't see you, but just in case."

He drops the sword he is sharpening. Kalyan actually loves working with metal and fixing equipment, so he lowers it begrudgingly. "You need to tell her the truth."

"I need more time. It's only been three weeks since I met her."

"More like nine years, Jatin."

"Exactly! Nine years of me being a homesick little brat." I slide into a chair. "That entire time I never really understood why she hit me. I mean, I know I said the wrong thing of course, mean things. But I didn't understand her perspective, how deeply I had cut her." I drag my hands through my hair.

"Please stop looking so pathetic. It doesn't suit you."

A laugh erupts from my throat like a gag, unexpected and harsh. "So you will do it, then?"

Kalyan looks determinedly at me, calculating. *Oh Gods, he is chewing something over.*

"What if she falls for me?"

I hit the back of the chair hard. It's moments like this when I realize I've given Kalyan too much confidence, or at least enough to outdo me. "What?"

"What if, let's say, I crafted some humble apology, was nice to her, she forgave me, thinks I'm her *fiancé,* and it just . . . worked out."

"You are cruel." That's also a lot of what-ifs. He didn't see her face that night on Pier Sixteen or in the restaurant afterward.

Kalyan picks up the sword again. "I did think she was pretty from the start if you remember."

"Gods, how are you this manipulative?"

He smiles at the weapon as he scrubs its hilt. "You've taught me a lot, Jatin."

I stalk from the room, but I'm not three steps away when he calls out, "You know if it comes to it, I'll do it. Just don't let that happen."

◇ ◇ ◇

I wait by the ice door like a stalker, feeling like that sleazy Underground manager cursed me into being one. Minutes phase into an hour until boredom and nerves take over and I grab some ink and parchment. With a swipe of purple magic, a floating slab acts as a desk so I can reply to my father's most recent letter.

I have received only two reports from him. One, he wrote to say he got to Warwick territory safely. Two, I reread:

> Dear Jatin,
>
> I am going to cut straight to it because I don't have much time. Twenty more citizens died before your uncle agreed to meet with me. Naupurian goats wandered over the Moolek border and were butchered (a few for bloodletting to the gods—Retaw in particular). The skirmish has grown into an argument over land once again. And, of course, how and which animals should be off-limits from bloodletting.
>
> Moolek has experienced tremendous drought and yet has not asked for any help. I guess he planned on letting people starve to death (the fool). Maharaja Moolek wishes to come to the palace to draw up a new amendment to the treaty. Which really should be us signing and enforcing the twenty-first treaty again. I have yet to understand why he would want to give up home advantage when I am already here. You should reread the twenty-one treaties before sending a reply. Let me hear your opinion on the matter. Of course, as always, if something urgent occurs inform me immediately.
>
> P.S. Good luck with Adraa.

Hughes shakes his head at me from where I sit on the floor. "She isn't *that* pretty, sir."

I guess I look rather pitiful, but it isn't like I'm not getting work done on the cold hard ground in the middle of the large tiled entryway. "Don't know what you are talking about, Hughes," I say, because it is all I can come up with. I go back to my letter.

I have reread all the treaties, all the beginning documents that tried to solidify our freedom from Moolek, all the violent tug and pull over the years until we finally broke free. Everything makes sense: Moolek's citizens' desperation due to the drought, the bloodletting, the argument over land renewed. Everything besides the fact that my uncle wants to talk of peace here, hundreds of miles from his lands. After articulating what I think needs to be amended or clarified in the twenty-first treaty, I stumble over my words. *Why? Why come here?* He's avoided meeting me for eighteen years already. *So why now?*

Footsteps sound outside the ice door and I jerk up. I slip the unfinished letter in my pocket. With a whisk of my hand, the tabletop evaporates and I'm standing, pacing, moving. I can't stay still.

I cast open the door, watching the ice fracture. Shards fall and splinter like glass.

Then Adraa steps through. Her expression shifts between confusion and maybe, hopefully, pleasant surprise. "Hi."

"Hey," I answer. I've been here all day and that's all I've got. Exactly how fast can someone become pathetic?

Adraa lifts the strap of the saddlebag. "I'm here to deliver the firelight."

"Jatin is busy right now, so you can give it to me."

"I should probably give it to him myself."

She's going to do it then, introduce herself to me, the real me. But I don't want that to happen. "I thought this would also be easier, so we could train together after."

Adraa's eyes brighten at that, and then dull just as quickly. "I should tell you something."

Blood. She's going to say it. But I'm not ready to tell her. My mind sweeps through all the interactions we've had since I've been here. Pretty sure she would still hate me. I've got to distract her.

"It's okay. I'll tell Jatin these firelights won't last the full two months. Don't think he will even notice."

"He's that busy, huh?" She looks to the stairs, and then sighs. "Still, I should meet him properly."

Gods, she doesn't want to meet me as much as I don't want her too. My chest tightens. This further solidifies my dread. *I think it would be worse—contempt.* That's what she had said. The word *contempt* bounces around my head.

"Rainbow."

Adraa swivels her attention back to me and away from those bloody stairs. "What?"

"Do you want to rainbow? It's something we did at the academy. Duel through all nine types of magic. Skip the colors your opponent can't do."

"I know what rainbowing is."

I smile broadly. "Good. You'll take the challenge, then?"

"So we would start with orange instead of red?"

"Yep."

"Okay, then. One." She points to herself as she drops the

225

saddlebag. "Zero." And she points to me like she's won something. I'd have to beg to differ. Relief and happiness soar through me and it feels like victory.

◇ ◇ ◇

Despite all my planning, I didn't ask the palace guard to stop their training for the day. My acts of deception shouldn't negatively affect everyone surrounding me. But now Adraa and I walk to the training field with a hundred men and women sparring or developing their magic. Kalyan isn't among them, even though he should be. Guess I negatively affected him with my tangle of lies.

Heads are already turning, one after the other. The men nearest us have lowered their weapons completely. Adraa is unfazed.

"Oh, that man is going to burn a building down one day if he continues to jerk like that when he casts red magic." She nods her head in indication.

I follow her gesture to a trainee jolting his arm upward every time he casts a small ball of flame. Nice assessment.

"He should focus on one hand at a time, hold it with the other if he needs to and concentrate on casting only enough fire to light a candle." She looks at me expectantly. "Be best if you tell him."

"Don't think he'll listen to you?" I don't know why I challenge her like this all the time. I can't seem to turn that part of me off when I'm around her.

Something sparks in her eyes. "No, I thought it would be better coming from a fellow guard." She pushes past me and onto the training yard. "But I guess we'll see."

I stare after her, a laugh bubbling at the back of my throat. How did I ever think she was anyone else besides Adraa?

"Raja Jatin?" a voice asks.

I whip toward my left to find one of the lead trainers. "Don't call me that today."

"Oh, right." He frowns. "Ah, sir, do you need something?"

"Start to clear the grounds please. We are going to rainbow." I nod toward Adraa.

His mouth falls open. "She's going to rainbow with . . . okay, whatever you say, sir." He calls to his fellow guards and trainers and they shuffle off the field. A big portion of them sticks around, clogging the perimeter. Oh Gods. Guess they want to see the show.

I peer over at Adraa, not wanting to interrupt her lesson. The kid nods wildly after seeing her demonstrate a small flicker of intense flame. She smiles at something he says and my gut wrenches. *It's nothing*, I tell myself. She has a right to smile at anyone she wishes. Then she touches his arm and holds on to his wrist. I take a deep breath. *It's a bloody lesson, Jatin. Get ahold of yourself.*

My guards stare from the sidelines, pointing, questioning. They really don't know who she is. Belwar has always had the custom of privacy, of not letting royals be introduced to the public until after the ceremony. That's how it is supposed to be, to ensure the gods' consent for the new generation of rajas and ranis before being named heir. But the gods have not denied a potential heir in hundreds of years. No one has died in decades. At the beginning of school, my name transcended my skill because with my parentage I would surely amass power. I was identified immediately, exposed. But I had the talent everyone expected.

To live a somewhat normal life, not having everyone know who you are at all times, it's what I've yearned for my entire life, what I falsely created with Kalyan at every opportunity. Is that why it's so easy for Adraa to lie and construct this Jaya Smoke identity? She's had practice at obscurity.

I laugh as the guardsman twists and flinches in embarrassment at the sudden emptiness around him. He bows to Adraa and runs off the field.

Adraa jogs back to me. "He listened. You can thank me for saving the barracks from burning down one day."

"Good, one less problem to deal with in the future."

She watches the crowd of guards awaiting our tournament. "Didn't realize we would have an audience."

I shrug. "Rainbows aren't too common. Most of them are only a four or five." I pause. "So, race for orange?"

"All right." Adraa places her obviously new skyglider to the side. Then, unexpectedly, she unknots her pink skirt, folds the fabric in half, and reties it around her waist. Now instead of falling a little below her knees, a breeze brushes the silk across her thighs. She's still wearing flying pants, but blood, it's like she knows exactly what to do to distract me.

I force myself to look away and bend into a running stance.

She whips her braid over her shoulder and looks at me. "I hope you aren't a sore loser."

Before I can reply, one of the guards yells and we are off.

"*Tvarenni!*" we both shout. My legs pump hard as the orange magic spreads into my muscles. Dirt slips beneath my shoes and

228

the training field whooshes past me. Adraa surges ahead and I urge my magic to work harder. But within seconds it's done and I've lost. Adraa has already turned to face me beyond the finish line. I duly tune into the roar of my Guard taunting me.

"Two." She points to herself. "Zero." She gestures to me, grinning. *Gods, why is that smile so aggravating and intoxicating at the same time?*

"It's only the beginning," I huff.

"Yeah, but I'm setting a precedent."

I remember now how much I loved competing with Adraa. Sometimes I would run across campus to get to my desk and write her. We were never friends exactly, but she was the first person I wanted to tell of my accomplishments. Other class-mates would ignore or taunt me. Father would say things like "that's nice" or "good job," but Adraa would get irritated. The more irritated she got, the more I knew I really had done well. It was empowering. But actually standing next to her, feeling my muscles yearn to cast more complicated spells? It's like the physical embodiment of all those letters and my body loves it, hums with genuine competitive energy. She isn't holding back either. Never before has someone gone up against me and not held back just a little. At the academy I could imagine the warn-ings behind closed doors: "Don't you dare hurt the future Maha-raja of Naupure. He's the *only* heir."

But all I sense from Adraa is pure fire behind her eyes as she scoops up air and blows it a hundred meters across the training yard and knocks down a target. I hate to admit I barely win yel-low magic, but it's the truth—barely.

I rightly take back my dignity when we get to green. Agsa

229

is known for its agriculture and Adraa is a city witch, born and bred. Growing trees, fruit and all, has always been an expertise of mine. I also win blue magic quite easily, but maybe that's to be expected knowing my father. I give her a big smile, not unlike the one she doled out to me. "What did you say earlier? Precedent, was it?"

Red mist swirls around her hand until a sword manifests and gleams like blood. "For purple let's actually duel." She doesn't say it too loudly, but the watching guards can sniff the whisper of a fight. They whoop in approval.

I gulp. I don't know if I can do this. "I don't want to hurt you."

"Just to first blood, nothing like the Underground."

I sigh in what I hope conveys annoyance, and then generate my own white sword. "Swords only." Gods know I didn't want to chunk daggers at her or swing an ax.

"Fine, *swords* only." Red smoke blooms into a second sword in her right hand.

Blood.

She lunges forward and cuts, aiming for my upper arm. I only scarcely make the parry, and use the close distance to swipe at her outstretched arm. She blocks with her other sword and pushes back at the same time. Fighting lefties is the worst. Adraa swipes again with a lunge to the right. At least I think she's a lefty.

I had watched her fight the Vencrin sailors out of the corner of my eye, but fighting her myself is different. She moves like fire, lashing, fluid, consuming. Together we weave and twist around one another. Jab. Parry. Twist. Slide. Duck. More ducking than I have ever done in any fight.

The guards on the sidelines are having fun, though, at my expense, of course. They holler cheerfully as I twist away from Adraa's sword, try to lock out the other one, and narrowly escape with an unscathed arm. I breathe heavily. Blood, she moves fast. In fact, we have skated around so much that a cloud of dust skims around our legs and nestles in itchy bundles in my throat. I cough.

Adraa makes another slice at my chest.

I retreat to regain distance. "You sure you aren't trying to kill me?"

"Never." She smirks. "In front of all these witnesses."

"Reassuring."

Pivot. Shift. Cut. Parry. Riposte. Parry. Adraa and I are too agile for this kind of fight. We both aim for the easy and non-lethal targets to draw blood. But she's too fast. I have to break this pattern we've created. With a quick flip of my hand I lower my blade and stab for her stomach instead of slashing. She jumps back and tries to sweep her blade in defense. Our swords skate up one another, white on red blending into pink, and our guards lock. Adraa whips her other blade forward, slashing at my face. I counter and angle the red sword away, another lock. For a moment, we are like statues, fastened together like ice. The crowd jeers.

"Want to call it even?" I ask, her face mere centimeters from mine.

"No," she huffs. She jerks back and I wrench my wrist at an angle, unlocking our guards and slicing into her calf. Adraa grimaces and her leg buckles. A roar erupts from the sidelines.

I pull away and drop both swords. They vanish in a puff of white smoke before touching the dirt. "You okay?"

"I'm fine," Adraa relents. She clutches her calf, stands, and shows the crowd of guards the blood on her hand. "To appease the bloodthirsty masses," she explains with an eye roll.

They cheer at my small victory. Adraa nods toward them. "I guess most bet on you."

I turn to see a few men and women exchanging coins. "Can't believe anyone betted against me."

"Yeah, well, it's not like you are their raja."

"Yeah, of course. That would be embarrassing. . . ."

Adraa sits down on the ground and begins to heal the cut on her leg.

I squat beside her, trying to forget the biting irony in her words. "You know what this means?"

Adraa continues to cast, ignoring me, then looks up. "That for someone who once told me guardsmen try to fight honorably, you don't."

"No." I pause. Was my move shrewd? I *did* warn her somewhat. I shake the thought from my head. "Four." I smile and gesture to myself, then to her. "Two."

"No, four, three." She twists her leg so I can see the smooth brown skin through the rip in her orange flying pants. There is no hint of even a scratch. "I haven't forgotten about your limitations."

I hold out a hand to help her up. "Yeah, and what are yours?"

"You're going to have to find—" Adraa stops, staring at our audience. I turn to see what, or whom, she's looking at. For a heartbeat I picture Kalyan in the crowd, but he's obeyed my request.

"What is it?"

"I just realized something."

"Yeah?"

She turns to me, her face bright. "Do you have a map of Belwar and a copy of my report?"

◇ ◇ ◇

I lead us to one of the palace tearooms. This one is on my mother's side of the palace and thus rarely used. Years after she died, many of these rooms were kept clean but untouched, like an artifact polished and then encased for study. I used to sneak in here and learn what I could. Fiddle with the array of birdhouses hanging outside each window (most are empty now), scan the shelves for the most worn books, and touch the silkiness of her yellow robes. I was allowed anywhere in the palace as a child, except the nursery.

"I didn't know whether this side of the house was used anymore," Adraa whispers, as if a ghost lives here.

"That's why it's good for our meetings. Also this." I gesture to the painting on the floor, my mother's huge map of Wickery gleaming in the sunshine.

"Now I understand when Maharaja Naupure said she strategized like a bird."

I start. I heard my father say that about my mother once. Once. "You know a lot about the Naupures, don't you?"

"Maharaja Naupure and I talk when I bring the firelight, so yeah, I guess," she agrees as she nudges aside a card table to reveal the entire map.

I don't push the issue further.

"You don't need to move the furniture." I lay my hands on the floor, whisper some black magic into the painting, and shove outward. The white mist of my magic soaks into the floor and the map moves beneath us. With another swipe, it zooms in on Belwar as if we're nose-diving on skygliders. I've always loved this room.

"It's like flying with you all over again," Adraa jokes.

I give her a teasing smile.

She plops down, sitting right on the illustration of her palace. "My report?"

I hand over the bundle of paperwork. With a few glances at her own map and simple purple spells, she throws her hands outward and small pinpoints fall upon the East Village. I examine the jumble of marks, trying to see what she does. "What did you figure out?"

"Limitations," she answers with a grin.

I slowly sit next to her. "What do you mean?"

"Firelight. It doesn't magically make its way to Pier Sixteen. With the drugs, any back shop or home could be used to make it or house it. I've tracked down one drug den." She lights up a marker. "There must be more. I just can't find them. That's what's so hard about all this. But only one person makes firelight."

"Adraa Belwar," I whisper, the sound of her name nice to finally say aloud.

She doesn't even flinch. "Yes, and with Basu out of the picture and not handing over his entire shipment, the Vencrin will have to buy it slowly or steal it. Which means . . ." She smiles wide, drawing a large circle that surrounds every reported drug deal. Then, slowly, she sketches triangles, connecting dots until the map bleeds. "Limitations."

I manifest my own magic, lighting up the key spots and outlining my own triangle—Pier Sixteen, the Underground, and Basu's shop. "You're right. Glowing balls of light with expiration dates are hard to move across the city unnoticed. They have to have a—"

"A warehouse or something." She smiles at me, lit up like I've never seen before. It melts me.

I zoom in even closer and our image breezes past temples, streets of squished houses, and market squares. There aren't many structures large enough to house such an operation. Time evaporates as we pick apart possibilities. Adraa has an answer for every building, proving she knows Belwar like the scroll of her Touch. Finally, I get to a tall rectangular structure near the East and North Village border. For the first time she pauses.

"That used to be a trading bazaar, but once a few bigger grand bazaars opened it was converted for the homeless and Untouched," she says.

So the perfect place for Vencrin to seize.

"We found it," she breathes. Relief releases her laugh. It's such a wonderful sound.

So we plan, discussing possible ambushes and her past tactics. I lean forward to point out the building next to the former trading bazaar that will be the best lookout point, and my hand brushes hers, by accident. I stop talking, and for a second, we stay frozen like that, my fingers covering hers.

Adraa looks up and our eyes connect. "You really don't care, do you?" she asks.

Gods, even simple contact with her and I become undone, unfocused on the facts and the mission before us. "What? No, I'm with you on this." I gesture to the map, forcing myself to look at our red and white pinpoints. *What was I saying, again?*

"No, I mean my arm. It doesn't bother you at all, does it?" She nods at our hands, causing my lips to curl upward with happiness.

I lean toward her. "You're right. Doesn't bother me at all." My gaze flits between her eyes and her lips. Gods, I want to kiss her, to mimic our hands. I think maybe, just maybe, she wants the same thing. But she wouldn't be kissing me, Jatin. She would think she's kissing a guard, and that would be a lie. A cold tremor hits me straight in the chest. A lie she wants?

A bell chimes and, *whoosh*, the curtain on the far side of the room unveils one of our maids. She yelps. "Gods, my apologies, I wasn't expecting anyone to be in here."

Adraa's hand slinks back to her side, and with a wave the red spikes on the map burst into smoke. "I should go." She flies to her feet.

I cast away my own spikes and send the map reeling out of the illusion and back to a mere painting. "Wait!" I yell as Adraa runs out the door and her footsteps echo in the hallway.

"Raja Jatin, I—"

I wave a hand toward the maid. "It's fine. Pretend this never happened." And I bolt after Adraa.

"Jaya, wait!" I yell again.

Ahead, Adraa slows and finally turns around, panic still on her face.

"It's fine. She's a maid. She didn't see enough to understand what we were planning," I try to reassure her.

Adraa looks down at her right hand and squeezes it into a tight fist. "I . . . maybe I should do this on my own."

What? So this is more than embarrassment. My brain fumbles through every possible way a single maid could have thrown me into useless guard territory again. No matter what has driven Adraa to this decision, I can't let it stand. I can't let her go out alone, knowing every drug dealer is looking to ambush her, to kill her. "After all that planning, everything we heard at Pier Sixteen, you would do this alone?"

"It's more complicated than that. Kalyan, you and I . . . I don't want anyone else to get hurt."

"And with me there, there will be a less likely chance of that happening. Please, tell me we are still partners in this." I can't help but beg at this point.

She withdraws. "Yes, fine. Partners. But nothing more."

Nothing more. It's not rejection. It's not even bad news. I've won, really. She'll listen to reason and won't go into the streets without me. But as I watch her turn and leave, it still feels like I've lost. And it's never quite hurt this badly.

◇

CHAPTER TWENTY-TWO

I Acquire a Name for Myself

Adraa

For the next two weeks, on every other night, we stalk the empty shell of what used to be the grand trading bazaar. It's seen better days. A web of cracks stretch across its rounded roof and arched windows. The sand-colored stone, which most of Belwar's buildings are constructed with, has faded along the top and blackened at the base.

By day five I'm sure this is the place. It may not scream Vencrin, but it both smells of ruin and bustles with activity, a combo that can only mean one thing. And if that weren't clear enough, I asked my North Village distributor to place firelight in the public lanterns that used to house sticky candles and dripping wax. At nightfall Kalyan and I witnessed each glowing light of comfort and warmth snatched from their containers. So now we watch in the heavy darkness.

Which normally wouldn't be a problem. I'm not afraid of the dark. Kalyan and I are both talented enough in orange magic to zoom in and see through the murk. No, the problem is Kalyan. For the past two weeks I've set boundaries. Don't get physically close. Don't sit, or Gods forbid lie, on the ground together. The darkness scatters my rules across the rooftop like they're a joke.

I thought my "nothing more" could halt *my* feelings at partnership. Nope.

Two nights ago Kalyan suggested that if we get caught we could pretend to be two teenagers messing around on a rooftop. I don't normally become engulfed in flames, figuratively, but my cheeks burned as I tried to play it off like that was a solid plan.

Then he choked on laughter and said, "I didn't mean it like that." Which meant that not only was I the embarrassed one but my mind is the one that went there, that jumped. I may not have voiced my rooftop rules, but I'm the individual pushing them over the ledge.

Before all this, I hid my identity to do one thing—gather information. Now, it's something else. The lie also lives out a fantasy. Kalyan and Jaya could be together, *could* fall in love. My birthday, edging ever closer, brings a whole different level of anxiety.

But I shouldn't think about this. I have a job. Watch. Plan. Then we will raid this makeshift warehouse. Once in I'll be able to find my firelight. I'll have proof.

The threat of ambush and the Vencrin leader's order to destroy us still hang thick in the air. Twice we have been attacked on our way here. Once, streams of magic pelted from the sky. The other attack was two blocks away, drenched in black magic. Eleven bodies fell.

Midfight, Kalyan and I developed a tactic for watching each other's backs, one we call rings: let one or two Vencrin come close, send them to the ground, and expand in small and steady increments. We also started to work on levels too, one of us on the roof, one on the ground. Assassins not only love jumping out of shadows but down from them as well.

I've stopped wearing my Red Woman uniform. Tonight, I've opted for purple flying pants, pink blouse, and lavender wraparound skirt, which is long enough for me to fasten and pleat over one shoulder like a sari. No masks. No shadowy costume that the God of Wodahs would be proud of. Just two teenagers . . . messing around.

Kalyan bumps my shoulder with his. Every particle of my being focuses on the tap like I'm an orange forte and my nerves have been enriched. At first it was just my hand that became warmer when he touched me. Now that feeling has swum up my arm and throughout my body these past weeks. It's beyond irritating, not to mention unprofessional.

"Someone's rounding the corner on our left," Kalyan whispers.

I swivel my attention, dragging my bloody senses away from the minimal contact. Kalyan's right. The hulking form of a man steps under an empty lantern and trudges up the road. Something about the walk and the frame has an air of familiarity I can't seem to—

No! My stomach bottoms out. A lump rams into my throat and I choke on surprise.

"I don't recognize him. Can you see his face?" Kalyan says.

I turn around and crouch so that nothing pokes above the roof's ledge. My lungs work overtime.

"Smoke?"

I can't answer.

Kalyan leans close. "Who is it?"

I look into his sincere eyes. "Beckman."

After I let the truth into the air I whip around because I have to make sure. Maybe he's just passing by. This doesn't mean he's a part of the Vencrin. He's too good. He's not a junkie and not once has he lamented about money issues. Maybe he has nothing to do with destroying everything I stand for.

One extra glance and I know it's Beckman. I'd spot one of the tallest and most solidly built men in existence. But I don't want to see him here. Anywhere but here. My knuckles ache from clenching them against the roof's edge. *Keep walking. Go home to your girls.*

He doesn't. Upon nearing the warehouse we've been watching for days, the one I saw Nightcaster himself slip into yesterday, Beckman slides under a curtain and vanishes. Something in me hollows out.

"I'm sorry," Kalyan whispers.

The term friend *is used loosely to craft allies.* My father's words ring in my ears. I guess that's what Beckman and I had done. To Beckman I was nothing more than a young cage caster in over her head. That night with Rakesh, the upper deck, the shame and terror—all meaningless to him. Still, I thought we were friends. Wrong. Always wrong. I can't seem to learn my lesson.

But it's more than that if I really comb through my feelings.

Beckman isn't just a friend but also the wizard connected to the worst, most terrifying moment of my life. And he saved me from it. How could someone like that be working for the Vencrin?

"Can I never trust anyone?" I look over at Kalyan and he appears as devastated as I am. "What?"

He stares at the alleyway. "I should tell you something," he finally voices.

"Did you suspect him?"

"No, I—" Kalyan's eyes widen at something over my shoulder. "He's out."

I whip my head around so fast my neck spasms. But I ignore the pain because Beckman is walking again. He stops at the corner, wads up something in his hands, and discards it in a bin.

"Do you see that?" I ask, finely tuned to each movement, each step. Then he's disappeared into the shadows.

"At least he's not a litterer." Kalyan rises to his feet slowly. "I'm going to check it out."

I grab his wrist. He stares at me until I let go. "Be careful."

Then he says the words I crave more than anything right now. "I trust you. Rings?"

"Rings," I affirm.

I watch Kalyan land in a cloak of black magic, grab the item, and then, just as fast, ascend to our hiding spot.

"What was it?"

Kalyan holds out a sheet of parchment. "We're famous."

I seize the thin paper. It takes a second to process the image is of us, or at least our vigilante personae. A drawing with no detail, just red magic swarming a female face. They've made my features more triangular and feminine than they actually are. Which must mean that no one knows much about me besides the fact that I'm Erif Touched and female. Guess my unoriginal name has done me some good. Gives nothing but the obvious away.

Kalyan's silhouette, right beside mine, is even more obscure. The cloud of white smoke has confused the illustrator to the point where Kalyan's brown skin could be misconstrued as three shades paler than it is, as if he were an Agsa native. My black illusion spell has turned out better than I could have ever imagined, for the both of us.

Atop, an inscription reads NIGHT AND THE RED WOMAN. It seems Kalyan has finally been saddled with his own unoriginal moniker. But why did Beckman have this? And why did he throw it away?

"What are you thinking?" Kalyan asks.

"Wondering why you got first billing," I joke, lying because the hurt is too much to handle.

He smiles that smile of his. "It's obviously catchier that way."

"Yeah, but they want me dead more than you."

He opens his mouth to retort, probably to say the death threat is equal at this point, but then closes it quickly. Instead he looks me in the eye. "Let's not fight about who the Vencrin want dead more."

He's right. I have more important things to worry about. Like if Beckman wants to kill me, too. Because if he does, our cage-casting showdown is only days away and I've handed him the perfect opportunity.

I've committed one of the worst mistakes an undercover operative can make—I've underestimated my target. The posters are a new level of brilliance, one I didn't think the Vencrin were capable of. Within a day the pieces of paper litter the streets. They hang from market stalls, on the windows of most restaurants, even from flying stations. Now, everyone who sees Night or the Red Woman can alert the Vencrin. We are being hunted through paper and blotchy ink.

Within mere hours the Red Woman becomes a household name. I know because she's discussed in my own home the next afternoon. Reviewed in the hallways, debated between patient beds, whispered about among palace staff as they go about their duties. Riya, with growing suspicion, wants to talk about her during any spare moment we take a breath from training. Eventually the news becomes important enough that it reaches my father's desk.

The parchment my father has facedown and tucked beneath other paperwork has to be one of the posters. It curls at the edges like wind has beaten it against the side of a building for too long. I tense on reflex, but I *knew* this moment was coming. Ever since Beckman's trash unfurled in front of me, I expected she, or rather I, would be brought to my father's attention.

He holds up the poster and clears his throat. "My daily meeting today was about the Red Woman. I'll have to make a statement soon about how we view her and what actions we plan to take. I'm sure everyone has heard the rumors."

"What do your advisors and the Belwar rajas say?" I jump in. I've been waiting impatiently for this moment. With open discussion I can obtain information without my overt curiosity becoming suspicious. I just hope my family sides with my other identity when it comes to what will be done.

"Most recommend that she be stopped."

I drop my spoon, and desperately try to steady my voice for the next question that needs to be asked. "They mean to kill her?"

"No, I think the Guard wish to understand her motives, then use her. They say she is a powerful red forte." He pauses and his eyes brighten.

Blood, does he know? Can he sense it? Can he see my hands bundling and twisting my napkin under the table?

"Adraa. You worked with many red magic users after you created firelight. Could you imagine any of them being the Red Woman?"

I choke back panic, thankful this time that I gave up eating. Still, I play with the curry dish, to present a false casualness. "Ah, not sure, I tested them only on the one spell, so I don't really know what any of them are fully capable of."

I feel Prisha's eyes.

"But you could help narrow down the suspects," Father barrels onward.

"Not *every* red forte came to be tested," I try to reason.

"Still. Talk to our Guard. See if you can help their investigation."

Mother leans forward. "I don't know. Mrs. Burman says this

Red Woman is only going after Vencrin. I'm so tired of all these Bloodlurst addicts in the clinic, some mere kids trying to increase their Touches and burning out forever. In Pire, those with power are meant to stand against those that abuse the gods' Touch. That's the whole purpose of our leadership."

My mouth falls open, and it feels like my brain has too. After all these years of "do this," "wear that," "stand up straight," my mother has finally approved of my actions. Of course, she doesn't know they're mine, but still. She supports Jaya Smoke, who in some ways is the total opposite of how my mother tried to raise me.

Prisha takes a bite of her dosa and nods. "I agree with Mother. They're criminals."

This from my younger sister! Now, if she *knew* it was me under that red mask, her opinion would not be of admiration.

Father's voice rises. "Even so, the Red Woman dishonors the truth accords. We have no real way of knowing what her goal is. She could be trying to undermine our right to lead."

Why would I try to take away my own destiny? My heart pumps hard and fast. My father truly thinks she is a commoner, seeking violence or a coup. For the millionth time I think of telling them about the Underground, about the cage casting, about Jaya. The words stick in my mouth. My tongue feels heavy.

"I would like to hear Maharaja Naupure's opinion on this," Mother says.

Father nods in agreement. "He is to return from Moolek soon."

Prisha leans toward me. "You know what that means. You

won't be able to get out of a formal engagement meeting anymore."

I give Prisha a dirty look, but she is right. Jatin and I would be expected to officially meet and our parents to make the last arrangements for the blood contract and marriage ceremony. They might even speed it up to generate a sense of unity and stability. Two weeks ago I had lied and told them all that Jatin and I met at my firelight delivery. But compared with my other lies and the fact my father holds a wanted poster so the thugs in town can smoke me out, my arranged marriage seems trivial. *I have more important problems than Jatin Naupure!*

I interrupt my parents' hypotheticals. "I think I know how Naupure will respond."

Father's eyes crinkle as he scoops up a handful of rice. "Yes, Miss Made to Be a Naupure?"

I roll my eyes, but continue. "On a personal level he wouldn't want a witch to be hurt or killed, but the idea of her . . . well, this Red Woman can investigate the Vencrin like no one else can."

Father arches an eyebrow. "Investigate the Vencrin? How do you know that is what she is doing?"

I'm sweating, dripping with anxiety. It's imperative I word everything clearly and fluidly. "It's obvious she is against them. As Mom said, only Vencrin members have been taken down."

"Even so, I need to make sure. The Dome Guard will test her with a truth spell."

I shake my head, hard. "Why is that the only way?"

"Because it's the law."

"A bad law. To have only Dome Guard able—" I stop myself,

247

realizing what I have said, how much my voice has risen. It's Father who separated himself from court and trial, giving the Dome Guard the power to cast truth spells and pass judgment.

His expression falls. "It's a balance of power, Adraa. Look to Moolek to see what happens without it. Without our power checked. With believing the forte system defines someone's worth. Soon one starts believing they are Godlike." He holds up the poster. "This woman isn't noble because she is powerful. In fact most of the time in life it's the exact opposite. She must be checked."

His green eyes convey only sternness. The fact he must use them on me now hurts. But I've hurt him too. *Bad law.* Heat rises to my face, the napkin rips in my lap, but I don't say a thing. I agreed with the truth accords, praised him for it at the time. Then I discovered my own truth: Even those meant to save us can be corrupted. Even the Beckmans of the world can slip.

Father compares the Red Woman to Moolek's power-hungry inequality? No. Blood no. I've seen the streets; I've seen the bodies in the clinic. My secret is the only way, as is my silence.

Because I know under my mask I will always protect our people.

Father's voice evens out, trying to infuse peace back into dinner. "For now, Adraa will help with the preliminary investigation and eliminate suspects with the Guard. I'll have the Guard question the Red Woman at the earliest opportunity. Best scenario, she is brought to the palace. Maybe you would like to question her too, Adraa?" He smiles in encouragement at the opportunity he has bestowed, trying to mend our disagreement, not understanding how it condemns me.

I can imagine the scene: me being dragged into the throne room and Riya or Zara scouring the palace. I shudder. "Sure."

Gods, I had a lot to answer for.

◇ ◇ ◇

My father's plan fails of course and not because I don't cooperate with the Belwar Guard. Or even because of the simple fact they are searching for someone right in front of them. No, it fails because, like my dad, they distrust the Red Woman. As soon as I finish the meeting I fly to Azure Palace, needing to vent and update Kalyan. We naturally wind up on the training field, as we do most days.

"So I think what you're telling me is we are screwed. We now have not only the Vencrin but also the Belwar Guard after us," Kalyan says.

"Pretty much. The Belwar Guard won't kill us, though, hopefully. That is if the right ones get to us. So, there's that."

"*Pavria.*" Kalyan shoots a blast of air at my chest. I slink to the left, casting my own yellow magic to intercept his gust. I don't know how Kalyan can talk and fight/train with me at the same time, but he can.

I take a moment to gather a breath as I kneel on the warm dirt of the Naupure training field. My right side cramps, squeezing and tugging at me. "We need to move up our timeline."

Kalyan tilts his head and I know what he's thinking. Watch. Plan. That's what is decided this time around.

But he can only rein me in so far. My birthday still lingers in warning like a piercing scream. Twelve days. Or maybe I should

249

be worrying about the approaching fight with Beckman. Three days. "We've taken too much time as it is."

He finally nods. "Okay. Tomorrow night, then."

I nod. Pause. *"Hilloretaw!"* I shout, and try to catch Kalyan by surprise with a stream of water.

"Vicalayati. Vikara. Himadloc," he says calmly, and the water swivels in the opposite direction, turns to ice, and falls to the ground, breaking in the dirt.

He ignores the shock and annoyance clearly written on my face. "And you are sure you can't get the Guard on our side? None of them seem to believe you?"

"What should I have said? 'Hey, believe me that the Red Woman only means to help Belwar. I know this because I'm her.' Should I have given them my entire mission file too?" I step closer to practice hand-to-hand combat, throwing two punches Kalyan blocks easily.

"No," he huffs. He throws a counterattack and I duck. "But we need them on our side, otherwise we'll never know who and how many are corrupted by the Vencrin."

I twist around him and step away. "That's the problem. I didn't know whom to trust. I went in, I tried to convince them. It didn't work out."

I throw the same punches again and then mimic a kick to his groin. He jerks backward reflexively and raises his eyebrows, giving me an expression of mock dismay.

"What? Just because you will probably be fighting a man doesn't mean he won't use that."

"Yeah, but *he* wouldn't look so pleased with himself."

I hold my side, willing the ache to disperse. "I bet he would look even more pleased. I didn't even touch you."

He laughs. "You make it sound like he's pleased because he got to touch me."

"Gods, you know what I meant."

"Sure I do, Smoke." And he winks.

I throw another combo. Our arms beat against each other as we block, attack, duck, swivel, block. The pain in my side intensifies, yelling at me to stop. When I go in again, I can tell I'm telegraphing.

Kalyan catches my arm. "You're slow today."

"Yeah, well." I yank away. "I'm always slower on my period."

Kalyan's face drops. Guess he wasn't expecting that. "Okay, so we have entered that stage of our relationship."

I clutch my right side and try not to laugh. Laughing makes it hurt even worse. "I must have felt like it was time, or my uterus did." I take the moment to drop to the ground and sprawl on my back. I need a break. The more I cast and use up my energy, the more my cramps seem to claw their way through my abdomen. At least I won't be on my period during my royal ceremony. Some god is looking out for me.

"Is there any pink magic that can help?"

"Yes, but it's a potion for this kind of pain and I left it at home."

Kalyan kicks at the dirt. "Right, of course." Awkwardness settles over him. Maybe I shouldn't have said anything. He sits down next to me in the dirt. "Guess I need to learn that one when I get married."

Unexpectedly, that last word bites and chews through my chest. Kalyan would marry one day. That shouldn't bother me. But a thought bubbles up and swells in my throat and then pops. He wouldn't marry . . . me. An image plays in my mind: Kalyan combining the herbs and infusing the potion with magic and love for his woman who bleeds and one day would give him children. Then logic evaporates the scene. "Wait, how?" I ask, sitting up and pressing my right side, as if menstruation can be stopped like a gushing wound. "You would need to be able to do pink magic."

"Oh, um. I've been studying."

"And you can do it? That's amazing."

He grins. "Does this mean you're impressed?"

I shake my head no, but a new nervousness tugs at my gut. Our eyes lock onto each other. This is dangerous. We're close and on the ground. The pain blew away the boundaries I've been so good about maintaining.

His eyes dart to my hands holding my side. "Can I show you something?" he asks.

"Right now?"

Kalyan jumps to his feet and offers a hand. I take it and haul myself up. This better be worth the pain.

We make our way toward the garrison, but instead of turning right for the entrance we go left. Left, which leads nowhere except the back of the building. The kind of place I imagine Guard members go to fool around.

"Uh, where are we going?"

"It's really close."

When we reach the end of the garrison, a small stone staircase greets us. I never knew there was a path here. Frostlight trees converge behind the building, their branches bending over the hidden path, shedding and littering the ground with flowers. With the sunlight streaming in, and the mountain breeze tossing the bundles of white flowers it feels . . . magical.

The pathway turns to the left and there lies a building, a strange little building with wooden walls and a— "Is that an ice roof?"

"Would you expect anything different from Maharaja Naupure?"

I laugh. "No."

We step inside, into a fully equipped medic center. To the right an array of plants spring from the ground and collide with each other in a torrent of leaves and flowers. The ceiling drips water onto the plants in a soft patter. To the left are shelves upon shelves of ingredients. Beetle legs, fish skeletons, goat hair, crushed rose petals, cumin, turmeric, tulsi, peppermint, sage— it's all here.

"I never knew this existed."

"After Maharani Naupure died, Maharaja Naupure created this for the troops and the staff. He wanted a full clinic to be closer to the palace."

"Of course," I whisper. A stab of sadness awakens behind my eyes and I blink hard to try to block the tears. I can feel the pain Maharaja Naupure cast into making this place. The shelves are smooth and soft, painstakingly carved. Every herb, spice, and flower is marked and precisely spaced from the others. The clinic is so full of every kind of ingredient imaginable and yet so void of people. Created too late. Not that this place could have saved Maharani Naupure; childbirth when difficult can go wrong too quickly for a potion to help. But it might have saved his daughter.

Kalyan rolls up his sleeves, showcasing the Touch that runs up his arms. I can't help but stare. Gods, I'm always staring at him nowadays.

"So what do we need first?" he asks.

"For what? Are you wanting to make an explosion spell or something for the mission?"

He gives me a bemused look. "No, but I think I should be worried that you seem to know how to make explosion spells. I'm talking about the potion, for you." He nods at my hand, still pressed to my side.

"Oh . . ."

Is he serious? He is going to create the daydream I just had. It's not like he knows what I was thinking earlier, but blood, the very idea he could read my mind. I look around to avoid giving myself away further. "Valerian root first as the base and that bottle of oil right there. Oh, and grab the ginger. And that big ashoka flower bunch." I pluck a cluster of peppermint leaves off a branch and search for the right kind of blood.

After I light the fire under a large cauldron, Kalyan urges me out of the way and onto a wicker stool. "Just sit there. Tell me what to do."

"No, it's fine," I protest.

"You'll be telling me what to do, Smoke. You love that."

254

I roll my eyes. "Okay, but don't poison me."

He rolls his sleeves up higher and grabs a mortar and pestle. "I guess that depends on how good a teacher you are."

Of all the potions to start a beginner on, this would be one of the last on the list. It's beyond complex, edging into convoluted and at times traveling to the land of torturous. But if he really wants to learn I won't stop him from trying. I explain the process of this particular potion, especially what needs to happen with the blood. He can't mess that part up.

And then, beyond my expectations, he does fairly well, listening each time I jerk from the stool to correct his technique. He only has to restart twice. Prisha had to restart eighteen times before Mother was satisfied. Which raises the question, how is Kalyan so bloody good at everything?

Twenty minutes later, the potion froths, hot steam floats through the air, a bird sings as it bathes itself on the roof, and Kalyan and I are working together as usual. And yet it's in a totally different way from fighting in the Underground or in the streets of the East Village. We are in our own little separate world. It's like there's no such thing as betrayal, political issues, or my fated marriage to worry about. Just me, cramping, and Kalyan trying to fix it.

"How do you remember all of this?" Kalyan asks as he slices the lump of ginger root with a white knife.

"Monthly practice."

"Ah, of course. And what about other potions?"

"Daily practice." I reach out and stop his hand. "You want each slice to be the same thickness, the exact same."

He cuts slower, more evenly, my hand guiding his for a couple of slices before I return to the stool next to his. "It also takes a great mentor," I say.

"Guess I'm out of luck, then," he says as he beams at the ginger. He does that sometimes when he teases me; he looks away and smiles at his own joke as if I don't notice it.

I let out a huff. Gods, that cheeky smile. "And I was about to say how well you are doing."

"Too late, Smoke, too late. I'm taking the compliment."

"Well, we are on to the hard part, so you can truly prove yourself. This is the spell." I grab a piece of paper and write it down. "It's best to say it calmly and move your hands like this." Index finger pressed to my thumb I wave and flip my hand.

"Should I watch for a color change?" Kalyan asks.

"Not with this potion. I know that sucks, but this one just bubbles more, if you're lucky."

Kalyan takes a few breaths. I can't tell whether he is being serious or teasing me, but I watch him intently regardless. *"Alpaya Pidaleah Zantahileah,"* he casts, and white magic drips off his hands like water as he twists them. Perfect.

One large green bubble expands and pops. Kalyan turns to me expectant and hopeful. "Did it work?"

I get up and stir the green liquid. It bubbles grotesquely. "Nope. Failed."

"Are you serious?" he asks from behind me, *close* behind me.

I use the wooden spoon to smell the potion. Peppermint overpowers my nose. Perfect. So it's true. Kalyan can do pink magic. He's an eight. "No, I'm only messing with you. It's good." When I go to sip the potion, Kalyan clutches my hand, which means he's kind of half hugging me. "Wait, are you sure? I don't want to poison you."

His warmth is like a fever. I untangle myself, stepping away from our jumbled personal space. "Gods, I'm not *that* bad a teacher," I answer, praying he doesn't notice how my body reacts to his. How I as a person react to him. Even still, I should be nicer. Let him in on how good of a wizard he is. But I've never been the reassuring type. Jatin, with his overwhelming cockiness, and our competition over the years kind of beat that out of me.

Kalyan, on the other hand, doesn't seem to have a problem complimenting others. "No, you're a great witch."

I pour myself a glass of the green sludge, careful to maintain my distance while eyeing him and his overwhelming sincerity. I mean, he's always sincere, his facial expressions so open, his smile bright, but today . . . Even Prisha grumbles when I ask her to make me this potion. And I shudder imagining Jatin's disdain if I ever inquired. I take a gulp, watching Kalyan watch me. This feels so normal, so relaxed.

My gut wrenches at a sudden thought. I don't want him making this for his wife. I don't want to think about how I've helped him woo her, like it . . . I shake my head. *It didn't affect you, Adraa. At all.*

"It looks like it's pretty disgusting," he says as he leans against the countertop.

I try to recover. "With practice I'm sure you can fix that." Gods, I cannot turn off my tongue. Even if I wanted to be kinder and to flirt I can't.

"Well, I was thinking. Could you substitute something for

the oil?" He scans the clinic, examining the jars and containers. "Or maybe add something. Sugar or, or, something to make it taste—"

"Kalyan?"

"Yeah?"

"Thank you for this. You're a kind person." I meant only to thank him. That last bit just spilled out. It—

Kalyan gives me a weird look, as if he's caught me in a lie. He bends toward me. "Kind, you say? So *not* an arrogant jerk?"

"I don't know. I guess you can be both."

He laughs. "Yeah, I suppose so. I suppose we all can be different depending on the situation or whom we are with." His eyes find mine again. This time I don't want to look away.

CHAPTER TWENTY-THREE

Caught and Catching Fireballs

Jatin

Adraá and I are friends now. I know that much for sure. Every day I will myself to tell her the truth and then life gets in the way. There's a new mission, we need to scout the trading bazaar, or I have to read reports and hold meetings with Naupure rajas all day. Then Beckman betrayed her and I couldn't do it, couldn't bear her loathing.

Naively, I thought I would know when or if she liked me as more than a friend. Like I would just know? Ha! What was I thinking? As if I have a plethora of knowledge about this sort of thing. Sometimes I can't see behind her wall of sarcasm and her determination to defeat the Vencrin.

But being her friend? It's everything, a connection I never knew I could experience. It's different from Kalyan and me, because every once in a while he reminds me how unequal we really are, even if I don't want us to be. Adraa and I were equals from the start, equals at lying to each other, equals at camouflaging our identities, equals at feeling like the world is our responsibility to fix. I think I finally understand her. She has moved away from the land of supposedly, into reality. But then she discovered how to bunk in my heart, for free nonetheless. I don't know how she did that, but I'm sure she didn't mean to. Even if she had, it would have been an impulsive decision, like every decision she makes.

We might only be partners and nothing more for the rest of our lives. I can't force her to like me like that and I would hate us together if it weren't her choice. I just need to be observant enough to know when she has made her choice.

It's hard, though, especially when most of the time I spend with her we watch the warehouse that might house firelight. Tonight, though, we're finally breaking in.

Adraa and I perch on the edge of the neighboring roof, looking down at the huge arched building we've memorized by heart. Sweat beads behind my mask as a humid wind engulfs us.

To the north, over the mountains, lightning blazes in the sky. Thunder grumbles in the distance like a wild animal. But here, it's warm and dewy and I can't smell anything but sea salt. These are not the conditions we talked about.

"You still want to do this tonight?" I know what her answer will be, but I want to make sure, for posterity's sake.

"We *have* to do this."

"Okay, then, let's—"

Something sharp stabs between my shoulder blades. "Not a word. Not a spell," a harsh voice whispers.

Beside me another wizard holds a knife to Adraa's throat. My whole body tenses.

I straighten slowly, but my own assailant's knife digs deeper. After weeks of gathering information and watching the empty bazaar from this very spot and *now* we've been discovered? *Of all nights!*

"Hands up," the voice says. "Slowly."

I obey, toggling between Adraa's position and how fast I could cast. It doesn't look good. Too risky. For a full minute the four of us stand, silent.

We just stand there.

Adraa huffs. "This is getting awkward."

The wizard holding her presses his red knife into Adraa's throat and she hisses in pain.

"Hey! Don't—"

The knife cuts into me and I jerk. "I said, 'Not a word.'"

"I think it's protocol for you to give your demands, you know, eventually," Adraa says.

The way Adraa is talking, these aren't Vencrin.

"I was sent to bring you two in for questioning. So we—"

"That's not going to happen," Adraa says calmly.

And if not Vencrin, then that leaves only one other option. I just hope they are the good ones.

"It's orders from Maharaja Belwar himself," the man behind me says.

Adraa scoffs. "We aren't going anywhere."

"Then you are going to have to answer our questions here."

"No."

"Hey!" I yell.

"What?" our assailants both shout.

"Can I at least turn around during this conversation?" I ask.

261

"Uh, sure. Slowly." The pressure of the knife releases.

I turn, hands still raised, to find a boy around my age, straight hair, strong jaw, an orange kurta with the Belwar crest that looks a tad too big for him. No wonder Adraa isn't worried.

"First, you two are going to take off those masks," the boy demands.

I glance at Adraa, who is gesturing with her eyes toward the knife in the guard's hand. It's a real knife, steel and all, which means—

Still too risky with the purple magic at her throat. I shake my head slightly.

She rolls her eyes and gestures again. As if yelling at me with her eyes will make me gamble her life.

"Hey. Masks. Off. Now."

Movement breaks the stillness. The guard holding Adraa grunts. A loud thud echoes. *Blood.*

In one clean swipe, I smash the guard's wrist and the glimmer of silver snaps into black smoke. An illusion. Gods, I hate black fortes. A whip of black smoke lashes forward and I call to the wind, blowing space between us and tearing at his purple magic. For a second he looks at me, then his arms blaze and darkness coats his skin.

Adraa steps forward and mirrors his stance, red flames and all. Lightning cracks the sky and the three of us glow. I shift, letting magic well up my arms to pull his attention toward me in the hope we can still talk our way out of this. "Listen, we are not your enemy. We're trying to help."

"We don't need your help," the guard says.

I sigh. "I think you do. There are guards working for the Vencrin."

The guard tries to hide his surprise. He fails, his hurt visible. "That's not . . . they wouldn't. How do you know that?"

I pause long enough for the man to realize exactly how we might know.

"It was you, wasn't it, that night on the ship? That started all this mess?"

"Yes. Both of us," Adraa answers. "And a couple of those men were guards."

"We can handle that internally," the man rushes, still hopeful. "We'll find and question them. So stop this. Or better yet, join the Guard yourself when you are old enough."

"Are you even old enough?" I ask.

He glares at me.

"We can't do that," Adraa replies in a stiff voice. "This is more personal than a fight for justice or cleaning up the Guard for you."

He steps toward her and the magic on my arms flares in warning.

He sighs. "Revenge, then? How typical. If the Vencrin have done something to you, then report it and we can—"

I interrupt, not liking the way he's looking at Adraa. Like she's the easier target in this exchange. Is he trying to get himself killed? "Sorry, you seem like one of the good ones, but I think the problem might be bigger than the Vencrin, and if we're right, the Guard can't do anything."

"Bigger than the Vencrin? Is there another player involved?"

I can tell Adraa is done with this conversation and so am I. "That's what we are trying to figure out," I say. "We are trying to get proof."

"Proof?"

I point down to the building. "That's one of the warehouses where they store the drugs. Like we said, proof."

The boy stares at both of us, and then at the den below. "You are up here in masks trying to *stop* the drugs? You two are just bloodthirsty do-gooders?"

I frown. "We aren't exactly bloodthirsty."

"Yes," Adraa says at the same time.

"Ah, I can't believe I'm doing this." He sighs and rubs his neck. "You've got fifteen minutes and then we are going in. And if we catch you . . ."

"We know," I say as I unbuckle my skyglider. "This won't be the end of our questioning."

◇ ◇ ◇

"Is your neck okay?" I ask Adraa once we are out of earshot.

"I know that guard," she whispers as we descend upon the drug den.

"Who was he?"

"Lady Prisha's head guard. His name is Hiren."

The name rings in my ears. Her sister's guard. "So he's one of the good ones?"

"Gods, I hope so. Because if he isn't and I find out—"

"He seemed genuine," I try to reassure her. Though it irks

me how willing they were to hurt her. It feels good under the mask, but it's a jolting reminder to know that without my name or title I'm . . . vulnerable. We both are.

"Yeah, and upset about the traitors."

We drop to the roof and our conversation transfers to hand signals as we target the arched window we've been watching for days.

"*Vrnotwodahs*," I cast, and we wait for the next bolt of lightning. After it splinters across the sky I slide to the lip of the roof, complete a dangle-and-swing movement, and land on the thick stone windowsill. Adraa follows right after, and I grab her waist to steady her landing. I smile at her in my arms, but she rolls her eyes and crouches in the shadows I've crafted. I refocus, trying not to think about the warmth in my hands.

Below us everything looks abandoned. Empty stalls, broken crates, and wicker boxes fill the chasm of space. Deserted trading bazaars don't get pretty makeovers. A few wizards walk underneath us and we lean back.

"Okay, they've passed. Do your thing," I whisper.

"*Vindati Agni Dipika*," she casts. Little rivulets of red fall from her fingers and descend upon the open warehouse. Then she waits, head tilted. I don't want to distract her, but after two solid minutes I'm curious. "Can you sense it?"

"Yes, but it's faint. I—I don't know."

"Then we go with plan B."

With a nod, we climb down the wall, finding handholds in the intricate designs carved into the stone. We drop onto the top of old trading stalls, me to the right, Adraa to the left.

A Vencrin stands ahead of us and I slink up behind him. With my hand over his mouth I cast a sleep spell and my magic dives off my fingers. The jolt of struggle sags instantly and I catch him from thumping onto the dirt. Along the other wall two more Vencrin walk down the aisle—my next targets.

Every few moments I spot Adraa's shadow gliding along the walls, silently taking down anyone who could alert the other Vencrin. One by one the stragglers fall. I throw a discarded curtain over one of the last wizards when a *thunk* echoes behind me, and a spell veers over my shoulder. The wood overhead cracks and falls. I turn to find Adraa standing over a witch's body. "You need to watch your back!"

"But you're doing such a good job."

"Come on. They probably heard that."

We run toward the wicker crates. As Adraa cracks open the first one, muffled voices swarm around the corner. Five wizards spill into view. Adraa and I spin to meet them.

"Rings," I whisper.

Adraa nods. "Rings."

With a yell, our two groups collide. A blue stream of water fires first and I fall back, knocking it away with half a shield, and it drenches the floor. Adraa breaks through their line and smashes a wizard in the face. Blood flies. It's chaos, but this time we aren't dodging through the streets. Spells hit walls, wooden stalls crash to the ground, and draped fabric ignites.

I lean and twist as an array of black spears fly toward me. One snags my kurta. Adraa has moved on to her second Vencrin and they're dueling with lashes of wind. My next spell nails the spear thrower and I run forward. A wizard takes a punch to the gut with a strength spell and the wind weaver falls. Adraa's foot presses his throat as she yells questions.

I grab the nearest wizard by the collar. "Tell me about the firelight!" I shout into his face. "Where are you keeping it?"

The wizard panics and I watch his eyes to see whether he'll give up a location with a flick of nerves. Instead he smiles, the grin splashing across his face in such an unsettling way the back of my neck prickles. Then I place the oddness of the expression. He's smiling not at *me*, but at something behind me. . . .

That's when I turn.

"Red!"

A fireball hurtles toward Adraa. I drop the wizard and cast, calling to the water already on the ground. I'm not fast enough.

Adraa turns and, with hands outstretched and flaming red, grasps the projectile. It's too much. She flies backward and into a ruined stall. Wood cracks apart and the fire roars. *No!*

I run through the gaping hole, jumping over splintered beams and sloshing through the water I sent after her. Three aisles over, in the rubble of wood and silk, smoke slinks through the air. No fire.

"Red? Red!"

Shuffling wood off herself, Adraa steps out from the plumes of dust. The glow of her magic still dances through her Touch, her sleeve burned away. Ash dusts her red mask; her hair spirals loose from her braid. But she's standing. "No one respects fire anymore. It's all 'throw it as big and hard as you can without thinking of the consequences,'" she says, shoving more planks of wood away.

I grab her into a hug, laughing. *Thank Gods!*

She pushes at my chest. "Night."

I turn. As the smoke disperses to reveal the thin barrier I threw up, a gaggle of wizards greets us on the other side. We miscalculated how many Vencrin there are here, because we're surrounded. They all wear heavy black or gray kurtas, thick boots, and arrogant smiles. Some fake-lunge and create big purple magic weapons to intimidate us. One wizard in front even lets his sword grow to the point where it clanks to the ground, and he frantically tries to pick it up.

"Tell us where you are selling the firelight and no one gets hurt!" Adraa shouts. The wizards cackle as they do the math. Forty, maybe fifty, against two. It doesn't matter if a few are dense. The odds are bloody awful and we all know it.

Adraa's arms blaze. "Do you have a plan?" she whispers.

I settle into a fighting stance. "We don't let them get close."

Crash!

Everyone flinches as glass cascades around us, each window breaking as a flier swoops in, donning the Belwar nine-pointed sun on their chest. I've never been so thankful to see a wizard who not minutes ago held a knife at my back.

CHAPTER TWENTY-FOUR

◇

I Fall

Adraa

Guess our fifteen minutes must be up, and good thing too. As a forest of nets and binding spells rain down on the gruesome horde before us, Kalyan and I punch our way through what moments before was an impenetrable circle.

"Cover me!" I yell as I run to the unopened wicker crates. Kalyan's arms blaze to white and his deep voice shouts as he faces the Vencrin who aren't running or fastened to the floor. I rip at the wicker fibers of two crates and they fray in my hands. Packets of Bloodlurst stare into my face. But no firelight.

"It's just Bloodlurst, crate after crate of Bloodlurst."

"We don't have much time, Red!" Kalyan shouts as he heaves a Vencrin over his shoulder and lets him crash to the floor.

"Blood. It should be here. I can feel it." But maybe the pulsing faintness I had felt earlier only means it was once here, once sat in these crates until it was shipped to Moolek or Gods know where. I need to question someone. I had almost broken that guy before the shooting fireball.

I gaze around at the havoc surrounding me. Balls of light and smoke stream through the air. Bodies are scattered on the ground. No one would talk to us before, when they had the numbers on their side. But maybe now . . .

Out of the corner of my eye, a black cloak flutters toward a window. And I know that cloak. I memorized that back. *Here? He's here?*

"Night!"

Kalyan whips up toward the sound of my call, white arms blazing.

"The leader." I point.

Kalyan's eyes widen as understanding hits.

"He's getting away. We'll leave the rest to the Guard. *Tvarenni!*" I shout, running toward the stairs. Kalyan follows.

When I hit the landing it's empty. I step up to the window, infusing Hubris the Second with magic, and then veer back. There isn't a balcony, only shards of broken glass and a sense of dread pooling in my gut. A crack of lightning illuminates the cloaked flier in the distance. He must have just . . . fallen.

Kalyan stretches to peer at the cracked remnants of the building as I gather some distance.

No second thoughts. If that wizard did it from this height, so can I.

"What are—? No! Red, don't." Kalyan reaches for me, but I've already pushed off. I'm already falling. A low curse follows.

"*Makria!*" I scream into Hubris. Red sprouts from my hands and into the skyglider, but even as I push Hubris beneath me, I don't feel the cushion of weightlessness. All that's left is fear, gravity, and the mad flapping of my kurta against my skin. Wind pounds in my ears. I spiral. *No. I'm—I can't.*

Fear of the fall brings you closer to the ground! Mr. Burman's voice bellows in my head. I must level out. *Whoosh.* The roof of a one-story house zooms by. *Blood. Blood. Blood.*

Fear of the fall—

I have one chance. With a yell, I squeeze Hubris with my thighs and thrust my hands downward, pelleting wind at the ground. Gusts of air ripple and dirt blusters into my face, and I'm . . . flying. The cushion of levitation has never felt so magical. I cough out relief and choke on fear in the same breath.

Above me a magic-infused skyglider glows white. Kalyan followed me. *And he got control of his skyglider much faster than—*

He skids to a stop beside me. "Do you have a death wish?"

I gulp for a few seconds, staring at the wind-rippled ground.

"I thought I was about to watch you die," he says.

I allow myself to glance over and regret it as soon as I read his expression. Anger, worry, alarm, they each find their own feature to weave in the pain I've caused. And that's with his mask on. "I'm fine," I sputter.

He snaps to one emotion—sadness. "Smoke—"

"He flew that way." I pour speed into Hubris and shoot forward. We've lost enough time as it is. And this is why my "nothing more" should be sustained. We can't care about each other like that. Trust. Rings. Nothing more.

Kalyan and I skim the rooftops, hovering between cover and the visibility necessary to find our target. He shoots me looks every few seconds. I feel his eyes, his concern. But I'm fine. I had it under control. Maybe.

For a few minutes I think we've lost our target, even with both of us casting sensory spells to heighten our sight and smell, even with our added speed.

Suddenly, a blaze of purple magic zooms in our direction. Kalyan and I veer in opposite directions. But it's not an arrow or another projectile; it's a hiss of smoke that whirls into letters, and writes a clear message in the space between us.

Stop or you both shall die.

My throat tightens. The wicker crates upon wicker crates of drugs in that warehouse pound to the surface of my mind with each heartbeat.

"He's trying to keep his identity hidden," Kalyan whispers.

"What?"

"He's afraid."

Before either of us can move, arrows soak the night sky in color. Kalyan shouts a warning, but I'm already swerving. Yelps and hollers of a fight surround us. The black-cloaked leader is no longer alone. Vencrin, a whole pack, rise from the streets of the East Village. Gods, where did these wizards come from?

Spells race through the air. I'm reduced to a bundle of instincts. Any flash of color and I jerk, dodge, and shield myself. Orange spears spiral toward me, and I duck. A red chain tries to ensnare Hubris, and I dip and twist. Block after block, the intricate alleyways of the East Village blur into peaked pillars, flat rooftops, and fluttering-curtained doorways.

Any and all possible backup are still fighting in the trading bazaar. Convenient timing on the Vencrins' part or stupidity on mine?

I'm shooting spells off behind me erratically, when a Vencrin darts from the street ahead. I swivel in a new direction. I can't even keep track of how many there are. Another Vencrin bursts into wild laughter as he shoots a boulder of purple magic at my face. Blood. I duck, and in a loud burst the spell hits the building over my left shoulder. An archway crumbles, mosaic tiles shatter, and dust plumes.

Kalyan flies in front of me with a shield and a spell aimed for the boulder thrower.

"We have to get out of here!" he shouts as both of us dodge streams of green and yellow curses. We zoom forward, one shielding as the other fires. Forget our ring strategy. This is speed and power and reflex smashing my heart into pieces. And I need Kalyan right next to me. Hubris is slick with sweat and I'm shaking. Finally, one spell hits a Vencrin in the chest and he falls with a soundless scream.

"Enough!" a voice roars. The horde halts and slowly the cloaked figure drops from above, hood pulled tight. Kalyan was right. He's hiding his identity.

I catch my breath, hovering in our standstill, and count. Fourteen.

"Tell us where the firelight is!" I yell.

He laughs and the black cloak shifts unnaturally. "It's all around us, girl." Out of the corner of my eye, my light glows awake in a nearby window.

"Why have you stolen it? What do you want?"

"Maybe I want rebellion. Maybe I want to turn a profit. Maybe you have no idea what you are talking about." He snorts. "I don't have to answer to masked children, especially ones I properly warned."

His skyglider wavers and finally I place why his cloak doesn't fall right. Why more than half of these wizards are hooded and shrouded in black. Why that wizard didn't scream.

"And I don't answer to illusions." Before I can even release a spell, the hooded figure puffs into smoke. *"Agnierif!"* I call to my goddess. Without hesitation an eruption of flames bursts into the air. The flesh-and-blood Vencrin shout and veer back as the bloodred fire roars through the alleyway. The others, the illusions, swoop, and when touched by flame they billow into smoke. Serious and complex black magic.

With a hiss, spikes of purple magic slice through the fire. Blood. I jerk, but Kalyan reacts faster. He pushes at my shoulder and I barrel to the left. As I right myself, the streaks of purple breeze past, their potential danger sizzling along my arm. I look to Kalyan to exchange a sigh of relief. But I'm greeted with more purple arrows. Impossibly more, coming from another alleyway. It's a trap. This whole thing was a trap. Kalyan tries to move, to avoid the net they have caught us in. One, two, three bolts slash through the trail of magic glowing from the end of Kalyan's skyglider. Number four hits his side. He cringes and slumps.

I see blood.

And Kalyan falls.

"No!" My body responds before I even think of twisting or diving. But I'm doing both, wind screaming against my face as I plummet. Hubris digs into my chest. My heart hammers against wood. Kalyan's wide eyes find mine. We both reach out, our fingers stretching, shoulders straining. Our fingertips knock against one another, but I can't grasp his. *Come on, come on!*

A clap of contact. His hand grips my wrist. I yell as I pull against momentum and gravity. Wisps of red magic slide down my arm and wrap around his. Strengthening. Supporting.

Too late.

We tumble against a roof a second later. His skyglider splinters and snaps. The sound of pottery smashing and wood cracking erupts in a flare of noise. I tuck in naturally, but the roof cuts me open. Each clay shell tile bites into my arms, my shoulders, my legs. I roll three, four times and then, finally, stillness.

Lightning fractures the sky once again and flashes against my eyelids.

◇ ◇ ◇

Groaning, I rise and search for Kalyan amid the strikes of lightning. One: a crater of shingles. Two: the shards of our skygliders. Three: his slumped body.

I open my mouth to call to him, but the whoosh and orange tail of a skyglider from above distracts me. *He will keep hunting us.* On instinct I cast out a sheet of black magic, whirling my hands in broad, clumsy strokes. A screen of red filters off my fingers, painting a picture of our mangled forms. An illusion glides close. Now, not having to convince anyone of its false humanity, the shadow creature wears a blank face, smoke unfurling at the edges. It looks as if it seeped out of a corpse.

It glides even closer. I freeze. If one curl of smoke, one tendril, touches the red wall, it will break my illusion. The thing sniffs.

"*Mrtywodahsssss,*" I breathe, elongating the spell for death until my illusion rises, bubbles. I'm adding an extra layer, splashing the smell of blood and decay into the creature's gnarled face before it breaks my original screen. The thing shudders and in a whoosh, it flies off. That's right: go tell your boss of our demise.

I slump backward, rasping in hiccupping panic. *Kalyan!* My whole body aches and whines, but I crawl toward him.

"Kalyan? Kalyan?"

He's not moving.

I feel for a pulse. "Kalyan!"

"Ah, that sucked," he wheezes.

I gurgle between laugher and a sob as I throw my arms around him. We're alive. We're bloody alive.

"Ow!"

Snapping back, I zero in on the hand holding his side, and the blood pumping between his fingers. "Gods, let me see."

Kalyan pulls his hand away to reveal a slash along his ribs, sternum to stomach. "Does it look as bad as it feels?" he asks.

"No. It probably feels worse."

Kalyan slouches with a wince. "Yeah, I'm going to agree with you on that."

"Just hold on." I tear at his kurta, ripping the cloth and exposing the wound.

"We've talked about undressing me like this, Smoke."

I keep tearing. "Have I told you you're one of my worst patients?"

"But the best partner?"

I smile at his banter. It's a good sign. I search on my belt, open a small orb jar, and smear the pink numbing lotion amid the blood. *"Ksatleah. Suptaleah."* My magic glows to life and plunges into Kalyan's skin. "This is going to take some time."

"I'm not going anywhere." Kalyan falls back and I hover over him, casting, numbing, trying. There is so much blood. Too much blood. But I've seen worse.

After twenty minutes of tedious work, the sky opens upon us and dumps the rain it has been savoring. Each drop breaks open my weakening illusion spell as I focus only on healing. My whole body stings with the water's contact, every cut yearning for attention. My shoulder throbs. The side of my head pounds. There are two massive tears in my flying pants. Within seconds my clothes are both tattered and adhered to my skin. "Blood."

Kalyan casts under his breath and a white halo instantly surrounds us. Raindrops swerve.

"You need to save your energy," I say.

"You need to see."

I can't argue there.

Kalyan stares off into the distance. "You should have kept following him. He'll be impossible to trace now."

"Like I would have just watched you die."

He stares at me, another understanding lining my words. "Careful, Smoke, or I'm going to start thinking you like me."

"You don't make it easy, that's for sure." *Could there be a more blatant lie?*

He reaches out and touches the side of my head and I freeze. "You're bleeding," he whispers, concern lacing his voice.

Raising my hand I feel the wetness, the sting, the throbbing I finally clue into. Gods, I feel awful. But having someone in front of me that needs my help dulls the hurt. "I'm fine."

He frowns. "That's what you said earlier."

"I'm fine," I reiterate. It's bad protocol for patients to think the healer is losing it or doubting themselves.

"You can tell me," he whispers. "We're a team."

"We are a team. The best team." At that his hand drops away and his eyes close. It's only minutes later, but I finish sewing up the slash. It'll leave a brutal but clean scar surrounded by smaller cuts and blooming bruises. I clench my hand, a limp tingling sensation alerting me of my impending burnout. At least I closed his wound.

"Kalyan?"

He groans in answer and then falls silent. The water wall peters out, but the rain has stopped for the most part, only last-minute drops, slow to the party, sprinkling on us.

"Kalyan?"

No answer. I check his pulse and bend over his mouth. After a jolt of terror, his breath brushes my cheek. Unconscious, then, too much shock for his body or too many numbing spells from me. Thank Gods. If he had died . . .

I push his wet hair from his forehead. He looks kind, even asleep, even in pain. Catching myself smiling I snatch my hand back. Dear Gods, it's too late for me. I'm in love with him.

CHAPTER TWENTY-FIVE

Embarrassment Has Its Day

Adraa

I awaken damp, sore, and with the sun streaking into my face. I adjust, seeking warmth and curling into it. Then last night's events tumble into my memory. My eyes fly open to find Kalyan: half-naked, one arm around my middle, cuddling me to his side. I spring and flinch and start all at the same time. Shop owners and others hungry to start the day swamp the street below. Carts rattle, goats and sheep bleat, right below the roofline a customer haggles over the price of turmeric. *Oh my bloody—*

"Whoa, whoa, whoa, don't worry. I cast an illusion spell. People are seeing an empty, undestroyed roof," he says.

The smear of white smoke shimmers in front of us. "Oh," I manage.

Kalyan tries to rise, but cringes and hisses through his teeth. "Oh blood. Yeah, that hurts."

"Careful or you'll rip it open." My hands immediately go to his side and then realize how intimate . . . I mean, I tore his kurta open last night. And the other realizations from last night fog my brain. I feel like I've been drenched with heat and awkwardness. Or maybe that's the burnout.

I whip my hands back. "Do you mind if I . . ."

"Check the stitching that saved my life? By all means."

I peer at the scar, which is only a nasty stitched line now. It's as good as, if not better than, my mother's handiwork. Gods, how much magic did I pour into this? "It's not infected."

He stares at me and I wipe my face and pull back my hair. I'm probably beyond a mess. I wish he would look away and imagine me without the cuts, the bruises, and the sleep deprivation. "What?" I finally ask.

"Has anyone told you that you snore?"

My mouth drops open and my face ignites. "Do I?"

His eyes crinkle as he laughs. "Just a little."

"How long have you been awake?"

"A while."

"And you let me sleep on you?"

He shrugs. "You burned out."

"You're the one that . . . Wait, how do you know I burned out?"

"You get really hot when you burnout."

That means he felt my body, pressed against his. I look away, my face flaming.

"How you feeling?" he urges as if this isn't embarrassing. As if our act of passing out against each other is nothing unusual. As if I'm not engaged to his raja . . . *Oh Gods.*

I stare at my Touch to avoid his gaze. Red smoke lights up my fingertips. "I'm able to cast, but still pretty out of it."

"Yeah, and tomorrow you have to fight." He rubs his eyes.

"Blood." The Beckman fight. Twenty-nine days have slipped by as I shoved it to the back of my mind. Now, tomorrow, I'll be facing him. "I never want to see another cage caster."

"We just spent the night together and you don't want to see me again? That's rough, Smoke."

"We didn't spend the night together," I huff. But it feels like air is trapped in my chest—awkward, light, flustered.

He gestures to the rubble of shingles and the twigs of our skygliders. Hubris the Second didn't have a long life.

"Shut up."

He laughs. His side must not be that painful.

I stand and brush off the dust. "We're going to have to fix this roof."

"And I need to fix my kurta."

◇ ◇ ◇

After mending the roof and sewing his kurta with a flourish of green magic, we descend into the street. I need to get home, but I need something else first. Can't exactly sneak into my room without a skyglider. And I'm not walking through the palace doors looking like this or without Hubris. My parents aren't *that* busy.

It's an average market day, which means within seconds a swarm of colors and people ambush us. The younger generation of Belwarians wears flying pants, with bright kurtas for males, and blouses and wraparound skirts for females. Saris and vests are still in abundance among the older, more traditional crowds. After that it's a jumble, with Pire Island's heavier cloaks and duller coats, Agsa's pastel palette, and Naupure's clean lines and silks.

My burnout disengaged the swirls of purple barrier magic infused into my Red Woman uniform. Now, Kalyan and I both look like black fortes infatuated with their own color. I'm not saying we stick out like sore thumbs, but we should get out of here as soon as possible. Wanted posters line the shop stalls.

"We're going to need skygliders," Kalyan says.

"I know a guy."

He arches an eyebrow. "You *know* a guy?"

"What? You don't?" Having a good skyglider guy is one of the reasons I'm still alive. I mean, Hubris died because I splintered it into a thousand pieces and stabbed a Vencrin. Hubris the Second created enough resistance for us to survive last night's fall.

"I've had only three skygliders my entire life," Kalyan says.

I stop, actually halt in place. The streets keep churning with people alongside me, but I'm at a standstill. It takes a second for Kalyan to realize and swing around. "What?"

"Three skygliders? *Three.*" Maybe I misheard. He could have said thirteen or even thirty.

"Yeah, three. How many have you had?"

I flounder, but regain a scrap of composure and reengage with the flow of foot traffic. "Ah, a few more."

He eyes me. I've made a fatal error, I know because he starts grinning. "Smoke?" He elongates the vowel.

"We have actual important things to talk about. Like what we should be doing next."

"Yeah, and we can discuss that as soon as you answer this one question." He guides me to a stop in front of a silken fish stall. An Untouched vendor with a booming voice calls to us, thrusting scales and the pearly white flesh outward. "One pound one silver," he pitches.

Kalyan, like any practiced shopper, ignores him. "How many?"

"What are you willing to do for this information?"

His head tilts as if my embarrassing myself acts as proper currency in his book. "What do you want?"

So many things. For us to not have failed last night. For my fight with Beckman to not be tomorrow. For the world to give us more time. Give *me* more time.

I can't voice a single one.

"The skyglider shop I like is only a block away."

Mittal and Muni's is your typical skyglider extravaganza. Skygliders, condensed down to their stump form, dangle from wooden pegs. In the far left corner the walls bend and shoot upward for three stories like a hollowed-out tree trunk so customers can test out different skyglider designs.

I've been coming here for years. But memory pulls to a year ago, when Mr. Burman bought me Hubris the First. Before that I ran through skygliders recklessly, to an extent I refuse to admit to Kalyan. Mr. Burman had held the skyglider aloft and said, "We are going to name this one." It had done the trick. That is, until Riya's and my world caved in. So as bells chime at our entrance, the smell of freshly crafted wood and pangs of nostalgia hit me with full force.

"Say, if it isn't my best customer," Mr. Mittal announces. He calls me that—best customer—because he forgets my name, forgets everyone's name. He'd probably forget his partner Muni's name, if it weren't painted on the sign beside his. Sometimes I've wondered if it's an act or if that's why Mr. Burman took me here. Today, though, I'm just going to be grateful and for once not question his forgetfulness or make a sarcastic remark. He zips toward us, hovering on the skyglider he uses to be able to see over the countertops and glide to the vaulted ceiling and flying tower.

"Hey, Mr. Mittal." I bend and press my forearm to his. "I need another one. Actually, make that two." I jerk a thumb to include Kalyan.

"Already?" His eyes widen. Of course *this* he remembers all too well.

I peer at his fingers, three of them wooden. How can a wizard criticize me about crashing a skyglider when three weeks ago he had only *two* magic-infused wooden appendages? "Huh, what happened there?" I gesture.

"Ah yes." He flexes his hand and then stuffs it into his pocket. "We can all be clumsy at times. That's why you are my best customer."

I fake-laugh. "I appreciate the nonjudgmental attitude."

He slaps the counter in approval. "Right, so what's your weapon of choice?"

"The best you've got."

He mock frowns, jumps back on his skyglider, and whiz-zes three stories up the tower. "How vague. Have I taught you nothing?"

"Come on, Mittal!" I yell up the tunnel. "You're going to make me go through the whole elementary checklist?"

"If it helps you not lose another one of my babies." He pouts, swiveling between selections and inspecting different skygliders.

I sigh and roll my eyes. He's a feisty little seven-fingered man. But by the gods how I love this place.

I finally notice Kalyan examining the front display case, one hand pressed to his torso.

I'm by his side in two seconds flat. "Are you okay? Did it reopen?"

"I'm fine. Just sore." He glances at me. "And yes, I'm sure."

I guess my urge to inspect remains apparent. Kalyan even releases his hand like that's proof. For the record, that's never proof. The memory of him pushing me away flashes. Him falling. The blood.

What it would be like to choose *my own fiancé?* I know that can't happen. And I still can't bring myself to tell him the truth either. The moment he finds out who I am is the moment I lose my best chance of discovering what's happening with my fire-light and destroying the Vencrin.

But I already gave up the plan, and the surefire way to dis-cover those answers for him, didn't I?

"What would you do if you weren't a guard?" I whisper.

He slowly lowers his hand from the nearest skyglider. "No one has asked me that before."

"Really?" A guard has the ability to choose his or her destiny. Riya has talked about guarding since she was ten, and some Touched put all their energy into one type of magic to ensure their forte. It's a valued occupation, and because of its reputation and stability no one is forced into service. I'd think Kalyan has it easier than me, who's clutching onto lies like they're safety platforms.

"Yeah, no one. It was expected my whole life. Family business." He faces me. "What would you do if you didn't serve the Belwars?"

I'm silent for so long I'm sure he thinks I've ignored the question. And I almost do, but then the words spill out. "I didn't cast until after my ninth birthday. And it took me another year to be able to generate magic in my right arm as well. So flying was a big deal. But even now I wouldn't say I love flying. I love skygliders." I brush the silken fabric tail of Mittal and Muni's first creation, a very simple skyglider with no curved handholds or streamlined extension, but still so much craftsmanship. "In a simpler life I would be an inventor like Mittal, and maybe one day create something that can fly on its own for the Untouched, for those trapped on the ground."

Kalyan seems to absorb my words, to weigh them. "Maybe one day, after all this, I could help you with that."

My birthday is ten days away. So though my heart hurts to admit it, I doubt that will ever happen. Yet we stand in this shop as if the future is open and what-ifs can be purchased off the walls. Mittal and Muni's does that, makes you feel like with the right skyglider you can fly off and do anything.

"Okay!" Mittal yells, swooping through the air. "Dual-streamlined extension, wind curvature, Naupure's highest-quality silk, and braided porous sites for quick infusion." He brandishes the skyglider. "Or as I like to say, the best I've got."

It's a thing of beauty. Stained red wicker. Sleek lines. Etched in the braided fibers are Touch designs that I've learned mirror those on Mittal's own wrists. I hand Kalyan his skyglider. "Like it?"

"I'll let the expert decide," he concedes.

Mittal coos at this proclamation and whacks his fist against the countertop, thinking Kalyan means him. "I like this one."

And just like that, my haggling flutters out the window, but at least I get Mittal to throw in wood cleaner and two sets of bubble air masks for high flying. But the little man knows he got us good; I'll never live this down. Mr. Mittal even waves as we leave, wooden fingers knocking against one another.

Kalyan buckles the skyglider to his belt. "Don't think you've gotten away with it."

I look over. "What?"

He smirks, actually smirks. "How many, Smoke?"

I carry on, barreling through the crowd. "Gods, you're persistent."

"Come on." He steps in front of me, arms open in a shrug. "I did almost die for you last night."

"Ah, I'm never going to hear the end of that, am I?" I duck around him. "How about this, I tell you and we don't bring that up ever again?"

His boots crunch in the dirt behind me. "Just to clarify, do you mean the part where I threw myself in front of that arrow or the part where we slept together?"

My pulse jumps. I hold myself back from clapping a hand over his mouth, instead going for a casual wheel around to make sure no one heard. "We didn't sleep together," I whisper-yell. "And both. We never mention either of those things!" He's driven me to panic.

Kalyan whistles. "It must be even worse than I thought." He pretends to ponder before, "Deal."

I stop, the market bubbling with barter and gossip. A troop of monkeys skirt along rooftops, adding to the chatter. "Thirty-seven," I mumble.

He leans down, invading my space. "What was that?"

I fold my arms. There isn't a way out of this. "Counting today." I nod to Hubris the Third hanging from my belt. "It's thirty-seven," I annunciate. "Happy?"

He doesn't have to answer. He smiles and it's so blazingly joyful. There is something wrong with him if this measly piece of information makes him this pleased. And maybe myself for letting it infect me, too. "You never disappoint," he says through his smile.

Twenty minutes later, I'm sneaking into my room and falling into bed.

And I can't sleep.

You never disappoint. I don't fully believe him, of course, but still—I don't disappoint. The females populating the kitchen would say Jatin's fake love letters that jabbered on about destiny would be considered more romantic than that statement. But for someone who feels like a disappointment and is struggling to never do so again? Kalyan's words produce . . . comfort.

I grab a pillow and yell into it. This is wrong. All wrong. My birthday approaches like a wild storm. I fight Beckman tomorrow. And I'm in love with a man I have no right to be in love with. Everything seems to be teetering on an edge and about to crush me. Yet, I still fall asleep imagining the warmth of my blanket comes from a different source.

CHAPTER TWENTY-SIX

◇

The Showdown of Champions

Adraa

Sims may be a sleazy Vencrin abettor, but he sure knows how to market a fight. Slogans such as RISING FIRE AGAINST THE IN-SURMOUNTABLE MONSOON pepper the walls in fake blood splatter. Black magic illusions of Beckman and me trying to rip each other apart artfully dazzle the crowd in anticipation. It shakes me to the bones, but it's impressive all the same.

One foot settled into the stench of the Underground, and Kalyan and I are already surrounded. Voices question my mental state, how I plan to win against the biggest fighter in cage-casting history. Kalyan, after that *one* fight, has risen through the ranks at the Underground, a personal favorite with witch viewers. Or at least with the few we have. Several female figures lob their support for the White Knight. Kalyan only frowns and points to the board, showing them he's obviously not on the roster. It's nice to pinpoint jealousy in the swarm of other emotions swallowing me. But once I shrug it aside, three other emotions wreaking havoc with my body demand attention. Fear clouds. Anxiety swirls. Anger bites.

I can't take it anymore. With a wave of my hand, I swerve through the mirth and retreat to the locker room. Normally, I would be happy to have a fan base because that means I'm more valuable to Sims. And more valuable to Sims means I can get more intel. But tonight? Tonight irritation and fear grip me like a second skin. Most of these wizards and witches have no idea what kind of operation they fund when they gamble here. These same people buy my firelight and pay taxes. Also, like me, they have no idea what kind of man Beckman truly is.

I shove the door to my room open and it slams against the wall. Sonna, a fellow female fighter, sits on the bench, meditating. One eye pops open as I enter.

"Hey, Smoke. Still dealing with those anger issues, I see."

"Hey, Mist." I follow her gaze to the dent in the door. "That wasn't me. This time . . ."

She laughs lightly and closes her eyes again. Blue smoke rises and falls from her arms like they're breathing.

The door opens again and Kalyan enters. He nods to Sonna, then turns to me. "Hey. Why did you leave?"

"Just wanted to get . . . settled."

He shakes his head. "I'm sorry. You shouldn't have to do this. It's not too late to back out. Maybe you should."

We stare at each other. "I can't." I miss this fight and Sims will hunt me down personally. I just have to get through it and not die.

"Could you two look at each other somewhere else? And

you do know this is the women's locker room, right?" Sonna snaps.

Kalyan looks left and right for a second, placing himself. "Oh, right. I'll be on the upper deck." He squeezes my hand and leaves.

I turn to find Sonna watching me. "You guys really are the perfect couple. He's powerful and you're pretty," she says.

"What?" I stare at her. "First, we aren't a couple. And second, I'm powerful too. Shouldn't that be why we're good together? I mean, we aren't even a couple, but if we were I would contribute more than just being pretty—"

"Jaya, I was talking about your personae. Smoke is alluring and sexy; White Knight is the powerful hero. Sims set it up like that, right? All that heteronormative crap."

"Oh . . . yeah, sure. Smoke and White Knight work . . . for the audience."

"Huh, so you do have a thing for him, then."

"No, I, ah, didn't understand what you meant when—"

Sonna laughs, a nice light laugh if it weren't aimed at me. "That bad, huh? Well, I wish you luck. Cage casters have the worst egos."

"I've got to get going."

"Good luck out there, kid." Her expression says the unspoken: *you'll need it.*

"Thanks, you too." It seems wrong to endorse Sonna's pounding Navin, but for cage casters that constitutes bonding.

As I push past the second curtain the roar of the crowd hits me. Cheers, sweat, the sloppy drunkenness all vibrate through the floorboards. "Smoke, Smoke, Smoke."

292

As I walk toward the ring, my memory flashes to Rakesh on the upper dock. His sticky, ugly words. His hands. His implication that I could not win, that I could not overpower him. The grip on my arm until Beckman had helped throw him off. Beckman had been there ever after. And then I had put on a mask, painted myself in an illusion of confidence until it seeped into my bones.

Beckman waits in the dome and I step inside to meet him. *Why did I let this happen? Why did he have to be working for them?*

"I don't want to do this, Smoke," Beckman groans as he bends his knees into a fighting position.

"Yeah, me either." The dome latches above with a thunk. For the first time in the ring I'm not angry. Fear lines my stomach and squeezes. Confidence leaves me on each exhale. Before, I could always envision my opponent as one of the men who hurt Riya's father. Now all I see is a father and my friend. Who tends to Beckman's injuries after a fight? Surely not one of his daughters . . .

I've seen his family. His youngest girl is obsessed with pigtails and rainbow ribbons that bounce along her back. Most little girls like rainbow-colored material before their Touch or forte presents itself. Riya loved to wrap them around her wrists and pretend she could cast all nine colors with me. And I'm supposed to label a man like Beckman a traitor.

I'm thinking about Riya too much because suddenly I see her, envision her in the crowd. She scowls like I know she would if she ever saw me in the Underground, bleeding and in pain for the amusement of criminals. I stare harder and the faces blur.

"Are you ready for the showdown of champions?" the announcer roars. The crowd responds in kind.

A cloud of blue smoke wafts above Beckman like a wave. *Focus, Adraa! Riya isn't here.* I conjure up my own magic and it swarms and lashes to look like fire.

The crowd cheers as blue and red streams blend into purple in the middle of the ring. The announcer drums up Sims's marketing material. I catch a joke about my height and stature even though I'm tall for a witch. Another about this being the show of a lifetime, about Tsunami dousing my flames. And yes, it leans hard on sexual innuendo. I tune it all out, awaiting one word, one sound.

"Fight!" the announcer yells.

Beckman leaps forward, a long staff in hand, one of his trademarks. I duck under his swing. Blood, really? Bringing out the staff first thing? Well, best to fight purple magic with purple magic. I create my own staff. But I'm not great at staff fighting, never been trained much. So when the rod slams into my stomach I'm unable to breathe, but not surprised. As I drop to the ground, Beckman rallies the crowd, and they answer.

"What are you doing? Get up," Beckman whispers as he turns back toward me.

"I don't want—" *I don't know how to fight him.* I don't even know how to think past the confusion and betrayal.

"In here, you don't get a say in what you want." Beckman bends over me and the staff presses down on my throat. I kick out in alarm, casting a strength spell. But then I realize I don't need it. To the audience it must look like he's killing me, but the pressure isn't full force. He leans in closer. "Fight me or both our covers are blown."

"You . . ."

"I was hired to protect you and I will not harm my future rani, but you have to make this look good."

For a second I let go of his staff and it presses on my throat. I feel like all the air inside me is gone. I feel like I'm going to pass out.

Doesn't want to hurt his future . . .

"Smoke," he whispers urgently.

First Kalyan and now this. Maharaja Naupure hired Beckman to protect me.

"Adraa."

I whip my eyes to his and the truth is embedded there. The truth and the lies.

"Puti Pavria!" I shout as loud and with as much intention as I can. My magic blasts from under the staff and a wind tunnel shoots up and out. Beckman goes along for the ride, straight to the top of dome, where I keep him plastered. *I'll pretend. I'll more than pretend!* With a twist of my hand, I release the air and Beckman thuds to the ground. I rush to him.

"I saw you at the Vencrin warehouse. Why were you there?" I hiss when I get close.

"To protect you."

What? "I don't need your protection."

He slams his elbow into my side, and I crumple backward. "Yes. You do."

I whirl and punch. He blocks. "Why should I trust anything you say?"

He slips around me, pulling my arm into a lock. "Because. I know everything and you are still alive."

I shake my head.

"Think, Smoke," he whispers in my ear. "How else do you think you fooled Sims all this time? Why do you think Belwar guards were there the very night you decide to raid?" He pushes me away and I stumble.

I twist back. "And the posters?" I ask as we circle one another. "You were the first I saw with them."

"Trying to get ahead of them, to stop production. I was too late."

Do I believe this? My gut says yes, but anger seethes. "I could have done this on my own. I didn't need—"

A volley of water catches my foot and jerks upward. With an echoing thump to the tune of the crowd screaming "Tsunami!" I land on my back. "Yes. You did," he says.

I jump up, flying with fury. The moment on the upper dock crashes into me again. Rakesh's strong grip on my arm. Beckman tearing him off me. The fear. No, the terror. And now, I don't know what's worse, the thought I was only saved because of my title or the knowledge that I'm a girl who's accomplished nothing. Vencrin still fill the streets. Drugs still flow right outside this arena. And I don't have any clue where my firelight is being taken.

Rage surges. Something snaps. They thought I needed protecting. They thought I couldn't do it.

"If you were truly here to help, then why didn't you?" I ask, pain choking the syllables. Swords materialize in a blazing swirl of red. I whack away at my fury and the colors converge in purple sparks between us.

"I had a mission," Beckman growls.

"As do I."

Swish, a scream of speed. Parry, a clang. Retreating, fast feet kicking out. Beckman dodging, punching. The crowd soaking up my fear and violence. Pretend. A show. Our entire friendship fraying in a smash of purple smoke. With a twist I slash, and it hits its mark, right across Beckman's chest. A streak of blood spatters the dome wall.

No. He was supposed to parry that, guard himself. He was supposed to . . .

For he is better than I am. I, who couldn't think for the pivotal seconds when Rakesh latched on and pushed me to the ground. I, who have failed for weeks. Victim. Attacker. Savior. Vencrin. The roles mush, bleeding together as I focus on the blood.

I stall, cast in stone, as Beckman fumbles. *No!* I reach out, not noticing the blue stream rushing toward me until *thud*, it pounds into my chest. For a second, time stops as pain erupts through me. Then I fly against the wall and my head flips back, slamming into it. My vision blurs and black dots float in front of Beckman as he steps forward, fear framing his face. I try to get up, but the black takes over.

◇ ◇ ◇

For the second time in the past day I awaken to the warmth of Kalyan. This time, he stands over me, and with a start, I realize the warmth comes from his pink magic, his white smoking hands holding my head. He chants. A stabilizing spell. Kalyan is performing a stabilizing spell.

"Hey," I whisper, clutching his wrist.

"Oh thank Gods."

Reaching for the pain in the back of my head, I rise to the familiar benches, dust, and body odor of the locker room. I'm weightless and heavy with fog at the same time.

"Is Beckman—"

"He's fine. Already gone. But he explained everything. He's not—"

"I know. I—" I stop, seeing we are not alone. Behind Kalyan stands my best friend. So, I did see her in the crowd; that frown was real. "Riya?" I shout a bit too loudly.

She sighs. "Gods, I'm glad you are awake."

"How . . . how did you find me?"

She stares Kalyan down. "I need to talk to her. Alone."

Kalyan gives me a look of concern. He doesn't want to go as much as I don't want him to. But when I nod, he raises the curtain and I'm left to explain myself.

Riya doesn't waste time. "You're the Red Woman, aren't you?"

The air in the room shifts. The thunder of noise from the Underground falls away. I consider lying for only a second. "Yes."

She exhales slowly. "How . . . how could you do this, lie to me, go off by yourself?"

"I'm not doing this alone." No need to tell her for months I was unaided in the Underground, beating up Vencrin and spying on how they worked, before Kalyan joined. Though I guess I had Beckman watching my back this whole time as well.

"Oh, not alone? I forgot. The Red Woman and Night. What do you even know about him?" Riya spits as she gestures to the curtain.

"What do you mean, what do I know? He's helped me." Helped me more than she can even imagine. And not because I'm Adraa Belwar, and definitely not because someone gave him a mission like Beckman's.

"He's *lying* to you. He's not who he says he is."

"What?" *Where the blood did that come from?*

"Have you seen his arms or the way he casts? I don't think he is what he says."

No. I can't let her debase the one person who fought alongside me without a hidden agenda or mission. "What are you even—"

"Because if you let me for one bloody minute, I *would* be good at my job. I could protect you. But no, you have to run off and save the world behind smoke and masks."

"I did this because of you, for you."

"Because of me?" A fresh dose of anger streams into her voice. "Oh, this is going to be good."

"I'm trying to find the men, the ones who hurt your dad, Riya."

Her expression falls. Whatever she thought my explanation was going to be, this isn't it. "Then who was it? What are their names?"

"After I started to investigate I realized how big this whole

299

thing was. I focused on the drugs and then firelight was being taken off the market and—"

She scoffs. "Don't pretend you did this for my father, then. Don't you dare do that!"

"I'm sorry. I'm so sorry. But all this is bigger than you or me or your father. It's about Belwar's entire future." When she swings away, I tug at her arm. "Riya, I think it's Maharaja Moolek. I have reason to believe he has corrupted our guards and is taking my firelight. I think your father, our teacher, was one of the first they silenced."

She jerks as if I've sucked out all the air in the room. "Maharaja Moolek? Adraa, that's why I'm here."

"What?"

"You were summoned to the throne room. Zara and I searched and searched and we couldn't find you, and then—" Her words spin faster until I think even she realizes they are out of control. And my best friend is never out of control. She pauses and I finally take in the strands of black hair falling from her bun, her wraparound skirt askew.

I lunge forward, dread filling me. "Riya, tell me, what has Maharaja Moolek done?"

"Nothing," she breathes. "But he wants to talk to you. Personally."

◇ ◇ ◇

I burst into the palace. I left Kalyan with a fumbling apology and only a sentence of information, which resembled an excuse more than an explanation. Gods, how I wish he could be next to me opening this door, though. On the way over I cleaned myself up and threw on garments worthy of the Belwar name, but you can't clean up shock like you can a bloodstain. It overwhelms my face. I might as well go in there with my red mask on with as much as my parents will be able to piece together.

But that doesn't matter so much as what in Wickery am I going to say to Moolek? Or, more important, what he has to say to me?

As I enter the throne room three heads turn in my direction. My parents look worried and annoyed. The third is a bulky man doused in green-bejeweled garments. His skin is light brown, lighter than even some of the Moolek rajas' I have met. He's strikingly handsome. Built like a palace, with a tall straight spine, layers of muscle, and adorned with decorations. But his eyes—they're watchful, predatory, the goose bumps up my arms yell. He's almost exactly how I imagined. And I don't think I've ever been so terrified.

A dark-green table has been crafted in the middle of the room, with chairs and a tablecloth that glows with the intricate designs of a Touch, overlapping swirls, branching crisscrossed lines, and pebbled dots. He has literally mapped out his blessing into the purple magic so we can witness it shine in the firelight that burns around us.

"I'm glad you were finally able to join us, Lady Adraa." He constructs another chair and gestures for me to take it.

I bow, placing two fingers on my neck. Never before have I

felt nauseated giving my respects. "It is a pleasure," I say, the lie dripping with pretend sincerity. Then I sit, perched on my enemy's magic, knowing at any moment he could break the spell. As if I hadn't already felt like I was walking into a trap.

"Yes, a pleasure. You are as stunning as everyone says." His eyes flip between my parents and me, and a smile I'm sure many would label as charming beams at the three of us in turn.

The retort *I know* comes to mind, as does Maharaja Naupure's laugh way back then. But I am no longer eight and I don't want this man knowing my true nature, the rebellious streak conjuring up questions and suspicion. "Thank you," I say, my face surely blanketed in disdain.

"Now that we are all here, I'll get straight to the point. I want to talk to you about an alliance."

We all pause at this word as if Maharaja Moolek has said something disgusting. But, well . . .

"What kind of alliance?" my mother says slowly.

"I find the best alliances are those made of blood, through marriage."

My heart thumps hard in my chest, as if it just woke up and must climb Mount Gandhak in one bound.

"I don't understand, Maharaja Moolek. You don't have a son, so I'm unsure what you are proposing."

But I understand. I understand *too* well. I recoil, wanting to be wrong. The next words come, though, unstoppable.

"I'm talking about between Adraa and myself, of course."

He bloody just said it. I lurch up from the chair and take a big step back, hoping that with it I can walk out of the room, rewind time, anything to retract the notion I would marry Maharaja Moolek, a forty-year-old manipulative creature of a wizard. The very man who might be fueling or funding firelight's disappearance.

"But you are correct," he continues as he, too, stands. "I do *not* have any sons. . . ." He smiles at me, his teeth bearing the word *yet* on his canines.

Blood! This cannot be happening. I glance at my father, trying to scream the word *dusk* with only my eyes. My parents rise.

"Our daughter has been arranged to your nephew, Jatin Naupure, for many years," my father says.

"And yet there has been no blood contract, not even a formal engagement meeting."

"Maharaja Naupure has been away, as you well know, and Adraa is not yet eighteen."

"Of course. Of course." Maharaja Moolek's eyes pierce me. "But I think we should give Adraa a choice in the matter, don't you?"

This is what I got wrong when I was eight and forced to climb a mountain. My parents want to grant me freedom, to fight for it. It was never blood contracts, marry Jatin or else. It was marry well and Jatin Naupure seemed to be the best candidate. But now, my father *would* let me choose with such good prospects in front of his daughter. Because how could I go wrong? Two powerful men are willing to marry me. I already know what my father will say too. So as he opens his mouth I can practically mouth the words. "We will let Adraa choose."

Everyone's eyes fall on me. Maharaja Moolek's and my

father's words are a cage, entrapping me. Choice has never felt so malicious. I can't breathe, let alone speak.

"Of course, you don't need to answer tonight. I'll give you time to think about it, Adraa. Let us get to know each other, shall we?"

CHAPTER TWENTY-SEVEN

◇

Return of the Rightful Ruler

Jatin

As I enter Azure Palace my thoughts keep snapping back to Adraa. She ran out so fast with her guard. And after that head injury . . .

I think I deserve to know what's happening. But no. Something in Riya's face told me I'm no longer to be trusted. She must know about us being Night and the Red Woman, but it doesn't appear that she knows who I truly am. If she had I would have gotten more than Adraa's worried look and the bland words: *I have to get back to Belwar Palace.*

I need to tell her because I can't keep doing this. The lying, once a wall to protect myself, has become a barrier that distances us.

I shove open the office door with a sigh. A figure stands in the shadows, rustling through the desk. Vencrin. Without hesitation, I cast a knife and it slices forward. A blue shield bashes the purple magic away and the weapon thuds into a wooden cabinet.

My arms flame in preparation, the makings of a spell ready on my lips. Then the intruder speaks.

"Planning to kill me?" The hallway firelight catches my father's face as he looks up with a bemused smile. "I didn't expect a welcome home party, but betrayal by my own flesh and blood is a little much."

My magic bursts into mist. "You're . . . you're home."

"A few hours ago." He steps toward me.

We perform a stumbling dance of "how should we greet?" before I place my fingers on my pulse and bow. It's even more uncomfortable than when I came home, as if our relationship has regressed. Then again, I did almost murder him. I have found that always kills the mood and stiffens the air. Sadness touches his eyes as I rise from my respects and I yearn to withdraw the last five minutes and somehow fix our dysfunctional shuffle.

Maybe it's me. Maybe when you want connection so desperately, people can see it.

He walks back to the desk and nods at the mountain of paperwork. "I forgot how messy you are."

"Looking for something?"

"The twenty-first treaty actually."

"I have it over here." I pull out the bundle. "And in these drawers are the plans for the new school and updates on the water system. And here is the bill about the Untouched. It's going to be bloody awful to pass, but it needs to happen." I catch my father smiling. "There is some order to the chaos," I try to say without sounding defensive and resentful. I can do this. For weeks I was the raja of Naupure and the Night of Belwar.

"I'd hoped so." He crosses his arms and leans on the desk. "You wrote about all the bills and plans. But tell me, how are you getting on with Adraa?"

It's the last thing I want to talk about. "It's a slow development."

"But no domestic abuse, right?"

I laugh roughly. "She hasn't hit me." But she has torn at my heart, almost died in front of me a few times, left me in the Underground alone wondering what the blood was going on. On second thought "slow development" doesn't sound right. I might have gone backward.

"Since we are covering all the big things that happened in my absence, want to explain this?" He holds up the poster with my masked face plastered on it. It looks nothing like me thanks to Adraa's black magic spell, but of course there's no denying it to him.

"You wanted me to be a part of it."

"You two have gone far beyond gathering information."

"Yeah, that's mainly Adraa. The night I met her she had the intention of ambushing a dozen Vencrin by herself."

He sighs. "I'm guessing you won't stop, even if I ask."

"You want me to *not* help her?"

He shakes his head and runs his hands through his thinning hair. Do I do that? Sometimes I catch myself trying to define our similarities or habits. And most of the time I come away with nothing.

"You are my only heir, Jatin. Three times, my brother reminded me his son, your cousin, has taken the ceremony over a year ago. They will find any way to dethrone you. Your death would make it beyond easy to disrupt Naupure's entire future."

"It might have started by helping Adraa, but now it's about helping everyone. Do you realize what these Vencrin are capable of? I want this. For once in my life I feel like a normal wizard who can make a difference."

He stares at me for a long moment. "You're a lot like her."

"Adraa?"

"No, your mother." He scans the big map on the wall and clutches his wedding bangle. "She didn't want the throne either. All the power-hungry people in this world and my family simply wants a normal life." His eyes jerk to me. "But that will make you a great maharaja, I think."

The mention of my mother not only stings, it scorches. It's as if my father only brings my mother up to unravel me. He doesn't speak of her. I learned not to ask. And now he thinks he can compliment me into submission. To blood with that. "I'm not stopping."

He sees something in my eyes. We face each other in silence. Whoever breaks first . . .

"At least tell me what you've discovered," he finally says.

I sigh, the tension of our silence unwinding slightly. "We've traced it. It goes from East District warehouses to Pier Sixteen. But we haven't found any evidence that it's Moolek stealing the firelight. And, more importantly, we haven't found out why it's being stolen. Adraa and I think it may just be to tarnish the Belwar name. Prove how unstable it is in the market so that Untouched resort back to candles and thus Moolek's ghee."

"Maybe." My father rubs his chin. "But you have no concrete proof yet?"

"No. None."

He sighs, a heavy sound that makes him appear even shorter, even older. "The trip was as awful as you could expect. Your uncle has never been a good man. But since he has taken power he has become worse than I could have possibly imagined."

"Where is Maharaja Moolek now? I thought he was coming to Naupure to re-sign the treaty."

"He did come. He is at Belwar Palace. He insisted upon staying there. That makes me nervous, of course, but I couldn't refuse."

My body turns to stone. Maharaja Moolek is at Belwar Palace. Which means . . . he's under the same roof as Adraa. "What does he want in Belwar?" I demand.

Anguish washes over my father's face. "What I'm afraid he has always wanted—Adraa."

CHAPTER TWENTY-EIGHT

◇

The Enemy and I Have a Talk

Adraa

In the past few weeks my dreams have amped up full force. It's stress. It has to be, and yet, in my dreams I live in a world of red. And in this place fear penetrates every part of my body like a sword gutting me. Something is coming. Something bad is coming.

"You must perform for the nine gods. You must complete the ceremony," a female voice hisses at me. She repeats it over and over. "It's the only way. Sometimes one must die so others can live," she says.

Listening to the voice makes the fear disappear. I try to hold back at first, try to explain how I need more time to determine the Vencrin threat. "I need to be the Red Woman!" I shout at the voice. By the end, every time, I give in as the fear swallows me.

The night Maharaja Moolek proposed marriage, the dream grew worse. The fear pressed in on me like fire.

Since I can't sleep, I train. But after white magic spell upon

310

white magic spell fails, I stop. I haven't performed my morning prayers in weeks. Guess in times like these most people would consult the gods. I might as well try too.

I walk to the temple slowly, not wanting to grovel to Dloc so early. Dread fills my gut like I'm an orb about to bust. Stress does that, feels like it's unending and limitless, like it will keep eating at you until nothing is left.

As I trudge up the steps, I'm surprised to spot Prisha praying.

Instead of calling out, I kneel beside her. She starts. "You're normally asleep this early in the morning," she says.

I guess she's more observant of my comings and goings than I thought. "Yeah, I guess I am. Do you come here every morning?"

"Most days."

I never knew she was so devout. What could she possibly be praying for that much? I've seen her in the clinic and on the training field with Hiren. At fifteen she has a good grasp on all nine types of magic, better than I was at her age. Back then, I was failing white magic consistently. Who am I kidding? I'm still failing at white magic.

"Were you ever scared?" Prisha whispers.

I stare at her. She doesn't look at me; she's still in the position of meditation, her eyes wide, gazing at Laeh's pillar.

"Scared of what?" There are just so many things now.

"Your forte." Finally, she turns to me. "I mean, did you want to be Erif Touched?"

"I didn't pray for it if that's what you're wondering. But I was scared. No, actually I was terrified. I thought I wouldn't be chosen at all. Since I was little, Mom and Dad and Maharaja Naupure told me they"—I nod toward the pillars—"were fighting over me. I was so afraid the gods would give up the fight and I would be left Untouched."

She nods, but I can tell it's not the answer she was looking for. My sister is normal; she never had to deal with the prospect of having a naked arm.

"Are you scared?"

She fiddles with some sand on the floor, building it into little mounds, dispersing it, and then rebuilding. "I don't want to be Laeh's. That's what I pray for every day."

I reel back. "You hate the clinic that much?"

"No, it's not the clinic exactly. I just . . . I just don't want to be like Mom. She's so trapped there."

"I wouldn't say that. She loves the clinic."

"Maybe. But, I mean, have you ever seen how some people treat her? Like she's their slave, expected to dole out potions every day. That because she is a woman, that's her one and only use. And I think Mom hopes I'm Laeh Touched so that I can take over for her. But I want to be strong, stronger."

"Pink healing magic is not strictly feminine, and it is not weak. It saves people's lives. Mom. You. Me. All pink users. We save people's lives. There is *nothing* weak about that."

She won't meet my eye as she plays with the sand. "I want to be wanted for me, not what I can do. Not what Belwar thinks I should do."

But what someone can do as a witch or wizard is connected inherently to their talents, their desire to devote oneself to specific types of magic. Pink fortes are always a welcomed skill, especially when trained by our mother. Prisha will always have a place in society. But I guess that's what upsets her. She doesn't *want* to fit in. She believes pink fortes are inherently lesser, weaker, feminine. Gods, I never imagined how different we are. She's so spoiled by her normalcy that she can't see how good she has it or how important pink magic is to saving Belwar, saving everyone. Once the drugs are off the streets, we will still need to help the wizards and witches who are in withdrawal or have damaged Touches.

"Prisha, it's only a one in nine chance you'll become a pink forte."

"I know, but . . ."

"And you would be more than a pink forte anyway. You are a Belwar."

Prisha pulls at her choli.

"Don't worry. You'll— Wait, is that my sari?"

She has the decency to look down at the orange fabric guiltily. "Ah, maybe."

A knot tightens in my stomach. Prisha knows my sleeping habits; she goes into my room unannounced and into my closet. What else could she have seen there? "Did Zara give it to you?"

"Not exactly."

Gods, I thought she was past stealing my clothes a few years ago. "So you just took it?"

"I always return it before you wake up."

Before I wake up? How often does she do this?

"That's not the point—"

"You're only worried I know where you go at night. But I already know about the cage-casting ring."

A chill runs through me. *She knows about the Underground? Does everyone know? Wait.* "It was you. You told Riya I sneak out."

She looks at me full-on. "Zara and Riya were frantic trying to find you when Maharaja Moolek showed up. I had to tell them."

"How do you—"

"I followed you to that window door once."

"You never said anything."

She shrugs. "It wasn't my business until last night. Actually, I've been covering for you on nights when Zara wants your opinion or Riya wants to talk."

I don't know what to say. "Thank you, Prisha. I—"

Footsteps echo on the temple stairs behind us. Prisha turns first and I see curiosity, then fear, grow in her eyes. I whip around. Maharaja Moolek stands by Wodahs's pillar, a gleaming smile melded to his lips.

"I was hoping we could talk alone," Moolek says to me.

"Prisha, go back to the palace."

"Adraa—"

"Prisha, go. Now."

With a few glances over her shoulder, Prisha steps off the temple stairs and disappears from my sight and, more important, from Maharaja Moolek's.

He steps into the temple and I circle naturally. *Don't let him get close. Don't show fear.*

"You don't have to be so worried about your little sister."

But I do. I know exactly whom I'm dealing with. And if he

really wants to marry into our family and I refuse, Prisha is only three years younger than I am. I don't want Moolek to entertain the idea of taking Prisha's hand.

"She's innocent in all this, yes? She doesn't know about you."
I still.

He tilts his head to the side as if weighing my emotions, reading me. I try to give nothing away, but he must have caught the flash of fear in my eyes. I have secrets and now he knows I do.

Maharaja Moolek jerks his hands forward and shouts a spell.

What the blood? "*Simaraw!*" I yell, hands crossed and thrown up before me. A lush green smoke flows out of Moolek's hands and forms into a meter wall between us. My red shield does nothing to save me. The wall of green passes through it like a ghost and washes over me. And then, nothing—no pain, no physical threat—materializes. I don't know the spell. The green smoke filters upward and disappears.

"Interesting," he whispers with a smirk.

My shield evaporates. "What did you do?" I sputter, unable to fully comprehend Maharaja Moolek casting against me in my own temple. "How dare you, in a temple before the gods—"

"There are such secrets inside of you."

Was that spell . . . ? I choke and try to recover as best I can. "As many as any teenage girl, I suppose."

He scoffs. "Naupure told me everything."

He couldn't have. He *wouldn't* have.

"Why should I believe anything you say? You are stealing my firelight."

"Stealing your firelight? I wouldn't let that abomination into

315

my country even if you paid me. Personally, I think it is a unique little invention, although my people would riot. Rajas would be at my throat at the very concept. But I'm glad you created it, my dear. It led me to you, illustrated your power."

I step back, unable to grasp what he is saying. "Then you really are only stealing it to ruin Belwar?"

"Are you not listening? I'm not stealing it. You have been misinformed. Who was it that told you I was responsible? Maharaja Naupure, I'm sure. The man hates me." Maharaja Moolek looks away and watches a monal pecking at the grass. "It's as if he forgets Savi was my older sister. As if her death didn't destroy me as well."

I always seem to forget Maharaja Naupure and Maharaja Moolek's connection. But regardless, that can't be where all the animosity stems from. Dozens of treaties and skirmishes over the years. Wizards killed, murdered. It can't just be because of Jatin's mother. This is a ploy. This is the man who is stealing my firelight. I shouldn't trust anything he says. And yet a small voice whispers, *You haven't found any proof that firelight is being taken to Moolek.*

No, no, Maharaja Moolek is practically evil. Maharaja Naupure always said . . .

Wait, Maharaja Naupure *always* said. He was the one who pointed me in the direction of Moolek from the beginning. He had all the answers. And he had Beckman watching me. But Maharaja Naupure has been a friend for over a decade. I can't think . . . he couldn't.

"I see you are piecing it together," Moolek says.

"No, no. *You* are scared of my firelight. No one else would want it."

"But I don't. Not now anyway. I have yet to convince my people to stop wasting animals on bloodletting or to quit destroying our limited fields." He steps forward. "But with you helping me lead my people I foresee a future for Moolek, a prosperous one that develops new spells and embraces a long-needed change."

He sounds genuine. Could he be this masterful at manipulation? Never in my life have I yearned to cast a truth spell and bind him in it.

"Why wouldn't you send red fortes for me to teach, then?"

He sighs. "Do you know how many hundreds of wizards and witches are fleeing to Agsa and Naupure each year? I'm losing talented members of society constantly. I couldn't afford to send them. Besides, the four primary fortes are honored in Moolek. To make one-fourth of them leave for even a visit would have been seen as weakness. I do want to change that, though. Trust me, I want to change that most of all."

He wants to change the discrimination, the prejudice, and the pain those who are not Touched by the four gods face every day in his land? I want this to be true so badly. But does Maharaja Moolek know this?

I can't think of any comeback that would hurt as much as the doubts swarming the back of my head, running and pounding behind my eyes.

"I'll let you think about my proposal, of course—"

"I don't need any more time. I'm not marrying you."

"Because you love the Naupure boy?"

I pause. "Yes."

"You hesitated, Adraa. You hesitated."

"I . . ."

"You love someone else?"

Kalyan's face flashes to mind. "No," I will from my mouth.

Moolek tilts his head. "It's probably a guard. It always seems to be a guard." He steps even closer, hands up in surrender. "I wouldn't touch you, Adraa. Not until you were ready. But as Rani Naupure you would be a wife, not a leader. A family with as much arrogance as that wouldn't let a woman lead. *I would.* As Rani Moolek, you could change the world. One-armed Touches are more common there than you know. My lands are the home of the first Touched, the originals, and it's common for the gods to fight over wizards and witches there." He pulls up both his sleeves.

What is he . . . ? Then the fabric slips away. I gasp and rock back on my heels at the sight before me. Maharaja Moolek, his arms . . . He's a one-armed Touch. His right arm is covered in fine black designs, while his left is bare, a reflection of mine.

"Htrae and Retaw, if you are interested. That's why my lands face drought. I'm not cruel, Adraa. I'm like you."

"I never . . . no one ever told me."

"It isn't public knowledge in this part of the world."

A thousand questions buzz in my head. The panic surges, but Kalyan's face resurfaces through the muck in my brain. "That doesn't change my decision."

Moolek sighs. "I believe you will come to regret rejecting my offer."

My body tenses. "Is that a threat?"

"Just the truth."

Does he think an intimidation tactic like that will change my mind? Will make me want to marry him? He has to be out of his mind. He turns to go, pushing his sleeves back down and walking toward the monal, who still searches for a morning meal. "You are wasted as Maharaja Naupure's puppet."

"I'm no one's puppet!" I yell after him. And I will certainly never be his.

He stops and half turns his head. "Are you sure about that?"

I fall to the ground as soon as he is gone, gasping for breath. What in Wickery was any of that? The truth? Well-rehearsed and rational lies? The desperate need to talk with Kalyan shoots through me like an arrow. Only to properly talk about any of this, I have to tell him who I am, who I really am.

But with Moolek here, proposing, threatening . . . I need to tell both Kalyan and Jatin the truth right now.

Who first? Kalyan. Definitely Kalyan. He's the one I've been lying to this whole time. Oh Gods, he is going to hate me. I don't care about Jatin as much, even though I should. All I can imagine is the look in Kalyan's eyes. Blood, it's like I'll be turning him into Jatin, turning him unfeeling and cold.

Before I even realize it, tears roll down my cheeks and I'm crying.

◇

CHAPTER TWENTY-NINE

I Learn the Truth

Adraa

"Excuse me?"

The young man looks up from cleaning his shoes and his eyes widen when he takes me in. "Hey, you're that girl, the one who rainbowed weeks ago! I won a gold piece that day, so thanks for, you know, losing."

I don't have time for this. "Great for you. I'm looking for Kalyan. Do you know where he is?"

"Raja Jatin's guard?"

"Yes."

"Ah, I think he's fixing a few swords." He points to a hallway. "First right."

"Thanks."

"Yeah, um, anytime. Hey, tell me the next time you'll be fighting—" His voice fades as I walk away and I don't care enough to try to listen.

The first door on the right is closed, but I might as well get in trouble rather than wander around this place forever. I open the door and four men twist. All noise and smiles fall. I anticipate the words before hearing them. This is going to be awful. "What are you doing here, girl?"

I sigh. How do any of the female guards around here not strangle some of these men? "I'm looking for Kalyan."

"Kalyan?" the guard says the name in surprise, sounding as if he never knew those letters could be organized that way.

"Yes." While he struggles with his interrogation, the younger man next to him calls into the adjoining area.

A tall wizard lifts the curtain and bursts into the room. "I've about got it," he says, gesturing to a sword in his hand. I go rigid. It's Jatin, standing there like this is nothing peculiar. Like sharpening a sword or aligning a hilt is no big deal. *Escape!* I scan for it.

The younger fellow, who called Kalyan, nods to indicate my presence. "You have—"

Jatin turns to me and with one look his face falls. "Oh Gods."

It's not a happy *Oh Gods.* No, this *Oh Gods* is resigned defeat. He can't know who I am, can he? And would he be this upset to finally meet me? I had him pegged right all along: arrogant and cold.

"I'm looking for Kalyan." Maybe I can salvage this and then escape.

"This is Kalyan." The young man gestures, so eager to help, yet missing the chill of tension overtaking the room.

Jatin's head falls and he shakes it. "Oh Gods."

"Kal, who is—" Without looking up, Jatin holds up a hand to the young man. "Just stop talking, Mulm."

Yes, stop. Stop everything. I need to understand. But it's all too clear, isn't it? My head spins. *I don't think he is what he says,* Riya had said. Two men in a royal carriage, one wearing the emblem of Naupure, and the other . . . the other a simple guard. He carried me in his arms, he made it snow in the underground fighting ring, and he's been my partner for weeks. The man before me is not Jatin Naupure.

I've never been so caught off guard in my life. My body doesn't like it. My lungs expand, but can't secure air. My knees lock unkindly. It's like a burst of burnout ramming up my spine. Swords line the wall in perfect rows. Bits of twisted metal are scattered on a worktable. I know which of the two I resemble.

"What is *wrong* with her?" one of the men whispers.

I can't stay in here. Maharaja Naupure. Raja Jatin. Were they in this together the whole time? I can't look at him; anywhere but him. I need to think, reorganize . . . everything. I stumble backward, my foot catching a wicker stool, which bangs to the floor. I flinch at the sound and then turn.

"Wait!" Kalyan, or whatever his name is, shouts after me.

I sprint down the hall. I don't know I'm casting speed into my muscles until I'm halfway across the training field. Sunlight wraps around me, a thin fall wind pushes my hair from my face, and yet I'm numb. My reality, the truth, it's all wobbling before me. First Maharaja Naupure might have betrayed me, and now this. I halt in my tracks, staring up at the palace. Gods, I'm eight years old all over again, scared of this massive structure and the boy who lives here. Where the heck am I running anyway? I need to—

Wham! Something hits my shoulder hard and I spin and tumble into the dirt. I try to catch myself. Pain greets me instead,

322

slicing up my arm. The bulky perpetrator falls on top of me, digging my wrist further into the dirt. A moment later, he rolls off, groaning. "I didn't expect you to stop."

I rotate and find Kalyan on the ground next to me. "What the blood?" I holler as I clench my wrist and choke down the pain. Gods, it hurts. Of all my falls and hits, this is when I might have broken something? For blood's sake.

"Are you okay?" Kalyan asks, his breath still shaky like he hasn't gathered it back yet.

I scramble to get up. I can't do this. I don't want to talk to him. My body, even in pain, still wants escape.

"Are you serious?" he growls as he reaches for me. "You're going to keep running?"

He tries to grab my arm as I lurch out of the way. He manages to capture my sari. With one tug I fall sideways and against his chest. Blood, he's strong. Instinctively, I jerk my elbow backward. It connects with his ribs hard; harder than I intended.

He huffs out a breath, but doesn't let go. Instead his grip intensifies and he uses the momentum to roll back, twist, and pull me with him. A moment later, he's on top of me, holding me down. "Just hear me out. I'm not getting fired over this ridiculousness."

I still. What the blood does he think he's doing? Does he know who I am? He must to chase after me as he did. Jatin and Kalyan must have planned this from the beginning. Their switch was all a trick.

He's on top of me. On top of me in the middle of the Naupure training field.

His chest rises and falls as the adrenaline dulls. I pause the spell I have ready to blow him off me, waiting to see when he realizes the precarious position he's placed us in. But then my wrist throbs for attention. "You're hurting me."

My whisper smacks some sense into him. He jolts, releases his grip, and tumbles to the side. I can tell he's shocked. It's like my hit to his gut spurred the primal defense system in him— sedate threat. Only now does he realize the "threat" he used his physical strength on. From the wide-eyed stare he's giving me, I think I've broken him.

I roll my wrist, flexing against the pain. Based on the lack of swelling, I think it's only a sprain. *"Mahlaeh,"* I cast as I finally get to my feet.

I stare up at the walls of the palace. At least the pain has stalled my brain long enough for me to think. I stumble ten steps before looking back at the guard. Gods, they look so much alike. I turn around. "Your ribs okay?"

His eyes jerk up to me; he's probably surprised I've decided to stick around. Hey, I'm surprised too. But if I don't get my answers now, who knows when I'll receive them. And I don't think I could face Jatin, the real Jatin, anyway. Gods, it's hard to wrap my head around that. The real Jatin, my fiancé, and the man who's been lying to me for weeks.

"Are *you* okay?" he asks.

"My wrist is fine if that's what you are asking."

"Only . . . partly. I'm sorry about . . ." He blushes. Good, I've unsettled him. Maybe he will give me the answers I so desperately need.

"If you want to talk, talk. *Your* name is Kalyan, right?"

"Yes, My Rani."

"Don't 'My Rani' me. A few minutes ago I thought I was engaged to you!" I stare at him full-on. Yes, they look very much
alike, but this boy appears younger than Jatin, maybe even
younger than I am. "How old are you?"

"Sixteen."

Sixteen? And he's Raja Jatin's guard? Would Maharaja Naupure have disclosed his plan to someone so young and inexperi-
enced or would Jatin and his father have commanded this guard
to do their bidding? Only one way to know for sure.

"Why would you switch places with him? What do you have
to gain?"

His eyes shift. "We should probably talk somewhere else."
Good point. We are still in the middle of the training field after all.

We trudge to the barracks because I'm sure not going into
the palace. But the barracks are full of guardsmen, brimming actually. "The only place I know is empty is my room," Kalyan says.

"Okay, then." I gesture.

"We shouldn't be in there alone. People will think—"

"After all this, you're *that* worried about my reputation?"

He nods. "Mine too. You do realize who you are, right?"

This is getting irritating. "Yes, I do, so don't make me give
the 'one day I'll be in command' speech."

Reluctantly, he leads me down the hall, ducking his head
each time we pass a fellow guard. Barely anyone even glances
our way, though. He seriously overestimates how often people
pay attention. Hiding in plain sight is strategic for a reason.

He leads me into the plainest room in history. A tidy bed and a clean desk sit in a boxlike room, which can barely be described as a living space. It's a closet. Vibrant blue curtains with the Naupure crest blow toward us as we enter. Okay, it's a closet with a window.

It's so different from my memory of Jatin's room at age eight. "You're very clean."

"I don't need much."

I spot Kalyan rubbing his ribs again as he sits on the floor. "You sure you don't want me to fix that?" I ask.

He lifts his hand from his ribs. "It's just a bruise." He stares at me. "I always thought Jatin was exaggerating when he said you punched him in the face the first time you met."

"He *was* exaggerating. It was a slap at best."

"Uh-huh, sure."

"Was it Maharaja Naupure who devised the plan for you two to switch places?"

He shrugs. "It's in my job description. When we travel I dress as a raja of Naupure to protect Jatin. But this situation with you . . . well, this situation is messed up, if you ask me."

I get it. He impersonates Jatin. If Belwarians idolized their heirs, Father probably would have wanted the same for me, too, although it would be hard to match my dark skin tone because of the Pire Island in me. "So Naupure doesn't know about any of this?"

"No, nothing," Kalyan says.

That doesn't mean Maharaja Naupure didn't tell Moolek about the Red Woman or try to get me to investigate Moolek this whole time instead of . . . him.

"So in the carriage, you were—" I gesture to his clothes.

"I was doing my job, protecting Jatin. We both thought you were some commoner, like a four, at most, burning out in an act of heroism."

"A four? Pshh, I should be offended. That was intense orange magic. So Jatin didn't know then?"

"No, neither of us even guessed."

"So when did he find out?"

"I believe it was the night you guys fought that ship full of Vencrin. I tried to tell him this was ridiculous. Believe me in that."

Jatin had known my identity for weeks. *For weeks.* I try to make sense of Jatin as I know him now compared with back then and in his letters. Blood, he's changed. And yet, in some ways he hasn't changed at all. I should have figured his arrogant smile and masterful casting could belong only to a raja. But he was so . . . kind. The complete opposite of unfeeling. The Jatin I knew wouldn't have partnered with me, wouldn't have followed my lead in fights, and definitely wouldn't have brewed a potion for my cramps unless there was a way to tease or humiliate me in the end. He was always about being better than me, right? He could never consider us equal. And yet, he did, which means I had my fiancé all wrong.

Even this guard, Kalyan, doesn't treat me as an equal. And isn't that what I found most attractive in the man I've fallen for? He saw me as nothing other than an equal, his partner.

"But why didn't Jatin tell me?"

"The truth?"

"No, I want you to lie to me again, for a few months at least."

"Sorry, I meant whether you're sure you want to hear this from me."

That makes me pause. Was it a game, then, a trick? "I need to hear it."

"Well, Jatin. Well, you know he . . ." Kalyan stares at me and frowns. "Jatin knew you hated him. You two have been competing for years. I've seen some of the letters." He shrugs. "So as unbelievable as it sounds, he was trying to change that. Trying to get you to be his . . . friend."

"He was trying to be my friend?" *Was that all?*

I walk over to the desk chair and collapse into it. Now I'm mad because that explanation kind of made sense. If I had met the real Jatin at the beginning I might have hated him, just out of spite.

Red tendrils of magic waft from my arms, careening in the air with no directive as my emotions buzz. I go back to the simplest of absolutes to try to re-sort everything I know. This tall man is a guard; the man I love, who wants me only as a friend, is Jatin. I've felt awful the past few weeks. Jatin made me think I was cheating every time I fell for him a little more. But he wanted me only as a friend, a partner. And I was the one this whole time saying partners, nothing more. *Gods, I'm so ignorant.*

"Can I ask you something I've been wondering?" Kalyan asks, breaking my raging thoughts.

"What?"

"Why all the secrecy on your part? Why didn't you tell us in the carriage that you were Adraa?"

On instinct I want to say it isn't any of his business, but the words stall in my throat. I sigh, trying to process all my horrible decisions since then. There have been so many. "In the carriage I was embarrassed. Later, well, later I wanted to maintain our partnership. I thought he was only a guard. And once he knew the truth, I thought he would look at me like—" I try to find a proper description. "Kind of how you've looked at me since I stepped into the barracks."

Kalyan turns away awkwardly. That's exactly what I meant. Gods, I am more than a damaged arm, a pretty face, or the heir to the throne. I'm even more than firelight's inventor, the Red Woman, or Jaya Smoke.

"I never deeply hated Jatin, you know. I just didn't want to marry him. He was so . . . irritating."

"Still is," Kalyan says, a small smile playing on his lips.

"Where is he?" He and I need to talk. About Moolek. About everything.

"Probably in his father's study."

His father's study. Those words smack into me. I start for the door.

"Adraa?"

I turn around, but itch to run.

"He's the best person I know. I would do anything for him, even help him in his weird mission to be normal." Kalyan lifts one pant leg to reveal grayish-white magic attached to his knee and slowly churning in the shape of a calf. "I owe him my life."

For a moment, all I comprehend is how intricate and precise the purple magic is. Then something clicks in my brain. I recall the letter, Jatin talking endlessly of how he helped search for people after a monsoon, how he found one boy trapped in a house, how they had to amputate his leg. I had forgotten the boy's name over the years because I had been so focused on how much Jatin had proved himself in Agsa, how much he was beating me back then.

"The Southern Bay Monsoon," I whisper.

Kalyan nods. "You have a right to be mad. Just . . . just hear him out, okay?"

I step back into the room. Here I am, wanting to be seen as more than a rani, and I have yet to apologize for seeing Jatin as nothing more than an unfeeling man. Of course I'd be wrong about this too. "I've misjudged you and I'm sorry."

He laughs lightly. "Because you thought I was Jatin, right?"

"Partly. Well, mostly."

"At least in the end I can say I was right."

◇ ◇ ◇

Like most times I have entered the palace, I encounter Hughes giving me a discouraging look.

"I'm going to talk to my fiancé. Don't announce me."

Hughes's eyes tighten, but he doesn't move as I vault up the staircase and rush through the hall.

I pull open the door without thinking. For what feels like the twentieth time today I'm startled. Inside, Maharaja Naupure and Jatin sit side by side engrossed in paperwork. Both stand immediately at my entrance, chairs screeching, papers diving to the floor. I wasn't expecting to find Maharaja Naupure here. But of course, *of course,* he is home if Maharaja Moolek is gracing us with his horrid presence at Belwar Palace.

Pure surprise splashes across Jatin's face, while a blazing grin pulls at Maharaja Naupure's lips. Normally I would return his smile. But I don't know whether I can trust him anymore. All my doubts come crashing to the forefront. Could he be stealing my firelight? A voice whispers *yes.*

"Not even knocking anymore," Maharaja Naupure says, with a knowing look at Jatin. He thinks I'm *that* familiar with his son. Ha, if he only knew.

"Sorry, I hope I'm not interrupting a father-son moment."

Jatin inhales, sharp enough for me to hear it.

"Kalyan told me where I might find you," I add.

Jatin steps forward, but I halt him with my hand.

Maharaja Naupure looks between us. "Are you two *still* fighting after all these years?"

"You could say that."

◇

CHAPTER THIRTY

Fighting for Forgiveness

Jatin

At first, I was surprised to hear the door open. There hadn't been a knock and none of the servants would dare enter unannounced. Then Adraa steps in and my heart smiles and collapses within a two-second span. How did this happen? How did everything go so wrong so fast?

I was anticipating telling her any day now, but in all the scenarios I ran through my head, I never imagined her this mad. Not when I explained myself, not when we had shared so much in the past weeks.

I have to say something. After all these weeks of lying I have to say something.

Like always, my father beats me to it. "Are you two *still* fighting after all these years?"

"You could say that," Adraa answers. "And I could tell you about it. Or you could tell me why I have found zero proof Maharaja Moolek has been stealing my firelight."

Is she serious? We're going to talk about Project Smoke right now instead of the fact that she knows who I am?

I draw toward her. "Adraa, we need to talk."

Her eyes cut into me. "Not now."

My father interrupts our standoff. "Jatin told me you two haven't found proof yet. There's the possibility it isn't Moolek getting the Vencrin to steal firelight. Maybe it's only the Vencrin."

"*Only* the Vencrin?" Adraa says, her voice hard. What's going on with her? She's using her interrogation voice.

"Adraa, what's wrong?" my father asks. I guess he can sense it too.

"I had a conversation with Maharaja Moolek this morning."

Blood. Adraa had to deal with Maharaja Moolek and discover I've been lying in the same day. Now I think I understand her anger. "Are you okay?" I ask.

She glances between my father and me. "No, I'm not okay. Maharaja Moolek, he . . . he made a strong argument that he wasn't responsible for stealing my firelight."

"He could be lying," I protest.

Her eyes bore into mine. "Yeah, you never really know when someone is lying."

My throat goes dry.

Adraa steps closer to my father. "You . . . you created Project Smoke with me. You suspected Moolek from the beginning. You helped me secure Basu as a distributor. You planted Beckman in the Underground. Were you manipulating me the whole time?"

"Beckman? Adraa, of course I wasn't."

"Then where is my firelight going?" she cries.

I can't stand seeing her this hurt. I reach for her and place a hand on her shoulder. "We'll find it. We'll figure it out."

She shrugs my hand off. "Don't touch me."

I flinch. "Adraa, please. Let me explain."

"Maharaja Moolek also proposed. He wants me to help make Moolek a better place," Adraa says in a rush.

I don't know if I've heard her right. Moolek . . . proposed. My uncle wants to marry the girl I'm insanely in love with. My stomach drops. I feel like I'm being stabbed. *What in the blood is happening?*

"What?" my father asks. "He did what?"

"He proposed to me. You know, marriage. Even consulted my parents about it."

"He's almost twice your age."

I unfreeze, stepping close to her. I need to fix this, immediately. "We *need* to talk."

"This is more important." Adraa swivels back to my father. "I want to know why you would have told Moolek. Why would you tell him anything about Project Smoke when he was our main suspect?"

"I didn't tell him anything."

I believe my father. Nothing in his letters even hinted he would have brought up Project Smoke.

Adraa's anger falls. "Then . . . Oh Gods, is it my fault? He cast this spell over me and . . ."

My father's eyes flash. "What kind of spell? Did it hurt you?"

"It . . . I don't know what the spell was. I thought it might have been to read my mind or reveal my secrets, but—" She looks between the two of us. "Oh my Gods. There's this small voice inside my head telling me I can't trust you. That Moolek is right."

"It will fade soon," my father reassures her.

I turn to him. "What was it? What did he do to her?"

"It's a complex black magic spell. It makes one susceptible to manipulation. He used to use it against your mother all the time when they were younger. In this instance, Adraa could be convinced to believe Moolek isn't the one behind the firelight shortage and start to suspect me." He pauses. "And persuade you to accept his marriage proposal as well."

Adraa clutches her head. "Gods, I don't know what to think anymore."

More easily convinced to accept his— "Did you? Adraa, did you agree to marry him?"

"I . . . I refused. He was upset about that, but I was able to say no."

My whole body relaxes. I knew it. *Thank the gods. She's stronger than him.*

"Well, the spell doesn't control people," my father clarifies. "Understanding and knowing it was placed on you will make it easier."

Adraa finally turns to me. "We should talk."

A mix of relief and dread churn my stomach. I think the next five minutes will define my life and my happiness.

◇ ◇ ◇

I lead Adraa to my room. As soon as the door closes, I hold out my hands in surrender. "Listen—"

She interrupts before I can say more. "I just want to know one thing. Were you trying to be my friend this whole time? Or was all this another way for you to mess with me?"

"Yes. I mean no, of course not." The words twist on my tongue. For saying she only wanted to know one thing it sure sounded like two questions with very different answers. Blood, this wasn't how my confession was supposed to go. "I was *never* messing with you."

The questions I asked after my discovery flit back into my memory. Every time we teased one another. *So tell me, what do you think of Jatin Naupure?* Does that count?

She doesn't believe me. I can see it in her face. Maybe those questions do count. I'm a complete idiot. I open my mouth to say so.

"You should be happy knowing you've won," she scoffs, and then heads for the door.

I panic, my body racing with energy. Gods, she's so wrong. If she isn't in my life I'm losing, losing everything. She can't run away without me at least explaining my motives and why I lied.

"*Bhitti Himadloc!*" I yell in panic. As the spell unleashes from my hands, I already know it's a mistake. White condenses to ice in front of Adraa and crackles as it springs up and envelops my door. It's wrong to trap her like this, but a small part of me yelps at the victory. I got her to stop; maybe she'll listen now.

"Are you serious?" she asks, wheeling around.

"Please, talk to me."

"I won't while I'm imprisoned. *Gharmaerif!*" she yells. A slash of red light dances up my ice wall. For a moment I'm startled into amusement. Is she really going to try to melt it?

"Why are you such a bloody jerk?" she hollers.

"I don't think I should answer that."

She responds with another fire spell. Melting ice drips to the floor.

"You're only saying that after knowing who I am, aren't you?" Her *Don't touch me* still rings in my ears. After all this time I haven't changed her perception of me. I'm still the senseless nine-year-old who was too competitive and full of himself. I was a fool to think Adraa Belwar could ever love me. "This, this is why I lied. I wanted you to get to know the real me, as I wanted to get to know the real you. At least before one of us punched the other in the face."

She stills, dropping her gaze, stopping her casting. She doesn't turn away.

"Please, remember you lied too. When we met you were Jaya Smoke, not Adraa Belwar."

That gets her attention. "I'm both," she says, her eyes finding mine. "And if you can't see that—"

"Yes, you are both and yet conveniently you never told me you were royalty. You led me to believe you were just another Belwar citizen, Adraa's *servant,* in fact."

"And you led me to believe you were a guard, Jatin's guard."

We both pause, staring at each other.

"I guess we're equal, then," I relent.

The hard lines of her anger dissolve somewhat. "What did you say?"

"That we are equal. We both—"

She peers past me to the shelves of tattered books and my orbs of magic, their light bouncing off the new reflective ice door. "You truly believe that? You, who on day one claimed I was not even a witch?"

Of course, she would bring that up. It all comes back to that. "Adraa, I was nine. I regret that more than you can possibly know. You think I don't know how powerful you are?"

I can't read her expression. Confusion maybe? *"Gharmaerif!"* she yells, and red brightens the entire room.

I reach out and stop her arm before she bathes my room in water. "Adraa, stop. You need to break the ice with white magic. You can't just heat it up. Or, well, I guess you can. But it's going to take you all day."

She tugs her arm away and bangs on the wall once more before turning back to me.

"I . . . I can't do it."

She can't do what? Stand the thought of marrying me?

"Am I really that horrible?" I whisper.

She gestures to the door. "I mean I can't break it."

"Oh."

Carefully, I step closer. When she doesn't protest, I take another step. I place one hand on the sheet of ice. "I'm sorry," I say.

"Hima Diavadloc," I cast. The ice cracks slowly around my

fingers and then splinters outward. Ice rains on the floor, splintering and cracking like a small replica of the ice door downstairs. I don't look at it, though, because Adraa is staring at me, and I at her. She's especially beautiful right now: face flushed, strands of hair falling out of her braid, strength and stubbornness radiating off her as she takes in heavy breaths.

"If you want to leave, you can," I say.

She doesn't move. "You aren't horrible."

"But are you . . . ?" I can't even say it. "Would you consider Moolek's offer?"

"No."

"So you would never—"

"Of course I wouldn't. Gods, Jatin, I like *you*!"

The world pauses, the entire bloody world. Adraa looks down at her hands, rubbing them together. "I realize you don't feel the same way. But somewhere in all this, even amid all our lies, I fell in love with you."

Everything lifts, spins, whirls. My heart beats so loudly it pounds in my ears. She loves me? "What do you mean I don't feel the same way? Adraa—"

"Kalyan told me you lied to stop our arguing and competitiveness so that we could become friends."

For blood's sake. Kalyan is a dead man. I will never let him live this down. Only friends? "Adraa, I've loved you since— I can't even pinpoint it, maybe since I met you."

"What?"

"I love you."

I don't know how long we stare at each other in silence. One moment our eyes are locked, and the next it's our lips. I can't even tell who moved first, but as soon as I start kissing her, I never want to stop. I push her against the door, one hand reaching into her hair, the other at her waist, pulling her closer to me. Gods, how I've waited for this, to feel her pressed against me. And blood, the way she feels. Her arms wind around my waist and her hands tug at my kurta. I groan. Adraa moans softly back. It's the most attractive sound I've ever heard. To think she is as undone as I am.

She smells like mountain air. Like each and every letter I raced to open. Her skin is soft, her hair is thick, and I get to kiss her.

"This is how we should finish every argument we have from now on," I whisper, catching my breath.

She arches an eyebrow. "We better not have another argument like this one."

"You're right. Let's restart. No lies." I tuck a few strands of her wavy hair behind her ears. "I'm Jatin Naupure, and I'm not a murderer or a mistress."

"Are you trying to remind me of all the embarrassing things I've said to you?"

"Well, they did make me come to know your rambling problem and your constant implications of how you could kill me." I smile.

"It's for your safety. You are more careless and accident-prone than I am."

"That's not true."

She touches my shoulder, right where I tore it, my jaw, the

340

scar along my torso from that night on the roof. "I thought we weren't going to mention that?" I whisper.

She smiles as she cups her hand to my cheek and I pull her toward me, kissing her again. And she kisses me back. She kisses me back.

CHAPTER THIRTY-ONE

◇

Stuck Between Truth and Lies

Adraa

I don't think I could come to my senses. Kissing Jatin . . . It's like trying to describe pure happiness or the feeling of warmth. Your chest is light and heavy at the same time. You can feel each breath of air and it is both rich and all-consuming. I'm taller somehow, stronger.

But then one name knocks us both back into reality. Maharaja Moolek.

It's like Jatin can read my mind, because we both reach for our skygliders at the same time.

"Do you have a plan? Or are we just barging into the palace?" he asks as we descend the stairs.

I look over at him. "It is my palace."

"Fair enough, but this is Moolek we're talking about."

"We question him without getting manipulated, or killed."

Jatin unsheathes his skyglider and it glows white. "That's the worst plan you have ever come up with."

I frown. "I know. Maybe we'll think of something better as we fly."

◇ ◇ ◇

We don't think of anything better. But we don't exactly barge into the palace. I thrust the doors open to the throne room only to find it deserted.

Jatin stares at the orange stone walls adorned with Belwar's nine-pointed sun glowing with the afternoon light. With the room empty, that sun appears foreboding. Like the rising semicircle could also be setting. "This is a warm welcome."

A curtain at the other side of the hall shifts, revealing Prisha. "Adraa! There you are. I was worried and I didn't know what to tell—" Prisha stops when she spots Jatin.

"Prisha, this is Jatin Naupure." I hurriedly motion through the introduction.

"Jatin Naupure!" Her eyes widen as she looks him up and down. Her mouth does that mischievous twist. "I thought you would be taller."

"And, Jatin, this is my rude little sister, Prisha Belwar."

"I hear the resemblance," he says as he gives her his respects.

"Hey," both Prisha and I say at the same time. After we exchange a look I laugh. She examines me like I've lost it. But it's Jatin teasing me, the boy who smells like frost and tastes like happiness.

"Prisha, do you know where Maharaja Moolek is?" I ask when I finally calm down.

"He's gone. He left right after talking to you in the temple."

"Gone where?" Jatin asks.

Prisha shrugs. "I don't know. I'm not stupid enough to tail him."

Guess we didn't need a better plan. There is no plan now. I turn to Jatin. "You think he came here to manipulate me? I thought for sure there were ulterior motives, like taking the firelight shipment or something. I'm not important enough to warrant a whole visit like this."

"You're firelight's creator, the only creator. If he is stealing it, you are important enough. You are the most important."

"But how are we going to find him?"

Prisha steps forward. "What's going on?"

I had practically forgotten about her. And as I open my mouth to lie, something dawns in Prisha's eyes and she jumps, waving her hands. "Wait— Oh my Gods. Hiren told me the Red Woman was after Bloodlurst and I thought that sounded wrong, but— You . . . you two are . . . *You're the Red—*"

As I lunge toward my sister and clamp my hand over her mouth, our mother billows around the corner. "Prisha! I needed that sheep kemp three minutes ago."

"I'll explain later. *Don't* say anything," I whisper before releasing Prisha.

My mother stops in her tracks. The smell of steamed vegetables meets us before she gets an arm's length away. I envision the potion she is working on retroactively. "Adraa, there you are. I need you to—" My mother finally notices Jatin. "Hello."

All I can think about as my mother talks is Prisha, who

holds the biggest secret of my life in her throat. "Oh, um, well, this is—"

"Jatin Naupure!" Jatin exclaims with two fingers to his neck and a bow.

My mother's eyes spin and then light up. "Jatin. It's so nice to meet you again." She thrusts out her forearm and he presses his against it.

"It's very nice to see you," Jatin says with a smile.

"Sorry, but I need to get back to the clinic. Prisha, get the kemp. Adraa, I really do need you."

"I'm kind of busy."

She gives me a look. Examines the two of us. For a second I register fear on her face. Then it disappears. "I have two patients with Bloodlurst poisoning. Two kids who flew deliveries all day. It's bad, Adraa."

I tense, anger lapping at me. I need to stop the Vencrin. I need to get to Moolek. I need to talk to Prisha. I need—

"What degree of burnout are they experiencing?" I ask, tugging up my sleeves.

◇ ◇ ◇

For the next two hours I cast pink spell after pink spell to stabilize a drug addict. Mother was right. It's the worst the clinic has ever seen. One is so red from windburn it looks like a rash. He keeps mumbling too, something about not being able to take any more.

Jatin volunteers to help as always. As I work on the Bloodlurst poisoning he helps craft a few of the other potions Mother has fallen behind on. When we pass each other in the confusion of patients, potions, and magic, he always catches my eye and smiles. I melt and solidify at the same time.

My happiness is only pierced by Prisha, who electrifies my nerves with every glance. I watch her piece together most of my story as the Red Woman. Of course, Hiren told her everything from a few nights ago. But I had forgotten just how observant my sister is. Her eyes scream questions and mine spark with what I hope communicates *Wait, don't say anything.* But when's the last time my sister listened to me? Jatin and I are doomed.

My chance to talk to her finally comes in the potion room as Mother yells enchantments a wall away. I stir a gooey salve, with Prisha layering it on kemp to create a bandage. Jatin is next to me, glancing between us, waiting.

"Prisha, let me explain," I whisper.

"Don't bother. I want in."

"What?" I must have misheard her. There's no way that—

"I want in. I want to join you."

I turn to face her fully. She mirrors me. "No. You can't," I say.

Jatin laughs.

I turn to him. "Why are you laughing?"

He leans toward me. "Because we literally had this same conversation in the Underground a month ago and you are still as stubborn as ever."

"Prisha, you don't even understand what's going on or what we're fighting."

She crosses her arms. "You think Moolek has stolen your firelight and you want to find out why and then get it back."

"Yeah, but . . . yeah, I guess that's most of it. But there's also Vencrin and—"

"You think Vencrin are the muscle behind Moolek's plans. That's why you fight in the Underground, to get close to them, right? It all makes sense now." There is no doubt on her face or in her voice. She waits for me to verify.

"Wow," Jatin whispers. "She's pretty good."

"Don't encourage her."

He raises his hands, but a smile lingers.

"I'm right, right?" Prisha asks with her signature smirk.

"Yes, pretty much."

"I knew the Red Woman wasn't bad. I've been researching her for weeks. But to think it was you this whole time." Pride shines through the words. Pride. Like after my lies I can be forgiven. Like she truly respects what I'm trying to do.

"I'm not going to tell Mom and Dad," she says calmly.

"I . . ."

Mother glides into the room. "I want that salve on the Bloodlurst patients immediately."

Prisha and I both twist around and spread the ointment on the bandages. Jatin joins us, squeezing my hand and lacing the wool with the brown goo.

My mother smiles knowingly. "I knew you two liked each other. You know, we never told Adraa to write to you, Jatin. She did that on her own. She would run off as soon as she received one of your letters when she was younger."

I give Jatin a sideways look. "I had to correct your arrogance or prove you wrong, that's all."

"Yeah, me too." And he winks.

"Well, I personally always enjoyed your letters," Prisha interjects.

Good Gods. Prisha is making it very hard for me not to throttle her. I push her shoulder, but her smirk only grows.

"I'm glad you liked them," Jatin says, laughing.

Mother smiles. "We just have to get through your ceremony now."

I try for a reassuring smile. Only Jatin catches that it's more like a grimace.

◇ ◇ ◇

Jatin and I wander out to the training ground, escaping the chaos of the clinic and my clever little sister for a few minutes. Of course any of the staff could be peering out a window. But they can't hear what we are saying.

"If possible, I feel as if I know you even better," Jatin says as the crisp air knocks into us.

"Was it watching me pour blood in a cauldron or freak out every time my sister even moved in our mother's direction?"

"Both. You know, your sister *could* help," Jatin says.

"I don't know if I can watch out for the both of you."

"That hurts." Then he gets serious. "When you turn eighteen, masquerading as Jaya won't be as easy. We need to think of another way to get information. Your sister—"

"My sister hasn't been trained in the same way. She's gifted, she's never had to worry about the ceremony or fighting for her life."

348

Jatin gives me a look. "Are you scared about your royal ceremony, Adraa?"

I step up onto the fountain, hang off Retaw's stone hand and swing to the other side. Jatin jumps up on the rim as well, circling with me. We start a game of chase, my mission to avoid, his to capture. He tries to win, to look me in the eye, but talking about my shortcomings in front of him? It's easier to not face him.

"It's weird hearing you call me Adraa."

"You prefer Smoke?" he teases.

"Do you prefer Jatin?"

I swing left and suddenly he's in front of me. I guessed wrong.

"Yes." He smiles.

"Good to know," I breathe.

"We said no more lies."

I take a deep breath as I tell him the truth about the last lie I've been holding on to. "I'm terrified."

"I hope you're referring to the ceremony."

I laugh unexpectedly. "I wouldn't say you are terrifying."

"Good, I don't want to get punched in the face again."

I lightly push his shoulder. "It was more like a slap and you know it."

He catches my hand and weaves his fingers through mine. It's very distracting. "Why are you terrified?"

"I—I don't want to fail."

He frowns. "You won't fail. Blood, you are the best witch I've—"

"*Himadloc,*" I whisper, and red drips off my hands and into the water below. With each splash of red smoke my spell courses through the water. It slows, gets a bit colder, and we both wait as a light frost glistens across the surface. Not even frozen. My cheeks flush. I never thought I would admit this to Jatin Naupure. Never thought I would showcase my greatest weakness quite like this.

"It's moving water. It's hard to freeze moving—"

"Don't."

"Well, I could help. It's sort of my forte." He smiles. "I would just need payment, of course."

"Payment?" I snort. "The future Maharaja of Naupure needs to haggle a few gold coins out of me?"

"Who said anything about money?"

I narrow my eyes. "What exactly do you want?"

"You . . ."

I stare.

And then he continues with a smirk. "To admit that I'm the best wizard in all of Wick—"

He doesn't get to finish his sentence because I lean forward and kiss him. He welcomes the interruption, pulling me closer so that our bodies press together. I pull back only an inch from his lips, dizzy with happiness. "I don't think I can agree to those terms. We said no more lies, Jatin."

CHAPTER THIRTY-TWO

◇

A Performance for the Gods

Adraa

Moolek has disappeared. All reports say he left the country. I don't buy it for a second and the fact that we can find little to no information proves to me he's still here, lurking. But with no leads and the wanted posters stuck to every corner I focus on my royal ceremony. Jaya Smoke might never be again, but I still have my mask. I'll find a way. I already have plans to talk to Beckman, this time as a rani.

Jatin is true to his word. For the next week he trains me. And for once in my life, under his guidance, I don't feel like a failure in white magic. I can't freeze moving water, but I can freeze liquids. I can't create snow, but I can control how it falls. Jatin smiles and reassures me that that will be enough. That I'm a nine. That I won't disappoint. It's everything I ever wanted to be and to hear. And in our bubble of training, and focus, and study, I almost believe him.

Yet, doubt still clangs inside my head.

Like all events one dreads and is unprepared for, my royal test arrives too soon. The night before I toss, turn, and dream myself into the land of red. I start awake each time, willing myself to think about anything but the ceremony, and yet it drags me back down. "You must go through with it," the red room voice commands, ringing with intensity, until dawn strikes through my bedroom in staggered streaks and I fully awaken.

Zara pounces onto my bed. "I couldn't sleep. All I could think about was how I could do your hair, and what ribbons we could use." After that, she gets to work, painting, braiding, and fastening me to look like a genuine Lady of Belwar. It takes hours. But I don't really mind it and before long I'm spinning in front of the mirror. "I have to say, you have outdone yourself," I tell her. Zara has taken nine colored ribbons and woven them in my hair, creating a cascading rainbow effect I cannot even comprehend.

"It matches your ceremony garments perfectly," she gushes.

She's right. My lehenga is red with golden edging. Swirled and beaded into the fabric are all nine colors of the gods. The dupatta is sheer and catches a rainbow of colors every time I move.

She snags my eyes in the mirror. "It's okay if you are nervous, but today you won't worry about how you look." I smile. It's moments like this when Zara is most endearing. Even if she is all for love letters, romance, and clothes, she still understands how I might feel the day upon which I must pledge myself to the gods. And I love her for it.

Riya enters as I'm staring myself down, willing the nerves to cease their war within my gut. "Wow. Adraa, you look—"

"I know, right? I did a good job, didn't I?" Zara gushes, dancing as she retrieves the leftover ribbons and hairpins.

I stall, then turn slowly. "It's time?"

Riya nods. "Yeah."

I gulp as I step outside the palace gates. Belwar glows in red. Red banners, red flags, red dye splashed over each threshold. They're wishing me well, celebrating my forte as the next generation to take up the Belwar mantle. But shouldn't they have waited until after the ceremony? Failure looms, like the banners overhead. It reminds me of the red room of my dreams. Maybe that's what my mind was doing as I slept, preparing me for this moment.

"This is where I leave you." Riya unbuckles her skyglider from her belt. "I'll see you there."

"Riya." I tug at her arm. For the past week we've barely talked, but I can't let it go any longer. "I know you are still mad I lied—"

She scoffs. "You've done more than lie. You've jeopardized yourself and jeopardized both Belwar's and Naupure's futures. If Dad—" She chokes. "If my dad knew about this he would be ashamed. He would have stopped you."

"Is that why you're so upset? You think you failed to protect me and he would have?" She won't look me in the eye. I hook my hands around her shoulders. "Riya, I became the Red Woman not for some thrill. I did it because . . . because when I was eight and scared beyond measure about being Untouched, your dad pulled me aside and said a true rani doesn't have to have magic or a God's blessing." Tears well in my eyes. "A true rani just helps the people."

Riya finally looks at me. "My father had a lot of sayings. He wasn't always right." She pulls away and reaches for her sky-glider. "And you are not an Untouched, you are one of the most powerful witches I know. Good luck today, but I don't think you need it. You are not eight years old anymore." In a burst of air and dirt she's gone.

I wipe my face as the dust settles. I won't regret my decisions because they put me in danger. It is my firelight. I'm responsible for how people use it. In time, Riya will see.

It's tradition for a royal to make the journey on foot and alone for one's ceremony. Then my family and friends will walk back with me to the palace, following behind to show they believe in my leadership. But for now I'm alone. And while the temple lies next to the palace, I have to take the long way, through the city, through the red-bannered street. I've never seen Belwar empty like this before. It's ghostly.

This is it. This is the moment when I'm supposed to be mature, sophisticated, powerful. An adult. It's never felt so untrue. All of this is just dress-up. Am I the only one who feels like a fraud? Or have other royals walked this path and doubted? Doubted everything?

It seems like days before I arrive at the base of the small hill and begin climbing to the top. The sun burns into me as if it's focusing a spotlight. I might spontaneously combust as bile bubbles up my throat.

The temple rises into view. Gods, the entire palace has come out for this. I've been here hundreds of times. This isn't any different. My feet drag my lehenga in the hot, dry grass. Who am I kidding? This is completely different. *Breathe. Just breathe.*

I spot Jatin in the crowd. His eyes widen as he gazes at me. He smiles. I try to smile back, but it crumbles. My parents stand closest to the temple steps. I walk up to them.

"You don't need to be nervous. You are going to be fine," my father assures me.

I just nod. I don't know what to say anyway. Nerves gnaw at the words.

He touches my chin. "Bright dawn, Adraa. Bright dawn."

This time I smile. I'm the only one freaking out here. My parents are trying to reassure me, and no one else looks scared. The dreams flare to life in my memory, but I push them back down. They're not an omen, but a blessing. This is my day, my dawn, and my destiny.

Yet, why does it still feel like a lie? *Stop! Stop overthinking this. Do this, prove yourself and you get everything you want. Your title, Jatin, happiness . . .*

I approach the temple, climb the three simple stairs and find myself in the center, surrounded by the nine columns of the gods. It's never felt so empty.

"By the blood of my blood I offer myself to be tested by the gods!" I yell.

Nothing stirs, not even the wind. Maybe the gods aren't listening. I continue anyway. "I vow to protect all those touched with your blessing." These last words feel weird coming from my lips. This speech is an ancient one, when the Untouched were thrown away by society. But nowadays? Helping the Untouched is important for Belwar's future and I don't exactly care for everyone powerful and Touched.

I try to clear my head. "Allow me to serve through you.

355

Allow me to offer my blood if I don't prove fit." A shiver runs through me. I hate that line.

From the first pillar on my right, a wave of heat crashes over me. Red magic.

It has begun.

◇

CHAPTER THIRTY-THREE

A Dance and Its Destruction

Jatin

It's nice to watch the ceremony instead of performing it. Waves of fire roll off the first pillar and crash into Adraa. But she's ready. Her arm glows bloodred and she swivels around the flame, elbows and wrists bent. It's a push-and-pull movement, a dance.

Today, wizards and witches are overly lazy, using only speech to call forth their Touch. But in the original times, casting was full body. I too performed in this way for the gods a year ago, and watching Adraa move reawakens the old traditions I've learned. Reminds me how much I inherently move my arms when casting.

Next comes a mountain of orange mist that collapses upon her. She yells spell after spell as she is forced to bear the weight of Renni's trials.

"She is doing well," Maharaja Belwar whispers to his wife. He squeezes her arm. "Trust her."

He's right. Adraa is doing well. She sweeps the yellow magic around her, turning and moving like the wind. Then her steps harden as a green smoke rises from the bottom of Htrae's pillar, the magic weaving and climbing like vines. Red unfurls from Adraa's hands and sways with the branches, untangling them. For this spell she doesn't shout, mirroring Goddess Htrae's more peaceful trial.

Retaw: Adraa moves with the gushing blue wave trying to capsize her.

Raw: Hundreds of purple arrows materialize from the next pillar and Adraa redirects them back into the stone from which they came. Quick. Precise. Perfect.

The sun beats down on us. It's already been more than an hour. She's so close now.

"Laeh is next. We have nothing to worry about here," Maharani Belwar says.

She's right. Pink happens so fast I don't fully catch it. One moment pink smoke encases Adraa and in the next it's gone. Finished. Pride inflates my chest. That's my Smoke.

"You've taught her well," Father tells Maharani Belwar.

Black magic quickly swallows the scene, slithering from its pillar in shadow form. Adraa moves low and fluidly, weaving the God's test with her own shadow. She turns into darkness and for minutes I can't see her dance. My heart spikes. Her parents don't seem concerned, though. In a flash she's back and the temple lightens.

"Well done. Nearly there!"

Only white left. Yet nothing happens. We all watch the pillar, awaiting the final test, but there's nothing. Whispers start to seize the crowd. Adraa turns around, and for the first time in hours, our eyes lock. And in her eyes, I see terror.

In a violent burst, white magic surges out of the pillar.

"Adraa!" I yell, but it's too late. She moves to perform the first step of a spell, but then she's knocked off her feet.

Maharani Belwar gasps beside me.

A spell readies on my lips. My father, sensing my body language, clutches my arm. "It would hurt her," he says.

Even knocked down, with a white fury building up against her, Adraa fights back. She stands, stamps one foot, and begins dancing. And yet it looks wrong. Her body wobbles in the casting. There's too much white magic. Surely Dloc never cast this much magic against me in my trials. A roar of wind rips through the temple. Many people retreat in fear.

"We have to do something!" I yell.

My father shakes his head. "She must work through it herself. If we intervene, she will fail."

My entire body clenches, all muscles engaged and yet motionless. I can't do anything. I'm useless.

Adraa is a blaze of color within a torrent of snow and wind. It's like when I first saw her all those weeks ago, lying on the ground in front of my carriage amid a sea of chaos. But back then, she raised her hand to notify everyone she and the boy were safe. Now, there's no reassurance, no sign, only the flash of red in the middle of vast whiteness.

"What's happening?" someone yells as we lose sight of her completely.

This is wrong. I have to do something. I step forward, feeling the icy breath of Dloc down to my bones. "Adraa?"

A flash of red fire hits the temple ceiling and the stone cracks. Ice swallows the opening and the rock splinters. Someone screams and the Belwar servants scramble backward.

"Oh Gods," I think my father says.

Maharaja Belwar and I catch each other's eyes, and without a word, we run forward. But as soon as I step into the freezing white mist, it disappears. A loud slurping sound echoes, and with a whoosh the white magic flies back into Dloc's pillar. Have I just ruined everything?

I spot Adraa a few meters away, the rainbow ribbons in her hair mangled and sliding down her back. The next moment is quiet. No one dares speak. She did it! She must have. Relief swells inside of me. We were worried over nothing. She's passed their trials.

"Adraa?" I call.

Why won't she turn around?

Another breathless second ticks by. Something's wrong. Dread swarms my throat and with a swallow it spreads throughout me. Why won't she turn around? Why won't she move? But she is moving, her body vibrating, shaking uncontrollably.

Before anyone takes another step, Adraa tumbles to the ground as if her strings have been cut. It's a death fall. Riya shrieks and Maharani Belwar screams bloody murder.

My body numbs. I don't know I'm running until I skid to a stop and fall next to her, the first by her side. With trembling fingers I touch her shoulders and gently pull her onto her back.

"No, no, *nooo*. Please, no." I lift her lifeless form into my lap and fumble at her throat to find a pulse.

The Belwars collapse on the ground next to me. My father stands above us with liquid eyes and one hand to his mouth.

"Give her to me," a quavering female voice demands.

Hope punches me in the gut. Maharani Belwar, the best pink forte in all of Wickery. She can bring Adraa back. She can save her.

"What can I do, Ira?" Maharaja Belwar rolls up his sleeves.

Maharani Belwar doesn't even glance at us. "*Laeh!*" she cries out, thrusting her hands onto Adraa's chest. Adraa jolts upward, but nothing else happens. Her head lolls to the side in a deathlike swivel.

Gods, no. No!

"Stay with me, baby. *Laeh.*" She shoots again. The pink magic dissolves into Adraa, raises her body in a jerk, and . . . And nothing happens.

Maharani Belwar turns to Maharaja Belwar and sputters, "Vivaan, she's not responding. In the clinic, in the clinic there—"

In one fluid motion, Maharaja Belwar scoops Adraa up in his arms. And in a flash of orange he's gone, with Maharani Belwar right after.

I stumble to pick myself up. My father and what's left of the other ceremony viewers sit on the steps, stunned. Adraa's sister is frozen. Riya, however, is already dashing toward the clinic.

"*Tvarenni!*" I shout, and shoot after her.

When Riya halts before a doorway I lurch to a stop and gape at the scene before me. Adraa is on the medical table, where a week ago we stood together helping patients. Everything has changed. The floor, covered with blood and broken bottles, makes me want to vomit. I'm thrust back to a time in which I stood at the threshold of my mother's room, watching horrified as screams shot from her ragged throat. Now it's just the yell of spells and a blaze of orange and pink smoke wafting over the body of the girl I love. Blood drips to the floor in a maddeningly consistent patter.

There was no wound. Adraa wasn't bleeding for the few seconds I held her.

"It's not hers," a voice murmurs.

What's happened? There was no wound before!

"Jatin!" Riya shakes me. "It's *not* hers."

Peering at the floor again, I get it. Bottles, potions, blood, it was all pushed off the table for Adraa.

As I step forward to do something, anything, Maharaja Belwar twists around and slams the door closed with a flick of yellow magic. I think I hear a soft apology, but the slam masks any other noise. I'm cut off from her. I'm useless.

Riya slumps against the opposite wall, tears shimmering on her cheeks. "She still thought I was mad at her. That's the last thing she'll ever—"

"No!" I shout. "No!"

"Will you wait with me?" she whispers through sobs.

"I'm never leaving her."

◇ ◇ ◇

Within minutes, Prisha, Kalyan, my father, and several servants find their way to our hallway of torture, where time eats at us until it devours something vital. A servant girl falls into Riya's arms, which renews Riya's tears. Hiren, that guard from the rooftop who wanted to arrest me, holds Prisha close. Kalyan sits next to me, silent and strong. My father paces, wanting into the room as much as I do, I'm sure.

My brain cycles through all my memories of Adraa and tries to hold on to every detail. Of course, I fail. I fail over and over again until even in my memories I can feel her slipping away.

When the door finally unlatches, it's Maharaja Belwar.

"She has a pulse. Ira is still at it, but even if she were to wake up . . . There's not much hope," he says, with tears sliding down his face.

I turn and pound my fist against the nearest wall.

This is my fault. Adraa recognized the danger when no one else did. What royal has ever died during their ceremony? It's been a century, maybe even centuries, plural. But she knew and I pushed her here, to perform for the gods and they beat her. No, they *killed* her.

"Son?"

I whack my father's hands off me and run. I make it to the training yard before I collapse to the ground. Frostlight blossoms flutter at my crash and then lie still. I crush a few in my hands. Curse the color white. To blood with it all!

"Damn you! Damn all of you. I loved her, you bloody bastards. I loved her!" I scream into the air. I don't know I even said the spell, but a freezing blast of ice shoots up into the sky and my arms go numb from the cold that bursts from my body. My whole body is numb, besides my chest, which grates like I'm being shredded by a hot iron. A surge of pure white magic keeps shooting out of my hands. It feels like hours of me exploding, hurling my magic into the sky and hoping the gods die along with me. Then I slump to the ground and sob.

My father finds me a while later. Without saying a word he collapses to the ground as well. Before I can process anything, he lurches forward and clutches me in a hug.

I have experience with loss. I know the pain, the torture, the ache. But when my mother died I was only four, too young for grief to rip through me in the same way. As I grew up, her death slowly sank its claws into me.

But this. This is branding. My world is crumbling before my eyes and I can't do anything to stop it.

Gods, this is what my father dealt with, has dealt with for years. One look into his eyes and I can tell the pain is ripping him open anew. I have only one other memory of him crying.

I take a shuddering breath. I don't know if I can live through today, let alone the hollow moments that will fill the rest of my life. I will never talk with her again. Never touch her. Never put pen to paper knowing she will read my words.

Bang! The ground roars. *This is because of me.* I created a storm from all the white magic I smashed into the clouds. Or worse, the gods are responding to my rampage and they have decided to yell back, to shake all of Wickery in answer.

Bang! Bang! again. Explosions and the sound of thunder pound the air.

I search the sky for the source of the noise and find it instantly. A dark-gray cloud spews from the mountains to the west, toward Naupure.

The earth shakes and my father and I shake with it.

Bang!

I stand to get a clearer view of the clouds and where they're coming from. No, this isn't because of me at all. It's Mount Gandhak. Mount Gandhak is erupting.

CHAPTER THIRTY-FOUR

◇

The Loss of a Loved One

Jatin

"Come on, Jatin," my father orders. We run back inside, down the hallway. The group huddling around the medical room peers toward us for answers. More people have gathered, including an older female guard who stands next to Riya and wears the sun crest of Belwar.

"What is it?" Riya and Kalyan both ask, and then glance at each other.

"Mount Gandhak is erupting," I say as my father barrels into the medical room. I follow close behind. The blood and herbs on the floor perfume the air with an iron tang. At first, I can't look at Adraa, but when I do, my eyes stick. She looks peaceful. Her hair lays like a spiderweb, loose, tangled, and ribbonless. I choke back a sob.

My father steps forward. "Mount Gandhak is erupting. I don't know how much time we have. I'm going to need your help for this. Maharani Belwar, I don't think we can do this without you."

"Erupting? It hasn't erupted in centuries. It's a dormant volcano," the head guard says.

"Not anymore," my father says grimly.

Maharaja Belwar looks between the one small arched window and us. The sky has already turned to deep red in the past five minutes. "I'll help, of course, but—"

"I can't leave her!" Maharani Belwar shrieks. "If I leave her now . . ." At her cry it dawns on me. He is asking her to abandon Adraa. My father would take away the little hope we have left for Adraa's life?

"Maharani Belwar has to stay with Adraa. She's the only one that could possibly—"

"She's gone, Jatin, and we don't have time," my father says, his voice nearly breaking.

A small body pushes forward and everyone looks. Prisha slowly pulls Maharani Belwar's hands off Adraa's body. "Mom, go. I will save her."

"Prisha, you— It's too difficult and you need to evacuate."

"*Sansria!*" Prisha shouts, and a blaze of light-pink smoke consumes her mother's darker pink. It swarms and then dives into Adraa's mouth. "I can do it, and I won't leave."

"I'll help too," a young woman dressed in a healer's uniform whispers as she steps forward.

"As will I. Tell me what you need, Prisha," Riya says, rolling up her sleeves.

The female guard, who I think is Riya's mother, based on their similar features, pulls at Riya's arm, holding her back. "You'll be needed on the ground, helping with evacuation."

"No, Mother. This is my duty, to protect her no matter what," Riya says.

"But she's—"

Riya jerks her arm free. "She didn't give up on Dad. I will not give up on her. Ever."

My father nods. "Maharaja Belwar, Maharani Belwar, we are going to have to contain the fumes. I believe it will take all three of us."

Maharaja Belwar whispers into his hands and wisps of orange smoke dart in various directions. "I'm calling to all my guards. If Mount Gandhak blows we will need green forte wizards to redirect any landslides."

Without Riya, Prisha, and that other healing girl, the rest of us run toward the training field. "Is Maharaja Moolek still here?" my father asks as we turn the corner.

"He left a few days ago," Maharani Belwar answers.

"It all makes sense now," I spit.

"What?"

"It's too convenient. Moolek is gone, Adraa, the most powerful red forte in Belwar, is . . . gone." A bulge of anger tangles in my throat. "It's not right."

"You would *accuse* our most powerful ally?" Riya's mother hisses.

I don't bother answering. I don't care. This is Moolek. I can feel it.

Riya's mother doesn't reply either, charging forward with plans. Assignments are yelled and thrown around like spilled rice. Riya's mother will lead those who can't fly to the docks. Hiren is sent straight there to make sure ships aren't leaving port without the maximum number of passengers. Kalyan is tasked with evacuating Azure Palace. He and I nod to each other before he bursts into the air toward our home.

And as I listen I don't hear a word of how we are going to actually stop this thing. My heart lurches. Without Adraa . . .

It's just me. Our duo cut down to one.

"I'm going to Mount Gandhak," I say as those of us left round the last bend toward the training yard and front gates.

My father whips in my direction. "Jatin."

"I'll freeze it from the inside. I'll stop the lava." My voice hardens so that I don't break in half. "No one else dies today." Now that I've said it I'm calm, maybe still numb. But it feels like it's the right thing. The Belwars each nod and Maharani Belwar even smiles through the tears still spilling from her eyes.

"No." My father's voice bites. "I can't lose you too." The sad part is I don't know whether he means my mother, my sister, or Adraa at this point. But now isn't the time to argue or to elaborate on years of protectiveness and restraint.

The ground quakes. The arches and stone balconies hold their shape, but dust and the sprinkle of rubble suggest total collapse. "I'm the only one that can do this. Please, let me be the raja of Naupure for once."

My father looks over at me like he's trying to memorize my face. Finally he nods. "You always were."

People gush from the palace and into the training yard at the same time we reach it. Guards burst from the other side of the yard. Everyone is talking or yelling. I can't hear anything but the roar splitting the sky in two.

When we stop in the training yard, Maharaja Belwar cups his

hands to his mouth and thousands of small pockets of orange light shoot into the sky. A few blaze over his shoulder and I hear bits of their message.

Mount Gandhak . . .
Evacuate to the docks. Fly if you can.
Rest assured we will . . .

But the message isn't getting out fast enough. I can already see streams of color flying upward around Belwar. It looks like the Festival of Color. But no, that's wrong. These are signals, all of them meaning only one thing: help.

The Belwars and my father board their skygliders and fly to the roof. It takes me a second to process, but then I'm right there with them, bounding upward and landing on the thick tiles behind them.

"Listen, everyone!" Maharaja Belwar's voice booms.

Chaotic chatter still consumes the air. Many people are already running out of the gates and into the street. I look behind me. The sky is crawling with skygliders. More fliers than I have ever seen in my life.

Guards and servants below us shout out questions.

"Is the Goddess Erif cursing us?"

"Did Lady Adraa fail the ceremony? Is that why Mount Gandhak is erupting?"

"Is she dead?"

"*Tar Vazrenni,*" Maharaja Belwar casts, and his voice enlarges. "*Listen!*"

Everyone stills and looks up at us.

"My daughter and her ceremony have nothing to do with what we are facing. Listen to me." He yells instruction after instruction about where wizards need to go. But I already have my duties. I look to Mount Gandhak. The gray cloud erupting from its top grows, pluming into layer after layer of mushroom-shaped spouts. The magnitude of what we are about to face, it's indescribable. And we don't have much time.

Only when Maharaja Belwar pauses at the end do I truly listen. "I'm asking you all to save our country. I cannot force you to stay, but we must work together. Trust in your rajas as the gods have trusted in us and our home will still be standing at the end of this day. We will not fail." He bows; his voice dims, and the last of us on the roof hear his final plea. "We cannot."

CHAPTER THIRTY-FIVE

I Come to Meet Death

Adraa

Danger

    Love

    Passion

    Blood

    Death

Red, all around me, saturating, dripping, covering every particle I can see. I hold up my hands. Only the dark-brown hue of my skin has been left its natural color.

I'm in a nine-sided parlor much like a prayer room, a demented prayer room. Wait. It's more visceral and real, but this . . . this is the room, the land of my nightmares.

"Adraa?"

I turn to find a woman glowing in red. Red skin, red sari, and even redder hair, lashing out like fire around her shoulders. The only color not permeated with blood is her eyes, her black-as-coal eyes. And they're staring at me. Before I can utter the words, my brain tells me this is Erif, Goddess of fire. I tumble backward and fall hard on my butt. *What the blood?*

"I can't believe I did it," she says with a gleaming smile.

Panic builds up in my chest. I can't breathe. There's no air in this room. I'm going to faint. The bloodlike walls blur. They seem to be melting, gushing, oozing.

"Oh!" the woman yells. A burst of red smoke smashes into my face. I gulp back life. After a few moments of silence, calmness wraps around me like a cool blanket.

"Sorry about that. I forgot, your body thinks you are still dying."

Still dying? Still dying! "Am I . . . am I dead?"

"No, not yet. But I had to take you out of there. Dloc was going to kill you."

The ceremony swims back to memory. Yes, I was trying to contain the blizzard, but it was too much for me. Frostbiting cold. There was so much pain, and then, then nothing but the color red. "I'm not dead, then?"

"What did I just say? You're not dead. You seemed smarter down in Wickery."

Well, this is great. I really hope this is a dream, because I don't want to spend the rest of eternity being ridiculed by a woman whose hair is literally smoking.

"This is a dream, right?"

"You're not physically here, just your soul."

"And you *brought* me here?" I scan the room. A giant fireplace sits center stage in the bleeding parlor. A set of wrought iron fireplace tools line the stone hearth. A few chairs and a table covered in satin look unused. "The nightma—I mean the dreams I've been having, they were you?"

"I can only open up this portal at certain times. And several possible paths led you to never performing the ceremony. So yes, I called out to you in your dreams. But even after all my preparation, I didn't think I could do it with Dloc attacking you. He's so melodramatic." Erif turns from me and tends to the fireplace, poking at the embers and the little tuft of flame.

I can't even fathom what she is saying. Dloc melodramatic? *Melodramatic?* "Are we just tools to all of you? Is my entire destiny based on your argument with Dloc?"

At my tone, her coal-black eyes snap to me. "Look, you don't have a destiny because I chose you to bless. I don't have that kind of control."

"You don't have that kind of control? But you did choose me. You decided to bless me. Didn't you fight for that?" I pull up my sleeve, showcasing my bare arm. "That's why I'm deformed like this?"

"Yes, Dloc was pigheaded, and we fought over your blessing. Yes, he still holds it against me, and thus, by extension, you. But you aren't deformed; you're just a little different. You are the one who sees yourself as deformed and you are the only one who can fix that," she scoffs. "Also, there is no destiny. There are only various paths and outcomes based on a collection of people's choices."

No destiny? I have *no* destiny?

Erif returns to tending the small fire. I can't take it, her poking, her prodding. Am I not even worth her time? Why in Wickery did she bring me here if not to talk to me? To only tell me my entire mindset was wrong?

I shove forward and grab the fireplace poker. "My life is worth more than this. Please, tell me what is going on. If I'm not dead, then why am I here? Can I go back?"

She pushes me with a white-hot hand. I fly through the room and slam against a wall. "This fire is your life, Adraa. If you wish for it to die, interrupt me again."

I stay silent, staring at the fire. My life? *That* is my life? The fire is small right now. One could even call it weak.

The next time the goddess speaks it is in a whisper. "I'm going to tell you why you are here, but we need to give your body and mind a little time to adapt. As for blessing you, it's as political and complicated up here as it is down there. I saw your strength, your position, and I wanted you to be under my name."

"More like wanted to use me," I say under my breath.

She hears nonetheless. "How have I used you? I didn't give you firelight. You came up with that spell on your own. You changed your world. I might have foreseen you *could* change it, but I didn't know how, when, or *if* you would. No one did."

"And yet I died at my royal ceremony."

Her eyes turn red. I step back on instinct. "*Almost* died. Almost! I decided to save you. So show some appreciation. And grow up, because we don't have time for all your problems. I need to warn you before it's too late."

"About what?" I swear, if the nightmares were a warning Dloc was going to kill me when I tried to perform the Royal Ceremony, I'm going to scream.

"I don't think you are ready to hear it yet. Almost dying and coming here is strenuous on the body. And this is my first time doing something like this. Do you want . . . tea?"

Something is wrong with her. "No." I sit on one of the satin-cushioned sofas. Maybe she's right; maybe my body *is* still messed up. The pain of the blizzard is only a memory, but it shoots through me regardless, as if it has soaked into my marrow.

Erif checks the fire one more time. "Your mother is talented. I knew she could do this. Your sister too."

"My . . . mother? Prisha? What are you talking about?"

"They are keeping your physical body alive. On the other side of the hearth."

I stare at the embers. In the smoke and ash I think I can see my mother hovering over my body. For a flash, Jatin's hollow expression flickers in the flame. I blink and try to stare harder, but the image is gone. "They think I'm dying?"

"Yes."

I stand up, bumping the table out of the way. "Please, put me back! You can't do that to them."

"I need you here. I need to warn you."

"Then tell me. For blood's sake, tell me."

Her eyes flick to the fire. It has brightened slightly. "I need to make sure you can pull through or none of this is worth anything. You will be worthless."

She means I'll be dead, truly dead. I watch my fire too; trying to breathe evenly, trying to fill my lungs with life. I go through the motions, but it's unnatural, like a fish out of water. For there is no air in this world and I don't have to breathe.

The fire pulses. Amid the flames, my body arches in a jolt. I see the edge of the clinic table and the smear of blood. I want to live.

"Good. Promising. Very promising." Erif spins back to me, her neck turning just past possible twist. I want to throw up.

"Mount Gandhak is about to erupt and it's because of your magic."

I shrink. "What?"

"Firelight, your firelight, was used to set Mount Gandhak to erupt. In the next hours the capital of Naupure will die and all of Belwar will be melted away."

My brain tries to process what she is telling me. Mount Gandhak isn't an active volcano. But Erif would know. She's a bloody goddess. And she reigns over one thing.

"It's happening *right now*?"

"Yes, it's starting. That's what helped me open the portal to pull you here for the first time."

And she let me yell for the past few minutes? She let me carry on watching my fire? She *is* demented. "Then send me back. Send me back now!"

"That's what I'm hoping we can do. I want you to save your country. But listen, this isn't a normal eruption. It is fueled by firelight. Smoke, ash, and lava will spew for as long as firelight continues to fuel the magma. Do you understand?"

"What? How . . ." Thoughts and fears explode in my mind. *My firelight? Will fuel as long as . . . that's two months!* "How do I stop it?"

"I may have blessed you, but you are the one who created

firelight. I never gifted my Touched with that kind of spell. You will have to figure it out, and fast. I'll try to help if I can."

Erif lifts the poker. "We shouldn't wait much longer. This is going to hurt a bit," she says, staring at the branding flame on the poker's tip.

Before I can make a sound of protest, she thrusts the poker into my chest. I croak out a gasp. It's fire and pain and . . . and . . .

I crumble, shock tensing and stalling my every cell. Why, why would she kill me again in this way? I have to help Belwar. The room spins. I'm zooming backward, away from the red room. The pain eases slightly. I feel my heart pump once again and realize that in the past few minutes my body stood silent.

"In the war to come, I'll be on your side!" Erif shouts.

"War? Wait, what war?"

"Just worry about the task in front of you. If you don't stop it, the war will be over before it even begins." She pulls the poker, ripping it from my chest. Grasping my shoulders, she tugs me toward her. "Good luck." And with a push I'm falling backward, into the fireplace. I scream out as my skin pulls and I'm sucked in.

My gut tightens. I'm going to be sick. A spot on my stomach turns back into the rainbow of colors of my royal ceremony garments. I'm flipping, spiraling backward until other colors bleed into being.

CHAPTER THIRTY-SIX

❖

I Awaken into Another Nightmare

Adraa
———·———

I come back to life gasping, my lungs starved and unable to purchase enough air.

Several shrieks of surprise vibrate against my ears.

"Adraa?"

"Is she really . . . ?"

"We did it," someone whispers.

I blink back tears, my entire body groggy except for a dull ache that pulses a vigorous tune: *I live. I live. I live.* Color and light glare around me and yet it's dark, gloomy. Only firelight lights up the three women huddled about me. I finally make out their faces. Zara, Riya, and my sister.

Riya swings one arm around my back to help me sit up. "You're okay. You're safe."

"I'm back," I choke out.

"This is impossible. Are you . . . How do you feel?" Zara asks. She's practically itching to take notes.

I begin to say that she can when Prisha leaps into my arms, crying. "Don't you ever do that again."

The earth shudders. A rumble like thunder rips through the air. Jars of herbs crash onto the floor.

"What the blood was that?" I ask, but I already know. It wasn't some death dream or hallucination. Erif was real; her warning was real.

"Don't worry about it. We need to focus on evacuating," Riya commands.

Prisha still cries in my embrace. Zara is calm enough to announce the truth, to tell me just how much I do need to worry about it.

"It's Mount Gandhak. It's erupting," she whispers in fear.

◇ ◇ ◇

"You can't go. I'm not losing you again." Riya pushes me away from Hubris the Third.

She won't listen to me. Even as I threw on flying pants and tried to explain Erif's warning, she wouldn't listen. "I have to go," I tell her.

"You just woke up. Your parents and Maharaja Naupure are taking care of the air. Jatin is already there. We need to evaluate and help guide the survivors to safety."

Jatin is already there? Survivors? I freeze, my stomach coiling. "Are you saying Jatin is *on* Mount Gandhak?"

The earth rumbles again. All four of us stumble, holding out our arms to steady ourselves. Zara clutches the nearest archway, praying silently, her head bent.

"No one made him go. They tried to stop him," Riya says, sounding desperate.

I don't hear anything but the confirmation. Jatin is on the volcano. He will be trying to stop Mount Gandhak like it's a normal natural disaster, like it's a mere avalanche. He won't know it's fueled by my firelight. Oh Gods.

"Riya, I will explain everything to you later. But right now, give me my skyglider or I will take it from you."

She steps away from me, shaking her head and sliding the skyglider behind her. "How are you so willing to die? If you fly to Mount Gandhak, you probably won't come back. You realize that, right?"

She's right. Of course she's right. But Erif is right too. I'm the only one who can possibly stop it. It's my spell. It's my magic. I died to learn that truth. I can't concede. "I know."

"You know," she whispers, almost to herself. "Maybe my father was right about you helping people, about what a true rani is." Slowly she brings Hubris around and holds it out to me. "I have to get him, and the rest of the clinic, to safety."

I grab Hubris the Third tightly. "Thank you."

Prisha runs into my arms. "Please, come with us."

"I have to do this." I squeeze her tight. "I love you." The earth rocks again and I hold on tighter.

My eyes find Riya's over Prisha's shoulder. "You'll get them out safely?"

"Yes." Riya presses two fingers to her throat, the message clear.

I grasp Prisha's shoulders, peeling her off me. "Hey, I just came back from the dead. I can do it again."

"You better," Riya whispers.

"Be safe," Zara calls. "And take these." She holds out the two bubble masks for flying at high altitude and ventilation that I bargained off Mittal. I probably won't need them. If my parents' magic fails we are all dead. But I take them and thank her all the same.

"No, please, Adraa," Prisha whines.

"I have to do this." And gently I pull away from my sister. "Goodbye."

With a nod to all three of them, I mount my skyglider. For once, frostlight petals seem to have deserted the training field and only dirt springs upward as I launch into the air.

◇ ◇ ◇

I balance on my skyglider, not fully able to process the destruction I'm witnessing. My world is cast in firelight. The sky is one large glob of darkness painted in bleeding red. Mount Gandhak is breaking apart, lava running down its slopes like angry scars. Its top fumes in a gray mass of clouds as big as my entire city. Instead of up and out, the clouds are rotating like a slow twister. Wrapped around the ash and smoke are coils of color: pink, orange, and blue swarming and shifting together. Maharaja Naupure and my parents are controlling the gas, keeping its heat and poison away from both cities. They're saving us from death, but they can't hold it back forever.

I fly through ash, weaving and bobbing around other witches and wizards desperately fleeing. They yell out at me as I pass. Am I lost, am I confused, am I stupid? They're probably all right.

Soon it's not other Touched I'm avoiding, but flying rocks. I swerve and veer, Hubris shaking with the amount of magic I'm pumping into its wood. Ash cascades down like thick rain. Then I hear it—a boulder has crashed into one of the flying stations suspended above the city. Yellow magic spinning underneath a block of lofted earth unravels. Rock and stone groan as the thing tears in half and crashes onto the city below. *Oh my Gods.* I squeeze my eyes closed. If this goes on another hour, let alone two months, we will all be destroyed. I have to stop this.

"*Simaraw!*" I cry out. The shield is of little help. I drop lower, blasting up and over the side of the volcano. On this side, part of the mountain gave way, a mudslide of trees and earth washed toward the sea. *Oh my Gods . . .*

Jatin is down there . . . somewhere. I keep flying, searching. Along the side closest to Naupure I make out a long white streak. "*Vardrenni!*" I yell. My eyes zoom in through the wall of gray and I'm finally able to make out what it is. Ice, a stream of ice. *Yes! Thank Gods.*

"*Pavria,*" I cast, and I hurtle through the air.

My feet skid on ash-coated slush as I land and buckle Hubris to my belt. Jatin stands ahead, freezing the lava as it flows and spews near him. The ground turns from hot red to cooled black to frozen white. He's trying to get to the top, infuse the thing with chilling ice. If I perform my own extinguishing spell we might be able to do this.

"Jatin!" I scream.

He doesn't hear me. I can barely hear myself.

A blast of heat and pressure rises up on Jatin's right. *"Chidu-raerif!"* I cry. My magic swarms the emerging lava and dives into the rock. The earth bursts with a burp instead of a vomit of fire.

Jatin looks at the bubbling earth, then swivels and sees me. The look on his face makes me want to cry. Those eyes hold both the torture of my death and the euphoria of my revival. Beyond any doubt, in this moment I know he loves me as much as I love him. I can't hear him over the roar of destruction, but I know what he is saying. He is yelling my name.

◇

CHAPTER THIRTY-SEVEN

Sacrifice to Save Someone

Jatin

I've resigned to die on this volcano if that's what it takes. For the first time in my life no voice holds me back, saying, *Careful, you are the future raja.* Maybe because in this moment I am a raja, and this is what I was meant to do—protect my country.

I know it's also the grief, consuming me, pushing me. *Adraa . . . is . . . gone,* my mind rattles, both unaccepting and inconsolable. But I won't die before I know this is over, that I have stopped Mount Gandhak from killing anyone else's Adraa. That means facing this thing, climbing up to the mouth and casting inside the belly.

I yell out freeze spells like never before. I unleash my anger, my pain, on this force of nature. It is just like me, exploding, bleeding its heart out. But something's wrong. This eruption is unlike that of a normal volcano, or at least what I assume to be a normal volcano. Pressure points arise throughout the landscape, as if the power of this thing seeks any crack in the earth to blast open. From what I can tell, the true monster has yet to blow, and yet the explosions and mounds of lava keep coming in bloodred geysers, and I keep casting.

A glint of red smoke soaks into the ground, and I turn. The earth chokes back an explosion that might have killed me. Ash cascading, heat soaking, thunder roaring, within it all Adraa's ghost emerges through the firestorm. She stands meters away with a hand raised as if she has just finished a spell.

A sob rocks my body in one heave. *Have I gone completely mad? Yes, yes, I have.* And yet this is a happy madness if she is here. I'm okay with whatever realm my mind has escaped to if it means Adraa and I can be together again. I've never wanted anything more in my life than for her to be real, for this not to be a mirage created by my grief and volcanic fumes.

"Adraa?" I scream. "Adraa!"

We run to each other as best we can through the minefield of boulders, gas, and lava.

And then her body slams into mine. She's in my arms. She feels real, so real. I can't stop touching her, squeezing her, feeling her hugging me back.

"Are you real?" I whisper.

"What kind of question is that? Of course I'm real."

"I thought, I thought . . ." The agony and joy of knowing I haven't lost her suffocates and fuels my lungs at the same time.

I cup her face and stare into her fiery eyes.

"I won't be late again," she says with a smile.

"How? How are you here?"

"I'll tell you later. We need to stop this."

A burst of heat ripples up my back, which means only one thing. Lava. Without thinking I cast an ice shield and tuck Adraa behind me. She has a similar thought, and puffs of smoke explode around the two of us, shielding us further.

"It's my firelight!" she yells.

"What do you mean?"

She points toward the top of Mount Gandhak. "The Vencrin or Moolek or both of them, whoever, they put my firelight *into* Mount Gandhak. That's why they were stealing it. That's why Mount Gandhak is erupting."

Those bastards! Were they willing to destroy us all? I want to ask how she knows this, but that doesn't matter right now. After weeks of working on the streets, we still hadn't discovered this plan, and now it's blowing up in front of our faces. I'd promised her we would find out what was happening to her firelight. We failed.

With Adraa by my side, safe and well, a part of me wants to grab her and run. We could still escape this. Both of our cities would die, but she and I would live. I would have her.

Adraa looks at me and I know she can read my hesitation. "Jatin, we are the only ones who can do this."

She's right. Gods, she's right.

"*Tuhinadloc!*" I holler, and cold white magic releases from my arms, creating a large sheet of frost at our feet.

We climb. I pave the way in a sheet of ice and snow. Adraa extinguishes the heat on either side of us. The past month of fighting together has taught us well. If I sweep low, she covers the sky. We work in rings like in a fight. Our mission is to cool the ground in front of us and then proceed, step by step.

"How exactly does your firelight make this any different from a normal eruption?" I yell.

"If we don't stop it, Mount Gandhak will continue to blow for two months."

My stomach drops out from under me. Two bloody months. "How do we stop it?"

"I don't know. Let's get to the top and try to force it. If you cool it from the inside and I work to release all the gas, it might work."

I nod. As we go, Adraa sweeps her arms upward and calls to nearby roots to groove out the earth. She builds a trench on the left side, and I follow her lead and create one on the right. Suddenly, I know we can do this. It is Adraa and me. We understand how each of us is going to move. We are powerful enough.

So we keep climbing, increasing our speed with each step we take. Finally the air becomes heavy with heat.

"*Tuhinadloc.*" I blast at the earth. It crackles against the blaze, forming a plate of ice. Meters above us, the lip of a brewing cauldron bellows. I can't see anything through the sheet of black and gray, but the smell of sulfur slams into my nose.

"I think this might be as high as we can get," Adraa yells, hand outstretched as if to block the sheets of ash trying to consume us.

"Is it enough?" I ask.

"Gods, I hope so."

Digging our feet in the ground, Adraa and I lock eyes and

nod. We move in sync, weaving the toxic air out of this pit. Ria, Htrae, Erif, Retaw. We chant to the main four. Anything to release gas, calm earth, dull fire, and welcome water. Nothing seems to help.

"I can't think of any more extinguishing spells!" Adraa cries.

"Do you remember the spell you cast against Ax that night I first saw you, in the Underground?"

"Which spell?"

"He was throwing purple flames at you and you contained them, like put them in a jar."

"Oh yes! Yes, of course."

"Well, if you—"

"If you ice it and I— Yes! Got it."

"On three, then." We don't have much time left. This is our last shot. One last big spell from the both of us. I look over at her. She's watching me, waiting for the count.

"Jatin? You ready?"

"I love you."

She bounces up from her stance. "Are you serious right now? Jatin, the volcano."

"Just needed to tell you."

"Well, I love you too!"

I smile. *If I have Adraa, we can do this.* "On three. One . . ." I breathe in.

"Two . . . ," Adraa exhales.

"Three."

"Himadloc!" I shout. The simplest ice spell I have. Then I build on it, adding all the layers of frost, slush, and snow I can

think of. A blast of white erupts from my hands. Out of my peripheral vision, a blaze of red spews from Adraa, and I hear her containing spell trying to quell the heat beating me in the face. Slowly, a sheet of red magic blooms over the peak of Mount Gandhak, suffocating the ash and enveloping the terror.

Yes!

I yell louder and louder, until my vocal cords ache and my throat turns to ash. My limbs are numb, my body wrapped in ice as my white magic runs not only off my arms but also down my torso. My sweat turns to icicles. I can't move with my magic anymore.

"Jatin, I don't think it's working!" Adraa shouts.

I open my mouth to agree, to spout one final ounce of encouragement, when *boom!* Mount Gandhak rejects our magic. Adraa screams. With a blast of heat, all the ice melded to my body shatters and I'm blown backward.

◇ ◇ ◇

The world blares awake. My ears ring. Ash floats from the sky in heavy heaps.

I struggle to right myself, to recapture reality. *Where the blood am I?*

Ah, blood. I clutch my side. Even the smallest of breaths stabs my gut. I think a few of my ribs are broken. *"Suptaleah,"* I tell my body as I seek out Adraa amid the ash. She's gone again.

"Adraa?" I scream. My lungs feel like they're about to explode in my chest, like bone fragments are piercing my air supply. *"Cyavateleah,"* I cast again, with more strength. The pain eases, slightly, as my body is told to forget the agony.

"Adraa?" I call as I stand. The gray darkness whirls.

"Jatin? Jatin! Where are you?"

Finally. "Adraa!" I move to the sound of her voice. Then there she is, only meters away. We run toward each other. Right as I reach her, the ground rumbles. I think Adraa and I have made it worse. This is it. Mount Gandhak has had enough of our antics. It's going to go.

"Are you okay?" we yell at the same time.

She nods. It's enough.

"We can't fix it with physical force."

"I know!" I yell over the roar.

Boom! Blazing, unnatural red fire explodes and interrupts the sea of gray. Adraa and I shield our faces because with this light, we can see everything. Orange, pink, and blue streams of magic wrestle with the clouds, but they can't stop the lava. *Gushes* or *explodes* is too tame a word for the fury before us. I stare into pure unyielding fire, a two-month-long inferno that will wipe out both our cities. Before it was my life crumbling in front of me with the loss of Adraa. Now it is the world, the physical world erupting. And we still can't seem to do anything to stop it.

"We have to move."

That's all Adraa needs for motivation. We run. My lungs answer with a piercing pang.

"Do you have any ideas?" Adraa yells.

I rack my brain. We could try starting over at the base and climbing, ringing the mountain in a shell of ice. We could create deep trenches. But I have a feeling neither idea will work. A wall or a trench would only buy us time, a few hours at most. We need to stop it completely.

"Can we corrupt the firelight? Make it so it won't last months." My right arm is numb with tingling spikes. I shake it. I meant to numb only my ribs. *I must have—*

"No, I made sure firelight's longevity could never be tampered with," Adraa says.

"We have to figure out something. A disadvantage even *you* couldn't think of." My foot slips and I stumble. I call to my orange magic for strength or precision. But nothing—my Touch looks dull and the numbness in my arm only sharpens. *What the—*

Pain swallows my head. I clutch at it with a gasp. My vision blurs. *What's wrong with me?*

"Jatin?"

"I'm fine."

But then I process what is happening, and fear shoots through me. So this is what it feels like to burnout, for your magic to collapse within you. Gods, it's worse than I could have imagined. I'm dissolving.

I meet the hard earth with a thud. Black wavering dots stream in front of my eyes. Pain engulfs my rib cage and squeezes, unwilling to forget any longer.

Adraa shouts and tugs me toward her. My arms lie limp at my sides, unmovable. My nerves seem to have liquefied.

I'm going to fail her, leave her here amid this destruction. I'm going to die. Her voice sounds far away. "Jatin! Just hang on. Just—"

"Adraa, I'm sorry. I'm so—" Before I can finish my sentence, the world goes dark.

CHAPTER THIRTY-EIGHT

◇

Mount Gandhak

Adraa

I should know how to save both my world and Jatin, but I don't. I hold Jatin's unconscious body in my arms, trembling as heat blasts my face. He's fine for now, just a bad burnout, I think, I hope. No matter what, I can't leave him on the ground to die without protection. I am left to choose—fight the volcano or save Jatin's life.

I'll try to help you, Erif had said.

"Help! Erif, help me! I don't know how to stop it."

Nothing happens. Lava surges toward us in the distance. All around me the earth cracks open and steam shoots in the air. Sulfur overrides my nostrils and burns them. Our parents . . . It must be becoming too much for them.

"Zaktirenni!" I yell to carry Jatin's weight. Gripping him under his arms, I pull him down the slushy slope he created to get us up here. With a few raw green magic spells, I dig a moat that connects to the trenches Jatin and I crafted. It might buy

394

us a few minutes. But I don't know what good it can do, really. I'm alone, with no plan. Panic blossoms angry excuses in my head. *Of course I couldn't do this. I failed my ceremony. I am no rani. What did Erif expect? She should have known I wasn't good enough.*

I touch Hubris the Third on my belt, then jerk my hand away at the thought. I bite my lip and let my screams take hold. Mount Gandhak isn't the only one that can explode. When I open my eyes, with one look at Jatin and the echoing shrieks of the earth burning my ears, it's clear. I won't leave him. And I won't leave my country to be destroyed.

I wish I could reverse this, undo every decision that led to this point. But I don't know if that would have been any better. Without Erif's warning I might have attacked this volcano like it was an average eruption. My head spins. That's what Jatin and I were doing, weren't we? Yet the bloodstained sky, the exact same color of my Touch, demands attention, howls my failures.

I may have blessed you, but you are the one who created fire-light.

Yes, I created it. Me! It responds to me. And that's what it has been doing. I've fanned my firelight with more of my magic and it fueled Mount Gandhak, it responded.

But how do you stop a fire? You deprive it of its energy. *My* energy.

That's it! I need to take it back. That's the only way to get rid of it. And I have done that once before. It's insane to attempt something like that again and on this scale, but it's the only way I see out of this.

395

I take a few deep breaths. If I'm going to do this, I need to do it right. First, I cast a bubble shield around Jatin. Thinking better of it, I bend down and latch one of Mr. Mittal's masks for high elevation and cast a circulation spell. In case . . . in case I don't make it, Jatin will still have the chance of breathing through the ash.

Then I stand, desperately trying to clear my head. What had I said in Basu's shop? I search for the words. It had all come on impulse, in anger. Panic.

"*Dadti Erif*," I try, motioning my arms toward the top of Mount Gandhak and then gesturing toward myself. The spell feels wrong on my lips, but it's close.

"*Pratidadti Erif. Yatana Agnierif.*"

And on it goes, with nothing happening, me experimenting with each syllable and hoping the right ones will come. Beneath me the hard ice has turned to brown slush, the snow mixing with the dirt. The heat of the earth soaks my body. Sweat drips off me as if I'm melting.

Meters away, lava rolls down the mountain and through our trenches. As it meets Jatin's ice it sizzles and steams and then the ground is gone, eaten up by my fire. Jatin and I will be surrounded soon, floating on a slushy iceberg amid a sea of flame.

I dig my feet into the muddy snow and move with my casting, the dance of the royal ceremony flowing through me. *This is my magic, my magic! And it's going to listen to me now, not anyone else. I won't let it be used like this.*

"*Yatana Agni Tviserif!*"

That's it. That's what I was missing, the direction. I don't just need to remove the firelight. I need it to *return* to me. I reach out my arms and snap them to my body continuously, pushing and pulling in each new direction I can.

"Yatana Agni Tviserif!" I roar, jerking with the intensity.

Then it happens. A small blur of red light shines in the distance, and hope blooms inside of me. I chant, calling and gesturing.

The light spins closer, closer and closer, until *wham!* It connects. The red light hits my wrist, sending me reeling sideways. I trip backward and choke on the words of the spell. The spot on my wrist, right on the first mark of my Touch, glows red and then swims up my arm until it fades. I clench my fist. Blood, that hurt, but it worked. . . . It worked!

I look over at Jatin. "Just hold on a little longer; I have a plan."

"YATANA AGNI TVISERIF!"

Three streams of firelight blaze toward me. I welcome them with a smile until they join my arm. They sting and force me to retreat, but I don't pause in casting. I don't think about the implications of what I'm about to do. *I must do this.*

As I continue to cast the spell, I expel my magic and my energy, but as each of my spells returns to me I gain back the magic I once used. I'm like a weighted scale, seesawing between weakness and strength.

Before long, hundreds of red streams of fire zip toward me and ram into my body, punching, kicking, each one knocking me down and building me up at the same time. Impossibly, they get even more violent. And I fall.

With each passing spell cast, my firelights feel less like light and smoke and more like physical arrows piercing my body. One hits me in the shin and my knee buckles. I stumble to right myself. Two jab me in the shoulder and I spin. I have to stand up again. Three punch me in the gut and I crumble. I have to keep going.

Soon I'm not only righting myself but I'm also clawing to get back up, to reaffirm my position and cast again. *"Yatana Agni Tviserif."*

One giant mass of firelight slams into me and I'm hurtled through the air. I'm a doll to this power now. I can't even control the landing. My right leg slips off the slush and twists at the wrong angle. Needles, thousands of needles, stab my knee. I grip the slush as I scream into the ground. Each of my muscles shakes uncontrollably in turmoil. I . . . I can't get up.

For some reason, Naupure's words from long ago surge through me. *Strength is more than standing.* He obviously didn't mean it in this way and yet—I don't need to stand to save the world. I just need to cast.

"Yatana Erif Agni Erif Tvis Erif!" I cry, embedding Erif into each word.

Like I thought, even without the movements or me standing, the firelight keeps coming as I cast into the dirt. There must be thousands.

Pop! The shield around Jatin shatters. I've come to the breaking point. With my body beyond even sitting up, my magic can only center on this one spell, with no room for anything else. I face Jatin but can't see anything behind the veil of red consuming my vision. It's like I'm with Erif, surrounded by the color of blood and destruction.

"Jatin!" I scream.

The firelight doesn't stop, though, and that's how I know I'm still alive and on Mount Gandhak. They pound me, throwing my body to and fro like a ship lost at sea. Each time my leg is jostled, intense pain wells and splinters through me.

The lights accumulate into one big ball of fire. I'm not lost at sea. I'm sinking. Red blazes over my arm, diving into each vein, each vein that pops out as if it's the tracks of lava running down this volcano. A putrid variation of reds swells and lashes out. My skin puffs in fluorescent hues. I . . . my arm can't take any more. My own blood is too full of magic.

Snap. My left arm breaks in what feels like a dozen places. From skin to muscle to bone, I'm being torn apart. My screams swallow all other noise, all other twig-sounding snaps.

Adraa. You must keep going! Erif's voice yells inside my head.

The heat rises and it's not just my arm anymore. My shoulder blazes. I tear at my neck, which feels like someone is cutting into me, branding me. When the pain hits my face I'm nothing but screams. It's too much. *Make it stop. I can't breathe.*

Adraa! I'm doing what I can, but you have to keep casting. You have to keep casting.

I raise my arm. I try to say the spell. It falls from my lips in a whimpering stutter. *No.*

If you ever have had a destiny, it is this. So be a witch and cast.

"Help him! Help Jatin. If you are a Goddess help us."

Sometimes one must die so others can live. It's you and him or millions of lives. Fight this.

"*Erif Yatana Agni—*" My voice cracks.

Adraa.

I chant. I chant through the razor blades ripping at my throat. I motion in the dirt what needs to happen. I have to keep absorbing my magic even if my soul flees back to the red room with Erif. For what feels like hours, red coats me in pain as I chant. Dying the first time was so much easier. But I guess it's always easier to die when you don't expect it. Knowing is much more terrifying.

But I can't think that. If I stop the volcano someone will come for Jatin; someone else will save him. If I stop the volcano my country won't burn alive. And so I chant.

I don't black out from the burnout overwhelming my consciousness. Years ago I learned to push myself beyond burnout and keep going, to stay awake. Now I wish for the unconsciousness, for the end. The pain both steals time and elongates it into torturous, immeasurable moments. In one last effort, I roll to where I last saw Jatin. I stretch my right arm until I'm touching his hand. He feels like ice, what I imagine death feels like. Maybe I am ice. Or maybe I am fire.

Either way he can't be gone, he can't. I continue to chant.

Adraa! You can stop. I think. I think . . .

I mutter, moving my lips endlessly even though there cannot be any noise coming out of me now. Feet crunch in the slush beside me, and then stop. Thank Gods! We are saved. Then dark-green shoes eclipse my view of Jatin. Slowly, the figure squats down next to me.

"I knew you were special."

No! Not him. Not him. I try to move, but it's useless. I'm broken.

"And somehow I just knew you would regret rejecting my offer."

Tears stream down my face until finally I greet the darkness and the numbness of black. It's over or I am.

Adraa?

Adraa . . .

CHAPTER THIRTY-NINE

◇

Awake

Jatin

I open my eyes. Then wish I hadn't. It feels like a pike is trying to split my head in two. I blink and try to rise. My head pounds even harder. My arms ache as if my bones have dissolved.

"He's awake!" someone shouts. Doors open, close, slam. Cheers sound in the hallway. *What is happening?*

Suddenly, the bed sags and my father comes into view, leaning toward me. "Jatin? Thank Gods. How do you feel?"

I peer into my father's face. "Ah, my head is killing me. What happened?"

"*Mukleah,*" he casts, and blue smoke unleashes from his hands and dives into my forehead. "I was hoping to ask you the same thing. But don't worry about that right now. How are you feeling? Everything okay besides the head? You broke four ribs, though they should be healed, and you have some bad bruises and, of course, a bad burnout. But other than that . . ."

Burned out. That's what happened. I burned out. My kurta is gone and a white bandage wraps around my torso. Sorting dreams from reality is one of the hardest things to do. Especially the kind of reality I last remember. Heat sucking at the air. Sweat beating down. Lava coming for us. Falling. And Adraa back from the dead and right next to me . . .

"Adraa! Where is Adraa?" I scan the room, hoping she'll barge through the door without knocking.

"She's alive. And she's doing well, considering . . ."

"Considering what?" I demand.

"Considering what she did."

"She did it, didn't she? Stopped the volcano. There's no other way I would still be alive."

"I'm not exactly sure what happened. One moment the Belwars and I were losing to Mount Gandhak. Then out of nowhere the mountain stabilized and stopped fighting us. When it comes to Adraa, I was hoping you could clear some things up. But that can wait."

My heart thumps. "No, tell me! What's wrong with Adraa?"

"It's just a rumor. The truth needs to be settled. She's fine, physically, a few . . . burns, but nothing that can't be healed by Maharani Belwar."

"What's the rumor? What needs to be settled?

My father pushes my shoulders down. "You need to rest. We can talk about this when you feel better."

"Dad, if it's about Adraa I need you to tell me now."

He pauses, then slowly smiles. "You haven't called me Dad in a long time."

I stall. "I guess I haven't."

I remember collapsing into his arms after Adraa died. Never had I felt closer to him than at that moment. Staring at his face

403

now, I notice the dark patches beneath his eyes. His hair is ruffled and unkempt. He looks awful.

He wraps me in a hug. His kurta scratches my face and the angle is uncomfortable, but I hug him back. This is what I should have done on my homecoming and when he returned from Moolek. But no, I had been awkward and irritated. Frustrated about all those years that I had been sent away; jealous of his warmth and friendliness with Adraa; and then hurt he had chastised me for doing the one thing that felt right. But I'd done my part in pulling away, hadn't I? After Mother died, we both retreated, me into studying, him into running the country alone.

"I'm proud of you, Jatin," he continues, without letting go. "There is a rumor going around that Maharaja Moolek says it was Adraa's firelight that caused Mount Gandhak to erupt, but . . ."

I pull back. "It *was* her firelight."

"What?"

"It was her firelight. That's what made Mount Gandhak blow or at least fuel the eruption."

His face drops. "So you are saying she—"

"No, it's not like that. It was her firelight, but she didn't put it there. It must have been Moolek. He used her magic. But Adraa stopped it. You say Mount Gandhak got weaker. She saved me. She saved us all."

"Adraa didn't save you."

"Yes. She did." She was the only one on the volcano with me. *If it wasn't her, then who could have possibly—*

"Maharaja Moolek. He's the one who saved you. He's the one who saved us all."

◇

CHAPTER FORTY

A Burned Destiny

Adraa

Pain. A red room. Jatin. A volcano. More pain. A pair of dark-green shoes.

"No!" I scream as I lurch awake.

"*Yatana Agni . . . ,*" I chant until my voice crashes into reality. It was a dream. I'm in my bed. Dull light blinds me. A thick grogginess wafts over my eyes.

Then the pain engulfs me. My neck and the left side of my face burn. Moaning, I clutch my face and find several cloths taped to my jaw and running down my shoulder. It wasn't a dream.

A rough voice curses. "Blood!"

I start. I'm in my room, but I'm not alone. Guards, two by the door and one by my window, overwhelm the space. They stiffen when I rise to a sitting position. One even reaches for his sword and curses again. Another runs out of the room. I blink, focusing on their uniforms, but the tree etched in green is easily identifiable.

Bile laps at my throat. Moolek's men.

"What is going on?"

Silence.

"Where's Jatin? Is he okay? Are my parents okay?"

The guard whose hand still hesitates on his sword looks to his fellow guard. "They said she wouldn't be awake for days."

"Quiet."

"Is Jatin all right?" I yell, louder.

"Go. Tell him," the guard orders the younger wizard, who retreats in relief, slamming the door behind him.

"*Raja* Jatin," the man chastises in a bitter tone.

"What?"

"It's Raja Jatin to you."

Is he serious? "Yes, fine. Is *Raja* Jatin okay?"

Nothing. He gives me nothing.

Frustration and fear bubble over. Why is this guard here? I begin casting a diagnosis spell to gather my bearings, but as the red of my magic swarms around me, a purple stream flies through the air. The wicker from my bedpost unravels and lashes out, gripping my right wrist in a binding cord. I yank against it and the wicker tightens. "What is this?"

A lavender haze drifts off the wizard's hand in warning. "Don't try anything. I'm not afraid of you."

"What do you have to be afraid of?" I yell, jerking at the cuff. When he says nothing again, irritation and confusion sharpen into anger. "Answer me! Why?" I yell.

Purple magic blazes. "Because two days ago you and your firelight killed one hundred twenty-nine people. *Because*, Miss Belwar, you are a danger to us all."

My people. One hundred twenty-nine of my people are dead. That's the number I'm going to live with for the rest of my life. My firelight.

But I stopped it. Didn't I? If Mount Gandhak were still erupting I'd be dead. We'd all be dead. Without a second thought, I break the wicker cuff with a sweep of purple magic. Intense heat flares up my shoulder and into my cheek. It slows me down—but only slightly.

My healed broken leg, now numb and wobbly, buckles under my weight, but I push myself to the window limping. I have to see.

"Stop!" the guard yells as I reach the window. I chuck a cuff of my own behind me, pinning the guard to the wall. With one heave, and a spasm of retching pain, I throw the curtains open.

And then I do stop, because the world before me is completely gray. Ash covers everything in grime. Beyond the palace gates, timber and roof shingles pebble the ground. Amid the gray, black marks scar dozens of homes. But there are still homes, still wizards going through the wreckage. Flashes of magic light up my city. They're cleaning up, repairing. And in the distance, Mount Gandhak sits peacefully. No fire or clouds storm from its peak. "I did it. I—"

"So. You are finally awake."

An icy chill pierces me because I know that voice. Slowly, I turn. And it's him. Just him. The guards have disappeared. A warm breeze wafts into the room, whipping my hair and brushing his cloak from the floor. The green satin of his clothes gleams in the gray world he has created. Jeweled accents on every cuff and seam reflect the dull light into my eyes, but I don't dare blink as I take in Maharaja Moolek.

"For a while I didn't think you would pull through," he says. "I'm glad to see I was wrong."

Red flames bristle across my hand and lick up my shoulder. It burns, every ache ricocheting to the bone. I slip one hand behind my back and cast a knife into being, but before I can finish the spell and conjure the weapon, a torture spell snakes through my arm, piercing the swollen flesh through to the broken bone. I crash to my knees, screaming.

"Careful now. I don't want to undo all my hard work pulling you off that mountain."

I pant on all fours as the pain subsides, but everything still spins. "You? You saved me?"

"Is that so hard to believe?"

Yes, that is hard to believe. Disgust worms through me. When I saw those shoes I knew he had come to kill me or at least gloat as I lay dying. But . . . If he did carry me off that volcano . . .

A poisonous fear makes my next words sound pleading. "If you saved me, then you must have saved Jatin too."

He laughs. "Ah, so you do care for my nephew. Interesting."

I raise my head. Our eyes meet. For what feels like a century we stare each other down. Every piece of information he absorbs is a stab to the gut. I don't want this murderer to learn one single thing, especially when it comes to Jatin. But it's too late. Moolek knows his next words could unravel me.

He turns and steps toward the window, walking past me like I'm nothing. "Lucky for you I needed you both alive."

I take a trembling breath. Relief stings my eyes. Jatin. Is. Alive. "Why? Why save us?"

"I'm sure you'll figure it out soon enough." Moolek's fingers brush the curtains. Everything stills, deathlike. "This is a beautiful view you have here."

The ache shooting through my body tells me even standing would be a hardship, but I have to know. I want to hear him say it. Quiet has engulfed the room, making my words loud. "You should have seen it before you destroyed it," I say.

"You think it was me?"

I rise to my knees and slowly, trembling, stand up. "I know it was." Moolek turns, watching me with little interest. "Erif told me," I lie.

I want to see him bleed. I want to see fear in his eyes. *Anything!*

At the goddess's name, he only raises an eyebrow. "Ah yes, I forgot. You had your first death. You *talked* to the gods. Once you've had your fifth I'll be impressed." He scoffs. "You still think the gods try to protect us. You do not yet know how the world works. None of you down south do. That's why you are all so weak."

Father's words echo in my memory. *Look to Moolek to see what happens without our powers checked. Soon one starts to think they are God-like.* God-like enough to take more than a hundred lives without a second thought. My agony boils over.

"*Agnierif!*" I yell, and a bolt of red smoke shoots from my hand and rages toward him, blazing into fire.

With a flick of his hand, a wall materializes. Then the shield bursts into green smoke and swallows my fire.

I jump to the side and twist, building a piercing arrow. I

throw. But Moolek isn't where I thought he'd be. Out of the corner of my eye, I see green flaring to my left. As the spear pierces the curtain, his spell hits me in the ribs. I crumble. Pain consumes me, mimicking the burn of my arm throughout my body.

"Like I said. Weak."

Right now, I am weak. I feel it. Burned. Bandaged. *Broken!* my arm yells at me. The anger doesn't care, though. It wants to keep screaming. "We are strong enough to stand against you," I say, my voice a wheeze of pain and hurt. I raise my hand and begin another spell, but a cuff of purple magic flies in the air and hits my wrist, pinning it to the ground.

Moolek steps forward. "No, you aren't. You think Erif is on your side, that she grants you some destiny that will stop me? Who do you think granted me the power to activate that volcano?" He pulls up his sleeve and a dense green smoke soars into the air. "And you think it matters that *you* know it was me?" He laughs. "You failed your royal ceremony, Adraa Belwar. Look at yourself. Hire all the Red Women you want. You are nothing of consequence anymore."

Finally, the words have been spoken, the answer clear. The God of Earth helped him as the Goddess of Fire helped me. He infused the volcano with my magic and then with an extreme amount of green magic he pressurized Mount Gandhak to make it erupt. I stagger under the weight of it all. Especially the words that ring truest: I did fail. I failed the royal ceremony. I failed in saving one hundred twenty-nine people. But how am *I* still alive? He saved me. Why . . .

Something glues together in my mind. That guard said I had

killed my people, that I was the threat. Lies, of course. But still, lies that he believed.

Lucky for you I needed you both alive.

It's all manipulation, planned from the beginning. Moolek wants me afraid, not dead, because he needs me. My firelight. *My firelight!*

I break the cuff and rise. He thinks I hired the Red Woman. He thinks I am nothing but a royal who—like him—believes I have a right to rule. Erif made one thing quite clear: there is only choice, not destiny. I choose not to cower. He will pay for every life he took, even if that kills me. "So it's my word against yours. But you forget the truth accords. My people will know what you have done."

"I forget nothing, girl. Nothing," he whispers. Yet, I can tell he holds back a shout. I've unnerved him. I'm still standing.

Without a second thought I rip the bandages from my arm, push back the pain, and let magic flare in a bloodred storm. I ignore my burns, and my feet find their stability.

Finally, surprise enters his eyes.

"I won't forget either. Remember that," I say.

A wash of green smoke sparks into the air. I brace myself. I took down a volcano. I can defend myself for a few minutes. A few minutes.

Footsteps smack the stone in the hall. We both still. I listen, trying to pick out whether they are my father's hard footfalls and my mother's quick steps or those of Moolek's men.

"That's my cue. I'll see you soon." Instead of firing at me, his magic churns around him like a vine.

No! I lunge forward, but all that's left of Moolek is the thick fog of green smoke whooshing out my window. *How . . . What kind of spell was that?*

The door swings open, smashes against the wall, and my parents stand at the threshold. They're okay. Before anyone can say a word, my mom dives forward and wraps me in a hug. My dad is not far behind. My legs finally give in and the three of us fall to the ground. I sag against them and take in their warmth and reassurance. They tell me of Prisha's safety, of Riya's well-being, of Jatin's healing.

It's Mother who pulls away first, staring at my neck. "I thought these were burns," she breathes, reaching and then hesitating to touch me. I turn until I catch myself in a mirror. Finally, I see what created Moolek's surprise. Not burns, though the sting is the same, but . . . my Touch. Above my shoulder the designs continue, now in bright red, swirling in an erratic tangle that skims and brushes over my jawline like tendrils of fire. I choke on a snaggle of laughter because it looks beautiful, and different, and horrible. But it also looks like Moolek's greatest fear, like I am still a woman of consequence, like I've been marked for a destiny.

CHAPTER FORTY-ONE

The Saturation of Rumor

Adraa

War brews with a rumor. Erif said as much, but I didn't think the next wave of attack would start like this, with word and whisper. After I took back my firelight, Moolek stopped the volcano. He's dubbed a hero.

And me?

As the stories say, I'm a corrupt, evil, power-hungry woman who was vanquished after killing one hundred twenty-nine of my own people. This is meant to break me. Watching green-uniformed men repair my city and bring in supplies. Being spit on the first time I enter the clinic to help the wounded. Listening as my people say Jatin Naupure, who at first was bewitched by my treachery, discovered the truth in time to help his uncle stop my evil designs. It's all quite brilliant, actually. This is why Moolek saved me. When a marriage to divide southern Wickery didn't work, Moolek blew it up instead and gave the world what it wanted—a villain. Mount Gandhak was a contingency all

413

along, though. I'm sure of it. A bomb set with my magic to either control me if I allied with him or destroy me if I didn't.

But because I know that, because I know every word spoken against me is a lie, I don't collapse. At least . . . not completely.

One hundred twenty-nine pounds against my skull. *My firelight* follows soon after like a nagging tangle of unbroken thought. The game was fixed from the start, but I still didn't play it right. I couldn't stop Moolek from killing my people. And even though one shouldn't blame the sword for stabbing, I'm slowly caving in on myself because, with my country thinking I killed them, it feels like I have.

I've been avoiding Jatin. I told him not to visit. I can't force my heart to stop caring, but I also can't prevent my brain from naming all the reasons we shouldn't be anything more than partners. So I don't face it. When the entire kitchen staff, Willona at the helm, brings me one of Jatin's letters, I thank them and fold it away to their chagrin. Zara and Prisha have thrown themselves into clinic duty. Everyone works as I heal, trying to shield me from more spit in the face, hurled insults, or worse, an assassination attempt. Like old times, long before murder entered our lives, I find the only person willing to talk through the rumors instead of skirting around them is Riya. And I can always find Riya.

She wrings out a clean towel and wipes her father's forehead. "You know, I think people were always suspicious that firelight cost next to nothing. It's easier for them to believe you planted firelight in their homes and betrayed them than old-fashioned goodness."

I release a hefty sigh. "I want people's first assumption to be

Belwar's goodness, not its gangs, drugs, and corruption. Now they think those things of me."

"Well, right now you are only one of those things. You aren't a Vencrin drug addict using Bloodlurst to amass power. At least"—she raises her eyebrows and smiles—"not yet."

I give her a look. "Funny." She's only half right, though. Some so-called witnesses are coming forward to say they saw firelight being shipped by the Vencrin, which links me to the drug ring. Where were those witnesses when I was scouring the streets as the Red Woman? And moreover, why is darkness so much easier to swallow than light?

"*Pravleah*," I conjure over my mother's spell.

"Thank you, Adraa," Riya whispers.

"You don't need to say anything. He's the only patient who isn't repulsed by me."

Riya stares at her father. The towel drips. "He *was* right, you know. That new Touch of yours. The ceremony. People's love. None of that makes you a rani. But to me, what you sacrificed . . ." She looks up. Before I can, Riya rises and falls on me, hugging me close. "I'm sorry," she says with a squeeze.

I hold her fiercely, clinging to her and noticing she wears a red choli, as if no matter what is said I still became her rani that day. "I'm the one that should be sorry. I shouldn't have kept any of it from you."

She pulls back. "You should know it was all just . . ." She glances at her father.

Guilt. Blame. Responsibility. Any of these words can fill in what she will say next, but it's the accumulation of all three.

Something unnamable that has been crackling at my skin for days. And since I know what she means, I interrupt her. "I know. You don't have to say it."

Riya lets out a laugh. "Thank Gods." She hugs me again. "But do hear this. If it's us against the world, Adraa, I'll be there beside you, as your friend."

I feel myself smiling for the first time in days. "I already knew that too."

◇ ◇ ◇

It's my mom who heals me. My leg broke, but my arm shattered. So instead of Zara or any other mender, it's my mom who comes every day with new bandages. We revert into a healer-patient relationship until the day I'm staring out the window at the ash and she breaks the thick silence with, "I've never told you much about my life on Pire."

I turn so quickly that the bandages she's using to rewrap my arm are yanked from her hands, and sharp stabs of pain run up my shoulder.

"Careful," she warns.

"You never wanted to talk about it. Never."

"Yes, well. The culture there is . . ." She pauses. "It's rough for girls, the gap between men and women more apparent. My father cried at my birth, that's one of the first things I learned as a child. I was told he wept in despair at having his first child born female. The only way a woman could become anything of real value was being a healer, so I became the best healer in the entire country and then I left as soon as possible. Your father thinks

416

he chose me, but I pushed for our arrangement, made myself be seen. He was so funny and handsome, but I also saw Belwar as my only chance to both escape and prove myself."

I look at my mother straight-on. The bend in her nose has never looked more prominent. By twelve, I had stopped trying to learn how she broke it and why it was never set. Had she refused to answer or had I stopped asking?

"Society tells us that as women we need a man to be something. We don't. And I'm so sorry, Adraa. I forced you into marriage and leadership. I had such doubts when we trudged toward Azure Palace that night and yet I didn't try to convince your father it was too early for you. We hadn't even seen what you could become." She tucks my plain right hand between hers. "Then I allowed you only one path, your father's and my path. And I almost killed you in doing so."

Never before have I truly considered telling my parents, especially my mother, that I'm the Red Woman. It has been a secret I never wanted them to know. Their wrath, their lack of understanding, and their guaranteed forbiddance kept me on guard. I could foresee it all unraveling before me at the slightest mention. Yet, right now, it falls to the tip of my tongue.

"Mom, it's okay. I wanted it. I wanted to be a rani. I wanted to change Belwar for the better. I even wanted to marry Jatin one day. But now—"

"You can still do those things."

"But I failed." The words ring ugly and then burrow, allowing a nasty seed of negativity to spring forward and grow. I failed. Failed.

"You saved the country. That isn't failure. And you will

continue to save us." She lifts my head, casting a calming pink mist as she wipes the tears from my cheek. "That's what the Red Woman fights for, right?"

I freeze, the flush of shame turning cold. *What did she just—*

"You—you know?"

Her small smile says enough. Her nod says even more. She knows. She knows and she's not yelling.

"How . . . ?"

"First, I'm your mother. Second, I'm much more than a medic around here. Who do you think hired Beckman? Who do you think sent Hiren and those trusted guards the night of that raid? Half of the people who line up outside the clinic are informants."

My Gods! I jump to my feet and pace. My mother . . . *my* mother . . . this whole time . . . "So basically you're telling me you not only know my secret but also everyone's in Belwar?" What had Prisha once said? Mom was trapped in the clinic, treated as a woman obligated to create potions and nothing more?

She rises. "Maybe not all of Belwar." A pause, a small shake of her head. "Please, don't think you have failed because even with all my intel I didn't know about Mount Gandhak or your firelight. That day you came to the palace with Jatin I knew you must be on the hunt for Moolek and I stopped you, guided you to the clinic out of fear. So if anyone has failed, Adraa, one could point the finger at me."

I've always thought my mother only cared how I was presented to the world. But this? This is way more than beauty and etiquette. I shake my head, trying hard to realign what I know. "I don't blame you. I feel like a part of me should be mad, but after everything that's happened . . ." Something hits me then and I whirl around. Beckman was her man. She protected me and yet . . . "But now I'm sure you're wrong. You think you allowed me only one path, but you let me find myself out there." My mother allowed me to understand I was fierce Jaya Smoke as much as I was Lady Adraa Belwar.

She presses her hand to my cheek, smiling. "Well, I'm quite fond of the Red Woman."

I hug her and for one crystal clear moment the failure and the rumors and the devastation slip away and I'm just a witch. Not a deformed heir drowning under expectations. Not an innocent monster sinking under blame. A witch, accepted for being and rising above both. I can feel the power in that.

"And, Adraa?"

"Yes?"

"I like your partner too." Mom lays Jatin's letter on my bedside table. "You taught him well, by the way. If he ever wants to work in the clinic he has my approval." She holds up a small jar, nods, and places it on the bedside table with a light clink before she closes the door behind her. I walk over out of curiosity at first, and I'm not disappointed for my effort. A note tied around the jar's lid reads *Thought you might need this soon.* Unscrewing the cap, I find the potion I taught Jatin to settle my cramps. Good Gods. He makes it *hard* to not love him.

When I can finally face it, I rip open the envelope and peer at the words: *To the girl who has many names, but favors the color pink above all others.*

Below that it's blank.

"*Gharmaerif,*" I cast, and with heat illuminating the message, I read my first real love letter.

CHAPTER FORTY-TWO

◇

Confronting a Choice

Jatin

The vigil is held two weeks after Adraa and I climbed Mount Gandhak and she reclaimed her firelight and saved us all. I stand on the volcano, alone. Layers of black sludge wrinkle the landscape. Down below a forest of trees spreads horizontally, a sea of broken stumps with no sign of greenery until it reaches the ocean, where the mountain slips away. From up here I have a perfect view of both Adraa's and my cities. From here I can see just how far the ash fell and the lava flowed. Brocade banners flutter over both cities, memorials to the fallen.

Night begins to drain the sky of its color, but the sun fights back, staining the heavy clouds with orange. It's peaceful as people gather in the streets, each holding a candle against the dark. It takes a moment to fathom that each little spot of light is a citizen. Belwarians to my right; Naupurians to my left. Once, seeing all that life, for which I'm responsible, would have driven uneasiness into my gut. Now, all I can feel is gratitude that so many little fires light up the coming darkness.

One day soon, my uncle will pay for the one hundred twenty-nine people who make it darker. Who, days ago, would have used the brighter and more reliable firelight instead of inferior candles.

I'm so distracted by the thought I don't spot Adraa until she lands next to me, the wind snapping at her skirt. We stare at each other until she pulls out my letter and the potion I made for her. "You know in any normal situation this is a weird birthday gift," she says with a smile.

Happiness engulfs me. I had thought with everything she might . . . I didn't know what to think. Only that she didn't want to see me. "I'll do better next year."

She laughs. "The fact that you even know my schedule . . ." She holds up my letter. "Though I think I've learned something even more interesting today."

I step toward her, closing the distance between us. "What's that?" I ask.

"All these years I thought you were trying to be corny when you sent me those *love letters*. But you *are* that corny." She looks down and reads. "Though 'punched me to my senses' sounds a little harsh. Can we finally acknowledge it was a slap at best?"

I shrug. "*Punched* makes a better story, and I had to go with tradition or you might not have believed the letter was from me."

I like this. I like that we can be ourselves once more, as if nothing has changed. But then again, everything has changed. We stand on a wasteland. I take another step forward. "But the corny part probably proves I always knew I loved you."

She waves the paper and her smile fades. "Are you sure you should?"

421

In the dawning light I see it. I had expected burns, but it's . . . it's her Touch. Fresh bloodred swirls swarm over her neck. Instead of a net of flowers and circles like most Touches, these lash out, swerving and weaving within themselves. It's beautiful.

I step closer and brush my fingers across the designs. "That's intimidating. But I think my ego can handle you being more powerful than I am. Pretty sure you always have been."

She leans into my hand, choking on a sound that's half laugh, half sob. "That's not what I was referring to."

"What, then? Moolek's lies? The royal ceremony?"

She pulls back. "Yes, all of that. The people still see you as you are—good." She gestures to the mass of candlelit mourners. "War is upon us, Jatin, and it might be better for Naupure if you weren't seen with me. If you"—she breathes in—"marry someone else."

My body reacts like I'm losing her all over again. Cold sweat. Hammering heart. But now it's accompanied by gruff irritation. She can't mean it.

"But I was hoping that we could still be partners." She holds out her left forearm, as if pressing my arm against it could erase our feelings for each other.

I contemplate her with a frown. Her eyes are wet. Her hand clenches my letter. She doesn't mean it.

"I'm not marrying anyone else." I swing forward and wrap my hand around her right elbow and yank her close. She tumbles into me, body against body. I lean forward. "You think we could ever just be partners?"

I stop, a breath away from her lips. I slacken my grip and

422

make the choice clear. Push me away or kiss me. I can't live in a middle ground where we work together, but I can't touch her.

We stare at each other. I know she gets it. We are meant to be together not because we were forced into it. We chose. I need her to choose.

"You're right," she whispers.

"I normally am."

"Let's not get too carried away." And with that she grabs my kurta and tugs me the few centimeters separating us. Her mouth connects with mine. I greet her eagerly. One arm wraps around her to pull her even closer, the other exploring the new Touch on her neck. It's like coming home and setting off on an adventure at the same time. Warmth radiates through my body. Thank the gods she listened to me. With her in my arms I feel like I can conquer anything.

Something lights up the sky behind my eyelids.

Adraa jerks to attention, turning to stare at a fierce pink light shooting into the sky. Even I startle, my fears flashing to the red blaze of Mount Gandhak invading the skyline. But it takes me only a second to understand. Oh Gods, it works. It actually works!

"Jatin, what—"

I spin back to Adraa. "I've been working on something. It's a signal. For everyone, but especially Untouched." I'm more than excited. A smile spreads across my face as I fish for my still-unnamed invention deep within my pocket. "You inspired it," I say as I pull out a cylinder with a small orb on top. Frost crystals glisten across the handle, but the orb shines red with Adraa's firelight. Repurposed.

"You bottled up your magic?" she asks, reaching for it.

"Better that than sitting in orbs around my room." I squeeze her hand. She hasn't realized yet. "But it's yours too, Adraa. It's firelight. I've gotten reports of people trying to destroy any orb they could find. Moolek's men were going around taking it too, so I sent all my guards to collect it. Kalyan, in particular, was adamant about the search."

She stares at the stream of light. Not pink, exactly. White and red wound together, streaking into the sky.

"And what does it signal?" she asks.

"That we're needed." I unlatch my second skyglider, and with a blast of white smoke it extends. "I could use my partner."

◇

CHAPTER FORTY-THREE

We Survive

Adraa

My whole life I fought to be good at magic. I worked hard for my success, and in the end, I failed. But that does not mean I will keep failing. I will not fail my country in the long term. For it is still my country, even if I will never rule over it as a rani.

I am alive. I am still here. And one day that will be Moolek's greatest failure.

I look at Jatin, whose face is masked in a white glow. "Ready?" he asks.

What a pair we are, the hero and the villain of Belwar standing at the spot that not days ago tried to kill us both. And nonetheless we choose to stand up and be together. I don't know what the future holds. I don't have a destiny, a predesigned path mapped by the gods. But I will rise again. Jatin and I, partnering as masked white and red vigilantes—we will rise again.

My magic gushes from my hands, and the red mask swirls into place. "Ready."

Author's Note

I can't pinpoint the exact moment my inspiration for *Cast in Firelight* hit. It was a mix of old and new ideas fused together. But I can tell you the world of the story came from my husband and our conversations about culture, children, and what it means to be an interracial couple.

I know some readers may be disappointed that this story isn't #OwnVoices. You may look me up and see my pale skin (and one of the most English names in existence) and wonder why I tried to craft a fantasy in which none of the main characters look like me. And for me the answer is simple: because these characters will look like my children.

I was honored to be accepted by my husband's family. And as a result of their generosity in teaching me about their culture and incorporating them into their family, I began, as fantasy writers tend to do, imagining a world that encapsulated my experience. Thus, *Cast in Firelight* was born as a blend of both my worlds (with a heavy dose of imagination stirred in, of course).

Thank you for reading *Cast in Firelight*. I am eternally thankful to those of you who allowed me to share the idea that *anyone* can be the hero of a story, especially those like Adraa, who may doubt their worthiness, who may fail . . . but who never give up.

Acknowledgments

As any author will tell you, writing a book is hard, really hard. I like to imagine it as a witch's brew. It calls for a pinch of talent, lots of determination, a heavy dose of luck, and most importantly, the affirmations and commitment of a team of supportive people. So without further ado, I now get to thank everyone who helped me, and try to fit it into two pages. For an overwriter like me, this may be the hardest part yet.

First, thank you to my agent, Amy Brewer, and the Metamorphosis Literary Agency. You took a chance on me when no one else did, and I still can't believe how far I've come because of you.

Thank you to my wonderful editor, Monica Jean, for advocating for me and letting me be a part of the amazing and brilliant Delacorte Press family. You truly made this book shine.

And to everyone on the Random House team who had a hand in making *Cast in Firelight* the book it is today—thank you! I couldn't have done any of this without you: Cathy Bobak, Lili Feinberg, Drew Fulton, Erica Henegen, Alex Hightower, Audrey Ingerson, Jenn Innzeta, Nathan Kinney, Kelly McGauley, Carol Monteiro, Dani Perez, and Tamar Schwartz. Special thanks to my copyeditors, Heather Lockwood Hughes and Colleen Fellingham, who made sure all my sentences made sense.

Casey Moses, thank you for your brilliant cover design. Virginia Norey, thank you for the beautiful map illustration. And to Charlie Bowater, who illustrated my extraordinary cover: I cried when I found out you would be bringing my characters to life and since that faithful day never doubted my book's outer aesthetic. We can all see for ourselves why I never had to worry.

DFW Writers' Workshop—to all of you, thank you. I try to communicate constantly how this organization changed my writing, brought me a slew of mentors and friends, and gave me a family. Most of you actually had a hand in helping me re-write this book and craft the query letter, and then introducing me to my agent. So let the name-dropping commence: A. Lee. Martinez and Sally Hamilton—thank you for your humor, your wisdom, and your publishing advice. Rosemary Moore, I'm so happy we are Delacorte siblings. Thank you for answering my every publishing question. Leslie Lutz, Brooke Fossey, John Bartell, Sarah Terentiev, Jenny Martin, and Taylor Koleber, thank you for not letting me slip into the dread and doubt of drafting, as well as for always being interested in my work. It means more than you know. Last but not least, Katie Bernet, every day I think about how lucky I was to sit next to you at my first DFW Writers' Conference. You're the world's greatest critique partner and the truest of friends.

Thank you to all my beta readers, especially Leah Hudson and Rachel Griffin, who encouraged me and reminded me on my worst days that this book was good enough, and subsequently I was. Also to Priya Kavina—thank you for saving me from loneliness after I moved across the country and then for rescuing every spell in this book from complete catastrophe. You are magic. Persephone Jayne and Sage Magee, thank you for creating a home in California and being the best "monster readers" a girl could ask for.

Thank you to my fellow #Roaring20sDebuts for your advice, inspiration, and encouragement. Thank you to Half Price Books and all my fellow book-selling colleagues who read my work and cheered me on!

Thank you to all my family for their love and support. Steve, I hope you know I couldn't have done this without you. You have defined what it means to be a supportive parent. Mom, thank you for encouraging my reading habits, letting me stay up late with a book, and nurturing the seeds of creativity. Though you might have done it too well. I believe I have been overwatered, and I think we should blame you. Love you guys.

And Rae and Dad, thank you for letting me hang out and travel with you as I began writing this book. I'm sorry I blew off our *Downton Abbey* marathons a few times, but as you can see, I had a world to build. I hope you will think it worth the sacrifice.

To in my in-laws, Gokul and Nanda Bysani, thank you for inspiring me and for modeling the strength we see in each and every character. This world was born because of your openness and willingness to include me in Indian tradition and customs. Finding Kaethan was lucky, but you guys are my own sort of jackpot.

I went funny in the dedication, but let me be sincere now. To my husband, Kaethan Bysani, thank you for inspiring me and supporting me through this book. No one had to deal with my emotions as you did, and you carried me through them all. I can always rely on you—especially, as you like to remind me, for your witty banter. (Of course, I will continue to argue that it's not as witty as mine, but I digress.)

Finally, to my readers, I hope this book entertained you above all else. Thank you for picking it up and giving it a chance, which allows me to live my dream.

Turn the page for a sneak peek
at the heart-pounding sequel to
Cast in Firelight!

PERISH IN SILENCE OR RISE IN FIRE

THE SEQUEL TO *CAST IN FIRELIGHT*

BOUND BY FIRELIGHT

DANA SWIFT

CHAPTER ONE

◇

I Meet Up with the Love of My Life and Almost Throw Him off a Roof

Adraa

The sky crackles with color. Magic jets into the air and explodes in mist and sizzling lights. The festival is in full swing. It's loud. It's blinding. And it's the best thing I've seen in the past two months.

Booths and stalls have popped up overnight. Ornate silk banners in the nine colors of magic are draped and fastened to every frame, making the brocade ones dedicated to the recent fallen scarce for once. The streets flow like a river as currents of wizards and witches hunt for the best food stall or for a good spot to shoot some of their magic in the air and add to the glazed smoke screen of color. Children and the Untouched who can't cast throw powders instead and splash their friends in the face. Although the real Festival of Color isn't for months, this impromptu celebration radiates joy.

It feels like forever since I've seen the populace let loose like this. But if I were to drop from my shadowed rooftop, their happiness would melt. And by all nine gods, that's the last thing I want. For weeks Belwar has been repairing and rebuilding the city, and tonight we celebrate the new western flying station, the reconstructed homes, the life still thriving in this small coastal country. If there is anything my people deserve right now, it's one night of peace, of safety. So I stay nestled in my hiding spot, my eyes on the streams of color bursting in the sky, but my attention drifts to the bloodred magic in my hands condensing into my mask and then disintegrating into smoke over and over again. I know I'm saying the words, pulling the magic from the intricate design of my Touch to create the spell that blurs my face and makes me the Red Woman, and yet I don't quit my muttering.

It settles the heartache.

As do the squeals of kids' laughter below me, sounding bright and full of life. I didn't realize how much I was depending on the festival to showcase how my people might be able to keep going. After my magic was used to cause Mount Gandhak to erupt, killing one hundred twenty-nine people, my country has trudged through grief, repaired the city, and, most achingly, accepted the suspicion that I, Adraa Belwar, did this to them.

I've been living behind my vigilante persona for weeks, and I have to stop myself from plastering the thing to my face once again, right now, and become . . . become anything but the villain the city thinks I am. But I'm trying. I'm trying to feel okay with being just Adraa Belwar for a solid minute and a half as my country celebrates its color and diversity and strength to live on after destruction.

Luckily, no matter what they think of me, I'm still here. Every night I slip past my added security and watch for any sign the Red Woman is needed. That I am needed.

A thud echoes behind me. Footsteps. I whip around, mask adhering to my face instinctively and the bloodred of my magic smoking in my palms as I ready a ramming spell to throw the intruder off the roof.

"Hey. Don't kill me. I brought you food," a familiar voice says.

The lights from the street below illuminate Jatin Naupure, my boyfriend. *Boyfriend*. It's strange thinking of him that way, considering he was my fiancé first, then a weird mix of rival, partner, and crush, though we were hiding our identities from each other for months. And now, he's just . . . my person.

My defense vanishes and my magic evaporates. "Okay. I guess I'll let you sit next to me."

"Don't act like you didn't save this spot for me, Smoke."

I smile at the truth of it. I even kept the shingles warm with some red magic. When Jatin sits a second later, I can tell he notices the heat, but he only smiles and hands over my bowl. Roasted silken fish sitting on a bed of rice and smothered in a spicy red curry wafts into my nose. I take the bowl greedily.

"How's our favorite sociopath?" Jatin asks, scooting closer to me.

I glance down at Nightcaster, who's buying a witch a lamb chop on a stick. It would be somewhat endearing, watching him try to impress her, if I didn't know the true Nightcaster. A cage-casting wizard from the Underground who couldn't open his mouth without saying something revolting. We've been following him for weeks hoping he will lead us back to some scrap of evidence that we can use to prove a group of criminals called the Vencrin and the ruler of the country north of us, Maharaja Moolek, are working together. Or at least that they worked together to try to utterly destroy our cities when Mount Gandhak erupted.

"He hasn't been punched in the face today."

"The night is still young." Jatin pauses. "And he hasn't seen us yet."

"True."

Down below, Nightcaster pulls his bicep into a curl. Even from here I can make out the tattoos that run up his upper arm, mimicking the swirled designs of the gods' Touch.

"Gods," I sigh. "It's sad just watching it." A breeze draws the scent of roasted silken fish back to me and I dig in. "Have I told you this is my favorite?"

Jatin takes a bite from his own bowl and smiles. "I think it was in one of your letters once."

I frown. "I don't remember writing that to you." Maybe it was when I was really young and the letters I sent to Jatin still felt like something my parents were forcing me to do. At the time I couldn't fathom accepting an arranged marriage with the most arrogant boy I'd ever met. When love felt like an absurd question and marriage a horrifying inevitability.

"No, I mean the parchment was stained with it."

I knock against his shoulder as he laughs. "Stop lying."

"I could show you. I kept them all."

I side-eye him, my gaze tracing his strong jaw and thick black hair. "You kept them all?"

"What? You didn't?"

"Well, yeah, I did. But you know that post in the Belwar courtyard where we train? I pinned them there as motivation to beat you. Can't say they were well taken care of."

"Even the love letters? I'm hurt, Smoke."

"No"—I soak the rice in the curry and take a big bite— "those I burned."

"I don't believe you," Jatin says, so casually my lie loses its footing.

I open my mouth to joke he's not the only one, but it rings too close to reality. For the past few weeks we've been patrolling the streets, responding to the signal that Jatin created and saving people. We've even made a competition out of it. But that's what I've been doing underneath starlight. In blazing daylight it's councils upon councils with my father and the five rajas of Belwar as they accuse me and call for a truth-spelling trial to determine my crimes.

"Adraa?" Jatin whispers, sensing like always when I've started to spiral and tangle in my own thoughts.

I shake my head as if to clear it. "Hey, thanks for responding to the signal yesterday. I couldn't manage to get out of the meeting."

Jatin pauses. "They still want the hearing?"

I can hear my heart hammer. "My parents are still trying to convince the rajas it's not necessary."

"They'll get through to them. And soon it will be behind us."

His words hit home. That's all I want—for this nightmare to be behind us. But even the roof we're sitting on now has ash embedded between the shingles. The air is saturated with the smell of soot instead of sea salt.

Jatin goes back to his food, scooping up the rice with his fingers. "I saved seven people, by the way."

I drop a piece of roasted silken fish. "What?"

He ignores me, but a smile plays at the corner of his mouth. "And you know what that means."

I shake my head, reconfiguring the tally. It's been hard to keep track after two hundred. "I still think I'm up by two."

"Nope, down two." He smiles full-on.

It melts me even though my inner competitor huffs in irritation. "Don't say it."

He leans in, close enough for me to feel his breath. "Winnin—"

I turn my head quickly to kiss him, interrupting his taunt. I taste the spice of festival food, and, as always, kissing Jatin fills me with happiness and a sense of wholeness. The food is forgotten. His hand roams over my jawline where the Goddess Erif extended and stained my Touch burgundy, like tendrils of lashing fire.

"You know, I've figured out that you kiss me to stop my teasing. It's not a good way to train me."

"Are you admitting that you are trainable?" I joke, kissing him again.

He smiles, but something across the alley catches his attention. I follow his gaze. A woman is lighting a candle in her attic.

The flame seems to totter against the night, as if one hard blow might light up the curtains.

I sigh, the ache returning. "That's a house fire waiting to happen."

"Adraa, you should know, that signal yesterday?" Jatin waits a beat. "It led me to a house fire."

A lump forms in my throat. Two months ago, house fires were a thing of the past because my invention, firelight, brought sustainable light to every household in Belwar.

I know I was the one to do it, to take my people's firelight back to stop Mount Gandhak when Maharaja Moolek infused the volcano with my magic, but the candles still punch me in the gut. I could make more firelight. Easily. But the spell I invented has been labeled evil, an abomination everyone believes I created not to help but to control my people.

I think I could live with that—the vicious misconceptions, my ruined reputation. But house fires? People in danger? I will myself to not cast my mask onto my face, blur out my features, and let Adraa Belwar disappear. Because my other self, the Red Woman? Belwar accepts her, has cheered her on ever since Jatin and I started patrolling in disguise. Belwar loves me when I wear my mask.

Jatin reaches over and clasps my right hand—the one not covered with my Touch—a gesture that I have come to define as not only comfort but also acceptance. Love. "Thank you, Jatin. For being there for my people."

He squeezes again. "I'm here for you too." His expression grows earnest. "I wanted to talk to you about something. . . ."

"As long as it doesn't involve the hearing, my reputation, or the fact that people still think I bewitched you into trusting me."

"It's none of those things. Though that last one is still open to debate if you ask me."

"Jatin," I chastise. "What is it?"

He turns serious again, glancing down at our entwined hands. "I . . ." He's practically stammering.

"Why do you look so nervous?"

He rubs the back of his neck. "Well—"

A light vaults into the sky, red and white twisted together that can only mean one thing: a call to Night and the Red Woman. The glowing blaze is Jatin's invention, a device infused with both of our magic for people to signal us when they are in trouble. It's close. So close that it distorts the colors of the festival, washing away the residue of fun and piercing me with surprise.

Jatin and I only have to glance at each other, and then we're clambering to our feet and running. I reach for my belt and yank out my skyglider, Hubris the Fourth. *"Vitahtrae,"* I cast, and red streams of magic seep into the sturdy wood. As its handle extends and its kited tail unfolds, I throw myself onto it, letting the yellow magic buffer my weight. Someone picked the wrong night to mess with my city.

CHAPTER TWO

Postponed Proposal

Jatin

Being engaged since the age of nine has some advantages, the main one being never having to propose. In the last ten years I don't think I ever processed how lucky or spoiled I was in the art of romance. But, by the Gods, it's bad. Three days ago, I got down on one knee after Adraa beat me in our weekly rainbow tournament, and she thought I had stumbled. She doesn't seem to mind my awkwardness, but she also has no idea that I've been trying to get us officially reattached for weeks.

I wouldn't say it's entirely my fault. We've been busy, the Red Woman and I. Every time my invention sings into the air, we fly into action. And it sings often. I've lost count of how many times it has conspired against me. My best friend, Kalyan, keeps a tally, though.

But then again, Adraa and I are doing what we do best. So here I am, slipping on shingles and unhitching my skyglider so we can dive into danger. Adraa is two steps ahead of me, already bringing Hubris to life. I cast my own extension and levitation spells, ghost-white clouds pulsing into the wood. A roof isn't the best spot for taking off, but that doesn't stop Adraa. Heck, months ago she jumped from a second-story window to chase a criminal. So I follow suit, hitching a leg over my skyglider and shooting into the chilly air.

The source of the signal comes from the East Village. Which could mean a lot of things, but given the Vencrin's ties to the docks near Belwar Bay, it's highly suspicious. Adraa must feel the same because she looks over at me. "Night, do you think—"

An ambush? Yes. I've been awaiting the day the Vencrin use our signal against us. "Signaling for the others now." I cup my hands to my mouth and a blur of white magic gathers there until three beams of light explode upward. But as I watch my signal impale the sky along with all the other bursts of magic from the celebration, my mistake becomes apparent.

"They won't see."

"Then it's just you and me. Like the good old days." I raise my forearm, waiting.

Adraa drops closer and bumps her forearm against mine. "Good old days? You mean three weeks ago?"

I mean every single day I get to spend with her. "What? They weren't good for you?"

She laughs. "I could have done without the one wizard who signaled us to get that monkey out of his yard."

There are some aspects of the signal I hadn't quite accounted for. "Monkeys are no laughing matter, Red."

She doesn't answer, and as we draw nearer to the site of the signal, I understand why. A mob of people inhabits the East Village square, bodies scrunched together, vivid festival clothing brightening the dying day. And they're chanting a phrase that stabs my ears and gnaws at my core.

End Belwar rule.

◇ ◇ ◇

We land silently a block away. People mill forward, pushing toward the square. A platform raised on wooden stilts sits in the middle of the crowd, with a banner depicting the Belwar emblem. Even in the dark, the image of the orange rising sun—Adraa's family's seal—gleams. Adraa doesn't waste a moment. Skyglider hitched to her belt, she's off, maneuvering between people like a dancer.

It takes a moment for me to catch up. "Red, stop. Let's go. No one needs us here."

One glance at her face and I know it's a lost cause. Her eyes scream determination. For weeks she's been desperate to help in any way she can. No signal gets ignored. And tonight won't be any different. "Someone might. I have to be sure."

I yearn to tear off my mask in order to blend in, but neither of us has that luxury anymore, especially Adraa. And at this point I wouldn't dare. This crowd already has their mantra; they don't need much else to push them over the edge. Adraa ducks her head and enters the fray.

The group keeps up their insistent chant—*End Belwar rule!*—and it makes me want to punch something. I feel caged in by their hatred and I can't even imagine how Adraa is feeling. I keep my eyes on the braid swinging down her back, but she doesn't look at me, instead peering around for the source of the signal and the reason we were called into this madness. But I think I know why. And though I hope I am wrong, my gut wrenches.

After sliding through layer upon layer of the mob, Adraa finally stops. "I don't see it anymore," she says, nodding toward where the signal has disappeared from the sky. Her hands shake, and something in me breaks then and there.

"I'm ending this."

She catches my arm. "No, someone here signaled for us. Someone here needs—" Adraa stops as her eyes fasten on the wide platform. I turn to see a wizard gliding down the makeshift stage until he reaches a podium. He wears his lankiness like it was a gift from the gods. His smile sours with each step as if he can't force a genuine countenance for a solid minute. But then again, I'm biased. I already want to knock his teeth in.

With a swift orange spell, his voice booms over the gathered crowd. "Welcome all. Welcome to all the true Belwarians. No matter whether you were born here or not, you came here today to bring light to the real problems of Belwar. We are here to make things right. And to do that, things must change." The crowd applauds. You'd think he had said something profound.

"So I say, no more heirs. No more abusers of power because they were born into power. We should choose. We should raise our voices and get our chance to decide. The gods have forsaken Adraa Belwar and she has forsaken us. She will only rule in ash and misery." The wizard grabs a handful of dust and throws it. It's almost laughable how staged this display is. But no one else is laughing. Worry slices through me and I lean forward and take Adraa's hand. "Come on, Red."

She shakes her head.

"Let us rise!" the wizard yells. "Tonight, as we celebrate our survival, individuality, and power, let us begin making that change. Let us put who we want on the rising sun and let it be a new dawn." He rears back and tears the banner in half. The onslaught of cheers is overwhelming.

"It's quite convincing," Adraa whispers, her voice dead. "My father would like the 'new dawn' part."

I grab her shoulders and swing her toward me. "Hey. Hey! Don't you dare listen to him."

"Why not? There are a few nonroyal wizards and witches out there who can utilize all nine types of magic. Besides, one can become powerful through self-discipline and self-study. The fact that I should rule—or I should have ruled—because of my blood is nonsense. They *should* choose."

"Maybe things do need to change, but that isn't what I'm talking about. They can only raise their voices today because you saved them. Don't forget that."

She pierces me with her gaze. A part of me wants to yell. Why does everyone in this country seem to be losing their minds? Adraa Belwar saved us all. We've been working for weeks to prove it. And I have to prove it, not just because I want to be with Adraa without reservation or even because she's a bloody good leader. If we don't, the whole world will fall prey to Moolek's manipulation. Then there will be no choice.

"You saved *them*. You saved *me*. Please, tell me you won't forget that."

A cheer swells around us as I await Adraa's answer. The crowd has spotted us at last. "The Red Woman! Night and the Red Woman!" they call out. Hands reach out and touch my shoulders, poking and prodding. The news of our arrival ripples through the crowd in energized whispers, and a moment later the orator raises his voice. "Red Woman! You have heeded our call. Come, join me."

So not the ambush we were anticipating, but just as bad. Sometimes, I hate being right.

"Go," a fellow wizard insists, pushing my arm. A mob has power. And not only in its ability to express the need for change or cause such change but also in its ability to shuffle. Without meaning or wanting to, Adraa and I are pushed toward the platform.

Hands reach to tug us upward. There's no escaping now.

"Welcome, honored guests. Welcome." The wizard places two fingers to his pulse point, signifying respect. But he doesn't attach a bow to it, which generates my contempt. My gut wrenches tighter. I have to hold back my desire to flee. Adraa stands firm, and thus so do I.

The wizard turns back to his audience.

"We, the people of Belwar, do not know your name, but we do know your service. And from that we gather you are genuine Belwarians, faithful, honorable, and true. But we wish to know:

Do you follow the Belwars, or"—he uses the word *or* not as an alternative but as a decree—"are you here for the *people* of Belwar?"

The crowd cries out in approval. "End Belwar rule!" they chant. "End Belwar rule."

Adraa steps forward, shoulders set. "I stand with Belwar."

The wizard smiles, but he can't even do that properly. It turns down at the edges. "And you, Night?"

"I stand with Belwar," I echo. In truth I should say I stand with the Red Woman, with Adraa Belwar, that she is a fundamental part of this place. Now if only the people here declaring the opposite would come to their bloody senses.

"They stand with Belwar!" the wizard roars, grabbing our hands in his and hoisting them up. I've never felt so paraded about in my life. And my father has orchestrated parades for that very purpose, so that's saying something. I'm following Adraa's lead on this one.

Adraa untangles herself and jerks back. Pride swells in my chest as I watch her, and I unlink my own hand. "I stand with Belwar, and that means standing by the Belwars," she shouts. "The family that came here to escape the discrimination of the North and built this city. I defend the family who will keep defending this country. *Prahtrae*," she casts, and her bloodred magic straightens the torn banner and sews it back together, piece by piece.

All is silent. For a second I think maybe they'll listen, maybe they'll hear her.

Then come the frowns, the boos, the cries.

"You are no hero."

"Adraa Belwar tried to kill us all."

"She's the monster of Belwar."

"My house was destroyed. Moolek's people are the ones who fixed it."

"The Belwars are traitors. All of them."

The orator scowls. "If you don't stand with us, then you shouldn't stand at all. *Nizlaeh*," he shouts.

I move to pull up a shield as orange smoke springs forward, but someone beats me to it. A purple wall stands between Adraa and the wizard. I glance up, where Adraa's head guard and best friend, Riya Burman, hovers above us, her skyglider's tail a burst of violet and her face concealed by Adraa's invented mask. Alongside her flies Kalyan, my head guard, who lands in a gush of white wind.

Riya swings a leg over her glider and drops from the sky into a kneeling position. The makeshift platform shudders down to its wooden bones.

Riya rises slowly with a glare like death. "Don't touch her."

I can't help but smile. My signal worked after all. Our reinforcements have arrived.

◇ ◇ ◇

Although we have Riya and Kalyan on our side, a square filled with people lies before us, and based on their repetitive rhetoric and the knockout curse just thrown by Sour Smile over there, I think they want our heads.

It isn't the first time we've been outnumbered. But it's the first time civilians are the ones gearing up for a fight. Riya isn't helping matters. When the orator makes a move toward Adraa, Riya lunges. A second later, a satisfying crack splinters out into the crowd as the wizard falls to the platform.

"Nasty man," Riya spits, brushing pink magic against her bruised knuckles, "you don't misuse the signal."

"Yes, but it looks like he has some fans," I say.

The crowd heaves forward with screams of rage. *"Sphuraw!"* I yell, creating a wall of curved shields with purple magic.

Adraa and Riya follow suit, crafting our barrier into a dome of bloodred, violet, and white. But it's not enough. A few over-zealous members of the rally have already jumped over it. And they aren't happy. One hurls pink daggers at my face. I dodge. Another fastens wood planks to his arms with green magic and rushes forward.

"Don't hurt them!" Adraa cries from the other side of the platform, blocking a water stream someone has crafted.

Another pink dagger zooms past my nose. "Tell them that!" I holler, freezing the wizard's hands in ice and kicking up a plank to hit the other man in the face. I wince as he falls with a bang. Fighting amicably is difficult.

Kalyan steps up beside me, five shields swirling around him like a turtle shell and catching a dagger and two spears.

"I'm guessing she said no," he says, deadpan. At this moment, he is the most annoying I've ever found him. And as my decoy and head guard, I've seen the guy every day since he was eleven.

"No, she didn't say no," I huff, tossing a wizard over our heads and back into the gathering crowd. "I haven't gotten the chance to ask. Wait—" I block three yellow arrows with a shield. "You thought she would say no?"

Kalyan shrugs. "Fifty-fifty."

"Fifty-fifty? She and I have been engaged for ten years and all you give me is fifty-fifty?" I lengthen my barrier, pushing wizards and witches from the platform. *"Bhitti Himadloc!"* I yell. Sheets of ice spring from my hands, surging upward and barring more people from entering behind us.

Kalyan crafts a whip and catches two more men who are trying to climb the platform behind the Belwar banner. "Ten years, and yet you still aren't engaged. Now she gets to choose."

"Of course, she gets to choose. But—" A wizard takes this moment to barrel over my ice barrier with a funnel of wind. I swing some ice at him, catching him midfall and hitching his flaming yellow hands to the floor. "She still chose me."

At that moment, across the makeshift stage, Adraa sweeps the legs of a witch, then skids, using the heat of her red magic to melt the lane of ice I've carelessly constructed. As she slides, she topples one wizard back into the fray. A flash of red mist, and two other wizards go down.

Kalyan nods in appreciation. "And you are lucky for it."

I can't keep the smile off my face, even when Adraa stands, whirls around, and slips again. "Must everything be ice?" she yells.

I shrug. It's my forte. What does she expect? But I sweep

my hands forward and call back the chunks of ice that divide us. "Happy?" I ask, even as Kalyan's sentiment warms its way through me. I will always be happy if Adraa Belwar chooses me. Now if only we could get a moment to ourselves so I can ask her properly.

Before Adraa can answer, her eyes widen and her hand rises. I turn, but it's too late. Another extremist has crept up behind us, a streak of a blue sword falling down on Kalyan and me. I don't even have time to raise a shield before a barrier of purple covers us. Riya bounds off the boundary above, spinning in the air and kicking a witch in the side of the face. The witch goes down, and Riya turns. "I'd be happy if you would all pay more attention to your surroundings. Gods, how did you survive without us for this long?"

"Obviously with much luck," Kalyan says. "Unbelievable amounts, even."

Adraa runs up. "That's the last of them that slipped in before we got the barrier up. Let's get out of here before anyone gets hurt."

"I think it might be too late for that," Kalyan says. The four of us turn to the barrier, surveying the carnage of splintered wood. Most of the crowd has scattered, but those inside our bubble shield are lying on the ground, knocked out or moaning. Dozens of wizards still pound against the shield, though. Many have glowing red eyes, which can mean only one thing. They're under the influence of the drug Bloodlurst and all that comes with it: more power, less control, and no concern for logic. I've never seen so many drugged.

Three wizards punch the wall with orange magic and the barrier's outer shell cracks. It won't hold much longer.

"What's wrong with them?" Riya shouts.

"They're angry. Their city has burned and they want someone to blame," Adraa says, glancing toward Mount Gandhak.

"Today is not the day to make them see reason." I nod to Riya and Adraa. "You two go first. Kalyan and I will back you up."

Adraa gives me a look. "What about you?"

"I've made it out of avalanches. I can make it out of this."

"After all this time, you're still rubbing that in?" Adraa shakes her head but readies her skyglider. "Be careful."

I smile. "I'm always careful."

Kalyan huffs beside me as he blasts more ice at the base of the shield.

I break the ice at the top and the girls zoom through the opening. The question for Adraa is still on the tip of my tongue, unasked and unanswered.

Kalyan watches me out of the corner of his eye. "Remember that pep talk I gave you earlier?"

"Yeah, you said it would be hard to mess up a proposal with the festival's romantic atmosphere," I answer, unleashing my skyglider once again and preparing to punch into the air so fast it'll blow back the multicolored dome.

"Forget what I said. I hadn't accounted for how bad you are at this," Kalyan notes as we settle onto our skygliders. "And for the record, that's quite bad."

"Well, there's one saving grace. I don't think she even

knows I was trying to ask." With that, Kalyan and I chant into the wood of the stage, coating it in white smoke until we appear immersed in a cloud. When we finally do blast off, the stage ruptures. Two holes puncture its middle.

I might not know how to propose, but at least I know how to make an exit.

Underlined

A Community of Book Nerds & Aspiring Writers!

READ

Get book recommendations, reading lists, YA news

DISCOVER

Take quizzes, watch videos, shop merch, win prizes

CREATE

Write your own stories, enter contests, get inspired

SHARE

Connect with fellow Book Nerds and authors!

GetUnderlined.com • @GetUnderlined

Want a chance to be featured? Use #GetUnderlined on social!